Rita Bradshaw was born in Northampton, where she still lives today with her husband (whom she met when she was sixteen) and their family.

When she was approaching forty she decided to fulfil two long-cherished ambitions – to write a novel and learn to drive. She says, 'the former was pure joy and the latter pure misery', but the novel was accepted for publication and she passed her driving test. She has gone on to write many successful novels under a pseudonym.

As a committed Christian and fervent animal lover, Rita has a full and busy life, but she relishes her writing – a job that is all pleasure – and loves to read, walk her dogs, eat out and visit the cinema in any precious spare moments.

REACH FOR TOMORROW

Rita Bradshaw

headline

First published in 1999
by HEADLINE BOOK PUBLISHING

First published in paperback in 1999
by HEADLINE BOOK PUBLISHING

16

ISBN 978 0 7472 58056

Typeset by Palimpsest Book Production Limited,
Polmont, Stirlingshire

Printed and bound in Great Britain by Clays Ltd, Elcograf S.p.A.

HEADLINE BOOK PUBLISHING
A division of Hodder Headline PLC
338 Euston Road
London NW1 3BH

This book is for all the courageous women I have known in my life, who have fought back against the tragedies and difficulties life has thrown at them and their loved ones and have continued to reach for tomorrow.

Prologue – 1920

'Da?'

'Aye, lad?'

'You ready then?'

'Aye, Aa'm ready, lad, more'n ready. Aa've bin tastin' that panhaggerty yer mam spoke about last night for the last hour an' more.'

James Ferry grinned at his son as he spoke, but there was no answering smile on the black, coal-encrusted face as it stared back at him in the concentrated light from his pit helmet, and the young voice was agitated when it said, 'Come on then.'

Eee, daft young blighter. James's strong, big-nosed face did not betray his thoughts, but his voice was slightly impatient when he said, 'All right, lad, all right. Steady does it.' Still, they'd all been young once. The thought followed immediately and brought a tinge of compassion to the rough northern voice when he added, 'Not long now.'

It was that dream their Molly had had the night before, that's what had done it, James said to himself as he followed his son and the other eighteen men of his section down the slope into the main roadway towards the pit cage. There they would be hauled up by the winding-engine man, packed in like sardines, along with the other sections – one of which included his second son, Philip, who was just fifteen years of age – that made up their shift at the Wearmouth Colliery.

Aye, Molly had brought them all wide awake in the early hours with her screaming and crying, but that would have been all right if she'd had the sense to keep her mouth shut, James reflected irritably. But, Molly being Molly, she'd had to go and blurt out the horror of the nightmare. Eee, she hadn't got the sense she was born with, that lass, she was as different to their Rosie as chalk to cheese, and it was nowt to do with their ages, as Jessie would have it. Jessie had spoilt the lass, that was it at bottom. Their Rosie had been fetching and carrying from when she was nigh on five and she'd always had a level head on her shoulders and a bit about her, but here was Molly still wasting her time playing with the other bairns and such like at nine. Aye, Molly was her mam's favourite all right, and the others knew it.

James's big body couldn't stand upright even in the main roadway and now, as he came to an abrupt halt by cannoning into his son's thin back, he said, 'What's the hold-up? Owt wrong?' as he lifted his head in the thick, dust-laden air.

'Dunno.' Sam glanced round frowning, his teeth gleaming white in his black, sweaty face. 'Old Bill said there'd bin a couple of falls last night near five, perhaps it's somethin' to do with that?'

'Aye, Bill told me about that an' all,' the man in front of Sam said over his shoulder in a loud aside. 'Not surprisin', is it? There's bin water seepin' there for weeks but the surveyor says it's all right. Mind, he don't have to work in the bowels of hell so why should he worry, eh? Ruddy rabbit warren.'

'Aye.' The light from James's helmet showed another

black orb as the man turned to face him, and he answered it saying, 'You're right there an' all, Sid. It's all production with the managers an' no questions asked as long as the coal's got out, but they'll catch their toes one day.'

'Aye, man, but it'll be our feet that bleed, that's what worries me,' the other man answered with a macabre grin, before his light flashed on the solid dank walls as he turned to face the front again. 'The viewers'll still be sittin' pretty, damn 'em.'

James saw Sam hunch his shoulders before standing perfectly still again. That blasted dream . . . He could have throttled Molly when she blubbered on about a bang and fire and them all being buried in coal. It hadn't bothered Phil too much; he wasn't one for thinking, their Phil, but Sam was different. He was more like Rosie, he was, in fact the pair could've been twins the way their minds worked. Still, Sam'd have to get over it, the sooner the better, and maybe it'd do him a good turn in the long run. He needed to harden up a bit; he'd been down the pit for nigh on four years now and he was still as soft as clarts at times. It was all right for a lass to go on about sunsets and green fields and the like, but a grown man of eighteen?

And then James heard the rattle of the cage coming down, and he was just opening his mouth to say, 'There you are, lad, we'll soon be tastin' your mam's panhaggerty,' when the rush of air alerted him to what was to follow seconds later.

The blast took him off his feet and flung him like an outsize rag doll against the shored-up wall of the main road, and he was dimly aware of more violent movement all around him through the grit and rocks and coal dust as bodies of men plummeted helplessly here and there as though thrown by a giant hand. There was a pressure in his ears that was unbearable, and a roaring in his head that took precedence over everything else as he struggled to remain conscious, fighting all the time for his next breath.

Sam? And Phil? As the sounds from the explosion stabilized into groans and cries for help, James made the effort to stagger drunkenly to his feet, his head reeling. Their Phil had been at the front of the men with Frank, the collier he had been assigned to when he'd first come down the pit some thirteen months before, and they would have got the worst of it there.

'Sam? Sam, lad?' He could barely speak for the dust in his mouth, his nostrils, his eyes, and he choked, coughing and spitting a few times before he said again, 'Sam? Sam, answer me.' He had to find his lads, and quick. There could be another explosion if the fire-damp hadn't finished with them, and that could mean flames or flooding if they weren't buried alive. Hell, fire . . . His blood ran cold. He had seen what the flames could do to a man years ago when he'd been involved in a rescue in this very pit just a few years after he'd come down, and he'd never forgotten the sight of those contorted, burnt bodies. Pray God it wouldn't be fire.

More men were lurching to their feet, some with injuries that were appalling, and James noticed – with a curious detachment that spoke of shock – that the floor and walls shone red in places from the light of his pit helmet, the coal a gleaming scarlet.

'Da?'

The relief he felt when he heard Sam's voice and saw his son attempt to rise from the mayhem nearly caused James to lose control of his bladder, and then, when he reached his side and saw what the razor-sharp guillotine of rock had done to Sam's right leg, he wanted to vomit.

'All right, lad, all right.' He forced himself to speak naturally as he knelt down at the side of what remained of his first-born's fine sturdy body. 'We're goin' to get out of this, you hear me, Sam? Phil too.'

'Where . . . is he?'

The severed stump was pumping blood and already Sam's eyes were glazing over but he didn't appear to be in any pain. There was nothing he could do, James knew that as he took his son into his arms, cuddling him close in a way he hadn't done since Sam was a child. 'He's all right, lad, don't you worry. You just rest a while an' then the three of us'll see about gettin' out of here.'

'Da?'

'Aye, lad?'

'Don't . . . don't leave me, will you?'

James breathed in very slowly and then out again as his grip on his son tightened, and his voice was uncharacteristically gentle when he said, 'No, lad. Aa'll not leave yer.'

'At least there's still some light,' Sam mumbled faintly, staring up at the lamp on his father's helmet. 'I . . . I've never told you afore, Da, but I don't like the dark. Funny that, eh, with me bein' a miner? But I don't. Rosie knows, I've told her,' he said, his voice becoming weaker. 'I can tell Rosie anythin'.'

'Aye, she's a bonny lass.'

'She's not like the others, our Phil an' Molly an' Hannah.'

James could see him slipping away in front of his very eyes and there was nothing he could do.

'On Sundays, on our walks Boldon way across the fields an' such with Davey an' Flora, you oughta hear our Rosie

5

talk, Da. She wants to make somethin' of life, does Rosie. Oh, she wants to get wed an' have bairns one day like all lasses, but she wants somethin' different from livin' round our streets. She's a canny lass.' Sam's voice trailed away on a sigh and he settled himself more comfortably in his father's arms.

James sat amidst the rubble and devastation in the suffocatingly thick air and his mind travelled on from his son's last words. Aye, Rosie was a canny lass, and she was one of them folk who'd been born with an old head on their shoulders. She'd take care of her mam and the other two all right. He shut his eyes tight for a moment before they sprang open as a shrill scream sounded from somewhere down the tunnel, the sound of which was echoed in the groans and laboured breathing all around him.

Those that could still walk were kneeling over injured friends or in some cases sons or brothers or fathers, and James noticed a heavily bloodstained Sid begin to drag an equally bloodsoaked miner back down the passage whence they had come. He couldn't see who the man was from the angle at which he was sitting, and when Sid paused at the side of him and said, 'He's bad, eh?' with a nod of his head at Sam, James merely answered, 'Aye, he's bad, Sid.'

'You need to get to the next air-door, man. You'll choke in here an' this might not be the end of it.'

'Aye, Aa know. In a while.'

Sid coughed and gasped before he drew more of the swirling grit and dust into his lungs as he said, 'You might not have a while.'

'Leave it, man.' James glanced down at the face of his son who appeared to be sleeping. 'Aa'll come when Aa'm ready.'

'It's no good goin' yonder.' Sid inclined his head in the direction of the cage for a moment. 'The roof's down.' They were both aware he was pronouncing a death sentence on Philip and the others who had been in front, but again James's voice was flat when he said, 'Whey aye, I know, Sid. You go, man, an' get outa this styfe. Aa'll be all right.'

It would take the rescue party all their time to break through the first fall before the remaining air went, James thought as he watched Sid depart through the gloom. If there was more to come they were as good as dead anyway, air-doors or no air-doors.

At what point his son's heart stopped beating James didn't know, but by the time the second explosion hit – with the force and thunder of an earthquake as it brought tons of rock, coal and slate crashing down into the maze of tunnels – he had been holding Sam's lifeless body close to his heart for some time, simply because he couldn't bear to let him go.

Part One

Changes

Chapter One

'Mam, I know it's hard, I do, but we've got to talk about what we're going to do. It . . . it's been three weeks now, and Mr Kilbride said he wants the house for another family at the end of the month.'

There was no answer or reaction whatsoever from the plump middle-aged woman sitting slumped at the scrubbed kitchen table, and when a full minute had passed with just the occasional spit and hiss from the banked-up fire in the blackleaded grate to alleviate the heavy silence, Rosie's voice was sharper when it said, 'Mam, do you hear me?'

'Mr Kilbride won't put us out on the streets, not that man. He's always bin good to us.'

'He was good to us because Da never missed a day's work in his life and always kept his mouth shut if there were any disputes and such like, and he'd brought Sam and Phil up to do the same.'

'Your da was no boss's man, Rosie Ferry.' There was a touch of animation in Jessie's dull voice for the first time that day and she raised her head, staring at her daughter out of swollen, pink-rimmed eyes.

Rosie stared back at her, exasperation vying with deep, gut-wrenching pity as she surveyed her mother, who had

11

seemed to age twenty years in the last three weeks since
Mrs Robson had first come banging at the door with
the news that the whistle was sounding at the pit. The
continuous whistle meant a disaster of some kind, and as
they had thrown their shawls about their shoulders, scooping
up Molly and Hannah as they went, neither of them had said
a word, but they had run through the labyrinth of alleys and
streets in Monkwearmouth towards Southwick Road without
stopping.

The January afternoon was raw, the odd flake of snow
swirling haphazardly in the biting wind, but as the four of
them joined the crowd that was gathering at the pit gates
Rosie and Jessie didn't heed the cold. It was noticeable
that the majority of the company was silent, the women's
faces white and pinched and the men's expressing strained
control, but Jessie spoke directly to one of the two deputies
manning the gate as soon as they were near enough.

'What news, Stan? Is it bad?'

'We don't rightly know as yet, Jessie.' Stanley Fowler had
been a lifelong friend of James and his voice was tight as he
said, 'There's bin a fall but most of the fore shift was up.'

'A fall?' Jessie's voice was shaking.

'Fire-damp.'

The dreaded words were enough to bleach the women's
lips and cause the men's faces to tighten further.

'Who's down?'

It was a man at the back of them who asked, Jessie had
turned to stone as she clung on to Rosie's arm.

'They're doin' a check but it takes time, man, you know
that.' The deputy's voice was soft and low; he knew the
man who had spoken and he had two brothers on the
morning shift.

'Damn owners an' viewers.' Another man's voice sounded, strident this time. 'Three-quarters of a million killed in the war an' they're aimin' at the same underground if you ask me. All them giant maroons fired, an' church bells ringin', an' fireworks an' dancin' an' the like, an' where are we now, not fourteen months later? Beggin' for every penny we get. It's all well an' good the King givin' old Lloyd George the Order of Merit for his services in wartime, but what about us? We kept the country goin' with our blood, sweat an' tears bringin' their black diamonds up.'

'All right, man, all right. Not now.'

But the old wizened miner was in full flow. 'Order of Merit! An' that's the man who called the rail strike an anarchist conspiracy an' then turned down nationalization of the mines. Too many pals of his have too much to lose, that's the thing. There's barely bin a month without a strike, an' why? There's nothin' else we can do, that's why. They pay nowt but lip service to safety—'

'*Jimmy*.'

Silence reigned again, an uneasy, tense silence broken now and again by a whispered word or two, or children crying in the cold northern afternoon as the bitter chill seeped into their bones.

It was quite dark when the first rescue party came up and the next one went down, and by then Rosie was a block of ice, every part of her frozen, and she knew she would never feel warm again. Sam and her da were down there, maybe Davey too, and it was more than she could bear. And Phil, he was just fifteen. *Fifteen*. And the pit might have taken them all. But they couldn't be dead – it was inconceivable that she wouldn't see them again, they *had* to be all right. And her mam, her poor mam. What would her mam do . . . ?

One of their neighbours had taken Hannah and Molly when it had begun to get dark, and now, as she stood cradling her mother in her arms, Rosie saw Davey Connor and her heart leapt. Davey was on the rescue party, he was *safe*. But Sam, and her da and Phil . . . ?

'You've been down?' she asked weakly, but she had seen it in his eyes, that look of desperate pity and compassion, and she knew that, whatever he might say, there was little hope for the others.

'Aye.' He cleared his throat, his young face under its mantle of black dust working slightly. 'Aye, I've bin down, an' it's goin' to be a long job, lass. Best take your mam home, eh?'

'I'm not goin' nowhere.' Jessie spoke for the first time in hours.

'Mrs Ferry, it'll be a long job, there's a good stretch of the roof down,' the young man said softly, 'an' it's no use you waitin' an' gettin' chilled to the bone, is it? Your man wouldn't want that. They might well be at the back of the fall, there's still hope, but it'll take time to reach them. Go home, the bairns need you.'

'Bairns?' Jessie looked up at him, her brow wrinkling, before it cleared and she said, 'I'm stayin' put, lad.'

'No, you're not, Mam. You heard what Davey said, they'll not have any news for hours yet and we can be back at first light. You're coming home and having something hot and getting a few hours' sleep. You'll be no good to Da and the lads in the infirmary with pneumonia, now then.'

Rosie didn't expect her mother to take any notice of her – Jessie was well known for her stubbornness within the family – so it was with some surprise that she glanced up at Davey again as her mother turned obediently in the direction

14

of home and said, 'All right, lass, whatever you think best,' without any more argument.

'Davey?' Rosie caught hold of Jessie's arm as she spoke – the older woman was already walking docilely away – and said hastily, 'How many? How many are down?'

'Your da's section an' some of the lads from five, the rest were up when it happened.' Rosie knew Davey Connor to be a fine, fresh-faced, good-looking lad, but at that moment he looked like all the miners did when they came up from the bowels of the earth – a barely recognizable creature from a different planet. 'Rosie, it could be forty-eight hours if not longer, you'd better prepare her.' He nodded quietly at Jessie's back. 'They're talkin' about establishin' a fresh-air base an' comin' in from a different angle an' that takes time.'

Rosie nodded, her breath a white cloud in the bitterly cold, frosty night as she said, 'Aye, I'll do that, Davey, and . . . thanks.'

'Oh, lass, lass.' He didn't say any more but he didn't have to. There are some heart cries that are too deep to express.

It was seventy-eight hours later before the first body was brought up, and a full week before they reached the last man. The rescue teams had worked frantically, long after any hope of finding anyone alive had gone, each man aware that the training he had gone through over and over again was now being used in a disaster the like of which he had never imagined.

It had snowed heavily on the day of the funeral and the whole town had lined the route to show their respect. Even Fawcett Street, with its wide road paved with wooden blocks and magnificent town hall, was subdued and strangely still.

But to the families concerned, many of which had lost their main breadwinner, there was only the long black line of horsedriven hearses, and the seemingly endless service when coffin after coffin was lowered into the hard, unforgiving northern earth.

But in a strange sort of way she had almost welcomed the funeral, Rosie thought now, sinking down into a straightbacked chair at her mother's side, and taking Jessie's limp hands in her own as she began to chafe them gently. During the terrible wait for news, and then the agony of each body being brought up from the black cavernous depths that had consumed it, she had really feared her mother was losing her mind.

Jessie's grief had been overwhelming. There had been times when the older woman had sat for hours without speaking, her hands picking at the fringe of her shawl and her eyes staring sightlessly ahead, and then others when she had ranted and raved like a madwoman and Rosie had had to physically restrain her. At her worst she had lashed out at little Hannah when the six-year-old had tried to clamber on her knee, knocking the child against the hard wood saddle where only the plump, flock-stuffed cushions had saved the little girl from serious injury. Even Molly, the undisputed favourite, had failed to make any impression on Jessie's deranged mind, and her two sisters had clung to Rosie increasingly.

But although the frightening mood swings had passed along with the funeral, the woman who had returned home with Rosie from the cemetery was not her mother. The big, buxom, rosy-faced Jessie had died in the mine along with her husband and her sons, and what remained was a silent, bitter shell.

'Mam, me da was a fine man, I know that,' Rosie said now, her voice soft. 'I'm just saying that Mr Kilbride knew which side his bread was buttered, that's all. And now Da – now things have changed, he won't put himself out for us beyond what he's already done. You have to see that, Mam.'

'Aye, perhaps you're right, lass.'

It had become Jessie's stock answer to anything that was put to her, and always spoken in the same dull, uninterested tone.

'Mam . . .' Rosie bit hard on her lip, shutting her eyes for an infinitesimal moment. 'Mam, you do see we've got to find somewhere to live? And Davey, he said that the hot potato man – you know, Mr Nebb who's the verger at Holy Trinity – well, he told Davey on the quiet that he knows of two lasses who are going to leave Bradman's jam factory in Hendon Street in the next week. They're going up Newcastle way, the family's moving there because their da's found work through his brother, but they're not telling the foreman before time in case he gets rid of them early.'

'So?' Jessie turned to look at her pretty, dark-eyed daughter, but Rosie had the feeling her mother wasn't really seeing her.

'So we could get in on the ground. I'm fourteen next week and Bradman's pays more than most. If we could get set on—'

'You're not sayin' I should work outside? Your da won't have that.' Jessie looked scandalized. 'The most he's ever allowed is me takin' in the odd bit of washin' when you bairns were all young an' money was tight. He's got no time for women who work outside or for men that allow it.'

'Mam, things are different now.' Rosie prayed for control

17

as she kept her voice quiet through the frustration and pain that gnawed at her every waking moment. What was she going to do? *What was she going to do?* Mr Kilbride had been at his most officious when he had called round the night before, his black eyes as hard as bullets, and their meagre store of cash was nearly all gone. There was just enough to buy food for the next few days and then . . . She bit down on the panic and fear that threatened to swamp her. There were men being laid off all over the place, there was even talk of a soup kitchen being set up in High Street East besides the ones in Boldon and Jarrow. Things were bad. *Da*, oh, Da. Tell me what to do.

'No, Rosie.' For a moment an echo of the old, stubborn Jessie was back. 'I'll take in washin', or maybe card them linen buttons like Annie does next door, eh? Anyways, who'd be here for when the bairns get home from school?'

'Mam, we're not going to *be* here, we're going to have to look for rooms elsewhere. And Molly can take care of Hannah, she's old enough. I was taking care of her at eight when Hannah was born and she'd only have to walk her home and keep an eye on her till we're back in the evening. They'd be fine.'

'Not be here?' Rosie doubted if her mother had heard anything else as Jessie, her voice high, repeated, 'Not be here?' as she glanced round the kitchen of the neat two-up, two-down terraced house.

Rosie, from the age of eight, had always included a nightly thank you in her prayers for the fact that she lived on the north side of the River Wear in one of the ordinary prosaic streets of terraced houses that made up the heart of Monkwearmouth. There had been complications with Hannah's birth, which had occurred in March 1914, just

18

five months before Britain was plunged into the Great War against Germany, and her father had taken Rosie, along with the other three children, across the Wearmouth Bridge to his mother's house in Sunderland's East End where the four of them had stayed until her mother was well enough to have them home again.

Of course Rosie had visited her grannie's before; brief visits which she had always enjoyed as her grannie's lodgers had tended to make much of the bright-faced little girl with the silky dark hair and deep brown eyes, but always with her parents and only for an hour or so at the most. Nothing had prepared her for sleeping in her grannie's kitchen along with Sam, Phil and Molly on a big flea-infested mattress that her grannie kept for the odd lodger who couldn't be fitted into the two crammed rooms upstairs; or for the cold and general filth in the dirty, overcrowded, insanitary house, which was only one of countless hundreds in the back-to-back tenement slums that made up the wretched East End of Sunderland.

She had cried against her father's broad chest when he had come to visit them the next day, but when he had told her, gently but firmly, that there was nowhere else for them to go – she knew her mam's mam and da had died afore she was born when her own mam was still a little bairn, didn't she? and her da's only brother had moved away years ago to escape the mines – she had gritted her teeth and endured the rest of the endlessly miserable visit without complaint.

But on her return home, to the small but immaculately clean house in Forcer Road where she shared a bedroom with Molly and her brothers – a big square of curtain on a piece of string separating their half of the room from the lads' section – she had cried again, but this time with thankfulness. The blackleaded grate, the big iron kettle that was always on the hob, the bright clippy mat in front of the fire on the scrubbed floor, the smell of Metal Shino polish and the broken flagstones her mother scoured with soda, all took on the form of heaven. Even the communal privy in the yard which they shared with the houses either side, and which all three housewives took turns in cleaning daily, became something wonderful after her grannie's foul, stinking square box that had caused her to gag every time she entered it.

There was poverty and there was poverty, and the lesson Rosie had learnt when Hannah was born had embedded itself deep in her young soul; so now, when Jessie's eyes came to rest on her and her mother said, her voice dull again, 'There's always your grannie's shakedown while we get sorted,' Rosie's voice was loud in her reply of, 'I'm not taking the bairns there, Mam, and anyway we want to keep as much furniture as we can, don't we? There's no money to get anything stored.'

'Aye, perhaps you're right, lass.'

Perhaps you're right, lass. If she heard that one more time she would scream. But then a flood of compassion and guilt lowered Rosie's voice as she said, 'I'll sort something out, Mam, don't worry. You get yourself to bed, you look all done in.'

'Aye, lass.' Jessie shambled immediately to her feet like an overgrown child, and again the change in her once vital and authoritative mother made Rosie want to weep. It just showed you never knew anyone, not really. Her mam had gone all through the war years, the dreaded Zeppelin raids and the rationing and all, with a cheerfulness that had kept the whole family on an even keel. She would never have dreamt in a million years that her mother would have gone to pieces like this, but from the moment Jessie had heard that whistle it was as though her life spring had snapped. And there was Molly having screaming tantrum after screaming tantrum and refusing to go to school, and Hannah – sensing the general atmosphere without fully understanding it – crying herself to sleep each night.

Alone now, and for the first time since she had opened her eyes that morning and begun the daily task of chivvying the family into some sort of normality, Rosie walked across to the old battered armchair in front of the range where her father had sat most nights on his return from the pit, and sank tiredly onto its thin, flattened cushion, her mind worrying at the urgent matter of work.

She'd take the tram into Hendon tomorrow if Mrs McLinnie would have Molly and Hannah for a few hours; she didn't dare leave the two bairns with her mother but she couldn't drag them round with her either. She could have a look and see if there were any cheap rooms going, although how they were going to pay the first week's rent she didn't know, and she could perhaps call in at the jam factory and make enquiries. Although she couldn't let on about the two lasses who were going to leave; Davey had been explicit about that when he had tipped her the wink.

Davey . . . Rosie leant back against the hard wood and shut her eyes. She'd always liked Davey Connor, Sam used to tease her about him unmercifully. Oh, Sam. *Sam.* She always did her crying at night when the others were in bed, and now the hot tears scalded her face but she made no effort to wipe them away. How could he be dead, her tall, shy, sensitive brother? It wasn't fair for him to have died like that, away from the sky and the wide open spaces he loved so much. She had watched him and Davey breathing in the fresh grass-soaked air on the country walks the three of them had shared on a Sunday afternoon along with Flora, and Sam had seemed to come alive as he and Davey had discussed their plans to get out of the pit and work on the land, and then on a Monday morning that dead look would come over his face again. She hoped he hadn't died in the dark, she couldn't bear to think he had died in the dark . . .

She scrubbed her face dry on her hessian apron after a time, her body still shuddering. Of course she missed her da and their Phil too – her bouts of crying invariably ended with feelings of remorse that her main grieving was centred around Sam – but she'd been so close to Sam. His dreams and Davey's had been so aligned to hers; they had shared her desire to escape these grim back streets where the only view of the sky was of a thin rectangle in between the narrow roads and alleyways. All the girls she had been at school with seemed to look only as far as marriage and bairns, that was the sum total of their aspirations. And when she'd used words like that – aspirations – they'd oohed and aahed and poked fun. Except Flora. Flora had always stood up for her even when her friend didn't understand what she was talking about. She was longing for Flora to come back from visiting her mother's family in Wales, things were always brighter when Flora was around, and if ever she had needed her friend's infectiously optimistic presence it was now. Although all this was going to hit Flora hard too; she'd always had the notion that Flora had a soft spot for Sam although she had never let on.

The thought of Sam brought the weakness into her mind and body again and Rosie pushed it away determinedly, rising abruptly and walking across the kitchen to slip the bolt on the back door before she banked down the fire still further. She had to be strong now, she couldn't afford to give in to her grief for more than the odd minute or so, there was too much to do. Her da, and their Sam and Phil, would expect her to keep the family together.

Her mam would get better in time, hadn't Davey said that very thing when he'd called round the night before with a sack of coal? She glanced at the fire which was now smoking profusely under its blanket of damp slack, and her face softened. They had been down to the dust and grime in the bottom of the scuttle before Davey had called, and she had been thinking she would have to use some of the precious hoard of money to buy fuel, but now they could manage for a bit longer. He was so nice, Davey. And Mrs McLinnie was good, bless her; she'd called round twice in the last week, once with a pan of rabbit stew and dumplings and another time with a bag of chitterlings and two pig's trotters, and one or two other neighbours had dropped by with small offerings. But people couldn't keep doing that, most of them were living hand to mouth as it was.

No, she had to take stock and get things sorted, and she had to do it by herself, that was becoming clearer every day. The idea of her going into service with the Chester family in Seaburn was no good now, not that she had ever really wanted to in the first place. That had been her da's idea, her being taken on as a kitchen maid in the big house, he'd had a bee in his bonnet about her being somewhere safe and secure. But her mam and the bairns needed her; her mother didn't seem able to make even the most elementary decisions any more and she couldn't leave them. Everything had changed.

She flung the thick braid of shining brown hair that hung down to her waist over her shoulder, straightened her thin shoulders and narrowed her eyes as she glanced once more round the clean, cosy kitchen that signified home. This stage of her life was over, it was over for all of them and she had to let it go – there were three people depending on her now and it was no good crying for what used to be.

But whatever she did, she'd continue trying to talk properly and learning about words as her schoolteacher, Miss Trotter, had encouraged her to do. Their Sam had understood about that when she had told him what Miss Trotter had said. 'You could be a schoolteacher you know, lass.' He had nodded at her, his eyes thoughtful, and in answer to her laughing, 'Go on with you, our Sam,' he had repeated, 'Oh aye, you could, lass, I'm not jestin'. I can't put me finger on it but you're different to the rest of us.'

Well, she didn't think she wanted to be a schoolteacher, not that there was much chance of that now anyway. But a few things had clarified after those Sunday talks. She still liked the idea of being married, but not the sort of marriage where she had one bairn after another and lived her life within four walls in a daily drudgery that would have her an old woman at thirty like some of the women hereabouts. And she wanted her husband to have something better than a subterranean existence in the bowels of the earth with the pit controlling whether he lived or died. She wanted . . . Oh, she wasn't sure what she wanted, that was the truth of it, but she would recognize it when she saw it.

She turned, her thick plait whirling about her shoulders, and left the room without further speculation.

Chapter Two

It took Rosie a few minutes to get the fire going again
the next morning, but eventually the glowing embers were
persuaded into life and more of Davey's coal, along with
half a bucketful of cinders, began to make the burgeoning
flames crackle and spit.

After filling the big black kettle and putting it into
the centre of the fire, Rosie stood close to the shining
blackleaded hob for a few moments, soaking up the warmth.
Not that the kitchen had had the bitter chill of the bedrooms,
she reminded herself silently, holding out her cold hands to
the blaze. There had been thick ice starring the inside of
the bedroom window this morning and her nose had felt
as though it was frozen over. The thought emphasized the
poignant difference a mere three weeks had made to their
quality of life.

Since Sam, and then Phil, had joined their da down the
pit they hadn't had to worry about money, Rosie reflected.
A good week, when both her da and the lads had worked
the full five-and-a-half shifts – although that had happened
less of late – had meant wage packets totalling nearly nine
pounds between them after stoppages, according to her
mother. Of course their Phil hadn't earnt as much as their

da and Sam, and the lads had still kept a fair portion of their earnings after they'd paid their board, but nevertheless her mam's housekeeping had run to fires in the bedrooms from October to April, plenty of good food on the table, and warm winter coats and boots each year in spite of the way she and her sisters had shot up.

Her mam doing up the front room had cost a fair bit, but her da had been happy to go along with it. He'd said her mam had had a bee in her bonnet about having a nice front room from when they were first wed and it was high time she had some new stuff instead of old hand-me-downs. But now . . .

Her musing on the extravagance of the new suite and square of carpet and curtains in the mausoleum that was her mother's front room was cut short by a gentle knock at the back door.

'*Davey.*' She stood in front of him, smiling widely. 'I was just getting things ready before I get my mam and the bairns up.' And then, a little flustered by the knowledge that she had shown her pleasure at seeing him too enthusiastically, she added more sedately, 'Come in, won't you, you must be frozen out there,' as she stood aside for him to enter then shut the door quietly behind him.

'It's a raw mornin',' he agreed, as he turned round to smile at her.

Oh, she was so *glad* to see him. The depth of her feeling made her heart pound and when he said, 'You look flushed, are you feeling all right?' she was glad she could say in all honesty, 'It was the fire, it wouldn't go at first,' with a nod towards the range.

He stood in the middle of the kitchen looking slightly awkward as he glanced round the silent room, and it was his faint bashfulness that enabled her to speak more naturally. 'I was just going to make a pot of tea. Sit down there and I'll have it mashed in no time.'

'Ta, thanks.'

Oh he was nice. He was so, *so* nice.

'I popped round on me way to work 'cos me mam had a bit of streaky bacon and a couple of sausages she thought you could use for the bairns' breakfast.'

Rosie glanced at the package he placed on the kitchen table and she could see there was more than bacon and sausages in it, and again her heart flooded with emotion. She knew exactly who had prompted Mrs Connor's magnanimity. 'Thank you.' She turned fully to look at him as she spoke and his eyes were waiting for her.

'That's all right.'

'I'm going into Hendon later to look for rooms.' Rosie placed the big brown teapot on the table as she spoke before filling a pint pot with tea and pushing it towards him.

He nodded his thanks before asking, 'With your mam?'

'No.' She raised her head and looked at him again, and she chose her words carefully when she said, 'She's not well enough yet, she's not up to it.'

He didn't like the idea of Rosie trudging round the streets by herself, and his voice reflected this when he said, 'You watch yourself, lass.'

'I'll be all right.' Her smile was bright but he didn't respond to it, and now his voice was soft and warm when he repeated, 'You watch yourself.'

Their eyes caught and held, and Rosie was never sure afterwards how long they continued to stare at each other, but she read something in his gaze that lifted her spirit until she glowed. When she turned her eyes away from his she began to shiver inside, but it wasn't with cold or fright or any other sensation she could put a name to.

In the next few minutes before Davey left and Rosie took her mother a cup of tea the conversation was of an inconsequential nature, but he touched her face lightly as he made his goodbyes at the back door, and again there was a promise in the hazel eyes that made her tingle long after he had gone.

'I don't *want* to go to Mrs McLinnie's, I want to stay here an' look at the picture book Mabel Fanshawe lent me. Mrs McLinnie's house smells.'

'You are going.' Rosie's voice was terse. She had had more than enough of Molly in the last fraught ten minutes to last her all day, and her sister had managed to dispel the last lingering thrill of Davey's unexpected visit with her tantrums. 'Now get dressed like I told you and help Hannah to button her boots, I've brought the hook up for you.'

'I won't.' Molly's head was up, her lower lip thrust out. 'Not if you say we've got to go next door. 'Tisn't *fair*.'

'Then you will go to school.'

'*I won't!*' The last was a shout.

'One more "I won't" and you'll feel my hand on your backside.'

'Huh!' Molly's deep sea-green eyes were hostile as they stared into Rosie's, and she shook the mass of golden-brown ringlets that fell to below her tiny waist as she said again, 'Huh! You're not Mam, an' you're not *that* much older'n me,' before pouting peevishly.

How could someone who looked so angelic, so ethereally lovely, be so awkward and stubborn on occasion? Rosie asked herself as she stared back into her sister's angry face. But a large part of this was her mam's fault. Her mother had consistently given in to Molly's tantrums since the child was a toddler, so proud had she been of the small golden-haired daughter she called her 'wee princess'. Well, the wee princess was going to have to knuckle down to it like the rest of them. There was nothing else for it.

'No, I am not your mam,' Rosie agreed grimly, 'but until Mam is feeling better I'm as good as. Now get dressed.'

'I like Mrs McLinnie.' Hannah, who had been sitting in a corner of the three-quarter size iron bed she now shared with Molly – Rosie having steeled herself to remove the dividing curtain and take up residence in the other bed the week before – had noticed the glint in her oldest sister's eyes, and recognized there could only be one outcome to this particular battle of wills. 'She always gives us lardy cake an' stickjaw.' The plain little face beamed at the thought.

'Aye, well I don't know if there'll be any cake or taffy today, Hannah, but you be quick, there's a good lassie.'

Rosie glanced at Molly's grumpy face as she spoke and as a dart of compassion pierced her irritation – this was a bewildering and difficult time for all of them – she bent and hugged Molly to her for a brief moment, feeling a return pressure of thin little arms as Molly leant her head against her sister's chest. Meanwhile Hannah was glowing with self-righteous obedience as she slipped from beneath the coarse brown blankets and pulled her calico-topped petticoat over the linen smock she slept in, her fingers hastily reaching for her woollen dress as the icy chill in the room hit warm flesh.

Hannah's shiver prompted Rosie to put Molly from her as she said, 'Come on now, get dressed with Hannah, it's freezing in here and the kitchen is nice and warm,' her voice soft and persuasive.

'All right, but I still don't want to go to Mrs McLinnie's.'

Rosie left them to it, but before going downstairs she popped her head round the door of her mother's room. Jessie was lying in the same position she had been in earlier when Rosie had taken her the cup of tea, her body straight and still under the thick faded eiderdown and her face staring up at the patchy ceiling, her eyes unblinking. But she had drunk the tea, Rosie noticed.

'I'm going into Hendon, Mam. Mrs McLinnie's said she'll watch the bairns.' There was no answer or even an acknowledgement of her presence from the bed, and after a long wait Rosie said, 'Mam? What we were talking about last night about finding rooms? We won't be able to take everything with us, and we'll need some money for the first week's rent, so I thought . . .' She took a deep breath. Her mother wasn't going to like this. 'I thought we could sell the sofa and the chairs from the front room.'

'*What?* What did you say?'

'We're not going to be able to have a front room where we're going and we never use it anyway, it makes sense to—'

'You'll not touch me front room.' Her mother had raised herself on her elbows under the covers and now she paused, dropping her head slightly towards her shoulder and screwing up her eyes before she continued, 'You hear me, our Rosie? Not me front room.'

'We might have to, Mam.'

'Never, not while I've breath in me body. It's took me years to get that how I want it an' I'm not lettin' that go for nothin' or no one. Your da knew how I felt about me front room, aye, he wouldn't hold with this. He'd tell you soon enough, so he would.'

30

The mention of her father was like a sword piercing her through and that, together with the fact that Rosie had lain awake for a good part of the night tossing and turning as her mind had worried at the mountain of that first week's rent – and the week's after it – until the thought of the virtually new furniture in its hallowed holy of holies had come to her, made her voice tight as she said, 'Face facts, Mam, *please*. It's rooms somewhere or the workhouse, we've nowhere else to go.'

'Eee.' The curtains were still drawn and the room was dim, its dark brown paintwork and faded wallpaper making it even more sombre, but her mother's eyes became pinpoints of light as she raised herself still further in the big brass bed. 'For one of me own to threaten me with that, I never thought to live to see the day. By, things have come to a pretty pass.'

'I'm not threatening you.' Rosie's stomach was trembling. 'I just want you to understand how things *are*. We were all right a few weeks back, we had Da and the lads' wages coming in, but that's all gone now. We don't have any *money*, Mam.'

'Huh.'

It was so exactly the sound Molly had uttered just minutes before that something of a revelation flashed across Rosie's understanding, something that shocked her into leaving her mother's room without saying anything more.

It was her *mam* that Molly took after, Rosie acknowledged, as she stood on the landing for a few seconds before walking slowly downstairs to begin preparing the family's breakfast of porridge and bread and butter. And she had never seen it before.

Suddenly a hundred and one little incidents from her

childhood, buried deep in the recesses of her mind, fitted together into one whole. Her da had always babied her mam, looked after her, even pandered to her at times, and on the one or two occasions he had denied her some whim or other there had been hell to pay for a while. It wasn't that her mam was a bad person, and she had loved her da and the rest of them, but there was a – Rosie searched for the words to describe how she felt – a singlemindedness about her in some ways, a childish determination to have things her own way and get what she wanted regardless of circumstances or people. And Molly was the same. The pair of them were a strange mixture, a really strange mixture.

Funnily enough, Annie McLinnie seemed to confirm that very thing when Rosie took Hannah and a sulky-faced Molly to her next-door neighbour after the two children had had their breakfast. Rosie had popped round first thing before the others were awake to see if the garrulous old northerner, who had a husband and five sons all in work at Doxford Shipyard – there had been three other sons too, but of the six who had been conscripted to fight in 1916, only three had returned after the war – could take care of her two sisters for a few hours, but Rosie hadn't gone over the threshold then, mainly because the men hadn't left for work.

'Hallo, lass. You want the missus?' Arthur McLinnie had been eating his breakfast when she had opened the back door after knocking once, and his cheerful, gnome-like face had broken into a smile on seeing her. Rosie liked Mr McLinnie, he was small and wiry and possessed of a geniality that was indestructible, and the four oldest brothers were all right – big, rough, a bit over-boisterous at times but kind – but the youngest son, who was the same age as Sam and Davey, made Rosie feel . . . funny. He had a certain way of looking at her, she couldn't explain it, but when Sam had told her a few months before not to be alone with Shane McLinnie, Rosie hadn't argued, despite the fact that she had played with the McLinnie brood from a bairn and treated their house like her own.

'You'll have a sup of tea afore you go, hinny?' Annie was all alone now in her kitchen, which had none of the scrubbed cleanliness of next door but nevertheless was warm and cosy after the bitter chill outside. 'An' I've a nice bit of fat bacon if you've a mind for a bite?' She indicated a large cut of meat lying amidst the havoc of what was obviously the remains of the men's breakfasts, and as Rosie glanced at the glistening white mound, on which there was only a thin streak of pink, she just managed to suppress a shudder.

'No, no thank you. We've just had porridge.'

'A sup then?'

'I'd like to, Mrs McLinnie' – it was true, she would like nothing more than to sit and talk with this old friend who had been like a second mother to her ever since she had first toddled into her kitchen as a tiny bairn, until Sam's warning to her in the summer – 'but I've no end to do, and I want to be back home before dark.'

'Aye, hinny, all right. The bairns'll be looked after, you know that, an' I'll look in on your ma after a bit.'

'Thank you.' The kindness had a weakening effect. It cut into the armour Rosie had to put on daily to cope with her private grief and pain whilst taking care of her mother and Molly and Hannah and trying to sort out the wreckage of their lives. She swallowed deeply before she said again, 'Thank you.'

When she opened the front door the air was bitingly cold and there was a raw wind blowing that spoke of snow. Annie

33

followed her onto the doorstep, glancing into the frozen street as she exclaimed, 'By, by, it's cold, lass. You go careful mind, it's a sheet of glass out there. An' Rosie?'

'Yes, Mrs McLinnie?'

'Don't you take the world on your shoulders, you know what I mean, lass? Your mam's a friend of mine as you well know, but it don't make me blind neither. I know it's early days an' she's still reelin' under the shock of it all, an' that's understandable, but Jessie's never bin one for facin' what she don't want to face. You get my drift? Your da had to be firm with her at times an' weather the storm to sail into calmer waters.'

Rosie stared at the blunt northern face and the weakness assailed her more strongly, causing her to blink a few times before she could say, 'She's finding it very hard.'

'Aye, an' so are you, I'll be bound. There's some folks who're givers an' some takers, an' that's what makes the world go round when all's said an' done, but it's as well to recognize the fact, lass. It needn't make any difference to the feelin' you have for 'em, just the way you deal with 'em, eh, hinny? An' while we're talkin' like this, I don't know what's made you a stranger to me door, an' I don't want to pry, but . . . is it anythin' I've said or done, lass? I haven't upset you in any way?'

'Oh, Mrs McLinnie.' Rosie didn't know what to say. 'No, no, it's not you, of course it's not you. It's just . . .' She didn't know how to go on, but she didn't have to.

'That's all right then, pet, enough said.' Annie patted her on the shoulder, her rough, flat-nosed face breaking into a wide grin. 'I'm not nosy, lass, an' I dinna want to know the ins an' outs of an old mare's backside, it's enough there's nowt wrong atween us. You go an' see what's about in

Hendon, an' I'll be sayin' a little prayer that the good Lord'll guide your footsteps.'

'Goodbye, Mrs McLinnie.'

'Goodbye, lass. An' watch how you go, mind.'

Annie stood and watched Rosie walk carefully away on the icy pavement and she was no longer smiling. It was as she had said, she wasn't blind, and she'd had a good idea all along what had made the little lassie stop coming round like she had since she was knee high to a grasshopper.

Annie narrowed her eyes after the departing figure and breathed in slowly, the freezing air cutting her throat. Every time she saw Rosie it made the unease she felt about her Shane rise up as bile in her throat, the taste of it reminding her of the bitter pain and outrage she had felt the day he was conceived. But then it was always there deep down, nagging away at her in the night watches when the rest of the world was asleep and Arthur was snoring his head off beside her.

But he was a good man, her Arthur. Oh aye, she could have done a lot worse than him. He had never looked at another woman to her knowledge, not even when she had had her bad spells after Shane was conceived and hadn't let him near her for nigh on two years. He had endured it all without complaint and in his own quiet way he had stood by her. She knew some of them who were off to see the priest at the drop of a hat, demanding he come round and add the church's backing to the man's demand for what he saw as his 'rights'. No, there weren't too many like her Arthur, not round these doors leastways.

Rosie had vanished from view now but still Annie stood there, her eyes unseeing as her mind returned to the problem that had become an ever-present torment in recent months.

She had worried enough when her oldest six lads had been called up, leaving only Shane and John at home. By, she had fair gone round the bend at times with what her imagination had pictured. But this worry, this was different, and aye – worse somehow.

She had learnt to live with the pain of Samuel, Jack and Hughie going, bad as it was she'd had no choice, had she. The war had taken them and that was that, and she did her grieving in private like many another mother. And she loved her Shane just as much as any of the others, aye, she did, but it didn't shut her eyes to the fact that something had been passed down in the genes, something . . . unnatural. And – God help them all – he liked that little lassie.

Annie turned abruptly, shutting the door and walking through the dark narrow hall into the snug warmth of the kitchen, there to find the two children sitting toasting their toes on the fender.

'I've told you about rozzeling your feet afore, now haven't I? You'll be gettin' chilblains the size of walnuts an' then you'll have summat to whine about,' she warned darkly, as Molly and Hannah brought their feet jerking down onto the floor.

They stared at her, and as she glanced their way she thought, The poor little blighters! Here's their world been turned upside down and their mam gone all to pieces. If it wasn't for that young lass just gone it'd be the workhouse for the lot of them, but Rosie won't let that happen. She was born with steel in her backbone, that lass, and she's been helping Jessie run the house and look after the younger ones for years, not that she's ever got any thanks for it.

'D'ye fancy makin' a round of singin' hinnie then?' As she addressed the two girls their eyes brightened. 'You,

Molly, you get the flour an' fat, you know where I keep it, an' Hannah, there's three pennyworth of currants on the shelf under the slab in the pantry. You fetch them, there's a good lassie.'

Aye, her Shane liked Rosie. As the children scurried away the thought was back. And there was something raw and ravenous about the liking. Eee, she was bad – wicked – to be thinking like this about her own son, may the good Lord forgive her. She walked across to the open fireplace and settled the kettle on the hob. She couldn't always be watching him, waiting for her worst fears to be realized. He was just a lad when all was said and done, she could be wrong. And mothers were supposed to think the best of their bairns weren't they? She turned to the girls, who were waiting with eager anticipation to make the scones, sleeves rolled up, and said, 'Come on then, get them aprons on, there's good lasses. Your mam'll have me guts for garters if yer go back all claggy,' and, putting all further thoughts of Shane out of her mind, fetched out her baking tins.

As Sunderland had grown in the nineteenth century it had absorbed the small villages of Hendon and Grangetown, which had been a pleasant rural area with the charmingly named Valley of Love and the spa water of the spring on Hendon beach, and by the beginning of the twentieth century it had become heavily built up. However, there was still a strong village sense of community in the area, and most of the residents knew as much about their neighbours' families and background as they did about their own.

This became evident to Rosie when, after taking the tramcar via Villette Road which passed under the bridge carrying the railway line between the South Dock and the

Penshaw railway, she ventured into one or two shops in the area and received the same response when she enquired about the possibility of rooms in the district. 'Rooms, lass? Oh, aye? You're not from round these parts, are you?'

It was after some kind soul had directed her to Hendon Road – 'You go an' have a look in the Co-op's window, lass, they've got cards in there, an' the London an' Newcastle Tea Company, they have a few an' all' – that Rosie felt she was getting somewhere, but by then it was past two o'clock and she could smell the forthcoming snow in the bitterly cold air. But she had to try and get something today, she thought desperately as she hurried towards the first address in Robinson Terrace. Whatever her mother thought about Mr Kilbride, she knew better, and he wouldn't be averse to turning them out into the street. They had stretched his magnanimity as far as it was going to go.

She liked the look of Robinson Terrace, but the two rooms at the top of the house had long since gone, the somewhat surly man who answered the door told her. It was the same story in Bramwell Road, and now, as she hurried to the last address in Benton Street, Rosie found herself praying as she slipped and slid along the icy pavements. She needed to get somewhere close to the jam factory, there would be no spare money for tram fares and the like, and hard though it would be to leave Monkwearmouth it made sense to find rooms on the south side of the river. But not the East End. Anything, *anything*, would be better than her grannie's.

In spite of all her scampering a grey dusk was casting deep shadows over the dark slate roofs of Benton Street by the time Rosie reached the lengthy street of terraced, red-bricked houses, and the first delicate snowflakes were dancing in the wind. It would be quite dark soon and she was going to be much later than she had planned, she told herself silently as she walked somewhat gingerly along the narrow, frost-covered pavement towards number fifty-four. But it didn't matter. All that mattered was getting rooms *somewhere*.

'Aye? What is it, lass?'

When the door to number fifty-four had swung wide Rosie had had her opening line hovering on her lips, but on her sight of the man who was standing in the doorway her mind went blank. He was a good-looking man, very good-looking; his wavy white-blond hair and deep blue eyes suggested a Nordic genealogy and his massive shoulders and big barrel chest spoke of strength, but it wasn't his handsomeness that caused her to gasp like a stranded fish. The top half of his body was magnificent, but it was carried on tiny, stunted legs that were no bigger than Hannah's and his height was well under five foot.

Rosie was aware she had to say something, *anything* – the poor man must have faced this sort of situation countless times in his life, but it was still awful for him – and she wetted her lips before she managed to bring out in a fairly normal voice, 'Good evening. I understand you have rooms to let?'

'Aye.' The brilliant eyes had narrowed on her face, and somehow the broad northern accent made his appearance all the more incongruous. 'By, you've bin quick off the mark, t'others only moved out this mornin'.'

'Did they?' She had to do better than this. Rosie took a deep breath and prayed her brain would unscramble. 'I . . . I only started looking today. There was a card in the window of the London and Newcastle Tea Company store.'

'Put there at ten this mornin'.' He nodded slowly. 'An'

who would be lookin' to live in the rooms then? Not just yourself?'

'Oh no, no.' She had an almost uncontrollable urge to clasp her hands together and wring them, whether with pity or embarrassment she wasn't sure. 'No, my mother' – it didn't occur to her she hadn't used the natural 'mam' – 'and my two sisters, my younger sisters.'

'Oh, right.' Something in his face relaxed and he nodded again, more briskly this time. 'You'd better come in for a minute, lass. It don't take much to have the curtains twitchin' in this street an' it's enough to freeze your lugs off out there.'

'Tha – thank you.' She didn't know if she wanted to go in. The 'for a minute' hadn't sounded too hopeful, besides which this had suddenly turned into something quite out of her sphere. Nevertheless, and mainly because she didn't want to hurt his feelings, she climbed the two steep steps and moved past him into the hall, following him down the passage once he had shut the front door and into a second room on her right. He walked quickly but with a shambling gait as he swung his big shoulders to compensate for his small strides, and again pity was at the forefront of her mind, but as she came fully into the room and glanced about her she forgot everything in her surprise.

It was a living room, that much was plain, but one the like of which she had never seen before. There was a carpet on the floor, and not just a square but a whole carpet stretching into each corner, and the swirling pattern of red and gold seemed to make the room glow. Two big armchairs, high-backed and deeply cushioned in a dark red material that matched the carpet, were drawn close to a blazing fire, and the gold velvet drapes at the window were pulled against the chill of the night and reached right down to the floor. A glass-fronted cabinet, complete with little figurines of shepherds and shepherdesses and the like, stood in one recess to the side of the fireplace, and in the other was a piano, its dark wood gleaming in the flickering light of the fire. Along the wall opposite the fire and five feet or so behind the chairs stood a big sofa with little occasional tables either side of it, and above the sofa there was a massive gold-framed mirror with fancy scrollwork and elaborate beading at the corners. A long bookcase, which reached to the ceiling and was crammed full with leather-bound volumes, stretched all down the wall that adjoined the room which overlooked the street, and the gold lettering on the spines of the books glowed in the soft light.

Rosie gaped, she couldn't help it. This room was a wonderland, a fairy tale, something you would read about in a bairn's book but never imagine seeing in real life. Her mother's prim, cold front room with its uncomfortable horsehair suite and small square of carpet was one thing – such rooms were a status symbol for those housewives fortunate enough to be able to spare the space in the cramped, overcrowded houses where families of twelve and more were not unusual – but this was so far removed from that as to be incomparable.

'Have a seat.'

Rosie came out of her stupor to realize the man was watching her, his eyes intent on her face, and she knew she was blushing as she sat down gingerly on the very edge of one of the chairs. But she needed to sit down, she was feeling very strange. Whether it was the heat of the room after the bitter cold outside, or the fact that she hadn't eaten anything since the few spoonfuls of porridge first thing, she didn't know, but suddenly the palms of her hands were damp and perspiration was pricking at her armpits.

'Thank you.' She could hear the wobble in her voice but she couldn't do anything about it. 'I'm sorry, but could I have a drink of water? I've been looking at rooms all day and . . .' Her voice trailed away as she fought the faintness, panic high. She couldn't faint, not here, not with him.

She was vaguely aware of him leaving the room but such was her physical distress that it barely registered. But then a cup of steaming liquid was thrust under her nose and a deep voice said, 'It's tea you need, lass, you look all done in. Get this down you while it's hot, eh? I'd just gone an' made a pot when you knocked at me door.' She opened her eyes, which had been tightly shut against the nausea, to find him by her side, his face just above hers as he looked down at her with kind eyes.

'I'm sorry.' She had taken several gulps of the strong hot tea and was feeling more like herself. 'I never have turns.'

'Nowt to be sorry for, lass.' He hadn't joined her by the fire but had seated himself on the sofa across the room, and Rosie couldn't help feeling he had sensed her initial reluctance to enter the house and understood the reason for it – even if she didn't fully understand it herself.

'It's . . . it's the heat after the cold outside, and I've been out all day. Not that it isn't lovely in here with the fire, it is,' she added hastily, in case he should misinterpret her words as criticism. 'I've never seen a room like this in all my life.'

'How old are you, lass?' His voice was soft now.

'Fourteen.' Well she was nearly, give or take a few days.

'An' why are you wantin' rooms?'

'We've got to get out of our house, Mr. Kilbride's got another family moving in.' She was gabbling, this was no good, she needed to start at the beginning. Rosie took a deep breath and began again. 'It's like this . . .'

He listened without saying a word, the blueness of his eyes expressing nothing, and she told him the whole story, but with a bit of embroidering about the jam factory, feeling if she didn't say they had already got the jobs there was no chance at all of the rooms.

There was a deep silence when she finished speaking, and it seemed to grow and stretch before he said, 'An' your name is . . . ?'

'Oh. Rosie. Rosie Ferry.'

'Do you want to look at the rooms then?'

'Can I?' Her voice was eager. Suddenly the idea of rooms in this house was desperately appealing.

'Aye, you can look, but afore you do I'd better explain how things are. There's two rooms upstairs, an' I live downstairs in this room, me bedroom, an' the kitchen.' He pointed to the far wall. 'The netty is outside in the yard an' each house has its own in these parts. The hatchway is cleared by the corporation at night, but I'd expect you to keep it clean when you use it. There's a fireplace in both the rooms upstairs, an' water for drinkin' an' washin' will need to be carried up from the washhouse where there's a tap an' a boiler for washin' beddin' an' the like.'

Rosie was impressed. At Forcer Road the tap was in the yard and regularly froze in the winter, needing pieces of burning paper pushing up its spout before it would oblige with a trickle of water, and the two washhouses were shared between ten households. Of course, here she would be lugging water up and down the stairs, but Molly would help, she'd have to. And they would have to bring hot food in when they wanted it, but again they'd have to manage. Her da used to say you could get used to anything when you had to.

At least she would be spared the paraphernalia of the weekly wash with the neighbours, she'd always hated that. The violent pummelling with the scrubbing boards and washing dollies always seemed endless, along with the mangling of the wet clothes and the constant chatter. Her mother enjoyed the communal wash though, along with the gossip and backbiting that always went on from the first firing of the boiler to the last item being hung in the yard or on the long rope her da had nailed across the kitchen for when it was wet outside.

'Right. Thank you.' She didn't know what else to say to the man. 'That . . . that would be fine.'

'Me name's Zachariah, by the way. Zachariah Price.'

'Zachariah?' She knew there was a Zachariah somewhere in the Bible, she remembered that name from Sunday School, but she'd never known anyone who was actually *called* that, and again it served to make him even stranger in her sight.

'Aye. It means "the Lord has remembered", so me mam told me when I was a bairn,' he said quietly, and then, his voice taking on what could be described as a lilt, he added, 'but He forgot more than He remembered with me as you can see, lass. I've always thought He must've bin halfway through makin' me when He was called away to somethin' more important, an' He forgot to come back an' finish the job.'

Rosie was utterly lost for words. She had met other people who were handicapped before but none of them had had such a wicked trick of fate played on them as this man, and certainly none of them had made light of their disability. And then, as she looked into his face and past the twinkling blue of his eyes, she recognized something – a plea, a need, an unexpressed groan from deep within to be treated as just another man – and it was in answer to that that she said, as she managed a slight smile, 'It just shows that even them at the top can need a poke in the ribs now and again.'

He stared at her for a moment and then he laughed. His head back he gave a great guffaw of laughter that suited his massive chest, and Rosie found herself smiling in response, naturally this time. She liked him. He might be a bit strange – and she didn't mean his physical appearance here – but he was a nice man for all that, and this amazing room suited him somehow.

'You go up an' see what you think then.' He was wiping his eyes as he spoke, his mouth still smiling. 'I only use the stairs when I have to; they're a sight too steep an' narrow for my likin'.'

'Yes, of course.' Rosie rose hastily, smoothing down her thick serge coat that had become too small in the last six months as her figure had begun to develop, and pulling her felt hat more securely about her ears. He would find the stairs difficult, of course he would. There must be hundreds of things he found difficult. 'I won't be long,' she added awkwardly.

'Take all the time you need, lass.' And then, as though the pop-pop-pop of the gas mantle had reminded him, he added, 'You'll be wantin' a light, it'll be dark up there by now.' He levered himself off the sofa and waddled out of the room, returning a few moments later from the direction of

45

the kitchen and handing her a lighted oil lamp as she stood waiting in the doorway.

The bare wood stairs were indeed steep and very gloomy, with a peculiar little twist three steps from the top that brought Rosie facing a small dark landing. She walked to the first door and opened it to reveal a room of perhaps eleven feet in length and nine feet wide. It was quite empty, apart from a small deep-set grate in the wall facing her which was enclosed within an iron framework that was unusually decorative. Two long, thin sash windows in the far wall overlooked the sloping roof of the kitchen and the small yard, and there were no curtains.

The second room was larger, encompassing the front of the house but on the same lines as the first, with an identical little fireplace and three sash windows this time. Again there were no curtains, but this room was brighter than the other one owing to the lamplighter having lit the street lamp that was positioned just outside the window. Rosie stood for a moment looking about her. Whoever the other occupants had been there wasn't a trace of them left, the floorboards were swept clean and there wasn't anything to say anyone had ever lived here. She shivered suddenly, the chill of the night making itself felt after the warmth of the room downstairs.

What was she going to do if she couldn't get them set on at Bradman's? Of course she could try the Northern Laundry in St Mark's Road and all the shops hereabouts, but work was so scarce. But she couldn't think of that now, she'd sort something out, she'd have to.

He was sitting waiting for her in exactly the same spot when she went downstairs again, and the sight of the small stunted legs dangling over the edge of the sofa brought such a rush of pity that she lowered her eyes quickly in case he saw it. 'The . . . the rooms are lovely.'

'Aye, well I wouldn't go that far, but they're clean an' bug-free, lass, an' that's more than you can say in some quarters, however much they might whiten the step an' bleach the pavement of a Saturday mornin'.' He was grinning when she looked up, and gestured to the seat she had vacated by the fire as he said, 'Sit yourself down, lass. You're welcome to another cuppa but it's syrup, not sugar, courtesy of the Kaiser an' this bloomin' rationin'.'

'No, no thank you, I must be getting home.' Rosie took a deep breath. 'Could . . . could we move in at the weekend?' Davey had said he could get the use of a coal cart and horse on Sundays and it would save paying for a flat lorry. 'Would that be convenient?'

'Aye, it'd be convenient,' he said with a slight emphasis on the last word as though she had said something funny. 'But don't you want to know how much the rent is afore you decide?'

Oh she was stupid, she was. What must he be thinking? Her face flamed as she continued to stand awkwardly just inside the door and she knew she ought to say something cool and sensible, but all she could manage was a tight bob of her head as she kept her eyes on the handsome face.

'Well I don't charge as much as some, with it just bein' the two rooms an' all.' He paused, his mind working rapidly. He could get six shillings or more from a family where the man was in work, but as far as he recalled Bradman's weren't over-generous to their lasses and there were the two little 'uns to clothe and feed. 'How does three an' six a week sound for now?'

'Three and six?' Her mother had said they'd been paying

ten shillings to Mr Kilbride for Forcer Road, and here the netty and the washhouse were their own, along with Mr Price of course, and the room overlooking the street was perfect for a sitting room. Rosie nodded quickly. She had no idea how she was going to meet the first week's rent, and if he asked for it up front like most landlords did . . .

He didn't. 'Right, we'll take that as read then, lass.' For some reason – and he couldn't explain it, even to himself – Zachariah was finding that the sight of this young girl was paining him. In spite of the unusually mature way she had about her it was obvious she was little more than a bairn, her body was only just beginning to take on the first signs of womanhood and her eyes were as innocent as a five-year-old's. The creamy-skinned oval face was pretty enough, and the dark brown eyes with their heavy fringe of black lashes were striking, but it would be an exaggeration to call her beautiful. And yet . . . there was something more than mere beauty shining out of this face, something warm and vital that was causing his guts to twist and his voice to sound abrupt as he said, 'I'll see you at the weekend if not afore then.'

'Thank you.' In spite of all the uncertainty before her Rosie felt as though a huge weight had been lifted off her shoulders. She'd found them somewhere to stay and that was a start. 'Thank you very much, Mr Price.'

'Nothin' to thank me for, lass.' Zachariah had always considered himself a levelheaded, charitable man, and it was doubly disturbing to find he was already regretting the verbal agreement. 'It's business, that's all. Straightforward business.'

'Yes. Yes of course.' They stared at each other a moment or two longer, Rosie's eyes faintly puzzled, and then she said, 'I must go, my mother will be worried. I'll let you know what time we plan to arrive on Sunday when I've had a word with her, if that's all right?'

'No need.' His voice was over-jolly in his desire to take the stiffness out of it. 'I'll be in all weekend, lass.'

As she turned in the doorway he slid off the sofa and followed her out into the cold hall, and perversely he found he was swinging his body so it exaggerated his shambling gait all the more.

It was quite dark outside and the snow was settling, a thin wispy layer covering the frozen pavement like a bride's veil, and Zachariah, in an effort to dispel the awkward atmosphere, remarked, 'Looks like we're in for a packet this time.'

After stepping down into the street Rosie turned to face him again and now she found the six inches or so difference in their height was evened out and her head was on a level with his, when she said, 'So they say but we've been lucky so far.'

'Aye, just so.' She could say they'd been lucky after what she had shared about her family's circumstances? He looked into her sweet face caught in the light of the street lamp, the shadow of her hat turning her eyes into dark pools of velvet, and felt something tighten in his stomach. 'Just so, lass.' She was a fighter all right, this one, and he'd always taken his hat off to them that bit back. He found he was suddenly glad he had agreed to rent out the rooms. 'So long, lass, an' watch yourself, mind.'

'Yes, I will. And . . . thank you again, Mr Price.'

Chapter Three

'Here we are then, hinny, this is your stop. Watch yourself, mind.'

It was the third time today she had had the last words spoken to her, but Rosie smiled at the fatherly tram conductor as she stepped onto the pavement. The tram only took Rosie as far as the corner of Mapel Avenue, there was still the trek down Chapel Lane before she turned into Forcer Road and home. She stood for a moment in the feathery white silence as the tram trundled away, the two men and one woman who had alighted at her stop disappearing into the darkness. It was strange how the snow changed everything. Rosie lifted her head and looked up into the swirling blanket above, the big fat starry snowflakes settling on her eyelashes as she blinked against their coldness. It could even make Chapel Lane a thing of beauty.

'Hallo, Rosie.'

When the shadow at the side of the wall of a house opposite the tram stop suddenly moved, Rosie actually squealed aloud before she took a hold of herself. 'Who . . . ? Oh, Shane. What are you doing here?' she asked sharply, her voice slightly aggressive with fright.

'Waitin' for you.'

Rosie found she couldn't move as Shane stepped out of his hiding place, and then, when he was standing in front of her, that nervous, disturbed feeling was back tenfold. 'Waiting for me?' She eyed him warily. 'How did you know I was coming on that tram?'

'I didn't.' He was big and solid and his broad face under its shock of abundant fair hair was smiling. 'I've bin waitin' for an hour or more since me ma said where you'd gone. She's given the bairns their tea an' took somethin' round for your mam too.'

'Your mother sent you to meet me?' Somehow Rosie couldn't imagine Mrs McLinnie doing that.

'No.' His voice was soft and low, and there was a quality to it that made Rosie want to start walking. 'That was me own idea.'

'Oh, I see.' She was standing stiff, talking stiff. 'Well you needn't have.'

'I wanted to.' There was a slightly argumentative note to his voice now that reminded her of when they'd been bairns playing together and it was oddly reassuring, relaxing her enough to answer fairly normally, 'Well, thanks, but it's only a minute or two home.'

'Aye, but you never know.' His voice was casual now and his tone ordinary, and it relaxed her still more.

'No, I suppose not.'

He was a tall lad, all of six foot and big with it, and when he took her arm and drew her along with him Rosie found herself thinking, he's well set up, good-looking even, so why don't I like him in *that* way? Nancy Brown does, she's mad over him, so Flora said. And Lizzie Hetherington's set her cap at him, apparently. Perhaps it was because she'd always liked Davey from as far back as she could remember? But no, her feeling for Davey didn't really have anything to do with the way she felt about Shane McLinnie. Even if she had never set eyes on Davey she could never have contemplated walking out with Shane. Not that he'd asked her, of course, and there was no reason why he should. She'd heard tell he had a lass down Southwick way, and he'd been courting Mary Linney in Roker before that. There had been some trouble about Mary but Sam had never told her what, although it had been after that that he had warned her to stay away from Shane.

'Me ma says you're lookin' to move to Hendon?'

They were walking down Chapel Lane and the snow was coming down thicker than ever, almost obliterating the houses on the other side of the road.

'Yes.' There was an inflexion in his voice that made her tone defensive as she said, 'We've got to.'

'Don't give me that, you don't have to.'

'What?' She turned to him, her mouth wide, even as a separate part of her mind was saying, Don't argue with him, don't annoy him. Just agree with everything he says until you're home and you can shut the door on him.

'You want to get away, don't you? From Forcer Road, from me.'

She felt her stomach begin to flutter, but her voice was firm and steady when she said, 'Don't be daft, Shane, of course I don't. We're moving because we need to be close to Bradman's. We . . . we've got work there, me and Mam.' Eee, he was the second person she'd lied to about the jam factory. She was pushing her luck here, it'd serve her right if they didn't get the jobs.

'Bradman's?'

'Yes, Bradman's.'

53

'Since when?' he asked a touch belligerently.

Frightened as Rosie was she wasn't going to put up with this. 'Look, what's the matter with working at Bradman's?' She forced an equally belligerent note into her voice. 'You know how we're placed now Da and the lads have gone. Money doesn't grow on trees.'

'Aye, aye, I'm sorry, lass, I didn't mean . . .' His voice trailed away and for a moment the boy Shane was back, the little lad who'd always made time for her even when Sam and Davey hadn't. Shane had never sent her home with a 'You go back an' play with the lassies, there's a good girl', or refused to let her go freshwater shrimping when the lads would skinny dip and the girls would watch them, wide eyed. No, even then Shane had treated her different and, bairns being bairns, she had played on it until the uneasy feeling she'd had since she was around ten or eleven had grown into something approaching fear.

They were about a third of the way down Chapel Lane and normally at this time of night the street would be thick with children dangling on makeshift swings they had strung together from the jutting iron arms of the lamp-posts, or playing tip the cat and bays – a northern form of hopscotch – with thick glass counters called pitchy dobbers, but tonight the near-blizzard conditions had them all indoors.

'You got anywhere in Hendon then?'

'No.' The lie was spontaneous and immediate and made Rosie realize just how much she didn't want Shane to know her new address.

'Aw, Rosie' – he stopped, taking her arm and swinging her round to face him – 'you know how I feel about you, lass. You do, don't you? You're nigh on fourteen, you're not a bairn any more, an' there's that Davey Connor forever sniffin' about.'

She was shivering inside and the dark street, mute and silent under its thickening white blanket, seemed terribly impartial to her plight, but she forced her voice to sound cool and matter-of-fact as she said, 'I don't know what you mean. Davey's a friend of mine, he was Sam's best friend—'

'Aye, aye I know that an' all, same as I know your Sam told you to steer clear of me. I'm not wrong, am I?' He peered down at her, the thick snow covering his hair and the shoulders of his cloth jacket making him seem even more at one with the pale muffled world she found herself in. 'Just 'cos Mary couldn't keep her big mouth shut, an' there were others she gave the eye to on the quiet asides me. There's any number of lads who could've fathered her bairn whatever she says, the fat dirty trollop.'

He had given Mary Linney a bairn? As Rosie attempted to start walking again Shane's hands came down on her shoulders, and it took all her willpower not to react. But she had to remain calm and show him she refused to be intimidated, she felt her safety depended on it. 'Sam didn't say anything about you and Mary, Shane, and I have to get home—'

'Oh aye, an' pigs can fly.' His hands tightened as he bent slightly towards her. 'Mary Linney, huh! There was no way I was goin' to be saddled with a fat plain piece like her, an' you know why, don't you? There's only ever bin one lass for me, Rosie. One lass I'm prepared to give me name to.'

Why wasn't there anyone about? Why had Mrs McLinnie let him come out? Oh, she wanted her mam.

'Say you like me, Rosie, just a little bit, eh?' She could

feel him trembling through his hands on her shoulders, and his voice was a hoarse whisper, his breath hot on her chilled face. 'I'd be good to you, lass. I promise you I'd never look at another woman, not if I had you. You'd want for nothin', I swear it.'

'Let go of me, Shane McLinnie. I'm warning you—'

'I can't think of anythin' but you, it fair burns me up at times. That with Mary, that was nothin', just an easin' of meself.' He was muttering thickly as much to himself as Rosie. 'It's always bin you, lass, from when you was a wee bairn.'

He had drawn her against him in spite of her struggles, his big muscled body subduing her as easily as if she was still the wee bairn he had spoken of, and even through the layers of their clothing she could feel his arousal. His knees, his thighs, his stomach, she could feel it all as he held her pressed to him, one hand in the small of her back and the other clasping her right buttock as he moved her against him, slowly exciting himself still more.

Fear had frozen her vocal cords but then, as he endeavoured to move her backwards into the shadow of the gable end of a house, she opened her mouth to scream, only for his to clamp down on hers in a wet thrusting kiss that almost covered the lower part of her face. Rosie was fighting in earnest now, her small fists battering the solid wall of his back as she twisted and kicked with all the strength of her slight, slender body, but at eighteen, and after four years in the shipyard, Shane McLinnie had the physique and strength of a man twice his age.

When she tore her mouth from his long enough to emit one desperate strangled scream the hand on her buttocks came across her face to stifle the sound, but her cry seemed to bring him to his senses. 'Whisht, Rosie lass, it's all right.' He was still holding her so close she could feel every inch of him, and the hand on her mouth was forcing her head back until she felt her neck would crack. 'I'm not goin' to hurt you, not you. Dinna panic.'

Don't panic? Rosie could feel the bubbling hysteria and she fought it with all her might, she couldn't afford to weaken now. But don't panic, he had said, when she felt he had been eating her alive.

As the hand clamped across her mouth released its pressure Shane said, 'Now dinna scream, Rosie. Dinna, lass.'

'Let – go – of me.' Again she twisted and writhed.

'Aw, lass, I dinna mean anythin', not really. Pure as the lily you are, I know that, not like some of 'em hereabouts who're at it the minute they're off the breast.'

Pure as the lily? But she had seen what was in his eyes and he hadn't been going to stop at kissing her, Rosie thought sickly. He had wanted to take her down, she knew it.

'I've got to get home.' She tried to push against the bulk of him but he wasn't ready to let her go. 'Please, Shane.' Please, dear God, please help me. Please, please . . . And then, as if in answer to that unvoiced prayer, she heard something and said, 'There's . . . there's someone coming, listen.'

They were standing close to the wall of a house without touching it and now, as Rosie saw the portly little man and even portlier little woman emerge out of the thick veil of snowflakes, she wanted to call out to them. But she didn't dare. Whether it was fear of what Shane might do, or the equally strong fear that the result of such an action would bring her respectability – the importance of which her mother had impressed upon her from when she was knee high – into question, Rosie didn't know. Whatever, she watched the couple hurry past, her eyes desperate.

And it was only as the white silence surrounded them again – Shane using the momentary distraction to his own advantage as he moulded her firmly against him, fitting her slight body into his with an ease that spoke of practice as he groaned her name before devouring her mouth – that Rosie felt a strength she hadn't been aware of before flood her limbs. It wasn't nice, it was dirty – *horrible* – that thing pressing and prodding against her belly. As the thought hit she pushed savagely at his chest, catching Shane totally unawares and almost sending him sprawling into the gutter. As he staggered back a step or two Rosie was vaguely aware of a dark shape on the perimeter of her vision, but in the next moment as her head swung fully round it was gone. *Someone had seen them?* Oh no, please don't let anyone have seen them. And then, as Shane made a move towards her again Rosie hissed, 'You stay away from me, Shane McLinnie. I mean it.'

She was speaking through her teeth, her eyes fixed on his face through the starry snowflakes as she told herself she couldn't cry, she couldn't betray any weakness to those narrowed eyes watching her so intently, or he'd be on her again.

'Aw come on, Rosie lass, be kind. You know how I want you—'

'You touch me again and I'll scream enough to wake the dead, I swear it,' she warned tightly. 'You go and see Mary Linney if you want that sort of thing.'

Shane held Rosie's gaze for some moments before he muttered, 'I dinna want her. How many more times? I only want you.'

She didn't say anything more, merely glaring at him as she brought herself away from the wall where she had been leaning for support. She had to get home. She wasn't safe until she was enclosed within her own four walls, but she must not run; she had to walk carefully, steadily. It was only her composure that was holding him at bay.

As Rosie began to walk along the pavement, the snow covering her black elastic-sided boots and brushing the hem of her thick serge skirt, Shane fell into step beside her. He made no further attempt to touch her and he didn't speak, but her heart was thudding like a sledgehammer as they reached the end of Chapel Lane. Forcer Road was poorly lit and never had the distance to number ninety-seven seemed so long, but then she could see her own front door and she had to restrain herself from breaking into a sprint.

She had her key ready in her hand and once they reached their respective doorsteps immediately inserted it into the lock, but he caught her arm as she stood on the step. 'You comin' in for the bairns?' His voice was soft and made her want to be sick.

'No.' She couldn't bring herself to look at him as she spoke but she was aware of his eyes sliding over her face, and it was all she could do not to scrub at her skin where they had rested as she almost fell into the dark hall, slamming the door shut behind her and leaning against it for a moment as she tried to compose herself. He wouldn't have dared to do what he'd done tonight if her da and the lads were still alive. Shock and anger were making her face burn and the bile rise like acid in her throat. Or maybe he would? Her eyes narrowed in the blackness. Aye, maybe he would at that.

It was some seconds before she straightened her back, but her head was still bent as her thoughts travelled on.

And what if it had been summer, and she hadn't been muffled up to the nines? What if he'd caught her in a back alley somewhere? Would he have treated her like Mary Linney, tried to force her even? She wouldn't put anything past him. Oh, she wished she knew more about all that side of things, bairns and marriage and all that, but her mam had never discussed anything with her. The little she did know she had gleaned from Flora, whose mam did at least answer her questions when Flora asked her. Rosie still remembered the terror she had felt the summer before when she had awoken in the middle of the night to find blood all over the bottom sheet. She had thought she was dying, that there was something wrong inside.

She could have asked Mrs McLinnie anything though, which was funny when you thought about it, with her being Shane's mam. Oh, he was horrible that Shane, filthy. She raised her head, gulping spittle into her dry mouth as she heard her mother call from the kitchen. And she was glad they were moving to Hendon now, she was. The other side of the world wouldn't be too far.

It was snowing and freezing hard when Davey Connor walked through the colliery gates and into the dark street beyond, and as he glanced round at the luminous new world he found the glistening white purity actually pained him. *He couldn't go down again, by all that was holy he couldn't.*

He lifted his hand in acknowledgement to the shouts of farewell from some of his workmates and walked steadily down the street without looking to left or right, but once he was clear of Southwick Road he had to fight the desire to run and run and keep running until he left Sunderland and the nightmare of the pits far behind him.

By, he felt odd, queer. He lifted his hand to his brow and it came away damp with sweat despite the freezing cold. There'd been a moment down there today, more than one if he was being honest, when he thought he was going to have to give the distress signal and get out as this feeling had engulfed him. He couldn't take it, he couldn't stomach going down into that black hell every day for the rest of his life.

The panic threatened to take him over and he turned off the main street, entering a cut between two houses known as Bog Alley that led to a small patch of waste ground which was used by the surrounding neighbourhood as a dumping site. Once he was out of sight of the street he leant against an old stack of rusty corrugated tin, drawing in deep gulps of the icy air as he willed himself to calm down. Damn it. *Damn it.* What was he going to do? This feeling, this terrifying, acrid blind fear that turned his bowels to water and made him sweat like a pig wasn't getting better as he'd hoped – it was worse if anything.

Every time he went down he could see the bodies, or bits of bodies in some cases, strewn about in the grotesque mayhem of death. Some of them had been unrecognizable, and that was bad enough, but it was the ones that still bore some resemblance to human beings that had affected him the most.

Old Frank Carter in the last section where the roof hadn't come down sitting with his bait tin in his hand for all the world as though he was going to eat his fill, but with all of his clothes burnt and melted into his blackened skin. And young Peter Fowler, it had been the poisoned air that had got him right enough; the look on his face . . .

Stop it. *Stop it.* 'That's enough.' He said the words out

loud with his eyes closed, but the picture was carved into the screen of his mind and there was no getting away from it. He had been fifteen, young Peter. *Fifteen.* And Rosie's brother Phil, still nothing more than a young lad. He was glad he hadn't been there when they had come to Sam. He couldn't have taken that and remained half sane. He snatched his cap off his head and tilted his face upwards.

There was an emotion threatening to burst out of his chest that was indescribable but he knew he dare not let it have free rein. Once out in the open he didn't know where the pain and anguish would take him, and he couldn't afford the luxury of letting go. And all this talk of what he was going to do – he shook his head at himself, his eyes springing open and his upper lip curling in self-contempt – he knew what he was going to do all right, what he *had* to do. He had to get over this, and damn quick too, there was nowt else for it. He was a miner.

He shivered, but it was the storm within that was causing his blood to run like liquid ice. Aye, he was a miner, and his da had been a miner, and his grandda and his grandda's da afore him. And the pit had taken each one of them in its own way. His grandda and his great-grandda had died of the coal dust eating into their lungs – silicosis they called it, according to one of Sam's books, but all he'd known as a bairn was that his grandda fought and gasped for each breath, his eyes wild at times as he'd died inch by inch. His own da had bought it in a mine disaster the year before Davey had first gone down. He had been one of three miners buried alive in a fall of side from a wet slip in the area where they had been working. They had brought him home that same day, almost to the time he would have returned from his shift, and his mam had taken hours laying his da out.

When he'd gone into the front room to see him he had found it difficult to believe the scrubbed white figure lying so still and serene was his da. He had been so clean, even his fingernails . . .

He levered himself off the mound of tin and shook his curly thick hair to dislodge its coating of snow. Before this last fall his life had looked so straightforward. There'd been Sam, who'd always been like a brother to him from when they had first played in the streets together as snotty-nosed bairns, and he knew Sam had been all for him and Rosie getting together when she was old enough to start courting. And that would have fitted into the plans he and Sam had in mind. Oh aye, Sam and Rosie had understood what made each other tick right enough, there would have been no difficulty there. And him and Sam would have made a go of that little farm they'd dreamed about, Castletown way maybe, or perhaps Herrington, and once Rosie had been wed to him she'd have been clear of these streets she hated so much and out in the country, and there would have been Sam's wife for company for her – whoever that might have been. By, them Sundays when the four of them, him and Sam and Rosie and Flora, had walked their legs off until the town was far behind them and the world had become a picture of brilliantly green fields and hedgerows and the like, seemed like another lifetime now.

He shook his head again but now the movement was savage. Whisht, what was he doing harping on like this? Sam was gone, the dream of their partnership was gone, and there was only grim reality left. And reality told him he'd be working underground and taking care of his mam for years yet, because one thing was for certain, the rest of her brood wouldn't lift a finger. Four older brothers he had, and three sisters, and they'd all cleared off and got married the first chance they'd had, leaving him with the old lady. Not that he didn't love his mam, he did, and he was only too aware of the hard life she'd had. And Rosie? The name caught at him with equal pain and pleasure. By, Rosie was special all right. The last few months had seen a change in her that plain fascinated him and something had been signed and sealed this morning. But – he paused in his thinking, breathing hard through his nose – he would have to wait a while longer before he showed his hand and asked her to start walking out. Sam and Phil had done a good job in warning the lads off, and he didn't blame them, it was only right and proper they'd looked out for their sister, but her innocence meant he couldn't rush her, especially with all she'd got on her plate now. No, he'd go nice and easy, but man – his breathing quickened as his pulse raced – she was going to be his.

'Course there'd be her mam and the bairns in the picture for a time but they'd sort something out, they'd have to. He couldn't wait until the bairns were grown up to wed her, that could be ten years or more and he'd go round the bend before then. He'd like to tie the knot as soon as she was old enough if she was willing. And her eyes this morning had told him she would be willing.

Davey straightened his back as the chill of the raw night penetrated his rough working jacket and muffler, congealing the perspiration on his skin with wintry fingers, and after shaking his hair once again, pulled his flat cap out of his pocket and stuck it on his head. By, the air smelt bonny the night – fresh, clean, like he imagined it must have done in the Garden of Eden if them stories in the Bible were to be believed. Sam had believed them. He caught at the thought, finding it strangely comforting. Aye, Sam had believed all right. He'd maintained it was man, not God, who had messed up creation, and they had had some right good discussions – if not arguments – about that and other things, and Rosie had put in her twopennyworth and all. Rosie . . .

Suddenly the longing to see her, if only for a few minutes, was so strong he could taste it. He'd nip round now on his way home and ask how she had got on in Hendon. The decision made, he turned swiftly and walked back along the narrow cut and into the dimly lit street again, his size-eleven hobnailed boots leaving deep indentations in the snow which was already an inch or two thick.

He took a couple of short cuts down the back lanes before he reached the alleyway that led through into Mapel Avenue, and as he neared the corner he saw two figures alight from a tram – a rotund man and small woman – who then preceded him into Chapel Lane. The couple were walking quickly, the woman holding on to the man's arm as she picked her way through the snow, and as Davey was in no hurry to overtake them he followed some twenty or so yards behind, aware the snow was coming down thicker than ever.

At some point – probably when he stopped to tie his bootlace – he lost them altogether in the swirling white cloud in front of him, but because they were still at the forefront of his mind he gave more than a cursory glance at the couple standing close to the wall of a house halfway down Chapel Lane as he passed. He couldn't see the woman – the man's back was obscuring her from view – but it was the unmistakable intent of the man and the intimacy of the entwined couple that caused Davey's head to swivel. They appeared to be fully clothed but what they were about was obvious, and then, at the same time that he recognized the man was Shane McLinnie, he heard him groan a name, *her* name, and caught just a glimpse of the small figure clasped in McLinnie's arms.

He stopped, he couldn't help it, and then he walked on quickly into the silent world ahead of him which almost immediately swallowed him up with blank anonymity.

Rosie. Rosie. His guts were twisting and he had the feeling he was shrinking, reducing down to a little speck of nothing. How could he have got it so wrong? How could he? And Shane McLinnie of all people? Didn't she know what he was like? Couldn't she see he was the scum of the earth?

He found he was swearing in his mind as he marched along, the profanities helping to burn up the sick churning that had stripped away all his manliness and brought a humiliation so deep that he didn't think he'd ever rise up out of it. And to think he'd refused Jenny Rowand when she'd offered it on a plate! And Hilda Casey, she'd been giving him the eye for months, along with her sister. But he'd had it in his mind to keep himself. *Keep himself.* He laughed deep in his throat, the sound bitter and low. Man, how they'd all laugh if they knew. Aye, they'd have a field day at his expense and love every minute of it.

He had passed the promenade at Seaburn, bare and desolate in the winter night and not at all like the bustling place of the summer months, when large numbers of bulky canvas tents were stored there and rented out to sun-seekers for the day, and walked on through the open fields past Whitburn Bay and into Whitburn itself, before reason asserted itself. His mam would be worried. He stood in the shadow of the gable end of a house and adjusted the muffler more securely round his neck as the wind blew the snow in mad flurries. Even if she assumed he'd stayed on extra he was never this late, he'd better get back.

It was gone eight o'clock before he caught sight of the sails of Fulwell Mill, and another ten minutes after that before he entered the back lane of Crown Street and then the communal yard that number eleven shared with the two houses either side of it. He noticed a piece of rag had been tied round the tap in an effort to keep it from freezing up. That'd be Mr Riley, he did the same every night and every morning it was frozen solid.

When he pushed open the back door Davey was immediately aware something was wrong. For one thing there was no evening smell of cooking coming from the blackleaded range and the fire was low, and for another Mrs Riley was sitting in his mother's chair to the right of the bread oven and she had been crying.

'Oh, lad, lad.' Mrs Riley sprang up at the sight of him, her hands going out towards him and her head bobbing. 'Where've you bin? Mr Riley an' our Douglas've bin scourin' the streets lookin' for you the past two hours or more.'

'Where's me mam?' He didn't answer her question. And then, when one hand went to her throat and the other clutched at her shawl, he said again, his voice sharp now, 'Mrs Riley, where's me mam? What's happened?'

'She's gone, lad.'

'Gone?' He stared at her stupidly. 'Where?'

And then, as her meaning hit him with the force of a sledgehammer, he groped at one of the straight-backed chairs under the table and sat down quickly, her voice coming at him through the ringing in his ears.

'You couldn't have done anythin', lad, not even if you'd

67

bin home hours ago.' Mrs Riley had her hand on his shoulder and was talking rapidly. 'I found her meself just after half four when I nipped round with a bit of bacon an' some stuff our Emily had got hold of.' Mrs Riley's married daughter, Emily, had a husband who dabbled in the black market, and as Mrs Riley's oldest friend, Davey's mother came in for a share of the contraband. 'Dr Maynard reckons she'd bin gone some hours, afore mid-day he thought. Heart attack.'

'A heart attack?' Davey looked up into the kindly face dazedly. 'But she was as fit as a fiddle apart from her rheumatism an' the indigestion keeping her awake some nights.'

'Aye, well the doctor reckons them dos she put down to wind was her heart.' Mrs Riley shook her head slowly. 'You know how she was about goin' to the quack. Wouldn't be told. Eee, it gave me a turn, I don't mind tellin' you, lad, findin' her like that.'

'Where is she now?' He couldn't take this in.

'In the front room, lad. She'd've wanted to be laid out there. Mr Riley an' our Douglas fetched in the trestle we used for our mam.' The hand on his shoulder was patting him as she talked. 'Mrs McClancy said she'd come in later an' help me do the necessary for your mam if that's all right with you, unless you think the lasses will want to do it? Or there's the undertakers?'

Davey thought of his three sisters and shook his head. 'No, Mrs Riley, I think me mam would've liked you to see to her.'

'Aye, I do an' all, that's settled then. We'll lay her out.'

'I . . . I must see her.' Davey lumbered unsteadily to his feet, his head spinning. He took a step towards the door and then paused, turning and taking the little woman's hands as he added, 'Thank you, Mrs Riley. Thank you.'

'Aw, lad, lad. You know how much I thought of her, closer than me own sister, she was. Bin through thick an' thin together, your mam an' me, an' the war was only a part of it.'

'I know, I know.' Now it was Davey who was doing the patting.

'I've got a bite of somethin' at home for you when you're ready, lad. It's in the oven, keepin' hot. You tap on the wall when you're ready an' I'll pop it round.' Mrs Riley wiped her eyes with the hem of her apron and bustled out of the door with her head down, pulling her shawl more tightly about her as the cold hit.

Poor Mrs Riley, she'd miss his mam. Davey stood for a moment in the kitchen and for the first time in his life he thought of it as empty. The lump in his throat became choking. He'd miss her too. She'd been a good mam, a loving mother, not like some round these parts who put on a show outside and became harridans and worse with their own menfolk. No, she'd been too giving if anything and his brothers and sisters had always taken full advantage of it. He felt something hot and wet drop onto the back of his hand and looked down at the teardrop in surprise. He hadn't been aware he was crying. He squared his shoulders, raised his chin, and prepared to walk through to the front room as the tears became a flood that coursed down his young face.

Chapter Four

It was a full five weeks after the pit disaster and eight days after Davey's mother had died before Rosie opened the door to Flora one cold February afternoon when Zachariah was out, and it was Flora who had to be helped up the stairs and into the sitting room as she burst into tears at the sight of her friend's face.

'I can't believe all that's happened, I just can't believe it.' Flora's pretty face was white, her grey eyes enormous. 'And me da didn't even write and tell us, he didn't say a word.'

The two girls were sitting in the bigger of the two rooms which now housed the kitchen table and two straight-backed chairs and the kitchen dresser at one end, and her father's old armchair and the five-foot wooden saddle with its flock cushions set in front of the fireplace at the other, with a space of four feet separating them. On the floor in front of the small grate was a large clippy mat, so heavy Rosie had difficulty in lifting it, and her mother's deep blue front-room curtains were hanging at the windows. Sam's small collection of dog-eared secondhand books were stacked neatly on a small cracket placed against the wall in one corner – Rosie couldn't bear to part with one of the painstakingly acquired little hoard – and a large orange box and a big ugly chest held all their clothes. There was absolutely no room for anything but the two three-quarter size beds in the other room.

Her mother's stiff horsehair suite had gone, along with the brass bed, the sale of which had meant Rosie needn't worry about the rent for a few weeks, and her father's Sunday suit and those of the two lads had swelled the coffers a little more.

Rosie shifted on the saddle where she was sitting with her arm round Flora's shoulders as she reflected, and not for the first time, that she knew why Mr Thomas hadn't written his daughter and wife about the accident. The tightlipped Welshman – who had a prestigious job at the Castle Street Brewery, which employed over two hundred staff and owned about a hundred and fifty licensed houses in the district – wanted his only daughter to associate with better than a mining family. The Thomases lived in a nice, terraced, double-bay-fronted house in the better part of Fulwell, which had its own garden front and back. Rosie had gone to tea there once and returned home with stories of the splendour and space, and the fact that Flora had a bedroom all to herself, but out of loyalty to her friend she hadn't mentioned, even to Sam, that she had hated every minute of it. Mr Thomas was a tyrant and his little mouse of a wife had scuttled about nervously in an atmosphere that had seemed to Rosie to be choking. Since that day she had felt desperately sorry for Flora.

So now she said, drawing Flora close for a moment more before moving to stand with her back to the glowing embers of the fire, 'Likely he thought it best. You couldn't have done anything being so far away and you would only have worried.'

'I'd have come home.'

Yes, she would have, and that was exactly why her father hadn't told her, Rosie thought perceptively. He couldn't control Flora as he could her mother and he knew it.

'Well you're home now.' Rosie managed a bright smile, Flora was feeling worse than she was right at this minute. 'And I can't tell you how pleased I am to see you.'

'How . . . how have you settled in?'

'All right.' Rosie shrugged, her face betraying none of the worry she was feeling. The jobs at Bradman's hadn't materialized, mainly due to her mother saying all the wrong things when they had gone to talk to the manager the day after Mr Nebb had tipped Davey the wink the two lasses had off and skedaddled. She had done it on purpose, Rosie knew it, and she hadn't pressed her mother to go with her on her subsequent searches for work. But it wasn't just the way merely living ate into their reserves that kept Rosie awake at night. She had thought Davey's manner – first when he'd told her the coast was clear at Bradman's and then when he had helped to move them in the coal cart – was due to his mother dying so unexpectedly, but now she wasn't so sure. They had been at Benton Street over a week and he hadn't called round once, and at his mother's funeral he had barely spoken to her except to announce his plans for the future.

Her thoughts prompted her to say, 'Have you heard about Davey's mam?' in as matter-of-fact a tone as she could manage.

'Davey's mam?' Flora's eyes sharpened on Rosie's face. 'No?'

'She died, of a heart attack.'

'*Davey's mam?*'

'The funeral was Thursday.'

'No.' Flora stared at her in open amazement, her full-lipped, wide mouth agape. 'I can't take all this in, I just can't.'

'And Davey's had enough of the pit. He—' Here Rosie had to pause in order for her voice not to wobble. 'He told me at the funeral he's thinking of leaving these parts now his mam's gone, getting right away altogether.'

'Well turn me over and call me Katie.'

The saying was a favourite one of Flora's and brought a smile to Rosie's lips despite the direness of the circumstances. 'Your da would go mad if he heard you say that.' Mr Thomas was always lecturing his outspoken daughter to conduct herself like a lady.

Flora shrugged unrepentantly. 'Everyone knows Katie Flanders has been no better than she should be since she's been knee high, now then. Aw, Rosie . . .' Flora shook her head bewilderedly. 'What's happened? I can't imagine Davey going off. I know you can never tell with lads but I'd have bet me last penny Davey was soft on you.'

Rosie averted her head – Flora's gaze was searching – before she said, 'Well that's what he said, Flora. And he was deadly serious.'

'Can't you talk to him?'

Rosie looked at her friend, her very dear friend, and her voice was flat when she said, 'No, I can't talk to him, Flora, 'course I can't, and you wouldn't if it was you.'

Flora nodded her acceptance of the statement, and as Rosie joined her again on the saddle the two girls were quiet, their bodies shoulder to shoulder as they sat staring into the tiny flames licking round the base of the fire. The bang of the front door followed by thudding footsteps and voices on the stairs brought Rosie to her feet. 'They're back.' Her mother had taken Molly and Hannah to see their grandma in the East End. 'You'll stay for a bite, Flora?'

'If you're sure.' Flora was feeling strange. When she had left Sunderland five weeks ago the world had been the same as it had always been. Granted, she had known she was going to take up the post of assisting Miss Wentworth in the office of W. Baxter and Sons, a small shipyard on the north side of the river, on her return from Wales, but that had held no surprise. Her father was a close friend of the Baxter family and the arrangement had been in place for months. But this with Rosie, her da and the lads dying and now Davey leaving, had turned everything upside down. Didn't Rosie care that Davey was going? Flora asked herself silently. Because *she* did, she couldn't bear to think she might not see him again. The pain that always accompanied thoughts of Davey – or more especially Davey and Rosie – caught at her throat causing her to swallow hard. She knew Rosie had always imagined it was Sam Flora liked and she hadn't disabused her friend of the notion. In fact she had actively encouraged it, because a blind man could see where Davey's fancy lay. And she liked Rosie – loved her – she was the sister she'd never had, which made things all the more confusing and horrible.

'What? 'Course I'm sure, you daft thing. Oh Flora, you don't know how I've longed to see you. I've missed you so much and everything has been so awful.' Rosie caught Flora's hands, her eyes moist, and Flora felt the coals of fire smoulder on her head. She couldn't be so nasty as to wish that she had got it wrong about Davey, could she? Especially when she knew how much Rosie liked him? But it was exactly what she wished and the self-knowledge was mortifying.

'Do you want one of Sam's books to remember him by?' Rosie said this last quietly as the door to the room swung open and Molly and Hannah entered at a gallop, and at Flora's nod, Rosie continued, 'We'll sort it out before you go and I'll walk with you to the tram. I want to tell you something.'

'What?' Flora didn't like the look on Rosie's face.

'I can't say now but it's to do with Shane McLinnie.'

'The dirty blighter!'

It was so exactly Flora, and so very definitely everything her father had tried to drum out of her, that Rosie found herself laughing as she clutched at her friend's arm and whispered, 'Shush, Flora, not so loud.'

'And you haven't told your mam anything about it?'

The two girls were making their way to the tram stop through dark streets where the frozen pavements were like glass.

'I couldn't, Flora, not the state she's in, and Mrs McLinnie is her friend. I wouldn't want to cause any trouble between the two of them. All round it seemed better not to worry her.'

'Well, remind me to show you a little trick my cousin Ronald taught me for putting a lad in his place if he gets frisky,' Flora said darkly. 'I haven't had the need to use it meself, but I can't think of a nicer bloke to try it out on than Shane McLinnie.' She made a sharp upward movement with her knee as she spoke and winked expressively. 'He'll get the message with that right enough.'

'Oh, Flora.' Again Rosie was laughing, but then her face straightened as she said, 'He wants to start courting me.'

'I bet he does, he's not daft, but you can do a sight better than Shane. By, even scraggy Aggie would be coming down a peg or two to walk out with him.'

Rosie grinned at the thought of the Sunderland fishwife who was notorious both for her loose living and vulgar tongue, but the laughter died as she said, 'He frightens me, Flora. Oh, I'd never let him see it, I've more up top than to let him think he's got the upper hand, but there's something about him . . .'

'And I dare bet his mam has told him where you live?'

'I suppose so.' And then Rosie flapped her hand almost irritably as she added, 'Anyway, he'd be bound to find out sometime, wouldn't he, and I'm blowed if he's going to make me hide away as though I've done something wrong.'

'Aye.' Flora nodded. 'Still, he can't do nothing if you keep saying no, and he'll get fed up in the end.' It was said with little conviction and Rosie didn't answer. She didn't want to waste the little time she had left with Flora before her tram came talking about Shane McLinnie. She didn't even want to think about him.

In the murky light from the street lamps the two of them continued to slip and slide their way along, clutching hold of each other now and again as one of them nearly fell and all the time talking. They passed a group of children about a game of mount the cuddie. Their cry of 'mountiekittie, mountiekittie, one, two, three,' at the player stumbling about with another child on his back followed Rosie and Flora down the street, and all but two of the little ones had no coats despite the bitter night.

It was as they passed the Dog and Rabbit on the corner that Rosie noticed the two little lads, who couldn't have been more than five or six, sitting huddled in the doorway of the pub, their bare feet blue with cold and encased in old holey boots that were falling apart. They looked frozen to death.

'You all right, hinnies?' Rosie stopped to stare down at the children as Flora continued to walk by. 'Shouldn't you be getting yourselves away home?' she asked quietly when they didn't reply.

'Me mam said we gotta wait for our da.' One of the boys, who was all eyes and teeth, jerked his head backwards towards the pub and even from two feet away Rosie could see the lice in his hair. 'He got his pay the night. We can't go home without him.'

'Poor little mites.' As the two girls walked on Rosie shook her head pityingly. 'What chance have they got, Flora?'

'Same as most round these parts,' came the stolid reply.

Rosie stopped abruptly, turning round and looking back at the public house with the flaking, creaking sign showing a snarling dog and a timid-looking rabbit above the doorway. She couldn't see the children now but she could picture them in her mind's eye huddled on the top of the cold stone steps with their thin little arms tightly round each other, in an effort to combat the raw chill with a measure of human warmth and comfort. Was it any wonder that bairns still died like flies round here? she asked herself bitterly. Why, only yesterday Hannah had come home from school half hysterical and Molly had informed them that little Millie Ross, who was just six years old, had had a heart attack in the middle of morning prayers and died. She had been ill with measles before, Molly had told them importantly when Rosie and her mother had questioned the children, and she'd only come back to school that morning, but she'd been all trembly and white in the playground and snivelling all the time. And now another child was dead, due to a lethal combination of lack of medical care, lack of food and – in Millie's case – lack of that most basic ingredient for a child's wellbeing, love.

'My bairns will have better than this.' Rosie turned to face Flora who was looking at her questioningly. 'By, they will, Flora.'

'Then you'd better set your sights on one of the gentry, eh?' Flora nudged her none too gently in the ribs and almost sent Rosie skidding off the pavement and into the road. 'Lucky that they're ten a penny hereabouts.'

'Oh aye, queuing at the door every night,' Rosie agreed, nodding solemnly at Flora and entering into the spirit of the exchange. 'Miss Rosie Ferry?' She struck a flamboyant pose in the manner she imagined a prospective suitor might, which brought a hoot of laughter from Flora. 'May I beg your company at the ball tonight?'

'Beg, eh? Ooo, la-de-da.' Flora was giggling helplessly now.

'What? You're just on your way out to the theatre?' Rosie's voice managed to express deep regret and obsequious civility. 'Then me poor heart is broken, Miss Ferry. May I enquire who the bounder is who's stolen your affection? Lord—? Oh aye, I know him, and he's not worthy to lick your boots, me dear.'

She eyed Flora with her head tilted slightly to one side for all the world as though she was listening to another voice. 'What? You want to present your friend, Miss Flora Thomas? Enchanted, I'm sure. I've heard of the lady's charm and elegance, of course.'

Rosie bowed low in front of Flora, who, in an effort to curtsey, found her feet flying up in the air as she slipped on the icy pavement with a loud squeal. She landed, legs outstretched and her arms supporting her, and let out a bellow of a laugh, and Rosie, her arms round her middle as she leant back against the wall, joined her, their breath white clouds in the freezing night air.

Oh, she was glad Flora was home, she was. Things were always brighter when Flora was around. And they would get through this, her mam and the bairns and her. They had enough money to last them for the next week or two if she was careful, even though the suite and her mam's big brass bed hadn't fetched a quarter of what she knew they were worth. And she would find work of some kind to keep a roof over their heads even if it killed her.

And Davey? The thought of the tall good-looking miner with his eyes of rusty green and wide smile made her heart skip a beat. Yes, and she'd sort that too somehow. She *couldn't* let him go.

Rosie found that vehement resolution was put to the test one night some three weeks later when she answered a knock at the front door when Zachariah was out.

'Davey.' Her warm smile of greeting dimmed when his face remained straight. She hadn't seen him at all in the last month and although she had tried to tell herself it was because he was busy, with his mam's passing and all, she had missed him terribly. And then the rush of euphoria at seeing him died away completely as he refused her invitation to come upstairs to the sitting room, his manner verging on the abrupt.

He had given up the rent on his mam's house starting the next day, he informed her gruffly as they stood in Zachariah's narrow hall, and he didn't see any point in remaining around Sunderland after that. He wasn't going back down the pit, that was finished, and with work of any kind being so hard to come by he thought he might try his hand at signing on with a ship. He wanted to travel a bit, see foreign parts, broaden his horizons.

'I . . . I'll miss you. There must be some work hereabouts you could find? Perhaps you could try at working on the land for a time like you and Sam always wanted?' It was as far as she dared go and even then Rosie felt she was being forward, all the worries which had tormented her since that morning in the kitchen five weeks ago crowding in with renewed vigour.

She had put him off in some way, she'd told herself a hundred times, as she had lain wide awake while the other three had slept. Or he had changed his mind about her and what he wanted, now he was free of all ties and could do what he liked. With things the way they were it wouldn't be just her he was taking on, certainly not initially, and what young man of his age wanted to be lumbered with a ready-made family? Or there might have been someone else who had taken his fancy. He was a good-looking lad and now his mam was gone it would be an added inducement to some of the girls hereabouts to land such a catch. Or . . . And so it had gone on, night after night.

Certainly since that morning in the kitchen he hadn't been the same, it was all tied up with that. And she hadn't imagined the way he had looked at her then, the promise his eyes had made that was in itself a declaration of intent. And up until that morning he had been so tender with her, so caring; but now that was all gone and she felt the loss like a physical pain. But she wasn't going to beg. Whatever, she wouldn't do that. He had to want her as much as she wanted him.

'Aye, I'll probably try me hand at farming somewhere or other, but there are other places than Sunderland.'

'Yes, I suppose so, but wouldn't it make sense to be close to friends and family – your brothers and sisters – for a while with your mam going and all?'

Davey shrugged broad shoulders, his brown eyes with their deep flecks of green hard on her for some moments before he said, his voice flat, 'How's the McLinnies these days? You have much to do with them now you're livin' on the south side?'

'The McLinnies?' It was all she could manage in response.

'Aye, the McLinnies.'

'No. No . . . not really.' Rosie could feel her cheeks beginning to burn and she stumbled over her words as she said, 'Of course with Mrs McLinnie being a good friend of my mam's she doesn't want to lose touch, especially after all that's happened. My mam feels lonely a lot of the time which is only natural I suppose.'

'Aye.' Davey's gaze narrowed on the eyes that always made him think of black velvet. So she wasn't going to come clean about Shane McLinnie? 'I had a chat with Shane the other day that made up me mind about movin' away.' He kept his voice steady and non-committal but it took some effort.

'Shane?'

But he had noticed the little start she gave at the name. 'Perhaps he mentioned it?' She must have wondered how Shane came by his black eye if nothing else, Davey thought, flexing the knuckles of his right hand which were still bruised and sore.

When he had sought Shane out four nights before it had been with the express purpose of finding out exactly how things were between the other man and Rosie, but when he'd found him in one of the rougher pubs down by the docks, the big steelworker had been cocky and full of himself. That in itself wasn't anything unusual, but Shane McLinnie's boasting about what he and Rosie had been up to had made Davey see red and the fight had been savage and furious. Had that bit of scum been carrying on with her even before Sam was killed, like he'd said? Davey asked himself now as he stared into Rosie's flushed face. A few weeks ago he would have bet his life she was as pure as the driven snow, but not any more. Damn it all, he had *seen* them, hadn't he. 'Begging for it,' McLinnie had said, before Davey had pushed the words down his foul throat.

'Why should Shane McLinnie tell me anything?' Rosie's face was about to burst into flames. But he couldn't know, not about that, could he? Even Shane would know better than to brag about what he had tried to do that night in the snow with Davey being such a close friend of Sam's, and anyway, unpleasant though it had been, nothing had happened, not really. 'I . . . I hardly ever see him.'

'Right.' Davey's thick brows came together and they stared at each other for a second or two in silence. Rosie wanted to lift her hand and cup his cheek, to place her lips on his, to ask him – beg him – to stay, but she was mute. His life was his own and he had every right to do with it as he willed, but she could scarcely believe this was happening. This wasn't the Davey she had known all her life, the gentle, kind lad with dancing eyes and a tender smile. This was someone quite different.

'I'll be gettin' off home then.' Davey's voice was gruff. 'I just wanted to let you know me plans, that was all, with you bein' Sam's sister. I'm away in the mornin' all bein' well.'

Sam's sister? *She was just Sam's sister.*

Rosie nodded slowly and she made no further appeal for him to stay although her stomach was sick as she bade him a stilted farewell on the doorstep. She continued to watch him as he marched off down the street and right until he turned the corner and was lost from view she half expected him to turn and wave, to pause and look back at her, to retrace his footsteps – *something*.

But then he was gone, and it seemed as though someone had extinguished a light deep inside her and all the world had turned grey.

Chapter Five

'You're goin' after a job at the *Store* you say?'

'Yes.' Rosie's voice was slightly defensive as she faced her mother before she turned abruptly to her two wide-eyed sisters whose ears were flapping as normal, and added, her voice sharper, 'Come on, you two, you'll be late for school again. Go and get your boots on, there's good lassies. And you, Hannah, finish your bread and dripping while you're about it.'

'You'll never get it.' Jessie sniffed disparagingly.

'Ta for the encouragement.'

'Well, I mean – the Store. Everyone's after a job there, you know they are.'

Everyone except her mother. Rosie kept the thought to herself but the frustration was biting deep. There was no reason at all why her mother couldn't do *something*, even if it was work at home like carding linen buttons or sewing hooks and eyes, but she didn't seem to realize that the little money they had left wasn't going to last for ever.

Rosie prayed for patience before she said quietly, 'Well, it's worth a try, Mam. The Co-op pay well and they treat their staff better than most.'

'Aye, I know that, an' that's why they can afford to be picky as to who they take on.'

'*Mam.*' Rosie took a deep breath. She couldn't let her mother get to her, not this morning, and now her voice was controlled again when she said, 'Like I said, it's worth a try.' And if this didn't work out she didn't know what she was going to do. Their main meal of the day for the last week had been potatoes baked in the ashes of the little fire in the sitting-room grate, with a slice of pig's pudding or a few chitterlings, as Rosie watched every penny.

They had been in residence at Benton Street for four weeks now, and in that time Rosie had gone after every single job she had heard about, only to learn they were long since gone by the time she had applied. Which wasn't surprising with more and more men either out of work or striking.

Not that Zachariah was pushing them. She had made sure she paid him the rent each week and when she had nervously explained that the jobs at Bradman's hadn't worked out, he had asked no awkward questions, merely saying, in that quiet way he had about him, that if the rent became a problem she must come and see him about it. But she couldn't take charity from him – he had been good enough about the low rent as it was and she appreciated that, more than he would ever know – and anyway, she needed a job in more ways than one. Her mother was driving her mad, and after the conversation with Davey a couple of nights before the two rooms had become positively claustrophobic. No, she was determined to get work, and please God it would be soon.

'Worth a try you say.' There was an odd note to Jessie's voice, high and yet at the same time flat, and it reminded

Rosie of Molly in her latest paddy first thing that morning when her sister had stated that it wasn't *fair* she couldn't have a party for her birthday in a few weeks' time, all the time staring at her out of great accusing green eyes that declared quite clearly whom she held to blame for her misfortune. 'Well, them that aim highest, fall furthest, as your da used to say.'

Oh, her mam! Rosie shut her eyes tight and bit hard on her lower lip before she turned in one sharp movement and called to Molly and Hannah who were squabbling in the bedroom, 'Come on, you two. *Now!*'

'Hannah can't find her knittin'.'

'What?' Rosie swung Molly about and pushed her back towards the top of the stairs as the young girl made to walk through to her mother in the sitting room. 'You're not going back in there, you're going to school. How many more times?'

'Hannah can't find her *knittin'*.'

Molly's resistance against her hands, and the quick and very definite kick backwards with one of her feet caught Rosie on the raw, and before she had even thought about it she slapped her sister on the backside. It wasn't a hard slap – it was more in the nature of a warning – but Molly's reaction was the same as if she had been knocked to the floor. She flung herself on Rosie, pummelling with her hands and all the time screaming, 'You dare! You dare skelp me, you dare! I hate you! I do, I hate you, an' I hate livin' here. I want to go home.'

Rosie was aware of her mother standing silently in the doorway to one side of her, and of Hannah emerging from the bedroom like a bullet out of a gun as she flung her arms round Molly's waist and got knocked to the floor for her efforts, but she didn't notice Zachariah until he pulled Molly from her, his massive chest and muscular arms subduing the sobbing child instantly although she continued to twist and turn in his hold like a demented rag doll.

'What's going on?' Zachariah was looking at Rosie as he spoke, but it was Molly who answered as she cried, 'I want to go home, I hate it here. You – you!' She spluttered at Rosie, a well of tears spurting from her eyes. 'You think you know everythin' an' you don't, you don't. An' you was always pushin' in with me da an' Sam an' Phil, makin' out they liked you best. An' I want to see them again, I don't want them to be dead.'

'Stop this.' Zachariah shook her, his eyes never leaving Rosie's white shocked face. 'You'll make yourself ill.'

'I won't!' And as Molly sensed where his sympathies lay she added, her voice as cruel as only a child's can be, 'An' you can let me be an' all, you Tommy-noddy. You can't tell me what to do.'

'*Molly.*' At the slang reference to Zachariah's lack of inches Jessie entered the rumpus for the first time, her voice sharp. 'You say you're sorry to Mr Price, d'ye hear me?'

'No I won't.' And then, as Molly realized the enormity of her crime, her sobs became a wail that threatened to take the roof off as she collapsed in a heartbroken little heap on the floorboards.

Rosie's heart was pounding so hard it was like a drum in her head and her mind was saying, How long? How long had Molly been feeling like this? She had tried to talk to her numerous times over the weeks since her father and brothers had died, but each time Molly had been quick with her rebuff and some act of naughtiness had followed. But perhaps she should have forced the issue, got it out into the open so that all the hurt and the confusion could have been dealt with and brought into the light. All this bitterness fermenting under the surface in a nine-year-old child was not healthy, and Molly was suffering as much at her mother's withdrawal as anything else.

'Molly, pet, now listen to me—'

'No, I'm not gonna listen, I'm not.' At her name Molly had clapped her hands over her ears, her face scarlet. Rosie indicated with a swift movement of her hand for Zachariah to carry the child into the sitting room, and as he sat her down on the saddle at Rosie's prompting, Rosie knelt in front of her and took the small hands in her own. She looked straight into the beautiful green eyes as she said, her voice weighty, 'Molly, I don't care if you hate me but I love you, I do. And so did Da and the lads, you know that. But they are gone now, they're gone and nothing can bring them back so we have to love each other all the more. Do you understand me, Molly? Everything I do I do because I love you and Mam and Hannah and I want us to be all right. I would have loved to be able to tell you we had enough money for you to invite all your friends at school for a birthday party, but we just haven't. And Da and the lads didn't love me more than you, Molly, but I was older and they talked to me about more grown-up things, that's all. You know that. You do, don't you?'

Molly tossed her golden-brown ringlets, her rosebud lips clamped together, but Rosie could see their quivering and she knew she was getting through.

'Molly, I would love to go home and have Da and the lads back and everything like it used to be, but I can't make that happen.' Hannah had sidled to Rosie's side and now she stood sucking her thumb, her other hand on Molly's knee, and as Zachariah watched the little tableau from across the room, his eyes on Rosie's earnest face, he experienced a physical ache in his chest as her gentleness touched him. 'And now we've all got to pull together as best we can, yes?' Rosie added persuasively as she hugged Molly to her.

'Yes.' And now, in one of the mercurial changes that had epitomized Molly from a baby, she threw her arms round Rosie's neck, hugging her back as she said, her voice tearful, 'I don't want to die an' be buried under the ground, I don't, Rosie.'

'You're not going to die.' Rosie moved Molly back fully onto the saddle again in order to look into her face as she added, her voice soothing, 'Is that what has been worrying you, hinny?' And, as Molly gulped and nodded her head; 'Molly, you're young, you're nothing more than a bairn, you've got years and years and years ahead of you.'

'Our Phil was only five years older than me.'

'But Phil was killed in an accident, a mining accident, you know that. You're not going to go underground, now are you?'

Molly shook her head. 'Is that why Davey is goin'? 'Cos he don't want to go down in case he gets killed?'

'Davey?' Even as Rosie said the name it dawned on her that Molly had been up to her favourite trick again, listening at keyholes.

'I heard him, the other night.' Molly knew she had given herself away and prevarication was useless. Besides, with Rosie in this mellow mood it was better to confess all now than later. 'An' you cried at the bottom of the stairs after he'd gone. Don't you want him to go?'

Rosie took a deep breath. Now was not the time to discuss Davey Connor and she was very aware of Zachariah's eyes on her as she said, 'It's sad when friends leave, Molly, and Davey was Sam's best friend, wasn't he? Now, we'll talk some more when you come home from school.' She wiped Molly's face with her handkerchief before she added, 'And I think you've something to say to Mr Price before you go?'

Apologies offered and accepted, Rosie chivvied the two little girls into their coats and down the stairs, and as they clattered away Zachariah, who was standing at the side of her on the landing, said, 'You all right, lass?'

'Yes, I'm all right. Thank you for your help, Zachariah.' It had become Zachariah rather than Mr Price at his prompting. What would he say, Rosie thought now, if she spoke the truth and told him she was far from all right? That she was being torn apart inside and all the little bits of her were striving to make some sense of the confusion that had become her life? Think she was going barmy most likely.

'The lass'll settle down in time, it's early days yet.'

'Yes, I know.' Rosie nodded slowly. 'And we'll get through. I've found the best way is to take it a day at a time and keep reaching for tomorrow. My da used to say that "trouble toughens and comfort corrupts".' She smiled as she added, 'But a little corrupting would be nice right now.'

By, she'd got some guts, this lass. If he'd been born with two strong straight legs he'd have moved heaven and earth to have her, in spite of him being a good few years older. That very first night, after she'd gone, he'd told himself he was a blasted fool, that he was imagining things, that love couldn't hit as quickly as that. But it had, oh aye, it had, and it *was* love – not lust, as he'd tried to convince himself ever since.

He'd had women since he was a lad of seventeen, and he'd only paid for it at the beginning when he'd thought an ordinary lass wouldn't look the side he was on. But there he had had a surprise. As the years had gone by he'd found there were quite a few who were willing. Granted it often started with curiosity; as his old mate Tommy Bailey had crudely put it, they were falling over themselves to see if his handicap had affected what was atween his legs. But the lasses had liked him too, one or two of them more than liked, but he hadn't loved any of them. And then when he'd met Janie, and her a well set-up widow with no bairns or family, he'd decided to settle down, as he'd described it to Tommy. At thirty, Janie had been five years older than him, and after ten years with a brute of a husband she'd had no inclination to tie the knot again. But she'd wanted company and someone in her bed now and then, and so they had found they suited each other just fine. Zachariah was fond of Janie but he didn't love her, although he was aware that over the three years their association had been going on he had come to mean more and more to her.

But how he felt about Janie, and all the lasses before her, was quite different to the way he felt about Rosie, and the thought of this little lass seeing him undressed, seeing him in his full glory as he put it to himself, was quite inconceivable. And the torment he had felt the last few weeks was as bad as when he'd first realized, as a little bairn, that he was different. Conspicuously different.

'Tommy-noddy, Tommy-noddy; big head an' little body.' Tommy-noddy. Oh aye, he'd heard that one afore and plenty more besides from some of the lads he'd been at school with, until he had worked his arms and his chest and developed his strength and the power in his torso to a point where they thought twice about tangling with him, small as he was.

'Zachariah?'

'Aye, lass?'

The front door had closed behind Molly and Hannah, Jessie had remained in the sitting room and the door onto the landing was closed, but Rosie still lowered her voice as she said, 'I'm sorry, about what Molly said.'

He didn't prevaricate. 'About me bein' a midget?' He forced his voice to sound airy. 'Likely that's how she sees me, lass, an' bairns are great ones for callin' a spade a spade.'

It had hurt him, she knew it had hurt him because she had seen the blow register in those beautiful blue eyes, but he would never admit it. She was surprised how much it upset her. 'She didn't mean it, you know, she lashes out when she's angry.'

'Aye.' He nodded now, and his voice lost its airy note for a moment when he said, 'I've never bin one for blowin' bubbles, lass, you know, like that song that was so popular last year? I know what I am, none better, so don't you be a frettin'. You've enough on your plate as it is.'

'Oh, Zachariah.' Her voice had a cracked sound. He was so kind, so nice, if she hadn't found this place they would be in dire straits by now. The thought reminded her about the interview at the Sunderland Equitable Industrial Society – the Co-op, or Store as it was always called by the locals – and when her expression changed and she said, 'I've got to be making tracks, I'm going after a job at the Store today,' he turned immediately, saying over his shoulder, 'Aye, you get along, lass, an' good luck.'

The Co-op in Hendon Road was a vital element in the local economy of the area, and more than that the inside of the building always had a warm and friendly feel about it; working there was a status symbol in itself. Rosie was vitally aware of all this as she hurried through the grey streets, her nervousness increased by the knowledge that if she could get taken on to the staff of the Store she would be well looked after, but that there would be plenty of other girls, and women, eager for the post. And some, no doubt, with experience.

As she rounded the corner into Hendon Road she almost slipped on the frosted pavement but then she was scurrying on again. She was going to be late, there was nothing else for it, and that would put the kibosh on the job before she even saw Mr Green in the grocery department. And she'd love to work there, oh, she would. Of course the hardware, greengrocery and clothes departments were all lovely, but on grocery the smells were so nice, mouthwatering. She didn't think she'd like to work in the butchery department – she'd be too aware of the slaughter yard at the rear of it – but she'd even jump at that if she was given half a chance.

She was panting hard when she pushed open the door and stepped into the bright interior, her gaze moving past the labelled shelves all down the right side of the shop where neatly packed packages containing currants, sultanas, sugar, flour, tea and a hundred other items besides reached up to the ceiling. A long polished wooden counter ran the length of the shop, and Mr Green was standing behind it at the far end, to one side of a stack of huge wrapped eighty-pound cheeses and a large beechwood cask of butter, busy grinding a measure of coffee for a customer.

Rosie stood for a moment catching her breath as she smoothed down her coat and nervously fumbled with her hat, and then she walked along the side of the counter, past the sets of brass scales, the massive tin box of corned beef, the bacon slicer and the vicious cheese wire on its big wooden block, and stood quietly to one side of Mr Green's customer as she waited for him to look up.

'Oh hallo, lass.' As the woman turned Rosie recognized one of her new neighbours in Benton Street. 'You all settled in now then? Findin' your feet?'

'Yes thank you, Mrs O'Leary.'

Zachariah had warned her to steer clear of this particular woman – 'twist the words of the Archangel Gabriel himself to cause a spot of mischief' was the way he had put it – so now, when the rough-hewn face continued to stare at her, and the bright beady eyes took in every detail of her appearance, Rosie found herself wishing Mrs O'Leary somewhere far away as she fixed her eyes on Mr Green and said, her voice as controlled as she could make it, 'Good morning. I called in yesterday afternoon and you asked me to come back this morning at ten about the position as shop assistant.'

'Ten o'clock?' Mrs O'Leary had noticed that this little bit of a lass wasn't over-friendly, and now she took great pleasure in saying, 'You're late then, aren't you, lass? It's gone ten past. Still, I dare say you had better things to do, eh?'

'Just wait there a moment and I'll see to you in a minute, lass.' Mr Green cut through the reply Rosie had been about to make, and she duly waited, her cheeks fiery, as he cut and weighed out five ounces of bacon and six ounces of cheese. Oh, that woman. That nasty old woman. She was bound to get short shrift from Mr Green now and she couldn't really blame him, and if she said she was late because her sister had been playing up that wouldn't look good either. Mr Green didn't want to take on anyone with home problems.

But she had to clear her mind now and concentrate on the forthcoming interview and that alone.

'Right, lass.' Mr Green was back in front of her again and now he lifted up a hinged block in the counter and ushered her through. 'Why don't you come through into the back for a minute and we'll have a chat. Agnes,' he called to a middle-aged woman with the most enormously swollen ankles who had been standing on a ladder stocking the shelves, 'you're in charge for a minute or two, lass.'

'All right, Mr Green.' The woman's voice was cheery and the smile she gave Rosie brightened the day for a moment.

Rosie followed Mr Green out of a door and into what appeared to be a small office which was situated between the grocery department they had just left and the hardware department adjoining it.

'Now, lass, you're looking to work for the Co-op, eh?' Mr Green's white overall was spotlessly clean, his collar and tie equally so, and it was this Rosie remembered most about him from the previous day when she had spoken to him briefly. 'Have you worked in a shop before?' His voice was brisk but encouraging.

'No.' She looked into the cleanshaven, austere face, the contours of which showed no sign that they had ever been wrinkled by a smile, and decided she had nothing to lose in being completely honest. 'I only left school a few weeks ago and my da had set a job up for me in service.' She didn't stand a chance of getting this.

'Oh aye?'

She went on to tell him all of it, forcing herself to speak clearly and concisely when she felt like gabbling, and when she finished he remained silent for what seemed like a long time before he said, his voice flat, 'And your mam? Is she working?'

'No. She . . . she isn't very well at the moment in . . . her mind. The accident has affected her.'

'Aye.' And then he reminded her of Mrs McLinnie for a moment when he said, his voice suddenly kind, 'I dare say it's affected you a mite an' all, lass. Well, the hours are from eight to six in the week and eight to five of a Saturday, and you'd start at fourteen shillings less stamp. You understand how the Co-op works? I dare say your mam has a divvy number?'

Rosie didn't dare to hope that he was offering her the job although that was how it sounded. 'Yes, yes she has.' Everyone had a divvy number, didn't they? And the dividend system was simplicity itself. With every purchase made you were given a small duplicate ticket with the amount spent and your membership number written on, and then these tickets were added up at the end of each quarter and the amount spent totalled up. With the discount at a shilling in the pound they had all looked forward to her mam's visit to the Store on divvy days, when the odd luxury or two would find its way into her mam's basket and her da would chaff her mam about them being up among the top nobs. Those days seemed a long time ago now. She pushed the weakening emotion the thought engendered aside.

'Aye, that's right.' And now Mr Green surprised Rosie and brought her eyes opening wide when he thrust his face close to hers and said in a loud stage whisper, 'It's high time you learnt how to deal with the Mrs O'Learys of this world, lass, and here'll be as good a place as any. You say you've got lodgings hereabouts?'

Rosie blinked. 'Yes, in Benton Street with a Mr Price.'

'Zachariah? Oh aye, I know Zac, I've known him since he was a bairn. Dirty trick life played on him, eh? But then there's something in this sins of the fathers, don't you think? God won't be mocked, lass, just you remember that.' And then, as though he had just realized he was talking too much, Mr Green's tone altered, becoming brisk. 'Anyways, to my mind Zac was due something for what he's had to go through an' I don't begrudge anything he's got. What say you, lass?'

'Yes, I suppose so.' Rosie didn't have the faintest idea what Mr Green was talking about but thought it best to agree.

'And Mary Price made sure the lad was looked after, you've got to give her that. Aye . . .' It was a second or two before Mr Green shook his head and his gaze cleared as he said, somewhat abruptly, 'Well, lass, I take it you can start Monday?'

'Monday?' It was all Rosie could do not to fall on his neck and kiss him, but she heard herself say through the fierce relief and thanksgiving that flooded her frame, 'Monday will be fine, Mr Green, and thank you. Thank you very much indeed.'

'Don't thank me, lass, you'll be earning every penny working here. They call me a hard taskmaster, you know.' And then he smiled at her, a nice smile, and again she wanted to kiss him and stand up and dance and sing. 'Come along and meet Agnes and Sally, you'll be working with them more than me most of the time, and Agnes will show you the ropes.'

When they walked back into the grocery department Agnes and Sally, a tall beanpole of a girl with a big hooked nose, were busy dealing with customers, and so Rosie stood to one side of a sack of flour near two little children. The tots were watching goggle-eyed as the little ball-shaped change boxes were sent whizzing along on wires by the pull of a cord, only to return like magic from a place unknown with the bill and appropriate change. One of the children smiled shyly at her and Rosie beamed back. She had a job. *She had a job.* And then, when she found she couldn't stop grinning, she bit hard on her lip in an effort to suppress her sense of euphoria. They'd think she was half sharp at this rate, she'd be out on her ear before she even dabbed her toe in the water. And she mustn't lose this job. Whatever happened, whatever it cost, she mustn't lose this job.

'So you're going to be working here then?' Once Agnes was free she bustled over to Rosie, her manner friendly. 'That's nice.'

Nice? It was wonderful, marvellous.

'Mr Green says you've just left school?' Agnes's face was curious so Rosie gave her a quick explanation of her circumstances, Sally joining them halfway through and listening intently.

'You poor little blighter.' This was from Sally, and in response to Agnes's '*Sally*' the other girl added, 'Sorry, Agnes,' with a wink at Rosie as she said, 'Agnes doesn't like any blighterin', do you, Agnes, and blasterin' is quite out of the question.'

'*Sally.*'

'All right, all right. Look, here's Mr Jones, he'll have a list as long as your arm. I'll go an' sort him out, shall I?'

'Yes please, Sally.' Agnes's voice was prim, but as Sally moved out of earshot she said to Rosie, 'Don't take any notice of Sally, she's a lovely lass really, salt of the earth, but she can take a bit of getting used to at first.'

Rosie's lips had been pressed together to prevent herself from laughing – the other girl had had a wicked twinkle in her eye that was infectious and reminded her of Flora – and now her voice had a slight gurgle to it when she said, 'She won't shock me if that's what you mean, Mrs . . . ?'

'Oh, call me Agnes, lass, we don't stand on ceremony here. Now, did Mr Green tell you about the delivery service?' And in answer to Rosie's shake of the head, 'Well, you'll be getting the orders ready for the lads and lasses who deliver them to start with, it'll get you used to where everything is and prices and such like without you having a customer waiting. The orders go out on a Thursday by horse and cart, and we've a list of regulars as long as your arm . . .'

'You got it?' Rosie had just finished telling her mother and as she came to a breathless halt the thought hit, ridiculous though it seemed in the present dire circumstances when every penny counted, that her mother didn't look overjoyed at the news of her new job, something that Jessie's tone seemed to confirm.

It had started to snow again as she had flown home through the frozen world outside the magic and warmth of the shop, and she had burst into fifty-four Benton Street, only stopping on the stairs long enough to call to Zachariah, who had poked his head out of his sitting room, 'I got it! I start Monday', before she had continued up to the landing and into their own sitting room. She had been taken aback to find her mother wasn't alone; Mrs McLinnie was sitting with her on the saddle in front of the fire, but she had blurted out her news nevertheless.

Rosie watched now as her mother rose to her feet and took the boiling kettle off the little steel shelf Zachariah had fixed above the fire, but she could not see the expression in her eyes, for her mother's lids were lowered, and it was Annie who spoke loudly into the awkward silence. 'That's grand, Rosie, the Co-op no less. Our Maggie, Arthur's sister's lass, has tried to get in more times than I've had hot dinners, but she's a sight too rough an' ready I reckon. You've done well, lass.'

Rosie smiled at her old friend but didn't refer again to the job, instead saying, 'How are you, Mrs McLinnie? And . . . and the family?'

'Middlin', lass, middlin'. Our Robert's gettin' wed next month, all of a hurry, you know?' She cast a meaningful look at Jessie who was busy brewing the tea at the kitchen table. 'An' Patrick an' John an' Michael are out with the joiners' strike, silly blighters. A reduction in wages is better than none at all with times so bad, eh, lass?'

Rosie nodded. Mrs McLinnie hadn't mentioned Shane and the name of her youngest son hung in the air between them.

'An' Shane?' Jessie asked from across the room.

'Oh, our Shane is all right,' Annie answered flatly. 'He always makes sure of that, does our Shane. There's men bein' laid off right left an' centre, an' Shane's still on full time an' doin' nicely.'

'Well, that's good isn't it,' Jessie said comfortably.

'Aye.' Annie answered Jessie but looked at Rosie as she said, 'But he's a mite too clever for his own good, an' that's what worries me, atween ourselves. Too many irons in the fire with our Shane, an' he's in with some right rough types. I'm not agen helpin' me housekeepin' along a bit, what with this rationin' hangin' on an' all, but there's a line you don't go over.'

'You mean he's on the fiddle?' Jessie turned from the teapot to stare straight at Annie. 'Serious like?'

'Oh, I don't know, lass.' Annie was clearly regretting saying anything at all, and she turned now, hitching up her ample bosom with her forearms before holding out her hands to the fire and saying, 'I like a nice fire, makes all the difference, don't it.'

This remark was addressed to Rosie, who nodded quickly. 'Yes, it does.' She had noticed her mother had used most of their remaining coal. So Shane was on the take? Well, that didn't surprise her, Rosie acknowledged silently as she took the mug of tea her mother offered her with a nod of thanks. And from what Mrs McLinnie had said it was more than the odd bit of moonlighting that most of the men hereabouts indulged in, given half a chance. Sam had told her ages ago that Shane was drinking with some of the Wearmouth dockers and the sailors, along with the dredger crew, and everyone knew there was business done in the pubs along the quays most nights. Still, that was his affair. She took a gulp of the hot sweet tea, which was almost black, as her thoughts travelled on. As long as he left her alone she didn't care what Shane McLinnie did. She had more important things to occupy her mind than *him*.

'. . . pleased to see you?'

'What?' Rosie came out of her thoughts to the realization that Mrs McLinnie had been speaking to her and she hadn't heard a word. And now her face was faintly flushed as she said, 'I'm sorry, Mrs McLinnie.'

'Nowt to be sorry for, lass. I dare say your head's full of the new job, eh?' Annie grinned at Rosie, her fat jowls wobbling, even as her mind was saying, The lass is too peaky-looking, bless her. But then, was it surprising? Rosie had taken on all of them and Jessie was more of a hindrance than a help, she'd be bound. 'I was askin' if you an' your mam would be of a mind to come to our Robert's shindig after the nuptials? Now, meself I wouldn't have bothered, an' our Robert's none too keen, to tell you the truth, but her mam' – Rosie took this to mean the future bride's mother – 'insists she wants a bit of jollification after, an' bein' as they run the Swan an' Crown they're havin' a do in the back room, private like.'

Rosie had only met Robert's intended once, but once had been enough, and now the memory of the fat, blowzy girl with fuzzy fair hair and hard gimlet eyes was at the forefront of her mind along with Shane when she said, her face and voice pleasant but firm, 'That's very nice of you, Mrs McLinnie, but I couldn't leave Molly and Hannah,' before turning to her mother and adding, 'but you go if you want, Mam. A night out would do you good.'

'Oh bring the bairns, lass, bring the bairns. Like I said, they're holdin' it in their back room, not the pub as such, an' the bairns'll be more than welcome. Connie's lot have got bairns comin' out of their ears – they breed like rabbits in that quarter an' no mistake – so Molly and Hannah won't be on their own.'

She would rather die than willingly put herself in a place where Shane McLinnie was drawing the same air. 'No, really, Mrs McLinnie. My da had a thing about bairns being round a pub, hadn't he, Mam? He would never let the lads anywhere near until they were working, when he said they were old enough to make up their own minds, and I know he would be dead against Molly and Hannah going into one.' This last had the advantage of being the truth. 'Isn't that right, Mam?' she added when Jessie remained silent.

'Aye.' Jessie's voice was grudging. James had been a staunch teetotaller although he hadn't minded her having a bit of the hard stuff or a drop of stout at Christmas and New Year, but it had always been a bone of contention between them that he wouldn't indulge now and again. Jessie would have liked to have made a night of it at the local as quite a few of the neighbours did on a Saturday night, but no matter how she had sulked or argued James hadn't budged. Of course him having his baccy was a different story, and he'd wasted a few bob on bets in his time, Jessie thought now with a touch of the old resentment.

'So I wouldn't feel right to take them now,' Rosie said firmly. Hypocrite! The accusing little voice of conscience brought hot colour working up from her neck, but, she argued back, what else could she say? I don't want to come to Robert's do because your youngest son is a dirty beast of a man?

'Father Bell will be there.' Mrs McLinnie spoke as though the priest's presence would turn the whole event into something holy, but then, when Rosie didn't respond, she added, 'But I understand, lass, aye, I do. Your da was a grand man an' likely he's right. There'll be a few oilin' their wigs I'll be bound.'

'The bairns could stay round your grannie's.'

'No.' It was too abrupt, and Rosie's colour intensified as she rose jerkily to her feet without any of her normal and natural grace. 'No, Mam. I've told you, I don't like the bairns staying there. Visiting for an hour or two with one of us maybe, but not staying by themselves.'

She had been through all this with her mother the weekend before. There was something about one of her grandmother's latest lodgers – a relatively young man who would have been good-looking but for his large, loose-lipped, wet mouth – that had unnerved her the last couple of times she had seen him with Molly and Hannah. It was the way he looked at her sisters, especially Molly. There was an element in his gaze that reminded her of the way Shane McLinnie eyed her, and she wasn't imagining it.

And Molly . . . Twice she had had to stop her sister from sitting on the man's knee when he had come down to her grandmother's kitchen, ostensibly to ask how they were all coping after the dreadful tragedy. Somehow Molly had always managed to sidle up close to his side. Of course, Molly was missing her father and her brothers, that was it. Rosie gave a mental nod to the voice in her head. She was just a little girl, an innocent bairn, and it was up to her mother and herself to protect the child. But therein lay part of the problem; her mother was so *unaware* these days.

Even when Molly had dropped the sixpence out of the pocket of her pinafore that same night when she was getting ready for bed, and, under Rosie's dogged questioning, eventually admitted that 'Uncle' Ronnie had given it to her, her mother had seemed quite oblivious to any possible implications.

'He said I could spend it on bullets or taffy for just me,' Molly had argued aggressively. 'An' anyway, I don't have to tell you everythin'.'

'No, you don't, Molly.' Rosie had looked down at her sister, at the deep sea-green eyes edged with thick lashes that curled like smudges of silk on her creamy skin, at the delicately arched eyebrows and luxuriant mass of golden-brown hair, and she had been afraid. 'But sixpence is a lot to give to a little girl.'

'That's why he said I hadn't got to tell.' Molly stared at her defiantly. 'He said you'd bray me.'

'I won't smack you but . . .' Rosie hesitated. This wasn't going to go down very well. 'I don't want you to accept anything else from Mr Tiller, Molly. Do you understand?'

'His name is Ronnie, Uncle Ronnie.'

'I don't want you to accept anything from Uncle Ronnie.'

'Huh.'

Altogether the whole incident had left a nasty taste in Rosie's mouth and it was back again now as she forced herself to smile at Mrs McLinnie and say, her tone as easy as she could make it, 'I've just got to pop in and see Mr Price for a minute but I'll be back before you go.'

'No rush, lass, no rush. You know what me an' your mam are like when we get jawin'. I'll be here for a while yet.'

Once outside on the cold landing Rosie stood quite still, her chin up and her eyes shut as she breathed in and out deeply, and then she raised her eyelids slowly, glancing round the sombre brown walls. She wasn't going to let anyone dampen her feelings this morning – not her mother, not Shane McLinnie, not her grannie's lodger, not . . . anyone. It hurt even to acknowledge Davey's name. *She had a job.* It would be a struggle to manage on fourteen shillings less stamp – Molly and Hannah both needed their boots mending already – but they would get by somehow. She had already asked her grannie to look out for a cheap secondhand coat for Molly, who'd grown a good three inches recently, from the old market in the East End, and Hannah would have to make do with Molly's coat which was still quite good. Her mother had paid a tidy bit for it not twelve months ago; she could afford to then, with her da and the lads all being in full-time work. Her own coat would have to be replaced before too long, the sleeves were halfway up her arms and the buttons were straining across her bust, but for the time being she would have to manage.

Rosie's shoulders slumped slightly at the thought of her threadbare coat, and then she straightened herself almost angrily. What was a coat anyway? There were others a darn sight worse off than her, and not so far from home either. Look at the wounded soldiers' victory procession last July – she had sworn to herself she would never forget that. All those men, lads some of them, sitting in the line of horses and carts and some of them missing limbs or eyes or both. She hadn't been the only one crying as the parade had gone by. She had her arms and legs and all her faculties, she was rich – *rich* – compared to them, poor things.

And then there was Zachariah. Her eyes looked downwards as though they could penetrate the floor and see into the room below. She had never once heard him whine or bewail his lot, although heaven alone knew he had cause. But it was funny . . . She had started to walk to the top of the stairs but now she paused, her chin coming down into her neck as her eyes narrowed. When you got to know him, when he started talking and making you laugh, you forgot all about his legs.

Funny that.

'What do you mean, she's not comin'?'

'Just that, she's not comin'.'

'Because her *da* wouldn't have liked it? That's what you're sayin'?'

Shane McLinnie had been feeling more than a little pleased with himself before he had entered the kitchen of ninety-five Forcer Road. He'd done a fair bit of business over the last few weeks, he always did when the Danes were over. They were hard to deal with at times, liked all the profit on their side and to hell with everyone else, but he was a match for them. Aye, he was that. He liked what he did, that was the main source of his strength. He enjoyed the excitement, the thrill of outwitting both the customs and excise and the foreigners he dealt with, for whom he had scant respect.

'Course there were some who were more dangerous than others, but he had been watching his back since he had first got drawn into the game as a bairn of twelve. And on the whole they liked him, the big, fair-haired, blue-eyed sailors from across the sea. They thought he was like them, that was the thing, and it was an image he had deliberately fostered over the years. They drank or gambled their profits away most trips, half killed each other outside the bars down in the docks some nights, and he drank enough, gambled enough and fought enough – just enough – to be counted as one of them. But he wasn't one of them, he was canny. He used them all but they couldn't see it, played them off one against the other and then sat back and watched the results. And all the time they thought they had the upper hand.

Aye, he was canny all right, and now another stack of notes had been added to the bulging tin box under the loose floorboard in the bedroom he shared with his brothers. He hated, *loathed* that room almost as much as he despised the other four inmates. He saw his brothers as big, stupid, blundering individuals without a grain of real intelligence between them, and the packed room, where every inch of space was taken up and the smell of human inhabitants was at times overpowering, disgusted him.

And to think he had once run himself ragged trying to get accepted as one of them. The thought slashed at him, bringing a hundred inexpressible, deeply buried emotions to the surface for a split second. Why had he always felt like a stranger looking in on this family? *Why?*

It didn't matter. He breathed deeply, mastering the resentment. The box under the floor was his get-out and a means to an end, and that end was Rosie. When he married her she was going to have her own home with its own privy and washhouse, and not one of the two-up, two-down hovels round this part either. No, he had the better part of Roker in mind for Rosie, perhaps even something in The Terrace overlooking the promenade.

He'd always fancied himself living in The Terrace ever since, as a lad of twelve new to the game of acting as a runner for one of the sea captains, he had delivered a package under cover of night to a house there, and been asked to wait in the hall by a uniformed maid while she fetched her master. By, it had been a revelation that night on how the other half lived. And after he had relinquished the booty, he had received a florin for his trip and been taken to the kitchen by the said maid and given a plateful of cold meat and potatoes and a glass of foaming beer, and the size of the room, as well as the gleaming brightness and warmth and general air of affluence, had set something in his heart. And Rosie would fit in fine at The Terrace; nothing was too good for her, nothing.

Annie had been standing looking at her son, and as always she found herself wondering what was going on in his mind. But now she shrugged nonchalantly, turning away from him as she said over her shoulder, 'Whether it's 'cos her da wouldn't have liked it or not, the lass isn't comin', Shane, an' that's that. Let it alone.'

Rosie liked his mother. Shane's eyes slid over Annie's broad back and his upper lip curled. He had often watched the pair of them having a crack in this very kitchen, but he was damned if he could understand the attraction. His mother was as coarse as any of the old fishwives down at the docks, she hadn't a thread of refinement in the whole of her bloated body. By, he wouldn't shed any tears the day he walked out of this filthy hole. But in the meantime, he might need her influence with Rosie, and it paid to keep her sweet.

His thoughts prompted him to walk across the kitchen to where his mother was standing stirring a big pot of thick rabbit stew hanging like a witch's cauldron over the open fire from a massive hook which swung out from the grate and, forcing a jocular note into his voice, to say, 'All right, arsey Annie, all right. Keep your pinny on, woman,' as he slapped the well-padded backside.

'Eee, you're askin' for it, lad, you are.' But Annie was smiling as she turned to face her youngest son. 'An' someone gave it to you an' all, didn't they, lad,' she added slyly, as she nodded at the black eye he had been sporting for days. She hadn't believed his explanation that he had walked into a door.

Shane grinned back at her, his broad face open and innocent. He could handle his mam. All it ever took was a bit of effort and she was all over him. The thought wasn't warming or even comfortable. It had ceased to be that a long time ago when he had started asking himself why she treated him differently to the others. Oh, she wasn't aware of it maybe, and she would certainly deny it if it was put to her, but there was something – something he couldn't put his finger on. It wasn't favouritism, not in the normal sense anyway. He had seen that in other families where one of the parents, or both of them, made meat of one child and fish of all the others. No, this wasn't that. It was almost as if – his mind struggled for a definition – as if she was *grateful* when he did or said things she would expect as par for the course from the others.

Oh, what was he griping about? He turned as he heard the others outside and made his way to the kitchen table as the back door opened. It gave him an edge, didn't it, and that wasn't to be sneezed at. He was just more canny than the rest, that's what it was, he could sense things the other blockheads were too thick to notice. Like with Davey Connor, he'd known exactly how to make him squirm with that story about Rosie. Connor had been putty in his hands. And Rosie steering clear of him with this excuse about the wedding, he'd sort that. He'd go round and see her himself. With Connor out of the picture the road was clear. A feeling of power broadened his chest. Aye, there was no one standing between him and Rosie now.

Chapter Six

'An' who is it that's askin'?'

Shane McLinnie at a hefty six foot was a good fifteen inches taller than Zachariah, but as he stood in the street looking down at the smaller man, who had one hand firmly on the half-open front door, it was Shane who dropped his eyes from the piercing blue gaze as he answered, 'Me mam's a friend of her mam's. I've . . . a message for her.'

He was lying. Zachariah regarded the other man steadily and kept his voice even and pleasant when he said, 'Aye, that's as maybe, lad, but you understand with them bein' women on their own I don't allow no visitors upstairs. Don't look too good to the neighbours an' they're nosier than most hereabouts.' Zachariah had never cared about the opinion of his neighbours and he wasn't about to start now, but he did care about Rosie, and there was something about this big strapping fellow in front of him he didn't like. 'Why don't you give me the message an' we'll go from there, eh?'

'I can't do that.'

'No? Personal like, is it?'

Zachariah saw his words register in the pale blue eyes and knew the other man was itching to knock him into next weekend – it was there in the flare of red under his

113

cheekbones and the tightening of his wide mouth – but he also knew that with Rosie upstairs this big lad would hold his hand. He was after her, even the way he had said her name betrayed it, and she might have something to say on the matter if her landlord was duffed up. The thought amused him.

'Aye, you could say that.' It was Shane's eyes that slid away again and he shifted from one foot to another before he said, 'Well if I can't go up you'd better call her to come down, hadn't you?'

'Aye, that might be possible if she's not seein' to the bairns. Why don't you give me your name, lad, an' we'll go from there.'

Zachariah watched the other man hold on to his temper with some effort before he rapped out, 'Shane McLinnie.'

'Shane McLinnie.' Zachariah moved his head slowly from side to side. 'I don't recall her mentionin' the name.'

'No?'

'No. Right, I won't be a minute.' And the next followed through on his gut feel. 'You don't mind waitin' out here, do you, lad, what with the neighbours an' all.' He shut the door before Shane had a chance to open his mouth and then stood for a moment staring at nothing before he turned for the stairs.

Once on the landing Zachariah knocked on the sitting-room door and asked to speak to Rosie away from the flapping ears of Jessie and the children, and by the time he had finished Rosie was standing with her fist pressed against her mouth, causing him to add, 'What is it, lass? You in trouble of some kind?'

'No, no, it's just that . . .' Rosie's voice trailed away, before she said in a rush, 'I hate him, Zachariah, he's – he's a horrible man.'

'Oh aye?' Zachariah sucked in his lips as his mind grappled with how to phrase the next question. 'Has he bin botherin' you, lass?'

Rosie didn't answer him directly but said instead, 'He used to live next door to us, his mother visited my mam today.'

Zachariah nodded. He had seen Jessie's visitor and thought she seemed nice enough.

'She's lovely, Mrs McLinnie, but Shane . . . I think he's always liked me but when my da and the lads were alive he didn't do anything.'

'An' has he tried to do somethin' since?'

Her face was all the answer he needed and Zachariah felt a murderous rage sweep over him that was quite at odds with his small stature. 'You leave him to me, lass. I'll—'

'No, no.' As Zachariah turned Rosie caught hold of his arm, her voice urgent. 'No, I'll see him, Zachariah. Please, I'd rather do that. And . . . and I shall just tell him to keep away.'

'An' you think he'll listen?'

No, but if she started running away now she'd be running from Shane McLinnie all her life. 'Yes, I'm sure he will.'

'Well just remember I'll be in me sittin' room, an' you shout if you need me, all right?'

'All right, thank you.'

Rosie went down the stairs first, knowing instinctively that Zachariah wouldn't want her to witness him bumping down on his rear end, and it was that same instinct that told her she had to convince Shane McLinnie, beyond any doubt whatsoever, that she didn't want anything to do with him. If she didn't, if she wasn't strong enough now, he would continue to pester her and lie in wait and she wouldn't know a moment's peace. She didn't know how she had come by the gut knowledge but it was there, along with the fact that he was dangerous, at least where she was concerned.

Once Zachariah was in his sitting room and the door had closed, Rosie took several deep breaths, her heart thudding and her stomach sick, and then she straightened her shoulders, pulling open the door with a determined flourish. 'Yes?' He was there in front of her at the bottom of the steps and such was his height that his eyeline was still above hers. 'Is anything wrong, Shane?'

'Hallo, lass.' His voice was soft, and now her heartbeat pumped her blood in gushing booms as she willed herself to stand still on legs that were threatening to shake. 'How are you doin'?'

'We're fine, but I'm just heating some water to wash the bairns.'

He nodded, and then gestured with his head towards the dark hall behind her. 'Aren't you goin' to ask me in for a minute?'

'Mr Price doesn't like visitors.'

'That's not what me mam said this evenin'.' He smiled but it was only a movement of his mouth. 'She said he was a nice little man.' He stressed the 'little', and there was the sort of laughter in his voice that invited her to join in his mockery.

'He *is* a nice man.' Rosie's face was straight and her tone was cool enough to wipe his face clean of amusement.

'Oh aye, but he only likes callers of the female variety, eh?' She thought there was an innuendo in the words, but when he followed with, 'He was tellin' me he don't like the neighbours to get the wrong idea,' she decided she must have been mistaken. Nevertheless his stance had taken on an aggressiveness.

'Shane, why have you come here?' She hoped he'd soon go, she didn't want him looking at her in that certain way he had that made her flesh creep.

'I want you an' your mam to come to Robert's do, that's all.'

'My mam is coming, didn't your mother tell you?'

'You. I want you to come.' His lips smiled again.

'I can't. I told your mother this morning.' She wanted to shut the door on him but he would only come back some other time.

'Aye, I know what you told me mam, but I'm sayin' *I* want you to come.' And then, before she could do anything about it or react in any way at all he had brushed past her, quickly stepping into the hall and pushing the door shut with his foot as he jerked it out of her suddenly nerveless fingers.

Rosie remained pressed against the wall and she stared at him like a mesmerized rabbit, the force of his dark personality so real she could taste it, before she pushed her shoulders back and straightened as she said, 'I want you to go right now. Zachariah doesn't allow visitors at night.'

It was as if her mentioning the other man brought a new element into the proceedings, because now the thickness of his voice dropped to a lower pitch and he growled, 'I don't care what that pint-size gorilla does an' don't allow. I came here to see you.'

'*No.*' As he made to touch her she sprang to the side, her voice sharp. 'You leave me alone, Shane McLinnie.'

'I'll never leave you alone.' It wasn't soft or persuasive as Rosie imagined a hopeful suitor might sound, but cold and threatening, as that other side of his persona

117

– which was quite separate to his love for her – took over.

They stared at each other for a moment without speaking and then as Rosie fumbled for the latch on the door behind her without taking her eyes off his face, Shane lunged at her. Instinctively Rosie used Flora's knee-jab on him and she put all her strength behind it.

She wasn't aware of calling Zachariah's name but she must have done, because the next moment Zachariah was out into the hall like a bullet out of a gun, a large piece of club-shaped wood in his right hand. 'Out! Out of me house, you filthy scum.'

There was no way Shane could comply. He was doubled up, his head almost touching the floor as his hands cradled the bruised flesh between his legs. It was some moments before his head lifted and even then his back was still bent, but he answered as though Zachariah had spoken the second before. 'I'll go when I'm ready an' I've things to sort out here first.'

'You'll go now.'

'An' you'll make me?' Shane asked with guttural contempt.

'Aye, I will. Have you ever seen the damage one of these can do to a kneecap, eh? An' I'm nearer to the object than most, as you may have noticed.'

'Don't make me laugh.'

'Oh, it wouldn't make you laugh, lad, not this. Scream maybe, writhe about a bit an' moan most likely, but not laugh. I took a man out down near the docks once, Charlie Cullen, maybe you've heard of him? Nasty bit of work, old Charlie, an' he thought I was an easy target, me bein' a bit short, like. He had weeks in the infirmary to reflect on his mistake an' I don't recall him botherin' me again,' Zachariah said almost conversationally.

Shane stared at Zachariah, and Zachariah could almost hear the other man's brain ticking over. It was clear the name Charlie Cullen meant something to him, and most folk who frequented the waterside had heard the story of a little fellow smashing one of Charlie's legs to a pulp some years back. Even now Charlie walked with a stick but he was still mean enough to command considerable respect.

'That was you?' This was after a vibrating silence.

'Aye, aye that was me,' said Zachariah easily.

'I don't believe it.'

'Only one way for me to prove it, lad, but I'm game if you are.' Zachariah smiled cheerily, his small legs astride and his powerful arms held slightly away from his body. He seemed perfectly relaxed, indeed one could be forgiven for thinking he was enjoying himself, and as Rosie watched the scene unfolding in front of her she had the feeling she was involved in a modern day David and Goliath drama.

It seemed Shane had come round to that idea too. 'I'm not wastin' time bandyin' words with a runt like you.' And then, his gaze shifting to Rosie, 'I'll be seein' you, lass.'

'No you won't, lad.' The words had been in the nature of a threat and Zachariah's voice was grim as he answered it.

'No? You her minder, then?' Shane's eyes sneered up and down the little figure standing in front of Rosie before he turned, wincing slightly as he did so, and opened the front door. He stepped out into the dark street without a backward glance, slamming the door behind him.

'I'm sorry, Zachariah.' As the door closed Rosie let herself fall limply against the side of the stairs and she

119

swallowed, moving her head a little before she said, 'He's mad, he's got to be.'

'Maybe.' No, this big brute of a man wasn't mad, likely it would be better if he was. You could lock the lunatics away. They remained quiet for a moment and then Zachariah said, 'Look, lass, I think we'd better have a little talk, you an' me. Come an' have a cup of tea an' get warm.'

Rosie hadn't realized she was shivering but now Zachariah had drawn attention to it she felt her teeth chattering, and she hugged herself as she followed him into the bright, glowing sitting room that always seemed to her like paradise on earth. It wasn't until she was seated in front of the roaring fire, a steaming cup of tea in one hand and a shortbread biscuit in the other, that Rosie asked the question that had been burning in her mind since the confrontation. 'Did you really have a fight with that man, that Charlie Cullen?' She found it difficult to reconcile the Zachariah she knew with the sort of man who was capable of hurting another human being so badly.

Zachariah's clear blue eyes searched her face and he took his time before he answered. 'Aye, I did, lass, but it wasn't so much a fight, it was all over in a minute or two. He's a bully, Charlie Cullen, one of the worst kind, an' he'd got a grievance agen me.'

'Couldn't you have reasoned with him? Talked him round?'

Zachariah thought of the veteran whoremaster who controlled umpteen brothels around the docks and beyond, and who had little girls as young as eight or nine working for him, and shook his head slowly. 'No, Rosie, I couldn't have reasoned with him,' he said gently. 'He thought I'd stuck me nose in somethin' that didn't concern me an' he was out to teach me a lesson.'

'And had you?'

He pictured Tommy Bailey's kid sister and the beating the girl had received when she had tried to get out of what Charlie had tricked her into, and shook his head again. 'No, lass, it concerned me all right.' He'd taken Jinny in until Tommy had been able to get her away down south, and he had paid for the little lass's lodging and food and such for three months until she was well enough to find work as a laundry assistant and make a new life for herself.

'I see.'

She didn't, and he could see that she didn't, and now Zachariah leant forward and gripped her finely boned fingers in his big hands for a moment as he said, 'Look, lass, that's a big world out there an' there's good an' bad in it, but some of the bad is plain evil, you understand me? Now, I'm no angel an' I've bin mixed up in some right goin's on in me time, but I've never willingly hurt someone if I didn't have to. Do you believe that?'

Rosie stared at him in silence. Did she? Yes, she did. She moistened her lips and inhaled deeply, nodding her head before she said, 'Yes, I believe you, Zachariah.'

'An' do you trust me, lass?'

She nodded again. 'Yes. Yes, I trust you.'

'Then I take it we're pals, an' pals tell each other when they're in trouble.'

'I told you, I'm not in trouble,' Rosie protested quickly.

Well, if she wasn't now she soon would be with that one hanging around. Zachariah brought one lip over the other and cleared his throat before he said, 'Lass, I might not be much but there's no one else as far as I can see, so why don't you tell me what this Shane McLinnie has bin up to, eh? Even if it's not much?' Shane McLinnie. He knew that name, but he wasn't quite sure where he had heard it or from whom. It could have been from one of his old pals who was still in the business. Aye, if he wasn't mistaken that was it. It wouldn't take long to find out anyway.

Rosie told him it all. She started with her initial unease of some years ago before relating Sam's warning and the most recent events, although she stuttered and stammered a bit over the incident in the snow. It helped that Zachariah was lying back in the chair with his eyes shut and his face expressionless, but her skin was still burning by the time she finished speaking and silence descended.

Some time later, when Rosie had gone back upstairs and Zachariah was alone, he found himself pacing the floor as he considered what to do. The lad meant to have her with or without her consent, that much was obvious, but exactly how dangerous Shane was he still had to find out. And he would do it quickly. There were enough of his mother's old contacts still around for it not to be a problem. And then . . . He stopped in front of the fire, staring deep into the glowing flames as he let his breath out in a soft hiss between his teeth. Then he would decide how to tackle this.

'You're sure about this?'

'Oh aye, I'm sure, man. You'd be lucky to get away with a fifteen-year stretch from what I can make out.'

Shane McLinnie stared at the landlord of the Lord and Lady – an incongruous name for a public house which was mainly the haunt of sailors, thieves and vagabonds – with a mixture of rage and bewilderment darkening his countenance. 'Who told you to tip me the wink?'

'One of the Danes, but don't ask me his name, they all look the same to me. Seems they've got one of the excise officers in their pocket an' he let 'em know so's they could make themselves scarce.' The other man's voice was philosophical.

'An' my name was mentioned?'

'Aye, man, I've told you, haven't I. Seems they've bin bidin' their time, you know how they work, watchin' an' waitin' until they're ready to haul in the net an' catch the little fish along with the big 'uns. But they're comin', if not tonight then the morrer.'

Shane swore, just once but very explicitly, before saying, 'What else was said?'

'Nowt else, but that's enough, ain't it?'

Aye it was enough, it was more than enough. Shane stood staring into his foaming beer as another customer claimed the landlord's attention. Where had he slipped up? He searched his mind quickly but could come to no satisfactory conclusion. He'd been careful, he was always careful; this had to be an inside job. Some of the scum he dealt with would sell their own grandmothers for a bob or two. He took a long gulp from his glass as panic churned his insides to water. Depending on how much they knew it could be a damn sight longer than fifteen years.

He turned, pressing his buttocks into the hard wood of the bar as he glanced round the smoke-filled room. There wasn't one pair of eyes that would meet his, but that wasn't unusual in this place where it was prudent to keep yourself to yourself and no questions asked. For this to happen now when everything was going his way. He ground his teeth together, his eyes narrowing as he turned back to his beer.

'Well? What you gunna do, man?' The landlord was back, wiping the rim of a glass on a none-too-clean piece of rag.

'Nothin' I can do, is there, 'cept disappear for a time.'

'Aye.' The other man nodded, his sallow face sombre. 'Them blighters are like me ferrets once they catch on to somethin', they never let go. Now meself I'd give America a go in your shoes, lad. I reckon Prohibition has opened the door to a good trade for them that's got their heads screwed on right, an' it'll be them that get in early that make the killin', you mark my words.'

Shane didn't bother to reply. He didn't want to put an ocean between himself and Rosie despite America's ban on booze the month before and the opportunities it offered. No, he'd disappear, but only so far and for only so long. A few years should do it. In the meantime he knew people who would keep tabs on Rosie for a price, and he'd pay for something else while he was about it. And now his face became ugly. He'd find out who'd done the dirty on him, and when he had a name . . . His hand unconsciously tightened on the glass in his fingers until it shattered beneath his grip, the jagged pieces cutting into his flesh and causing him to glance down at the red stain spreading out from his fingers.

When he did, blood would flow.

Part Two

All That Glitters . . .

Chapter Seven

The last three years had seen some changes at Benton Street, not least in Rosie. At seventeen, her figure now had the ripe softness of womanly curves – her full high breasts, small waist and long long legs beautifully proportioned – and her creamy pale skin, heavily lashed dark eyes and thick shining hair, which she wore in a silky, chin-length bob, gave her the appearance of maturity. But it was in Rosie's mind that the paramount transformation had taken place, and this was due in most part to Zachariah's friendship.

He was a surprisingly intelligent and informed man in spite of never having ventured further afield than Gateshead, and, recognizing Rosie's desire to learn and attain knowledge, he had been only too pleased to become her tutor. He had encouraged her to devour his considerable collection of books in the process of which, and without conscious effort on her part, her grammar and articulacy had improved in leaps and bounds. He introduced her to the thought-provoking realm of mythology, and increased her knowledge of history and geography at the same time as giving her her first taste of the classics and Shakespeare. And Rosie drank it in.

Wednesday evenings were devoted to current topics, and

1920 saw Rosie debating the escalating violence in the north of Ireland as Sinn Fein vowed to make the British government of Ireland impossible through an arson campaign culminating in street battles in Belfast, and discussing the fact that in October, as every mine in Britain became idle due to the coal miners' strike, one hundred women were admitted to Oxford for the first time to study for degrees.

Through 1921 and 1922 Rosie and Zachariah considered – and argued about as often as not – topics as wide-ranging as the first six women being allowed into a divorce court as jurors (here Rosie took exception to the fact that only the men on the jury were allowed to see some 'abominable and beastly' letters and pictures because the judge feared they would terrify an unmarried woman), the swift rise of unemployment along with the upsurge of pay disputes and strikes, the first birth control clinic being opened in London and the government's concern that the increasing decline in morals was a direct result of the skirt-length being raised.

By January 1923, when the Nazi Party held its first rally in Munich led by a fiery little orator named Adolf Hitler, Rosie was able to argue intelligently and rationally against what she considered Zachariah's unreasonable distrust of the new German National Socialist Party, and she thoroughly enjoyed doing so. Indeed she sometimes felt she only came fully alive in Zachariah's Aladdin's cave, even though she gained great satisfaction from her job at the Co-op, where she had recently been promoted to supervisor when Agnes's failing health had forced her to leave. But her discussions with Zachariah provided an escape route from the narrow confines of northern community thinking and of caring for the family; and here Rosie felt she had three children in her charge rather than two, the oldest – her mother – causing the most concern of all.

Like tonight for example. Rosie had just got home after her weekly excursion to the cinema with Flora and Sally to find her mother sitting huddled in her shawl with a blanket over her knees, although the April night was not a cold one, and with Molly out goodness knows where. '*Mam.*' Rosie made an impatient movement with her head. 'How many times have we agreed that any nights I'm out you keep the girls in so that we both know exactly where they are?'

'Oh, go on with you.' Jessie flapped her hand dismissively. 'There's nowt wrong in lettin' her play out, she's nowt but a bit bairn.'

'That's just it, she *isn't* a child any more.'

'Not a bairn? Aw, stop your blatherin', lass. You don't know what you're on about.'

Jessie's puffy face was red but Rosie suspected it was less to do with the heat radiating from the open fire than the fact that her mother had consumed the contents of the grey hen while she had been out. Apparently the large stone waterbottle had been half full of beer when she had left the house earlier, although Rosie hadn't been aware of it. Hannah had just told her, after she had popped her head into the bedroom to check the girls on her return, that their mother had sent herself and Molly to the Dog and Rabbit when they'd returned home from school that day. And now the grey hen was lying on its side by Jessie's chair.

'Mam, listen to me.' Rosie knelt down and attempted to hold the fuddled gaze with her own. 'It's half past ten and that's much too late for Molly to be out on her own. Did she say where she was going?'

'Goin'?' Jessie blinked up at Rosie as she tried to focus

her gaze. She was fully aware Rosie didn't like her drinking and she resented it bitterly. It was the only bit of comfort she had, she told herself morosely, and she was entitled to it. But Rosie always had to try and put her in the wrong, like this now with their Molly. She wasn't well, no one seemed to understand that, and as for Dr Meadows saying there was nothing wrong with her when Rosie had made her pay him a visit . . . He was a quack, that was it. A charlatan.

It was useless. Rosie straightened as she remained staring at the slumped figure in the chair. It had been the worst day's work Mrs McLinnie had ever done to invite her mother to the party after Robert's wedding. It had been there Jessie had discovered she could forget her troubles in drink, and from that evening, when two of the lads had brought her home so intoxicated she couldn't stand, the craving had been with her. But no, it wasn't Mrs McLinnie's fault, she corrected herself in the next moment. It would probably have happened sooner or later. In fact she had wondered more than once if the reason her father had been so opposed to having drink in the house or visiting the pub was because he had sensed her mother's innate weakness. Whatever, over the last three years her mother's drinking had had the effect of slowly alienating Molly and Hannah, Rosie thought sadly, and now it was her they turned to for maternal love and support.

Rosie became aware that Hannah was at her side as the child tugged at her sleeve, and as she began to undo the buttons of her coat she said, 'Yes, hinny? What is it?'

'I . . . I think I know where Molly is but . . . but she said I hadn't to snitch else she'd skelp me.'

Rosie became still and, looking straight at her sister, said in a quiet voice, 'This isn't like telling tales, Hannah. Where is she?'

'But she *said*.' Hannah's voice had a quiver in it; Molly could hit hard and she was frightened of her.

'Come here, pet.' Rosie took Hannah across to the other side of the room, pulled one of the straight-backed chairs out from the table and sat down, drawing Hannah between her knees as she said again, 'This is important, hinny. Where is she? Tell me.'

The plain little face framed by its two plaits of mousey-brown hair crumpled. 'I think . . . she's at me grannie's.'

'Gran's?' Rosie's eyes narrowed. Tuesday was her grand-mother's night out with her old cronies and they never missed going to the Archer's Arms where a little ragtime band played on Tuesdays and Saturdays. She'd half expected Hannah to say that Molly was out with Robbie Black from the next street. She had got the impression her sister liked the tall, gangling fifteen-year-old who had just started work at the kipper-curing factory and now had the added allure of being a working man. 'Are you sure, Hannah?'

Hannah nodded. She was sure, and now her worry at the late hour induced her to say, 'An' she – she's bin meetin' Uncle Ronnie after school sometimes, afore . . . afore we come home.

'What!'

'They make me wait somewhere an' then our Molly comes back for me an' she tells Mam we've bin playin'.'

This was getting worse by the minute. 'How long has this been going on, Hannah?'

Hannah wriggled a bit, rubbing her nose and twisting one plait round her fingers before she said, 'I dunno. A while.'

Oh, God, please don't let this be what I'm thinking.

Please, please, please. Rosie could feel the panic closing her throat and she forced herself to say, in as quiet a voice as she could manage, 'Have you ever . . . ? Has Uncle Ronnie ever asked you to do anything you don't want to do?'

'No.' It was immediate and carried the ring of truth.

So while she had been at work thinking her mother was taking care of the children they had been out on the streets after school, with Molly doing goodness knows what. And Molly had been clever. Or rather that man, he had been clever. But he knew she was only a young lass of barely thirteen and he was well over thirty, although he didn't look it. Oh, she had to find her. She had to get Molly back here and find out what had been going on.

'An' . . .'

'There's not anything more?' Rosie's eyes returned to Hannah's face as her sister spoke.

'No, 'cept . . .' Hannah wriggled a bit more. 'When me mam takes us to Grannie's an' Molly an' me go outside to play while they talk, Molly don't always play. She sometimes . . . goes upstairs.'

She didn't believe this was happening. Please, please, God, don't let her have allowed that man to touch her, Rosie prayed frantically.

'An' he gives her things.'

'Things?'

'Money an' things.'

Jessie was now snoring her head off, the guttural sounds from her throat vibrating the air, and Rosie suddenly had the urge to fly across the room and take hold of her and shake her and shake her until her teeth rattled. Every day, *every day* when she came back from the Store she would ask her mother how the bairns were and if they had come straight home from school, and every day her mother had nodded. And she had promised to keep the children with her every minute they were at her grannie's too. And all the time this had been going on. But no, she was jumping the gun here, she didn't know what 'this' was. It could be nothing. It could, it could be nothing.

Rosie had risen to her feet and now, as a thought struck, she looked down at Hannah and with a catch in her voice she said, 'These things, what did Molly do with them?' She knew every inch of these two rooms they called home – she cleaned them from top to bottom every Sunday afternoon because her mother wouldn't lift a finger, and while she was doing that Molly and Hannah would clean the washhouse and scour the privy and brush the small yard – and there wasn't anywhere to hide ill-gotten gains. Perhaps Hannah was mistaken, maybe Ronnie Tiller just gave Molly a few sweets now and again and the odd sixpence to spend on herself.

'She keeps 'em in her dolly bag.'

Rosie thought of the rainbow-coloured bag her mother had knitted some years back with odd scraps of wool and, realizing she hadn't seen it for some time, said quietly, 'And where is the bag?'

'She's hidden it. She gets it out when she thinks I'm asleep, she thinks she's *so* canny, our Molly.'

'And you know where it is?' At Hannah's nod, Rosie said, 'Show me.'

When Hannah led the way into the bedroom and squeezed her body down the narrow aisle between the two three-quarter beds, one of which was used by Molly and Jessie, the other by Rosie and Hannah, Rosie said nothing, but when her sister squatted in front of the little fireplace she let out a soft 'ahh'. It was impossible to light a fire in the room with the beds situated as they were, and Molly had hit on the perfect hiding place, she told herself silently, as Hannah fished out the now black bag with an 'Ugh, it tain't half hacky, Rosie.'

Her heart was beating like a drum as she took the bag from Hannah's soot-smeared fingers and she stared at it for some seconds before raising her gaze to Hannah, who was looking at her with wide, frightened eyes as the enormity of her betrayal to Molly dawned. 'She'll bash me face in.' Hannah sat down very suddenly on one of the beds and her voice was a whimper when she repeated, 'She will, she'll bash me face in.'

'No she won't, I won't let her, I promise.'

The contents of the bag were wrapped in a piece of rough cloth, and as Rosie unfolded it on the floor, the two of them kneeling either side of the rag, hemmed in by the beds, she found she was holding her breath.

'Ooo, Rosie.' Hannah's brown button eyes were wide. 'Why did he give her all them bits? An' look at the money, all them shillin's an' half crowns.'

Molly. Molly, Molly, Molly, what have you done? Rosie kept her gaze on the little hoard of jewellery, cheap trinkets for the most part, and the collection of sixpences, shillings and half crowns the rag had held, but in her mind's eye she was seeing Ronnie's smiling face as it had been a couple of months ago when she had last been at her grannie's. As she worked every Saturday her mother took the girls on the routine visit once a week, but that particular day it had been her grannie's birthday so she had arranged to meet them at the terraced house in the East End when she had left the Co-op.

She had only been in her grannie's kitchen two minutes before Ronnie had made his appearance, and he had been full of oily congratulations about her promotion, his white teeth flashing as he had smiled and nodded, and his manner ingratiating. And yet there had been something – an inflexion in his voice, a certain look in his eyes perhaps – she hadn't been able to put her finger on, but that had made her feel almost as though he was laughing at her. And he would have been, wouldn't he, if all the time he was— She caught herself abruptly as panic churned her stomach. She didn't know how far things had gone, now then. This could be something or nothing.

'What you gonna do with it?' Hannah was staring at the glittering heap with something like awe on her face, and as her hand went out to touch a gaudy necklace, its brilliant red stones twinkling in the dim light, Rosie made them both jump as she hissed, 'Don't touch it, don't, Hannah.'

'Why?' Hannah had shot back as though she had been burnt, sprawling onto her bottom and smacking the side of her head on the iron base of one of the beds.

How could she explain she felt the lot of it was contaminated, foul? Rosie found herself staring into Hannah's little face as her mind raced. She couldn't, but oh . . . She pressed one hand into the corner of her mouth, contorting her bottom lip out of shape. She wanted to kill Ronnie Tiller. Rosie swallowed deeply, and now she had to force the words out as she said, 'Just don't, that's all.'

'No, all right, Rosie.' Hannah didn't understand what was going on but she had gleaned enough to know that there was something bad about Molly's treasure and she was frightened.

Rosie was on her feet now and Hannah scrambled to hers

before moving forwards, stepping over the sparkling pile on the floor as she reached out her arms to this big sister who had become mother and father and whom she loved best in the world. As Rosie's arms went about her and she was pressed tightly into her sister's body Hannah wanted to cry. What had their Molly done now? She was always spoiling things, and everything could be so nice if Molly wasn't always going in a mood. And it was usually because she wanted something or other.

Molly knew they had to watch every penny so Rosie could pay the rent to Mr Price and keep them clothed and fed, but she still yammered on and on when she wanted something until it ended in a barney. Look at last week when Rosie had given them their paste eggs for boolin' after the Easter parade; Molly wouldn't join in with the rest of the bairns when they'd all bowled their eggs down the slope at the park, and she had chuntered on and on about how she would have been picked to lead the procession if she'd had a new rig-out, until even their mam had had enough and clipped her ear.

'Come on, get yourself to bed, pet.' Rosie put Hannah from her and forced a smile as she added, 'If you're quick I'll bring you a spice wig in and a sup of tea for your supper. Would you like that?'

'I'm not hungry, Rosie.'

Normally the offer of one of the teacakes with currants that Hannah liked so much would have sent her scurrying under the blankets, and now Rosie's voice was very soft as she said, 'Come on, hinny, don't worry. It'll be all right.'

But would it? By eleven o'clock, and after Rosie had settled her mother in bed, Molly's whereabouts had taken precedence over everything else, even the matter of the contents of the dolly bag. She had thought of one scenario after another, and each one worse than the one before. She couldn't sit here another minute, she had to *do* something.

Then the turmoil was temporarily frozen as Rosie heard the front door open and close again. She listened, her ears straining and her head cocked towards the sitting-room door, but when she heard movements from the room below her body sagged and the agitation returned tenfold. It was only Zachariah returning from playing darts with Tommy Bailey at the working men's club. Would Janie have been there too? The name pierced her anxiety briefly and brought her gnawing on her thumbnail.

It had been Tommy who had told her – oh, it must be some six months back or more – about Zachariah's lady friend, one night when he had called round and Zachariah was out. She'd often wondered since if that had been the prime motive for that particular visit, because it had almost been as if Tommy was accusing her of something, of some unkindness, when he'd said, 'Zac's just told her he wants shot of her, upset her good an' proper it has, an' him an' all. I've known Janie for years, even afore her an' Zac got together, an' she confides in me. She can't understand why he wants to end it when he won't give her a reason beyond he don't feel the same any more an' he wants 'em to be just pals. She was good to him an' all, didn't matter to Janie about him bein' short, she looked beyond that. She's taken to turnin' up at the club whenever she thinks he might be there, tryin' to wheedle her way back in.'

Rosie had wanted to ask Tommy why he was telling her all this but she hadn't liked to. Something in his manner had stopped her. She hadn't known quite what to say but had ventured, 'Well, perhaps she will?'

'No, lass, no.' He had fixed his eyes on her. 'I've known Zac all me life an' there's no changin' him once he's made up his mind about somethin'. I've got me own idea about why he finished it but Zac's a deep one an' he don't discuss his private affairs with no one, not even me.' There followed a pregnant pause when Rosie felt he was waiting for her to say something, and when she remained silent he had said, 'Still, there's nowt I can do about it, but it's a cryin' shame. Janie suited him.'

Rosie had pondered about the matter for days before putting it behind her, but since then it was as though a door had opened in her mind and she had been unable to see Zachariah in quite the same way. Before the incident with Tommy he had just been Zachariah – her friend, teacher and confidant too at times. But after Tommy's revelation about this Janie who loved him she had begun to see him as a man and it had disturbed her. It was probably the conversation with Tommy which had prompted her to ask Mr Green about Zachariah's parents shortly afterwards. She had never forgotten her employer's comment about 'the sins of the fathers' at her interview. Mr Green had been embarrassed at first but he had told her briefly, and stressing that no one knew for sure, that it was the general opinion of folk hereabouts that Mary Price had never been married. ''Course she wore a wedding ring, and she liked to put it about she'd been wed across the water, in his country, but folk aren't daft, lass.' This second discovery had bothered her less than the first but it had all added to her disquiet.

Still, all that was Zachariah's business, it was nothing to do with her. Rosie stretched wearily. But now he was back she'd go and ask him to keep an ear open while she went round her grannie's. She couldn't sit here another minute, but there needed to be someone available to let Molly in should her sister return while she was gone.

'Are you barmy, lass? There's no way you're walkin' the streets by yourself.' Zachariah's tone was adamant.

'I'll be quite all right.'

'Aye, you will an' all, because you're not goin'. If there's any lookin' to be done I'll do it. What's the old lady's address?' And then, as he took in the stubborn line of her mouth, he added, 'See sense, lass, now then. You're no bairn an' you know the sort of women who are out this time of night on their own, I don't have to spell it out. It's not goin' to help the lass if somethin' happens to you, is it? Give us your grannie's address an' I'll be off, an' ten to one she'll be knockin' on the door the minute I'm away.'

Rosie gave him the address and once Zachariah had left she sat without moving in the splendid red and gold sitting room, her knees tightly together and her hands joined on her lap as she stared into the glowing embers of the fire. Her mind had stopped questioning what Molly had been up to. She knew. Deep in her heart she had known even before she'd shown the dolly bag and its contents to Zachariah and seen the way his mouth had tightened. Had Ronnie Tiller actually taken her down? It seemed likely, but whether Molly would admit to it was a different matter.

Perhaps she shouldn't have gone out tonight? But no, she couldn't stay in every night, she just couldn't. The weekly excursions to the Kings Theatre in Crowtree Road with Flora and Sally were her one indulgence, and they always brought back fond memories of the Saturday afternoon matinees when she was a child. Sam and Davey had taken her and Flora and any of the other children who had their pennies for the entrance fee to see the silent films, and they had all scampered up the stone steps to the top of the gallery, there to sit on low forms as they goggled at the film and watched the pianist banging away at one side of the theatre on the old piano.

And now both Davey and Sam had gone. She had scarcely been able to believe it that day – over two-and-a-half years ago now – when Flora had come round almost hysterical with the news that the ship Davey had been on had sunk off the Bay of Biscay. She hadn't even known Davey had signed on. She'd often wished since that Flora had never started work in Baxter's shipping office because then they wouldn't have known. She could have imagined him out in the world somewhere, alive, happy, perhaps working towards buying that little farm he and Sam had dreamt of, without the shadow of the pit hanging over him.

The darkness that the thought of Davey's death always produced came over her and Rosie shrugged it away impatiently as she jumped up from her seat and began pacing the floor. No dwelling in the past. That brought weakness and she needed to be strong now more than ever. She was going to continue to try to hold this family together no matter what was hurled against them, and there were plenty of others worse off than them these days with more and more men being sucked into the deadly mire of unemployment and despair.

She still had to watch every penny, with the four of them to clothe and feed and the rent to pay, but with the extra two-and-six a week the supervisor's job had brought, and the other rises she'd had since starting work, she was now managing to pay Zachariah five shillings a week rent – something she had insisted on despite his vehement objections that he didn't want a penny more than the original three-and-six. Of course most weeks she was robbing Peter to pay Paul out of her eighteen shillings less stamp, and the long hours, six days a week, could be exhausting on occasion, but she had been fortunate, so, so fortunate, to get set on at the Co-op and she knew it. If she'd got work in a factory she would have been lucky to clear ten shillings, and the laundries and such paid no better.

A sound from the street caused her mind and her body to stop, but when there was no knock at the door Rosie resumed the pacing, but now all her energy and will was concentrated only on her sister and she was praying.

Some miles away Molly too was praying, but it was to her sister, not her Creator, that she was calling. Oh, Rosie, *Rosie.* She was walking blindly through the dark night and she had no idea where she was going. Rosie, tell me what to do, tell me what to *do* . . .

It had been all right at first when she had got to her grannie's. Ronnie had been waiting for her like he always did when she managed to make it on a night he knew her grannie and the others would be out, and they had gone straight upstairs. She liked it better when they did it at her grannie's, she always felt scared when he met her somewhere else and they went to the waste ground at the back of the chemical works or walked down past Ryhope to the sands or the fields. She didn't mind what she did at her grannie's so much, but some of the things he still wanted when they were out . . . You couldn't, you couldn't do things like that in the open. Well, she couldn't.

Ronnie had said she was beautiful, that she was his own bonny lass and that he'd wed her as soon as she was old enough and take her away from these parts, but it had all been lies.

She rubbed her hand across her wet salty face as she called out to her sister again, but the vivid pictures on the screen of her mind wouldn't go away. She had been sitting on the side of Ronnie's grubby bed – she hated that about her grannie's, the smell of the bed and the general filth and squalor – and she had just finished dressing when the door had opened. She had been frightened they had been found out by Fred or Gerry, the two men Ronnie shared the room with, because she knew they would tell her grannie and her grannie would tell Rosie, but she had never seen the three big men who were standing in the doorway looking at her. She had glanced at Ronnie, and he'd had a funny little half-smile on his face, his eyes bright, and then she had known – even as she hadn't quite been able to believe it – and a terror so great as to be paralysing had gripped her.

He had watched. Ronnie had watched the whole time. Molly made a tortured little gasping sound but her footsteps didn't falter. He had *enjoyed* seeing what those men did to her. And afterwards, when they had all put money on the bed and told her to buy herself something nice and that she was a good little lass, she had wanted to die. She had pulled on her flannel petticoat and her dress and coat, but she hadn't been able to find her drawers or one of her socks, and after pushing her feet into her boots she had half fallen down the stairs in her desire to escape. And then she had started running.

'You all right, hinny? You shouldn't be out this time of night, where's yer mam or yer da?' The old man was bent and thin, and the wrinkled face was kind, but the sight of him was enough to send her running pell mell down the long narrow alley and further into the web of back streets and passageways surrounding the docks.

When Molly reached the docks themselves she stopped running. As always at eleven o'clock on a weekday night the waterfront was populated with a collection of ne'er-do-wells, and there were men who called out to the enchantingly beautiful girl as she passed, but Molly ignored them all. Indeed it was doubtful if she even heard them. It was the dark black water that was drawing her on to the edge of the quayside.

She couldn't go home again, not after what had happened. The thought spun in her head as she looked down into the faintly swishing water. They would want to know where she had been and she couldn't bear to tell them and see their faces. She shuddered violently. No, she couldn't go home.

'Bit close to the edge, ain't you, lass.' She froze at the sound of the deep male voice just behind her and then, as a pair of burly arms went round her waist lifting her off her feet, she began to struggle and scream. The sailor's companions were offering increasingly ribald suggestions as to what he should do with her, and he had just clamped one big paw across her mouth stifling her cries, when another voice said, and quite quietly, 'Let go of her.'

She was free in the next instant, and as the sailor was saying, 'Aw, Charlie man, I was only lookin' out for the lass, she was a sight too near the edge,' one of the two women standing with the said Charlie reached out and drew Molly to her.

'You've had yer fun so sling yer hook.'

Again the voice was very quiet but the sailor and his pals didn't need to be told twice.

'You all right, hinny?' Molly had seen Charlie nod at the

woman who had her arm round her, and when the woman – who was dressed very brightly and had lots of hair piled up high on her head – bent down and looked into her face her voice was soft as she continued. 'You come with us, pet, me an' Jessie'll look after you.'

Molly blinked at her.

'Jessie?' The name registered through Molly's shock. 'Me mam's called Jessie.'

'There you are then, lass.' And as Charlie gestured again the two women moved either side of Molly and began to walk her along the quay with the man bringing up the rear as he limped behind them.

It was only a minute or two before they entered a house near the docks and there were more women sitting in the room immediately off the street, but her new friends led her past them without speaking and into a smaller room. This room was warm, even cosy, with a big coal fire and thick rugs on the floor, and when the woman called Jessie pushed her down in an armchair in front of the roaring flames and said gently, 'Come on, lass, you tell old Jessie what you're doin' here this time of night, 'cos I can tell you're a nice little lass,' the tears began to flow again.

'I . . . I'm not nice.'

'Oh aye, aye you are, hinny. Now you tell me what's wrong an' we'll see what we can do about it. Won't we, Lil?'

Lil nodded, her bleached hair looking as though it would crumple like dried-out grass if it was touched.

It was after Molly had related the events of the night that the man appeared again, as though he had been waiting behind the door, but he didn't approach her, merely handing Jessie a tray on which reposed three glasses of what looked like wine. He touched one of the glasses with his finger as he said, 'Get the bairn to drink that, it'll do her good.'

The cherry wine was very sweet and Molly drank it with the two women sitting either side of her as they talked soothingly, and with the warmth from the fire and the feeling that she was safe again she suddenly began to feel very sleepy. So sleepy she just couldn't keep her eyes open . . .

Every time Zachariah paid a visit to the East End he found himself reflecting that he wasn't surprised Sunderland still had the highest infant mortality rates in the country.

How was it, he asked himself as he loped as fast as he could through the cobbled back lanes with their oozing lavatory hatches and heaps of rotting rubbish, how was it that the wealthy shipbuilders and mine owners – most of them patrons of the arts and architecture – could shut their eyes to the way whole communities were forced to live? But they did, oh aye, they did all right, and with over one-and-a-half million men unemployed nationwide, and it getting worse by the day, the outlook was bleak for Geordies.

It was all well and good for the Glasgow socialists to send MacDonald that congratulatory telegram on his election as Labour leader saying 'Labour can have no truck with tranquillity', but would they be living in filthy, stinking slums while they made their fine speeches on the Opposition front benches?

He doubted it, he thought grimly, although there might be a few who had experienced soup kitchens and the soul-destroying means test first hand. Certainly they were better than the other two – the Liberals and the Tories – although that weren't saying over much.

By the time Zachariah turned into Fighting Cock Lane and continued through the labyrinth of alleys and narrow courts beyond he was panting hard, despite being a very fit man, and he was inwardly cursing Molly. She was nowt but trouble that one, he said to himself as his foot slipped on something unmentionable and he nearly cannoned head first into the brick wall of a back yard, the stench from within giving him a pretty good idea of what he had just stepped in. And the mother, Jessie, wasn't much better. By, Rosie had her work cut out all right and he wouldn't blame her if she upped and walked out on the lot of them. But she wouldn't. His eyes narrowed in the darkness as he felt his way along a cut between two streets that was as black as pitch. No, she wouldn't, not his Rosie.

Whisht. He made a clicking sound with his tongue against his teeth. He couldn't afford to think like that, even to himself. She wasn't his Rosie, she'd never be his Rosie – he had her friendship and that was enough, it *had* to be enough. He'd had the privilege of watching her mature into a lovely young woman and had played a part in broadening her mind, and he was thankful for that. The word mocked him with the serenity it suggested. There was nothing calm or peaceful about the feeling that burned him up every night and ate into his days, and he couldn't count the times he'd been near to taking up with Janie again simply to ease his body's torment. But Janie deserved better than that. It had been for her sake – Janie's – that he'd made the break in the first place, he thought too much of the lass to use her, and that's what it had turned into in the end. And she was a bonny enough lass and good company too, she'd meet someone else soon enough. There would be plenty of men who'd consider themselves well blessed to have Janie's favours.

As Zachariah emerged into Stone Street where Rosie's grannie lived he took a minute to lean back against a house wall and get his breath. He hoped he'd find Molly here with the old lady. His eyes narrowed as he realized he was worried about the bairn herself as well as how all this would affect Rosie. Half the time he wanted to wring Molly's neck, and the lass had got a tongue on her as sharp as a knife, by, she had, but there was another side to the bairn too.

She'd spent hours tending that baby spuggy she'd found fluttering about in the street, and against all odds the house sparrow had made it. He'd wondered if she would let it go – she'd had it nigh on four weeks and got right fond of it into the bargain – but came the day she'd opened the lid of the little cage he'd knocked together, and he'd never forget what she'd said as they had watched it flit straight up into the sky. 'He was made to fly. He doesn't want to stay around these parts an' be caged, he wants better than that.' Funny, but he'd got the idea then she wasn't talking wholly about the bird, and the look on her face as she had spoken had bothered him for days.

He straightened abruptly, irritated with his thoughts, and moved away from the wall with a shake of his fair head. Aye, well the same road that led upwards could lead downwards depending on which direction you were facing, and there were choices to be made all through life, even for a lass as young as Molly. Molly didn't have something that was inherent in Rosie's character – strength of purpose, self-dignity, fortitude, call it what you will, it wasn't there. There were people who made things happen and others who let things happen to them, and he knew which side of the coin he placed Molly.

He looked down the narrow dark street where the houses

seemed to lean over the greasy cobbles and felt a sense of foreboding. But he was running ahead of himself here, likely as not she'd stayed too late with her grannie and had been frightened to come home in the dark. There was many a grown woman who would think twice about walking these streets once the sun went down.

Molly wasn't at her grandmother's, but by the time Zachariah's banging on the front door had woken the old woman the whole house had been raised, the result of which being he met Ronnie Tiller for the first time.

The lodgers, all six of them, had gathered in the kitchen along with Rosie's grandmother, and after Zachariah had finished speaking they all shook their heads soberly. The old woman said nothing at all, she had imbibed a sight too freely at the Archer's Arms earlier that evening and it was doubtful if she was aware of anything that was being said as she sat slumped in a hard-backed chair, her eyes half closed and her mouth slack.

Ronnie Tiller was standing at the back of the others and just inside the doorway, and now Zachariah spoke directly to him as he said, 'An' you, Tiller. You're sayin' Molly wasn't here the night? Is that so?'

'Aye.'

'An' you'll be tellin' me next you haven't been givin' the bairn presents, money an' such, eh?'

'Presents?' Ronnie's eyes flickered and as Zachariah's gaze didn't falter he mumbled, 'Aye, I might have given her the odd penny or two to spend on bullets, I feel sorry for the lass with her da dying and all. That's not a crime is it?'

'No, *that's* not a crime.'

'And what does that mean?'

'You know exactly what it means so don't mess about

with me, lad. You've bin leadin' the little lass on . . . or worse.'

For a full ten seconds no one in the room moved or spoke a word. The other five men were digesting the significance of what had been declared and the two combatants – because it was clear to everyone now that that was what they were – continued to stare at each other.

'Look, man,' one of the lodgers, a middle-aged man with a heavy growth of beard spoke, rubbing his face uncomfortably, 'I dunno what's bin goin' on but you want to watch what you say unless you can prove it.'

'Oh I'll prove it all right,' said Zachariah evenly, 'but for the moment the main thing is to find the lass. So you're all sayin' she wasn't here the night?' he asked again, his gaze sweeping over the troubled faces of the other men now.

'There was a special do at the Archers, we all went along 'cept . . .' It was the middle-aged man who had spoken, and as his eyes turned to Ronnie all the others looked the same way.

'I was out an' all. You know that, I wasn't here when you all got back, was I?' There was a pugnaciousness in Ronnie's voice that sounded forced. 'Me an' some pals went for a drink, you can ask them if you don't believe me. I haven't seen hide nor hair of the bairn for days, not since she was last here with her mam and the other 'un.'

Zachariah's eyes were as hard as blue diamonds but he recognized that there was little else he could do right at this moment beyond search the house and netty which, as he had expected, produced nothing. However, he turned to the middle-aged man as he was leaving and said, 'You'll keep your eyes an' ears open?'

'Oh aye, man, aye. An' we'll have a scout round the

morrer an' ask a few questions. The old biddy across the road could tell you the colour of what comes out of your backside the way her curtains twitch.' The man's voice was weighty with meaning and Zachariah nodded to it. It seemed Ronnie Tiller's co-habitants trusted the man as little as he did.

He left quickly after that, and he didn't glance Ronnie Tiller's way again, but he found his fingers were itching for his club all the way back to Hendon.

Chapter Eight

'But where do you think she could *be*, Mrs McLinnie?'

'Eee, I dinna know, hinny, but I'll get the lads enquirin', they know a few sorts atween 'em. With our Patrick an' John laid off, an' Mr McLinnie an' Michael on short time it'll give 'em somethin' to do, instead of gettin' under me feet half the day.'

When Annie McLinnie had heard the knock on her back door just after she had come downstairs at her normal rising time of half past five, the last person she had expected to see standing in the yard was Rosie Ferry. And the lass had looked bad, as white as a sheet, which wasn't surprising when she'd had no sleep for twenty-four hours. She still looked bad. This last thought prompted Annie to push Rosie down into one of the hard-backed kitchen chairs as she said, 'Look, lass, you're havin' a sup afore you go, an' a bite of somethin'.'

'I really thought she might be here.' Rosie's voice had a cracked sound. When Zachariah had arrived home at gone two in the morning without Molly, Rosie had been filled with a dread that had increased hour by hour, and the only ray of hope had been the possibility that Molly might have gone to Mrs McLinnie's. Since Shane's departure goodness knows where just after they had moved to Benton Street, Rosie and her mother and the two girls had acquired the habit of visiting the McLinnie household for an hour every Sunday afternoon once the cleaning at home was finished, and she knew Molly liked all the attention the McLinnie brothers gave her.

'Lass, you know what bairns are. The gliff our John an' Patrick gave us when they were brought back by the constable after bein' missin' for two days, an' them not a day over ten years old. An' all 'cos Mr McLinnie had said he was gonna bray 'em for breakin' me vase. He brayed 'em all right, the pair of 'em couldn't sit down for a week.'

'But this is different.'

Aye it was, it was different. Annie busied herself mashing the tea but her mind was racing. She had always said Jessie would have trouble with that one, her Molly, now hadn't she. And this little lass here couldn't be in two places at once, bless her. Rosie worked all the hours under the sun as it was. By, old James would turn in his grave if he knew the state of things, he would that.

'Here, lass, get this down you while it's hot.' Annie pushed a steaming cup of tea under Rosie's nose. 'An' help yourself to sugar, I've just picked up me rations for the week so there's plenty. An' you're havin' a shive of stotty cake to keep you goin', you won't be no good to any of 'em if you're bad, now then, lass.'

Once seated at the big wooden table opposite Rosie, Annie said, 'What about that pal of yours, Flora? Might the bairn have gone round her house? You never know with bairns.'

'No.' Rosie shook her head. 'She wouldn't know the way there, Mrs McLinnie. Molly's never been to Flora's.' She hardly ever went there either, Rosie reflected silently as

Annie nodded her head and took a sip from her own mug of black tea. Since Flora had started work at Baxter's shipyard Mr Thomas had got worse about what she did and whom she associated with. Perhaps partly because Rosie suspected the son of the firm, Peter Baxter, was sweet on her friend from little remarks Flora had let drop, and Mr Thomas knew it and wanted the relationship to grow. Upstart that he was he didn't want this Peter put off by Flora being best friends with a miner's daughter. Not that Flora seemed to return this Peter's interest despite the fact that courting a lad like him would be a huge feather in her cap. But Mr Thomas had made Rosie feel thoroughly uncomfortable on the odd occasion she had visited his house, and on the last visit, some months before, she had determined not to go again. By unspoken mutual consent Flora always came to Benton Street now, or the two girls would meet at the cinema or in High Street West where they would spend an hour or two wandering about the shops, and of course in the summer there was always the beach at Roker.

Flora's house was a very unhappy one. In spite of her overwhelming concern for her sister, Rosie found the nagging suspicions, which she now realized had always been there at the back of her mind but had only dawned fully on her consciousness in the last couple of years, were at the forefront of her mind for a few moments. She'd tried more than once to broach the subject of Flora's home life tactfully with her friend, but Flora had always been evasive and changed the subject as soon as she could and Rosie didn't feel she had the right to press her misgivings any further. And of course she could be wrong, she might be imagining things. Certainly Flora had everything she wanted materially, she supposed her friend's family were quite rich compared to many round here and there was no doubt she benefited from Flora's generosity. Some of the clothes that Flora handed down to her were almost brand new and were a life saver with money being so tight.

'Come on, lass, get this down you, you look like death.'

Rosie came out of her thoughts to find Annie's anxious eyes on her face, and she forced a quick smile in response even though the lead weight in her heart was making eating difficult.

She was a plucky lass this one; all her da. Annie's thoughts materialized as she said, her voice bracing, 'Now try not to worry, hinny. The bairn'll probably turn up the day, she might have got playin' with some school pals or somethin' when there was no one at home at your grannie's, an' kipped there.'

Rosie nodded silently, but if she had spoken her thoughts she would have said she didn't altogether believe number eleven Stone Street had been empty while her grandmother was out last night. And Zachariah didn't think so either, although as yet there was no proof to the contrary. Anyway, it was the story Zachariah had been told and now, with this last remaining hope proving fruitless, she had no course but to go to the police station and let officialdom take over.

Oh, Molly, where *are* you? Her stomach turned right over and she pushed the last morsel of the slice of stotty cake – a large flat cake of bread baked in the bottom of the oven and one of Annie's regular stomach-fillers – to one side of the plate, straightening her drooping shoulders as she said, 'I'll have to go, Mrs McLinnie.'

'Aye, aye all right, lass, an' if we hear anythin', anythin' at all, I'll send one of the lads round sharpish.'

Arthur McLinnie had opened the door to the kitchen and

caught his wife's last words, and now he looked at Rosie as he said, 'Owt wrong, lass?'

'It's Molly, Mr McLinnie. She didn't come home last night.'

'No?' He cast a sidelong glance at his wife before he said, 'An' you've no idea where she is?'

'The lass wouldn't be knockin' at our door at this time of the mornin' if she did, now would she?' Annie's voice was abrupt but without real sharpness, her Arthur was a great one for stating the obvious but it had ceased to be an irritation in the years after Shane was born, when she realized he put up with a great deal more in their marriage than she did.

'Likely she's kipped down at one of her little pals' houses, lass.' Arthur had ignored his wife, and then, as Rosie said, 'I don't think she would do that, not without telling us,' he shook his head slowly. 'Lass, there's no tellin' what bairns will do. Our lot have put us through hell at times. Tain't that right, Annie?'

'Aye, that's what I told her.'

'She'll turn up, lass, don't you fear. Me an' the lads'll have a scout round in a bit, how about that? An' I'll skelp her backside afore I send her home, eh?'

'You? You never so much as clipped one of ours round the ear unless I made a song an' dance about it. Soft as clarts, you are.' Annie's voice was abrasive but her eyes were soft as she looked at her husband, and he in his turn seemed to take his wife's admonition as a form of compliment as he grinned at Rosie and said, 'She knows me too well, lass. Aye, she does that.'

Rosie smiled at them both before she said again, directly to Annie, 'I really will have to go.' And then, 'Goodbye, Mr McLinnie.'

'So long, lass, an' don't you be frettin'. She'll turn up.'

Annie and Rosie moved together to the back door, and when Rosie felt herself enfolded in a quick motherly embrace before Mrs McLinnie pushed her into the yard saying, 'Now dinna fret, lass, dinna. She'll be turnin' up like a bad penny, you mark me words,' it made the lump in her throat suffocating.

She swallowed hard, then turned quickly, taking Annie's hands in her own as she held them tightly and said quietly, 'Thank you. Not just for today but for everything. You're such a good friend, Mrs McLinnie.'

'Aw, go on with you, lass.' But there was moisture in Annie's eyes as she watched Rosie walk across the communal yard and open the rickety wooden gate in the five-foot-high brick wall. She'd get the tram and go and see Jessie later once she'd got the lads and Arthur sorted. She was bound to be in a state. Eee, bairns . . .

Annie continued staring out into the empty back yard long after Rosie had waved and disappeared after shutting the gate behind her. Bairns either sent you barmy or broke your heart or both. And you never knew whether to say owt or keep your mouth shut, you couldn't win. Look at their Robert's wife for example, Robert still didn't like to hear a word against her but the lass was nowt but a brazen huzzy. Barely wed three years and already he'd caught her carrying on and likely as not it weren't the first time. And she had her doubts about the bairn – it didn't look like Robert, or none of their side come to that. But she could cope with Connie. Bad though it was it was straightforward like, not like the other – their Shane.

The chill of early morning penetrated Annie's layers of clothing and she shut the door before pouring herself another cup of the black tea she favoured – Arthur having walked through to their bedroom with a bowl of hot water and his cut-throat razor while she had been seeing Rosie off – as her mind continued to worry at the thought of her youngest son. She'd nearly gone round the bend when Shane had first disappeared without a word to anyone, and it had been months before he'd let them know he was all right. Even then he hadn't said where he was or what he was doing. Perhaps it was better she didn't know at that. Annie's eyes narrowed and she made a deep obeisance with her head to the thought. Aye, she dare bet on it, but he was still her own flesh and blood and he'd been a bonny babby. Blood was thicker than water, when all was said and done.

Zachariah was thinking much the same thing later that morning when he made his way to Blue Anchor Yard situated in the East End's quayside As he passed the old Elizabethan custom house there were the usual handful of snotty-nosed bairns, fishwives and rough-voiced ne'er-do-wells hanging about, but his eyes were searching for one particular face and he found it just inside the open doorway of the tall three-storey building.

'Zac.' Alec Piper could count the people he had time for on one hand, and this small man in front of him was one of them. 'What you doin' round here, man?'

'Lookin' for you.'

'Oh aye?' Alec's bright sharp eyes, set in a face as lined and wrinkled as old brown parchment, narrowed. 'You'd best come away inside then.'

Blue Anchor Yard was close to the 'Death House', the building where any bodies found in the Wear – a regular occurrence – were kept initially, and once Zachariah told

Alec what he was about, the other man shook his head slowly. 'She's not bin found in the water, man, not yet at any rate, but I'll keep me ears an' eyes open. You think she's bin done in then?'

Zachariah shrugged. He didn't know what he thought except that if this ended badly it was going to break Rosie's heart.

'The coppers bin told yet?' Alec asked quietly.

'The sister, Rosie, is seein' to that, but I wanted to see you. I need your help, man.'

Alec nodded. There was nothing he didn't know about the goings-on on the quayside, and his network of contacts stretched from the East End to the north side of the River Wear, through Monkwearmouth and right up to the great breakwaters at Roker. He had fingers in every pie, from a tasty trade in smuggling to a sideline in the Roker promenade pickings, but Zachariah liked him and more than that he trusted him. It had been Alec Zachariah had gone to about the business with Shane McLinnie, and with just a few well-chosen words in the right quarter the matter had been dealt with. And Alec had chosen men who could keep their mouths shut too, in spite of the tasty bribes for information that had followed from McLinnie's spies.

Once Zachariah left Blue Anchor Yard he walked deeper into the terraced network of hovels stretching from the quayside. Most of the human occupants of these houses shared their living space with an army of fleas, rats, mice and cockroaches, and as he passed an open doorway, where a young woman was sitting delousing several children by pouring paraffin over their hair and then cutting it all off, his mind flicked back to the report in the paper he had read a day or so ago. The National Birthrate Commission was calling for sex education to be taught in schools, and was calling for specialized teachers to present this 'difficult and delicate' task to young children. Then, as now, his reaction had been acidic. It might be necessary for the rich and wealthy, even for families like Rosie's where some decent standards and propriety had been upheld, but in these quarters? The bairns here knew all there was to know about everything from when they could crawl, most of them party to their parents' copulating from birth as whole families shared one room. And the report had gone on to urge for a better diet, better recreation facilities and more sunshine – it'd be funny if it weren't so tragic, Zachariah thought bitterly. What chance did any bairn born in these conditions have to better themselves?

'Hey, canny man, you lookin' for Nick?'

Zachariah had been about to knock on a certain house door but now his hand stilled as he looked down on the young boy at the side of him who couldn't have been more than five or six years old. 'Aye.'

'He ain't in.'

'No?'

The child's hair was streaked white with nits and his clothes were nothing but rags, but there was a light in his eye and something about his grin that was appealing. 'No, but I know where he is.'

'Where's that?'

'How much's it worth?'

Well, perhaps the odd child would better themselves, Zachariah thought wryly as he said, 'A penny?'

'A penny?' The little face frowned up at him.

Oh aye, this one would definitely go far. 'Two?'

'Sixpence an' I'll tell yer.'

'*Sixpence?*'

'All right, all right, I was only funnin'. Threepence.'

Negotiations completed Zachariah was directed back the way he had come to Low Street, where he found the said Nick, another old and useful acquaintance, who had the lowdown on every thief, extortion racket, pimp and prostitute operating on the south side of the river, and who could gather information from stone itself when profitable.

Then, having done all he could, Zachariah made his way back to Benton Street, there to find Annie McLinnie comforting a half-hysterical Jessie who had been sent into a fit of the vapours by the ignominy of having a constable call at her door.

It was about two o'clock that same day when Molly opened her eyes, and she felt as though she was clawing her way up through layers and layers of thick, cloying cotton-wool as she struggled to keep them open. She was in a room of sorts, but it was so different to anything she had ever visualized that she couldn't quite believe she was really awake. She lay perfectly still in a trance-like state for some good time, her arms and legs dead weights and her mind numb, before she exerted herself enough to rise on her elbows and glance about her.

Where was she? What had happened? Then with the effort of movement her mind cleared and she jerked into a sitting position on the wide, silk-covered bed as her hands went over her mouth to stifle the scream she had been about to utter. It had been that drink the man had brought in to her and the two ladies. It had tasted sweet and nice, but odd, and the minute she had finished it her head had begun to swim and her tongue had felt too big for her mouth. She didn't remember anything after that.

She glanced round the room again, her green eyes wide and frightened and her hands still pressed against her lips. By, she was thirsty; she could drink a jug of water straight down, she could. There were two small tables either side of the headboard, draped in a silky material that matched the soft pink covers, and now Molly reached towards one of them, on which stood a tall water jug and fancy glass, and she poured herself a drink which she consumed in several frantic gulps. After pouring herself another glass and drinking it more slowly, she again glanced about her.

She'd never been in a room like this; who'd have thought it? She didn't know people had rooms like this in real life. It was beautiful, so, so beautiful – like something Rudolph Valentino would live in. Rosie didn't know she'd got in to see some of his films – *The Sheik* was her favourite, he'd made her feel all funny in his Arab headdress and flowing robes – because she knew her sister would have said she was too young with all the hoo-ha of him being shocking, but Ronnie had known the cinema manager . . .

The name checked her thoughts and brought her scrambling off the bed, the unusual feel of carpet beneath her bare feet causing her to glance down briefly as she made her way to the window, which was luxuriously draped with thick gold velvet curtains with elaborate tassels. Fancy people using beautiful material like this just for curtains, you had to be rich to do that, didn't you?

When she pulled the drapes aside she found thick iron bars at the window, and now she swung round as she glanced round the room again and began to whimper deep in her throat. Why had they put her in here like this? The brilliant chandelier overhead set in a mirrored ceiling that caught every tiny movement from the room below, the long gold-embossed dressing table and velvet stool, the flamboyant silk covers and mass of cushions and pillows scattered about the big bed suddenly stopped being wonderful and became terrifying. And she could smell herself. She glanced down at her dress which had been torn in her struggles last night. She had the smell of Ronnie's friends on her – it was fishy, thick, horrible.

The door was locked, but she had half expected it to be, and after battering on it for some time and shouting and shouting she eventually gave up, walking across to the bed again and climbing under the silk covers, which she pulled up to her chin as she sat propped against the voluptuous pillows. She glanced up at the ceiling in the midst of her tears, and in spite of her fear and confusion became arrested by the sight of herself, her hair spread out around her in a shimmering golden arc and the silky covers adding to the ethereal beauty of the scene. Eee, she looked like a princess lying here, she did. She wriggled a bit, appreciating the slinky gleam of the silk as it moulded to her shape. She did, she looked lovely. And then the radiance dimmed as a different image, one of subjection and brutality, flashed into her mind.

'All right, lass?'

The start Molly gave jerked her up and round in the bed, and she huddled against the ornate headboard with her fists clutching the covers to her throat and her eyes wide and staring before she managed to gasp, 'I . . . I didn't hear you come in.'

It was the man from the night before and he nodded his balding head slowly, the little bits of hair sticking out above his ears in wispy grey curls giving him a slightly ludicrous air, like a clown. But there was nothing comical about his face, or his eyes, which were of an unusual dark steel grey and very piercing. He stared at her now until Molly, becoming unnerved by the overt scrutiny, began to cry, and then he waited a moment before saying, 'No need for that, lass.'

'I want to go home.'

'Do you, lass? That's not what you said to Jessie an' Lil, now then. You told them you couldn't go home, didn't you, that your mam an' your sister would skin you alive for what you'd done.'

Molly's head drooped, and in a low voice she said, 'I do, I want to go home,' but her voice was less certain now.

'You're a bonny lass, you know that, don't you.' It was not a question and Molly didn't speak or raise her head in the pause that followed. 'An' from what you told Jessie you're no green bairn. Now them scum last night, you need protectin' from that sort. If they want it they should pay right good for it, you get me meanin'? That way it does you some good an' all an' you can afford to be choosy. An' if you're canny . . .' This time Molly raised her head in the silence that followed. 'If you're canny you can make on that it's the first time an' such, some of 'em will pay a small fortune for that with a lass as young as you, even if the bairn is as plain as a pikestaff. An' you ain't plain, lass, far from it.' And then, changing his tack, he said, 'You like me room?'

Molly nodded, startled by the question.

'This is nothin', lass, nothin'. I know one or two who have gone on to have their own gentleman in their own place, maids an' everythin'. Does that appeal?'

Molly wasn't quite sure what he was saying now and so

she just continued staring at him as her teeth gnawed at her lower lip.

'You think on, lass. You could do a darn sight worse.'

Molly drew in a short shuddering breath. 'Are you goin' to keep me here?'

'For the time bein', lass, for the time bein'. Like I said, you're under me protection now, an' I want you to think about what I'm sayin'. There's hundreds, thousands, live an' work an' die in two rooms with a pack of brats about 'em an' their stomachs always full with the next one. That's what they call wedded bliss, lass. Is that what you want? To wed one of the nowts round here an' live in muck an' filth? You're a long time dead, lass. Remember that.'

He waited a moment and when no rejoinder was forthcoming limped to the door and knocked twice. 'I'll be sendin' Jessie in with a bite, lass, an' I'm sure you'd be likin' a wash an' a pretty new dress, eh? I've a few you might fancy, an' there's a real bonny one of white lace an' silk. How does that sound?'

And then as the door was opened from the outside Charlie Cullen smiled, in the warm fatherly way he could adopt with 'his' bairns when he chose, and nodded at her before leaving.

When Jessie came she fussed and soothed Molly, helping her to bathe and change into the new clothes and then sitting by her while she ate a meal of black pudding and bread and cheese. 'There, hinny. That's better, ain't it? You have a bit of a sleep now, an' I'll see if I can sort you out some chocolates later if you're a good lassie. It's roast chicken for dinner, you like chicken, don't you?'

Molly nodded. She had only tasted chicken a couple of times, at Christmas – the rest of the year it was scrag ends and rabbit and the like – but she liked it all right, and *chocolates* . . . Her eyes gleamed at the thought.

'That's right, 'course you do. You're not goin' to give old Jessie any trouble, are you. Now I'll be back later an' I won't forget them chocolates.'

Once she was alone again Molly curled up in a little ball amongst the covers, but she wasn't frightened any more. She stroked the silk of her new dress, her fingers caressing the softness as her eyelids grew heavy, and within minutes she was fast asleep.

'Rosie? That man over there? He says he wants to speak to you, lass.'

'What?' Following her early morning visit to Annie, Rosie had been on her feet all day, added to which it had been deliveries, and with Beryl – the young woman who had taken her job when she replaced Agnes – off ill, and Mabel having gone home early due to an argument with the cheese slicer which had resulted in Mabel almost losing the tips of two fingers and fainting flat out on the floor in the process, it had meant she and Sally hadn't had time to draw breath.

'*Rosie*.' The tone of Sally's voice now checked her, and Rosie raised her eyes from the long list of orders she was inspecting and looked fully into the other girl's face. 'He said it was important, lass.'

'Who said what was important?'

'Him.' Sally inclined her head towards the door of the shop where Nick Pace was standing just inside the threshold and to one side of a stack of large round cheeses that had recently been delivered. 'It might be somethin' to do with your Molly, mighten it?'

'Carry on taking the orders through to the stock room.'

Rosie was already walking towards the tall thin man whose hawk-like gaze was narrowed on her face.

'I'm a pal of Zac's.' Nick never wasted time on unnecessary niceties. 'He came to see me this mornin' about the bairn an' I've heard a whisper, but he's not home an' I've gotta get back. Tell him to come an' see Nick tonight, all right, lass?'

'Oh please.' Rosie found herself clutching hold of his jacket. 'Can't you tell me? She's my sister.'

Aye, and that was exactly why he couldn't tell her. 'Just tell Zac, lass.' Nick had to prise her fingers from the lapel of his coat – for a little 'un she'd got a grip like the rent man on a Friday night. 'Tell him I'll be in Oldman's, he knows where it is.'

'Rosie?' Sally was at her elbow as the shop door closed behind Nick and the bell stopped tinkling. 'Trouble, lass?' And then, when Rosie just stared at her as her mind drew forth and considered one horror after another, Sally said, her tone bracing, 'Come on, canny lass. When life skelps you on the lug, you don't offer the scab your backside an' all, as me old gran used to say. Mind you, me gran was full of sayin's like that, an' no one could ever understand a word she said.'

'Oh, Sally.' Rosie leant limply against this tall, thin, ugly girl she had come to like so much and smiled shakily. 'You really are one on your own.' From the day Rosie had started work at the Co-op Sally had made the days full of fun and amusement with her own wicked brand of humour, and when Rosie had introduced her to Flora, and the two of them had hit it off like a house on fire, Rosie couldn't have been more pleased.

'Aye, that's what Mick says.' Mick was Sally's intended,

a big, rough Irish lad of nineteen who had a brogue so thick you could cut it with a knife and a heart of gold. Having horses in his blood, he worked in the Co-op stables, which had been built to house the many horses that were used in the delivery service. Sally often said that the only reason Mick had started courting her in the first place was because she resembled one of his beloved horses. 'Well, was it about Molly he called?'

Rosie swallowed deeply, and after she had told Sally what Nick had said there was a moment's silence. 'I'm not happy about Zachariah going alone, Sally, not if there might be any trouble. I think I'll call on Annie on my way home and see if the lads are available tonight.'

Sally nodded. 'Aye, lass, good idea, an' my Mick'll go along of him an' all, you know that, an' he's got a couple of brothers who could bend iron bars with their teeth.'

'Really?' Rosie wasn't surprised. Mick's family was vast and all the men seemed to be great bruisers.

'Aye, ugly great so an'-sos they are, an' they like nothin' better than a good punch-up. I've seen 'em break a man's nose without turnin' a hair. Zachariah'll be all right with them.'

Rosie smiled wryly, but she agreed with the general principle and so it transpired later that evening that while Zachariah, Mick, his brothers and the McLinnies made their way to Oldman's – a well-known bar and ginshop close to the foul-smelling chemical works – Sally and Flora came round to sit with Rosie, Jessie and Hannah and keep them company. And with Sally and Flora in residence the hours, in spite of the dire circumstances, were not without their moments of humour.

The women heard the men return at just after ten, and it

seemed as though a giant hand kept each one pressed in her seat as the footsteps sounded on the stairs.

Jessie hadn't touched a drop of beer all night although everything in her was calling out for its numbing power to obliterate the consuming guilt and fear she had felt since awakening that morning, with her usual thick head and furry tongue, and finding Molly gone. This with Molly was her fault, oh aye it was, right enough, and that's what the lot of them were thinking behind their comforting words. She knew, she wasn't stupid. But it was easy for them, wasn't it, they hadn't lost a husband and two bairns who had been flesh of her flesh. What did they know, what did any of them know? They were young, they'd got youth on their side, but she . . . She'd lost her man. Her life was over. It was all very well for Annie McLinnie to say she wasn't playing fair by Rosie and that she should get up off her backside and do something. Oh, she wouldn't forgive Annie for that, by, she wouldn't. And there Annie was, sitting pretty with her Arthur and five great hulking sons to look after her, well, four not counting her Shane. Annie didn't know she was born and she'd told her so in the minutes before the constable had knocked at the door. And the shame of that. It'd be with her to her dying day, and she hoped that was soon. Aye, she did. She hadn't been a wicked woman, all her life she'd tried to do her best, and now all this had come upon her while some of them got away with near murder and still the sun shone down on them. And their Molly, aw, Molly. What had happened to her?

Rosie was asking exactly the same question and she had been trying to prepare herself all night for the possible answer. One thing was for sure, there was something dark and nasty at the bottom of all this. She had told the police all she knew, but according to the constable who had called round earlier that evening Ronnie Tiller had flatly denied giving Molly anything but the odd penny or two to spend on sweets. She didn't intend to leave the matter there, though. Oh no.

And then the door swung wide.

'Oh, Zachariah! You've found her.'

'Bloomin' hell, Mick. You look like you've done a few rounds with Jack Dempsey.' This was from Sally.

'Molly. Molly, lass. Aw, me bairn.'

The sudden babble of voices that greeted the two men entering the room was deafening. Rosie moved forward, motioning for Mick who was holding Molly in his arms wrapped in a thickly padded silk embroidered eiderdown to place her sister on the saddle in front of the fire, and then she took her into her arms, holding her tight before she drew back a little to look into the small white face. The huge green eyes stared back at her, a mute appeal in their shadowed depths, and it was in answer to that that Rosie said, as she straightened and made way for her mother and Hannah to hug Molly, 'She's back, and we can go into the whys and wherefores later. Why don't you put Molly to bed, Mam, in a minute, and you and Hannah stay with her while I have a word with Zachariah downstairs.'

She glanced meaningfully at Jessie, who was now sitting on the side of the saddle with Molly in her lap, and her mother – after opening her mouth to argue and then catching Rosie's eye – said, 'Aye, lass, aye. I'll do that,' as she continued to hold Molly close.

Mick had walked back to the open door after depositing his cocoon on the saddle and was clearly anxious to be gone, and as Zachariah said, 'I'll be downstairs when you're ready, lass,' Flora and Sally hugged her in turn, without speaking, and joined him.

'I can never thank all of you enough for tonight, you know that, don't you?' As Rosie spoke her thanks she noticed Mick was sporting a cut lip and a rapidly swelling black eye, and that Zachariah also bore evidence of some kind of violent altercation, and it caused her to add, 'The others? The McLinnies and Mick's brothers? Are they all right?'

'Aye, lass, don't worry about them.' She had spoken to Zachariah but it was Mick who answered, and he continued, 'You get the bairn to bed an' I'll make sure these two' – the sweep of his hand included Flora and Sally – 'get home all right.'

Once she was alone with her mother and sisters Rosie chivvied them into the bedroom. She asked no questions and Molly proffered no explanations, but once Molly and Hannah were tucked up in bed and her mother was undressing, Rosie sat and stroked the children's faces for a moment before she rose. Under the eiderdown Molly had been clothed in a white lace dress that was now lying on top of the covers, and it was only when Jessie climbed into the bed the three of them were sharing, and Rosie, as she made to leave the room, reached for the dress and the eiderdown, that Molly seemed to come to life.

'No, leave them, I want them.' She clutched at the flamboyant material of the eiderdown as she spoke. 'I want them on me bed.'

'All right, lass, all right. You shall have 'em, don't fret.' Her mother indicated for Rosie to leave and after a moment she complied, but not without a feeling of reluctance. The eiderdown was undoubtedly expensive but it was garish, even vulgar, and it filled her with dread. And the dress, where had the dress come from? She had wanted to grab them off the bed and out of Molly's grasp and rush down to the yard and burn them, that was how she felt about them, she told herself as she shut the bedroom door. But she would deal with them in the morning, there had been enough emotion for one night.

She stood for a moment in the silent sitting room which had been filled to capacity just minutes before and looked about her. Everything appeared the same. From the open fireplace the fire was glowing a deep red, its flickering flames sending dancing shadows over the dimly lit room and mellowing the age of the furniture. It gave a certain grace to the hard wood saddle and a regalness to her mother's oak dresser at the other end of the room it could never aspire to in the harsh light of day; now the plates and dishes glinted and glowed like expensive china and everything in the room looked soft and inviting.

But things *were* different. Something had shifted in the last twenty-four hours and it was all to do with Molly's disappearing. She had to deal with this truth about Molly that was staring her in the face, and, of necessity, try to make her mother *see*. But first, first she had to find out what was what from Zachariah. Her heart thudded and raced. And then tomorrow, no matter what, she was going to see Ronnie Tiller.

For his part Zachariah didn't know how he was going to tell Rosie the circumstances in which he had found Molly.

When he had finished talking to Nick earlier and discovered who was holding the bairn he had felt sick to his stomach, and then the other side of human nature – the good side – had warmed him briefly when Nick had refused the

171

handful of notes he had pushed at him with, 'Nay, not this time, man, not for this. I canna abide yon scum meself, an' I've heard he uses the tawse on the young 'uns, aye, an' worse, to keep 'em dancin' to his tune. But you need to move fast, man. The word is he's for movin' her, he always does that with new ones he gets at first in case any interested parties come lookin'. He'll skedaddle her to one of his other houses an' that'll be the last you see of the bairn, especially if he knows the family have bin lodging with you. He'll look at it as gettin' one over on you for the business with Tommy Bailey's sister.'

Zachariah had recognized it was good advice, and once he and Mick and his brothers, along with the McLinnie lads, were standing outside Oldman's in the filthy narrow cobbled street that stank of rubbish and human excrement, he had decided to act immediately and go straight to the docks. And the others had been with him, to the last man.

They had posed as customers at first, but once the fighting had started it had been nasty and vicious and what with the squawking from the women and the shouts and cursing from the men it had been bedlam. But once they'd bulldozed their way through the establishment below, it had just been a matter of searching the bedrooms above until they found her. There had been more than one bairn of Molly's age and under in the fancy rooms, however, and he would never forget some of what he'd seen. By, he just wished Charlie had been around – or maybe it was better he hadn't been. They'd all agreed they could have seen themselves swinging for the filthy rotten scum.

The knock at his door was so soft he wasn't sure if he was imagining it at first, but when he opened it Rosie was standing in the hall, her eyes as black as midnight and her body straight and stiff. And Zachariah found himself beginning to babble.

'Come in, lass, come in.' He gestured into the room where the fire was blazing a greeting as he continued, with a nod at the newspaper lying on the sofa, 'Old Stanley Baldwin's cut sixpence off income tax, I see, an' a penny off a pint of beer, in the budget. Fat lot of good that'll do for the fourteen thousand men unemployed round these parts, mind you. I can't understand—'

His over-hearty voice was cut off as Rosie, her face and manner gentle, put a hand on his arm and said, 'I know you mean well, Zachariah, but . . . but I want you to tell me. Where did you find her?'

'Oh, lass, lass.' The words were seemingly wrung out of him.

'Please, Zachariah, I have to know, you see that, don't you? And don't keep anything back. I want to hear it all.'

Rosie was white-faced and her countenance was stiff by the time he had finished. She was sitting next to Zachariah on the sofa, her hands clasped in his, and her flesh was as cold as ice despite the heat radiating from the glowing coal. 'I'll get you a cup of tea, lass. It's bin a shock.'

'Thank you.' It was a mere whisper, and Rosie was still sitting in exactly the same position when Zachariah returned with the tea some minutes later, but after several sips her colour became more normal and she relaxed back against the flock-stuffed cushions with a deep sigh. 'Did she say anything?'

'Not much.' He was relieved the look of intense strain had lifted; for a minute he had thought she was going to pass out on him.

'Did she cry?'

'No.'

He didn't add that Molly's whole attitude had bothered him, the more so since he had had time to think about it. Of course the bairn had been in shock, he could understand that after being incarcerated in one of Cullen's brothels, and when she'd refused to say what had happened the night before or how she'd been picked up, that could be down to shock too. But . . . when they had burst into the room and seen her lying in that great damn bed, a half-empty box of chocolates at the side of her and the remains of a meal on the tray, she hadn't appeared over-pleased to see them. But he could be imagining things here. Everyone reacted differently to stress, and the bairn was only just thirteen, when all was said and done.

'Where would we be without you, Zachariah?'

Her voice had been very soft with a little throb at its centre, and Zachariah rose swiftly, moving to stand with his back to her for a moment or two before he turned and said, after forcing a quick smile, 'You'd be just where you are now, lass, copin' with what life doles out an' doin' all right at it.'

'I can never repay you for what you've done tonight, you know that, don't you?'

'I don't want repayin' so that's all right.'

Rosie smiled back at him now, rising from the sofa and putting the cup and saucer on one of the occasional tables as she said, 'I must get back, they might need me.' And then Zachariah froze, his whole body seeming to become still, as she took his hands in hers and said, her face straight now and her deep brown eyes looking hard into his, 'You are the one person in all the world I can rely on, Zachariah. I can see why your friend, your Janie, cared for you so much.' And before he could bring any reply out of the chaotic whirl his mind had fallen into she was gone.

Chapter Nine

Flora knew, as soon as she stepped into the hall after waving goodbye to Sally and Mick on the doorstep, that her father was waiting for her. The awareness, which caused the hairs on the back of her neck to prickle, was unexplainable, but born of years and years of such encounters, and it caused her stomach to turn and the palms of her hands to perspire.

She made no attempt to go straight to her room to avoid the forthcoming confrontation, knowing such prevarication to be useless. Her father was quite capable of forcing the door to her bedroom and had done so on more than one occasion in the past when she had tried to escape him.

'Well?' Flora had barely taken one step into the sitting room before her father spoke, and it was clear he had been spying on her from behind the net curtains when he said, his tone threatening, 'And who was that scum you came home with?'

'If you are referring to Sally and Mick, they are friends of mine.' Flora met his gaze without flinching, her body quite still and straight.

'Oh yes?' Mr Thomas was standing with his back to the fire, his hands behind him as he held the bottom of his jacket up over his large backside, and he swayed a couple of times on his heels before he said, 'And are you going to tell me where you have been all night?'

'I've been at Rosie's.'

'Rosie's. I might have known she was behind this.'

'Behind what? I've just visited a friend's house, for goodness' sake.'

'Don't give me that. I suppose the little trollop made sure there were plenty of lads there, eh? What was it? A party of some kind?'

'No!' Flora's tone was indignant now. 'I went there because Rosie needed me. There was a domestic problem.'

'I don't doubt it with the rabble she mixes with.'

He was a cruel man. A very very cruel man. Flora stared at the dark angry figure in front of her. He knew exactly how Rosie was placed, he knew the struggle she had had to keep her head and the family's above water for the last three years, but all he had ever done was to snipe and cast aspersions. 'That's unfair and you know it. Rosie is a decent person, she always has been.'

'She's not of our class and *you* know that.'

'*Our class?*' It was a strategy of his, this goading, but she couldn't help retaliating. 'What class do you think we are, for goodness' sake! We're working class, Da, whether you like it or not, and if you weren't such an upstart you'd be proud of the fact.'

'Flora, please.'

Her mother's voice was low but of a quality that made Flora turn from her father – who had straightened at her words, his furious face flushing turkey-red – and say to the small, thin-faced woman in front of her, 'I'm sorry, Mam, but I can't help it. He's so bigoted, you know he is.'

'I'll give you bigoted, my girl.'

178

Her father was undoing his belt as he spoke and Flora knew she had played right into his hands again in losing her temper, but she fought the fear that always gripped her in these moments and her voice was a low vehement hiss as she spat, 'You dare! Just you *dare* try that one more time and I'll do for you, I swear it.'

'Is this the kind of language you've picked up from your guttersnipe friends, eh?' Llewellyn Thomas's voice was quivering with the force of his anger. 'Well, it's the last time you disobey me on this matter, I'm telling you. You don't associate with the likes of Rosie Ferry again and that's final. I'm not having our reputation sullied by your low acquaintances.'

'Our reputation?' Flora was glaring at her father, her back bent and her head straining upwards as she faced the man she loathed and detested. '*Our reputation!* What reputation? Who on earth do you think you are anyway? And Rosie is a fine person, she is.'

'You'll do as you're told.' His belt was out of his trousers and he stood, his feet a foot or so apart, with the leather strap held taut between his hands. 'And I think it's high time you were reminded of that.'

He was mad. He was, he was mad. The terror Flora had fought against all her life, and which was all tied up with the military-looking man in front of her, was drying her mouth and causing the sweat to prick in her armpits. She could still remember the first time her father had beaten her, when she'd been no older than three or four. It was burnt into her memory. And she could also recall her overwhelming bewilderment as she had screamed and cried and tried to escape the murderous belt that her mother hadn't tried to help her, had done nothing beyond pleading with him to stop.

But two or three years later, when her understanding had developed far beyond her years, she had come to recognize the significance of the sounds coming from her parents' room some nights and why her mother occasionally wore long-sleeved, high-necked blouses on the hottest of summer days and winced if she was inadvertently touched.

He was a hateful man, a sanctimonious, harsh upstart, and yet everyone thought he was so upright, so moral, so *righteous*. He paraded his standing in the community – the fact that he owned this house, his managerial post at the Castle Street Brewery, and his authoritative position as a deacon in the little chapel in Monkwearmouth – like a row of medals across his chest, and in a way they were. Her grandfather, and her great-grandfather, had been in the armed forces, and her mother had told her once that it had been expected Llewellyn would follow his three older brothers into the army or navy. But he hadn't. Her mother hadn't appeared to know why, but Flora suspected it was because her father liked his home comforts too much to give them up for the rigours of army life. But he had aimed to create his own little mini-battalion in the privacy of his home, and rarely a day went by when he didn't berate her mother, in some form or other, for the fact that she had failed so miserably in her duty to give him the quiverful of sons he had required.

And her mother didn't seem to have any strength to stand up against him; perhaps she never had had any and that's why he had chosen her for his wife in the first place? She was of the old school that decreed the husband was lord of the wife, be he tyrant or saint, in all things, and that it was her duty to serve and obey without question. She didn't seem to have a mind of her own at all.

Was it any wonder that she herself had so loved to be round at Rosie's house when she was a bairn? This place might have the luxury of a bathroom and inside netty, but she had always known she would have swapped her comfortable lifestyle – the spacious bedroom all to herself, the wardrobe of clothes and the trappings of middle-class wealth – for Rosie's cramped little two-up, two-down house where there had been warmth and laughter and love.

She hated her father and she wished he was dead.

It was a thought that had been at the back of her mind for years and was all the stronger for being unvoiced. The humiliation and pain that went hand-in-hand with his thrashings was always there. How many times had she told herself she didn't need to feel such degradation? That he was nothing but a dictatorial, inhuman bully? Hundreds. Thousands. Nevertheless it was shame at her own weakness that kept her lips sealed about the years of beatings, not fear.

But she was seventeen now, and she wasn't standing for it any more.

He was advancing on her in the same manner as always, slowly, even calmly, but this time Flora took two rapid steps towards him and something in her stance checked the tall broad figure wielding the belt. 'I meant what I said. You try hitting me just one more time and I'll do for you, and I don't mean physically,' she ground out through clenched teeth. 'I'll tell Peter. I mean it, I will, and he'll believe me. Oh yes, he'll believe me all right. And that goes for Mam too, you touch her again and I'm straight to Peter and his da.'

'Why, you young—'

'And your boss at the brewery, Mr Barrett. I'm sure he'd be interested to hear about the goings-on here. And your cosy chapelite cronies? They're not above a bit of nice juicy gossip I'm sure, in spite of all their piety. I'll do it, I will, 'cos I've had enough.'

They were looking at each other now, the big, solid, moustached man and the slender young girl, and such was his surprise that he could say nothing. Even when the explosion came it was blustering and without weight. Flora didn't answer him, there was no need; besides which her stand had taken her as much by surprise as it had him, perhaps even more so. She was actually awed at her temerity and amazed at her daring, but in those hours when they had sat and waited at Rosie's house for Molly to be found, and she and Sally had acted the jesters as though it was just another ordinary evening, she had found herself hating all men. And when they had brought Molly in, wrapped in that gaudy bedspread or whatever it was, and she had looked into the young face that somehow wasn't so young any more, the hate had begun to bubble up in a way that had made her want to hurt someone. No, not someone – she had known who she wanted to hurt. *And she wasn't going to be a victim any longer.*

She left the room steadily, not rushing but taking her time, and as she did so she glanced once at her mother's white, drawn face, but the other woman's distress did not cause her to pause or falter. She had stepped over a line tonight, and although it had been the means of extricating herself from the power and authority of her father, it had also had the effect of distancing her from her mother. Her mother was too petrified of him to cast her allegiance with her daughter and they both knew it.

A few minutes later as she stood in her own bedroom, her arms crossed and her hands gripping either side of her waist, Flora looked about her. This room was full of appeasement. It was seeping out of the pretty bedspread and matching curtains and the big thick square of carpet in the middle of the room. It was in the small bookcase filled with expensive books and the gramophone in one corner, its stack of records lining the shelf above. She had all the latest hits – 'Chicago', 'Limehouse Blues', 'I wish I could Shimmy like my Sister Kate' – and they had all been bought by her father. Everything in this room had been bought by him. It was the same with her mother; when her father had spoken of buying a wireless set last week, with a loud-speaker instead of headphones so they could all listen to it, she had known her mother would be wearing concealing clothes and moving carefully. Oh why, *why* couldn't her mam fight back just once? Tears were trickling down Flora's face now but she made no effort to brush them away as she stood, swaying slightly back and forth, in the middle of the room. But she wasn't going to be bought off any more, and neither was she going to be intimidated into keeping quiet. She *would* tell Peter or Mr Barrett if her father raised his hand to her again.

Oh . . . She walked across to the bed and sat down abruptly on the flowered coverlet. She wished she was Rosie. She did, in spite of all this with Molly, and Rosie's mam being like she was with the drink and all, and Rosie having to watch every penny; she still would give everything she possessed to be Rosie. What was that bit in the Bible that her old Sunday School teacher had been so fond of? Oh yes: 'Better is a dinner of herbs where love is, than a stalled ox and hatred therewith.' Some of the other bairns had laughed at Miss Brent but she had known exactly what the old maid had been getting at. By, she had.

Part Three

Marriages and Homecomings

Chapter Ten

The traditional Egyptian house was two-storeyed and rectangular, built of brick moulded from mud, and the flat roof was supported by big palm rafters. The tall, broad-shouldered man standing looking down into the sun-baked fields below, where a line of family laundry, drying from a rope held between two ancient fig trees, fluttered gently in the sun and light breeze, could have been mistaken for a native of Cairo by his dress. The long flowing galabiya was of white linen and the man looked comfortable and relaxed in it as he stood eating from a small bowl of rice, lentils and pasta liberally sprinkled with white, crumbly and highly salted goat's cheese.

The meal finished the man turned, and immediately his greeny-brown eyes set in a face that was unmistakably foreign, and his light hair bleached golden brown by the fierce sun, proclaimed he was not an Arab, although his nut-brown skin was as dark as any national's.

Why was he putting off the inevitable? Davey Connor narrowed his eyes as he stared up into a sky as blue as the cornflowers back home. *Home.* He moved restlessly, his tanned brow wrinkling, but today he couldn't keep the lid on his thoughts as he usually did. Today they were determined to escape and have free rein and it was something of a relief to let them go.

He had been away for almost five years but he felt he'd aged five decades, aye, and then some. When he looked back on the ignorant and naive lad who had left Sunderland he didn't know whether he wanted to laugh or weep. Left? The word mocked him with its dignity. It had been an ignominious retreat at best, but he hadn't realized it until the day when he had acknowledged he'd exchanged the hell of the pit for an equally precarious existence under the jurisdiction of a complete madman.

When he had signed on the cargo vessel bound for the Suez Canal four days before his nineteenth birthday, after three months of working on the Culler tugboat in Tynemouth, he had counted it as good fortune. He'd wanted to get right away from Tyne and Wear and all it held, and the Mediterranean, with the exotic-sounding names it encompassed, had seemed perfect. Two days into the voyage he had understood why none of the more experienced sailors had wanted to sail on the *President* – its captain, a great brawny giant of a man with skin like weathered leather and the biggest hands Davey had ever seen, was an unbalanced tyrant.

The crew of twelve had had their work cut out to manage the big cargo vessel and it didn't help that most of them were young landlubbers like himself. Captain McGrathe had worked them like dogs, nineteen or twenty hours a day, until they had dropped.

He could still picture the turret ship in his mind's eye, its big deck raised along the centre rather than flush in an effort to reduce the deck area and lower the passage charges at the Suez Canal, and hear the piercing screams of

Micky Rawlings, one of the lads whom Captain McGrathe had had flogged for some minor infringement of the rules. He'd decided then that if he lasted until Port Said he would jump ship and forgo the payment due when they returned to England, even if it meant he was stranded in a foreign country with no money or belongings and just the clothes he stood up in.

It had been mid-June when the ship had arrived in Port Said and Davey had felt he'd sailed into an oven. The air was desiccated and scorching, but when the ship had docked just before sunset and the Mediterranean had become a saffron sea, the sun dropping into it surprisingly quickly like a juicy ripe Egyptian orange, he had been hooked. His past life – Sunderland, Rosie – had faded to an impossible, half-remembered dream, an illusion so far removed from the blazing hot world of colour and light he found himself in as to be unattainable.

It had been surprisingly easy to jump ship during the night, and he had determined to make his way across country towards the Nile in an effort to lose himself in this new land.

The cordiality displayed by the ordinary Egyptian people to this stranger in their midst who had been unable to speak a word of their language had both amazed and humbled him. He had discovered hospitality was almost a sacred duty in their culture, dating back to the times when nomadic tribes frequently roamed the deserts – harsh places even at the best of times – and with a relentless sun beating down all day, and nightfall bringing a sharp drop in temperature and producing shivering cold, he'd been glad of the unwritten law that food and shelter be given unquestioningly to any stranger.

It had taken him almost eighteen months to work his

way to the ancient city of Cairo, positioned at the apex
of the fertile Nile delta some hundred kilometres south of
the Mediterranean coast, and in that time he had tried his
hand at whatever employment came his way. He'd spent a
couple of months gathering dates from the tall palm trees
in one place, a few weeks ploughing fields in another, but
eventually he arrived at a small farm on the outskirts of
Cairo in January 1922, penniless and virtually in rags.

And he had been fortunate, he knew that now. Egypt's
land was rich in natural fertilizers and bore fruit the whole
year round – wheat, rice, corn and flowers thrived during
the winter, cotton and sugar in the spring and fruit in the
summer – and owing to an outbreak of cholera having taken
Mohamed's – the owner of the farm – three sons and wife
and daughter two months before he had arrived, the wiry
gnarled Egyptian had been hard-pressed and glad of another
pair of hands.

Davey had toiled long and hard in the fields surrounding
the farm using methods introduced some five thousand years
before, but still effective. He had become accustomed to the
shaduf, a device with a weighted lever used to raise water
from the river Nile into the irrigation canals running between
the crops, and the *saqiyya*, a water wheel drawn by oxen.

The sight of his fellow workers ploughing the fields and
women carrying home the harvest on the backs of donkeys
had satisfied something deep in his soul, and he had earnt
first Mohamed's respect and then his friendship with the
zealousness of his commitment to the farm and his work.

In return for his services Mohamed had given him shelter
and food in his own house, along with a small wage, and
Davey had told himself he was content in this country of
a thousand minarets, where the nights were scented by

the sweet white jasmine flowers and sun-warmed crops, and visits into the city echoed with the sound of the muezzin's voice calling the faithful to prayer. His former life underground in the dark bowels of the earth only surfaced in the odd nightmare, now his waking hours were spent in the warm clean air, and for the first year or so he had revelled in it despite the occasional hankering for England's green countryside and rainy summers. He still revelled in it, but . . . He sighed irritably. She was always there in the back of his mind, his northern rose, and the urge to find out where she was, what she was doing, who she was with was gnawing at him.

Aw, man. He shook his head now, angry at himself. Life was good here, he had fallen on his feet, and he'd be stark staring barmy to throw it all away and go back. Ten to one she was married to Shane McLinnie, she might even have had a bairn or two now despite all her fancy talk of what she wanted out of life. Talk, it had all been talk – women were good at saying one thing and meaning another. And he knew a bit about women now, certainly a darn sight more than when he had left Sunderland at any rate. But none of them had meant anything, not even the first, a little sloe-eyed beauty who had crept into his bed one night in his date-picking days when her husband was away.

Damn it! He threw the bowl down onto a large rectangular piece of wood that served as a table where it spun crazily for a few seconds before coming to a shuddering halt. How did you get someone out of your head and your bones? He had tried, heaven knew he had tried, but that dark-eyed, pale-complexioned ghost refused to go.

If he had known then what he knew now things would have been different. The sun was beating down on his uncovered head, its heat considerable, but Davey was back in Sunderland on a cold snowy winter's night. He should have moved heaven and earth to take her away from Shane McLinnie, played him at his own game, done whatever it took. Rosie had been like a lamb to the slaughter, that was the truth of it, and what had he done? Skedaddled off in a fit of wounded pride. He had been a fool. He'd left the gate wide open for McLinnie, damn it.

He raised his head sharply, his face – which looked a good deal older than his twenty-three years – grim and tight. He would go back. He had known all along that he would go back, hadn't he, and it was time. Aye, it was time all right. But he was a different person to the young, bigoted northerner who had never ventured further than South Shields; he had changed. And no doubt Rosie would have changed too.

His eyes narrowed but his mind was made up. Whatever, this stage of his life was over and he had known it for some time, but first he had to tell Mohamed and that wouldn't be easy. The old man had been good to him at a time when he had desperately needed it, and they had become close. He would stay until Mohamed found someone to take his place, but not a day longer. He was going home.

Chapter Eleven

'What do you mean, she's gone?' Rosie had just got in from work and had had to battle her way home through frozen streets where the wind cut through you like a knife, and the little particles of ice in the wind had stung her face raw. And that after a day of gloom and doom when everyone had been feeling so low due to the terrible Scotswood disaster. Even Sally had been subdued, which was saying something, Rosie thought ruefully. With the older girl's wedding day approaching at the end of April, Sally had been irrepressible the last few weeks. Even Mr Green had been helpless the other morning when Sally had serenaded the lads and lasses who had come to take the deliveries with a rendition of 'Fascinating Rhythm' whilst jigging about doing her own version of the Charleston. But the Scotswood flooding was awful, *terrible*, and when they'd announced yesterday that all hope was abandoned of rescuing the thirty-five men in the waterlogged mine in Newcastle twenty miles away, it seemed like the whole of Tyne and Wear had gone into mourning. And it had made her think of her da and the lads. And then she'd thought of Davey . . .

Rosie forced her mind back to Hannah as she realized she hadn't received an answer to her question, and then, as Hannah's face crumpled, she quickly drew her sister to her, saying again, 'What do you mean, hinny? Where's she gone?' as another part of her mind, a quite separate, deeper part said, No, no, not that, not again. She wouldn't put us all through that again.

The last two years had been turbulent ones for Rosie. Oh, not on the outside – on the outside life had gone on as it always had. She had continued working at the Co-op, taking more and more responsibility when it was offered to her until it was generally acknowledged she was Mr Green's right-hand man, something her eleven- or twelve-hour working day reflected, along with her increased wage packet. But Rosie didn't mind the long hours on her feet or the hard work, in fact rarely a day passed that she didn't thank the Almighty for that portentous morning in March five years ago when she had first set foot inside the Store.

She loved her job: the warm and friendly feel that was a hallmark of the Co-op's dealings with staff and customers alike; the way shoppers felt comfortable to stand about and gossip in what was virtually a meeting place for many housewives; the company of Sally and the other staff, and even delivery and divvy days when they were all rushed off their feet. And events like the local flower show or the Hendon carnival at Hendon Burn, when all the staff would get together and dress up some of the delivery carts and cart horses – Damsel and Daisy being two firm favourites – and turn themselves into harlequins or Red Indians and the like, were pure magic.

And in her spare time there were the weekly excursions to the cinema with Flora and Sally to look forward to, or sometimes the three girls treated themselves to cream cakes and a pot of tea at Binns cake shop and restaurant in Fawcett Street. And once or twice – on the rare occasions they felt they could afford it – they would take the horse cab in Thomas Street to the Winter Garden. Rosie didn't know what she enjoyed most out of those times, being driven along in the cab by the driver who sat in the front, the rim of his top hat worn and thin so the yellow cardboard underneath was visible, or the hours spent at the Winter Garden when they would wander, arm-in-arm, round the beautiful turreted glass conservatory and view the tropical plants and flowers, the aviary and the pond full of goldfish.

Her other evenings were spent either at her little treadle sewing machine, bought from Turner's pawn shop, making the family's clothes and brightening up the two rooms with pretty new curtains, covers and cushions, or in Zachariah's sitting room. His latest tuition had been a study of Chaucer's *The Canterbury Tales*, and Rosie had ached at the tragedy of *The Knight's Tale*, and found herself somewhat shocked at the bawdiness of *The Miller's Tale*, much to Zachariah's secret amusement.

Along with Chaucer, they had followed and discussed in depth the ignominious demise of Britain's first Labour government in 1924 under Ramsay MacDonald which had survived for just ten months, Zachariah insisting that Labour's ship had been scuttled deliberately by foul play by the Conservative Party whom he hated with a vengeance. 'The country'll regret gettin' rid of 'em, you mark my words, lass. Look at the McLinnie lads, standin' idle on street corners along with some of Sunderland's finest, an' the shipyards sinkin' deeper an' deeper, an' the mines an' all. The dole queues are the only things that are thrivin' these days. Aye, the writin's on the wall plain for everyone to read, we're runnin' headlong into disaster.'

Rosie agreed with him, but in stark contrast to the increasing number of unemployed beginning to gather at every street corner and swelling the soup kitchens, she had never been busier. She washed the family's clothes and bedding and endeavoured to keep her mother and the girls looking clean and well turned-out in the continual fight against poverty, and she fought alone, as Jessie declined further into apathy and drunkenness.

Rosie had hoped with all her heart that the incident which had occurred when Molly was thirteen would shock both her sister and her mother into changing their ways, and with Molly all the outward signs would indicate that this was so. But try as she might – and Rosie did try – she just couldn't bring herself to believe that the pliable and amenable girl who had materialized in her sister's frame the morning after the rescue – and after Rosie had followed her instincts and burnt the eiderdown and the white lace dress – was for real. She'd paid a visit to the East End to see what she could uncover when Molly had refused to reveal anything of what had occurred in the previous twenty-four hours, but she had been too late. Ronnie Tiller had done a moonlight flit and left owing her grandmother several weeks' rent. It was an unsatisfactory conclusion to a deeply disturbing series of events, but there was nothing more that could be done, in view of Molly's insistence that nothing had happened at Charlie Cullen's establishment and that she was perfectly all right.

But something that stemmed from that night's happenings continued to cause Rosie more disquiet than everything else put together. And she couldn't talk about it to anyone, not even Flora, much as she would have liked to. It had happened in those few seconds before she had left Zachariah's sitting room, when she had taken his hands and looked deep into the piercing blue eyes. It was as though all the unsettling feelings she had been having for months had crystallized in one heart-jolting moment and she had understood, as she'd mentioned Janie's name, why the thought of the other woman had bothered her so much. She liked him. She liked him very much, and not just as a friend or companion either. It had sent her scurrying upstairs in a state of panic at the time and she had lain awake most of the night convincing herself she was mistaken. But she wasn't. And he viewed her as – what? A friend? A pupil? Worse, someone in need of his charity? And even worse than *that*, a daughter substitute?

In the following weeks she had been alert for anything – a gesture, a look, his tone of voice – that might indicate he felt something for her beyond friendly affection, but there had been nothing. And lately, in the last few months, she had given up looking. She'd tried to tell herself that what she felt was deep gratitude, but then, when she considered the circumstances of that night and the fact that he might have been hurt rescuing Molly, she knew it was more than that. She didn't know if it was love, exactly – if it was, it was nothing like the seesaw of ecstasy and pain she had felt for Davey – but it certainly wasn't mere gratitude or friendship either. It confused her, it bewildered her, but such was the feeling that it induced her to refuse the tentative advances of other lads, who appeared little more than bairns beside Zachariah. She *wanted* to meet someone; Sally had Mick, and Flora was halfheartedly courting Peter Baxter now, but the thought of seeing someone just for the sake of saying she'd got a lad didn't appeal, even if she had been tempted once or twice lately.

Now, as Hannah remained huddled against her, Rosie said, 'Have you told Zachariah she's gone?'

'No, he's out, an' Mam said to wait till you got back anyway. There's . . . a letter. A little lad delivered it a while back.'

'A lad?' Rosie put Hannah from her and looked into the child's tearstained face. 'Who? What lad?'

'I dunno. He just come to the front door an' Mam said she took the letter an' he'd gone. It was just afore I got back from school.'

'All right.' Rosie straightened her back as though throwing something off. 'Let's go and see this letter.'

It was brief and to the point.

I'm going away where you won't find me, Molly had written in her round, childish scrawl, *and I'm not coming back. I'm sorry but I can't stand it here any more* – by this Rosie wasn't sure if Molly meant Sunderland in general or her home and job as a packer at the kipper-curing house, something the beautiful dainty Molly had loathed since day one in spite of the fact that she had been very fortunate to secure it with the desperate unemployment in the area – *and I'll go mad if I stay. I'm not clever like you, Rosie, and I want nice things before I'm too old. I love you but don't try to find me. This is for the best, I know it is. Goodbye, Molly.*

Goodbye, Molly? Rosie stared at the paper in her hand and then turned to look into the softly lit room she had struggled to make so nice. It felt as though all her efforts over the last few years – the back-breaking hours at the little sewing machine, her scrimping and scraping to give the girls little treats for Christmas and birthday presents, her endeavours to give Molly a pleasant and pretty environment – had been for nothing. She had gone. She wasn't a little bairn any more and she had *chosen* to leave, and she had a pretty good idea how Molly was considering getting those nice things of which she had written.

'I've told Hannah Molly'll be back when it gets dark an' she's hungry.' Jessie was raising a glass of beer to her lips as she spoke and her voice was already slurred. 'She's nowt but a bit bairn.'

No power on earth could have stopped what followed. The feeling that boiled up in Rosie was a conglomeration of fury and bitterness and even hate, and it enabled her to speak the words whose very truth made them sword-thrusts into the heart of the woman who had borne her.

'Don't you realize what this means? Are you so far gone that all you can see is the bottom of that glass?' she asked weightily as she walked across the room to stand in front of her mother's chair. 'She's gone and she isn't coming back, Mam. She has planned this. And she is no bairn, not Molly.'

'What are you sayin'?'

'You know what I am saying.'

'May God forgive you! Aye, may the good Lord forgive you because I won't. To say that our Molly, your own sister, could . . . Aw, I can't say it. It would foul me lips.'

'You stupid, stupid woman.' Rosie was speaking quietly but her voice was heavy with such despair that it caused Jessie's bloodshot eyes to open wide. 'All that with Ronnie, the money and everything. Why do you think a man like that would give her money? But you wouldn't accept it, would you, and not because of Molly. No, you were frightened that if you faced what she was up to it would interfere with your drinking yourself silly every night, and nothing must come in the way of that. Why do you think I've tried to keep such a check on her the last few years? Because I wanted to spoil her fun, is that it? She wasn't having *fun*, Mam. And all the times I've talked to you and you have made excuses for her has led to this.'

Rosie flung her arm wide as she pointed to the window. 'She is out there somewhere and she isn't coming back. Oh, it's no good talking to you! Drink yourself to death if that's what you are bent on.'

She turned away and as she did so Hannah, who had been standing just inside the room, ran to her saying, 'Rosie, Rosie, get her back. Oh, Rosie, please get her back.'

What would all this do to Hannah? Oh, she shouldn't have gone for her mother like that in front of her. The guilt that swamped Rosie extinguished the fury, and she hugged the child tight to her, muttering soothing endearments into the small head as they swayed together in the middle of the room.

This wasn't like before. It was a full minute later and there had been neither sound nor movement from the chair by the fire. Molly had made her decision, but she had to at least *try* to see her and talk to her, even if it was useless. Rosie's glance took in the grey hen propped at the side of the rocking chair and she said quietly, as she put Hannah from her, 'Look after Mam for a bit, hinny, all right? I'll be back as soon as I can.'

It was gone midnight, and after her visit to Zachariah's sitting room when she had asked him to make enquiries about Molly, Rosie had returned upstairs and dished up a dinner no one had eaten before putting Hannah to bed. She had said very little to her mother and her mother had said nothing to her, but neither had she taken another drink.

Rosie heard Zachariah return from his excursion into that other twilight world he had some understanding of just as the mantelpiece clock struck the half hour, and after a quick, 'That's Zachariah back, I'll go and see if he has any news,' which her mother acknowledged with an inclination of her head, she ran downstairs.

The door to his sitting room was open and he was waiting for her. He looked weary, weary and sad, as he waved his hand for her to be seated whilst saying, 'Your mam an' Hannah asleep?'

'Hannah is. My mam's still up, she wanted to wait for news.'

He raised his eyebrows at this, and Rosie said quietly, 'She's very upset, Zachariah. I shouldn't have said all that earlier.' She had related the conversation word for word when she had shown him Molly's note and he had made no comment then, but what he said now was, 'I disagree, lass, it was long overdue, besides which you are only flesh an' blood,' before he flung himself down in one of the armchairs by the fire, its bright warmth cheering after the icy cold and bitter wind outside.

'You look frozen, I'll get you a hot drink.'

'No, leave it.' As she made to rise from the sofa the tone of his voice stopped her in her tracks, and she was conscious of thinking, I don't want to hear this, I *really* don't want to hear this, as she sank down again without another word and faced him, her hands clasped in her lap and her back straight.

'I think I'd better tell you straight out, lass.' And then he paused as though in refutation of his statement before he continued, 'It's what we suspected after that note. She was seen earlier, this mornin' in fact, down at the quayside.'

'The same place you found her before,' said Rosie flatly.

'Aye. It appears she was knockin' 'em up or that's what it looked like. They sleep late in them places. But it must've bin her an' she caused quite a stir by all accounts. Anyway, she was in there an hour or two an' then out she comes with Charlie an' a couple of the lasses an' off they all went. None of 'em have bin back since.'

'Where did they go?'

'No one knows. Charlie's got a good few broth—' A moment's hesitation and then, 'Houses dotted around.' Zachariah could have kicked himself for the slip.

Brothels. He had been going to say brothels and Molly was in one of those places. It was one thing to suspect the worst, it was quite another to have it confirmed so baldly, and now she was thinking of her da and the lads and saying in her mind, I'm sorry, I'm sorry I've let you all down. Oh, Da . . .

'Rosie?' Zachariah's voice brought her eyes to meet his. 'If she's gone with Charlie's bunch an' she don't want to be found then likely as not she won't be.'

Rosie stared at him with great dark eyes as she thought, But she's been so sweet the last couple of years, we've got on better than we ever did. There had been none of the tantrums and harsh words that had characterized Molly's early years. Had she been planning this all the time? No. No, she couldn't think that, she just couldn't.

'Rosie?' Zachariah had moved to sit at her side. 'Now listen to me, lass, you've nothin' to reproach yourself for, you hear me?'

She shook her head, her distress overwhelming her for a

moment and causing her to push at his hands as he went to take hers, and it was in that moment, with her senses heightened to near breaking point, and Zachariah's guard temporarily down, that Rosie saw the look on his face and a veil was lifted from her understanding. It stunned her. For one moment it actually stunned her and she lay back limply on the sofa as he continued to talk to cover what had become an embarrassing rebuff as far as he was concerned.

Why hadn't she realized before? She should have. She had got so used to him cracking a joke to cover up any awkwardness about his small stature that she had ceased to look behind the words, and besides, she simply didn't *think* about the fact that he was a bit short any more. She hadn't for years. But he thought of it, of *course* he thought of it. And she'd called her *mam* stupid . . . The revelation had brought a quietness, and now she knew exactly what to say.

'You're probably right, Zachariah, and I know she'll be sixteen soon, she's not a little bairn any more.' She reached for his hands then and held them as she said, 'But I'd still like to try and find out exactly where she is, if that's all right with you.'

'Me?' His eyes had narrowed slightly at the tone of her voice which was soft and low, and in marked contrast to the flat painfulness of moments before. 'Of course, lass. It goes without sayin'.'

Too much had gone without saying. Rosie took a deep breath and now her voice was softer still as she said, 'You've always been here when I needed you, haven't you, Zachariah, through the good times and the bad.'

Dear God, dear God . . . It wasn't blasphemy; Zachariah was calling for a strength outside himself as he forced a quick smile and drew his hands from hers before rising and walking over to the fire. She had no idea what she did to him and it was her very innocence that made her cruel. He steeled himself and turned to face her, his voice robust as he said, 'Lass, you'll get through this, don't you worry. There's a strength in you that fair amazes me at times.'

She looked straight at him now, and after a moment she said quietly, 'I was worried about you, going down to that quarter by yourself tonight with that man, Charlie Cullen, knowing who you are.'

'What?' He blinked, and then grinned as he said, 'Oh aye, Charlie knows me right enough, but there's good an' bad at all levels, lass, an' I've a few pals down there an' all. An' I can hold me own in a spot of bother. They always say the little 'uns are the worst, don't they, an' if nothin' else I've proved that.'

'Don't.'

'Don't?'

She continued looking at him steadily as she said, 'Don't talk about yourself like that, about your height, as though you've always got to make a joke of it. You are more of a man than anyone else I know.'

She saw his eyes open very wide, his face naked and vulnerable, before he breathed out slowly through his nose, his eyes narrowing as he said, 'Thank you, lass. It's nice of you to say it although I doubt it's true. But thanks anyway,' before he turned from her.

'Do I appear young to you?' asked Rosie quietly.

A blank pause and then, 'Young, lass? No, you don't appear young, not silly young anyway, even though I'm near old enough to be your da.' He turned back to face her then but Rosie could see it was an effort.

He was smiling, but although he wasn't touching her,

and there was no visible proof of it, she could sense he was trembling. She stared at him long and hard, then she said, 'You're doing it again, aren't you?'

'Doin' what?'

'Trying to put an obstacle between us.'

'Tryin' to . . .' His face was unsmiling now, and she watched him take a deep breath and then release it very slowly before he said, 'Rosie, lass, you're nineteen an' you don't appear young to me, all right? But you're tired an' it's bin a day an' a half. Go on up an' get your head down.'

'No.' It was now or never, she'd never find the courage to do this again, but if she didn't say it he never would, feeling as he did. 'No, I won't go.' She watched his eyes narrow still more until they became slits of blue light and she knew he was wondering what was afoot as she rose slowly to face him. When she spoke her voice was low and rapid. 'I love you, Zachariah.' There was a small inarticulate sound from him and then silence as she continued, 'I've loved you for a long time but I know you won't say anything to me so I've got no choice but to say it to you. There, it's out.'

Zachariah remained standing still, his face blank, and if it hadn't been for that one tiny echo of what was in her own heart she would have thought she'd got it horribly wrong and his regard for her was only one of friendship.

She took a long shuddering breath. 'Zachariah?'

And then, as she made a step towards him, he jerked away from her with a violence that spoke of deeply suppressed emotion, and his voice vibrated with the depth of this feeling when he said, 'Go on upstairs before you say anythin' else you'll regret when you're yourself again.'

'I *am* myself!'

He had stepped back from her before throwing his body

into the armchair behind him and now he leant forward, his elbows on his knees and his head in his hands as he said, 'This is because I got Molly out of that place afore an' you was grateful an' tonight has raked it all up again. Whatever you say you're not thinkin' straight. How – how long have you known how I feel about you?' He didn't look at her as he spoke.

'I didn't know until tonight.'

Zachariah swore, just once but the sound was ugly, and then he said, 'Human sacrifices went out with the dark ages, lass. Now get yourself away an' we'll forget this ever happened.'

Forget it ever happened? Rosie didn't know if she wanted to hit him or kiss him but such was the feeling flooding her chest that she didn't trust herself to speak, and so she fell down on her knees by the side of his chair and leant her chin on the padded armrest as she reached out and held on to his arm.

'Rosie.' His voice was dragged up from the depths of him. 'You don't know what you're doin' to me, lass.'

Yes she did, she wasn't a bairn any longer and working with Sally had been an eye-opener in more ways than one. She knew what marriage entailed, the close proximity of the body and the linking of the flesh, as well as the joining together of two minds. She stared at his averted face, wondering how she could say it without appearing any more forward than she had already.

He wasn't making this easy. The annoyance that came with the thought enabled her to open her mouth and say quite sharply, 'You don't know what you're doing to me, either, it works both ways you know. I should never have had to speak first, my mam would be horrified if she knew.'

He did look at her then and there was surprise etched on his face. Before he could glance away she said quickly, 'I do love you and I think it's insulting you don't believe me. And it's nothing to do with Molly or anyone else, I'm not a child and I know how I feel. I love everything about you: your intelligence, your kindness, your generosity. And you're handsome, you know you are, you must look in the mirror sometimes. And your smell, I love your smell; it's clean and fragrant, not like some of the men who come in the shop and make me want to fumigate the place afterwards.'

None of it had come out as she'd wanted it to, but he remained looking at her for a good few seconds before he said, 'An' these? What about these?' as he gestured at his legs. 'Do you love these an' all, 'cos bein' married means more than sittin' readin' an' learnin' together in the evenings you know. Have you considered what bein' wed to me would mean?'

She wanted to fling her arms round his neck and kiss the hurt of thirty-three years away, so poignant was the feeling that gripped her, but she knew he would misconstrue it as pity. That could come later. And so now she waited a moment before she said, her voice very level, 'If you didn't have any legs at all it wouldn't make any difference to me, and there are plenty of lads that came back from the war in just that condition. You're a darn sight better off than them, now then.'

His head jerked, his neck stretched slightly, and then he said, 'Lass, you don't really know me. You think you do but you don't. There's things about me mam an' da—'

'If you mean about them not being married, I've known they probably weren't for a long time, but that's nothing to do with knowing you as a person and I *do* know you. As for

207

your mam and da, I'm sure they had their reasons but that was then and them, and this is now and us. I don't care that they weren't married, Zachariah. I don't care about anything but you.'

There was a long screaming silence before he said, his voice shaky with the fierce emotion that was threatening to burst out of every pore, 'Rosie, are you sure? Now think on, lass, because I couldn't stand . . . If you need time to think about what you've said . . .'

Now she allowed a smile to touch her lips for the first time and in answer she reached up and put her mouth on his. It caused such a swell of desire in Zachariah that he had to check himself from pulling her to him and ravishing her mouth, but his trembling must have been apparent because her voice was soft with understanding when she said, 'Zachariah. Oh, Zachariah.'

And now he did pull her up and onto his lap, his strength formidable, and as his mouth became fierce Rosie knew a brief moment of panic as Shane's clumsy assault flashed through her mind, and then she relaxed with a little sigh, her lips opening beneath his as she thought, This is Zachariah, *Zachariah*, and she loved him.

Chapter Twelve

Rosie married Zachariah on Saturday, 25th July, on the same day when violence erupted at a Miners' Gala from a crowd angry at the mine owners' demands for longer working hours and lower wages, and Davey Connor boarded the good ship HMS *Admiral II* bound for England's green, familiar shores without a backward glance at his adopted country of the last five years and with excitement filling his heart as the ship sailed. The wide expanse of blue-green, froth-crested waves, the endlessly clear sky above and the smiles and elation of the other passengers all seemed to offer a promise, the precise nature of which he wasn't sure of but which he felt he would understand once he looked into Rosie's face. And so he stood at the bowrail of the massive passenger ship with his hands gripping the smooth steel and his heart beating with the force of a sledgehammer.

Now he was underway, now he had actually made the break and committed himself to going back, he couldn't believe he had waited five years to see her – and home – again. And yet Rosie had always been with him somewhere deep inside, in the secret recesses of his heart, along with the desire to hear his native tongue and walk familiar northern streets again. He had known he would find her one day, even as he'd fought against the knowledge. And why had he fought it? he asked himself. For a whole host of reasons, but the main one – the one that superseded any other – was the realization he had made the biggest mistake of his life when he had left England. And he would stop at nothing to put things right.

He had not questioned what 'putting things right' would entail, not yet; it was enough for now that he was going home. The fact that he only had two sets of clothes to his name and a few pounds in his pocket after he had paid his second-class fare could be dealt with. Anything could be dealt with – once he had seen Rosie. It was all that mattered.

It had been a happy wedding day.

The marriage had taken place at St Barnaby's, mainly to please Jessie, who was a lapsed Catholic, but a Catholic nevertheless, and although the service had been a quiet one without the paraphernalia of bridesmaids and such, Rosie had looked lovely. She had been adamant that she wanted to marry Zachariah quickly and without any fuss, and for his part he would have marched down the aisle the day after they had declared their feelings for each other if it could have been arranged.

Rosie had taken Zachariah's breath away as he had turned from his position at the front of the church at the side of Tommy Bailey to see her walking towards him on the arm of Joseph Green – Rosie's employer having become a dear friend over the years. The simple white dress in a soft light fabric had just skimmed the top of her ankle-strap shoes, and the lacy little white cap on her shining dark hair and small posy of pink rosebuds had completed the picture of ethereal innocence. Rosie had made the dress herself, a wealth of dreams in every stitch, and as she reached Zachariah's side and the two of them looked at each other, no one present could have doubted it was a love match. Not that Rosie's family and friends had questioned it, after the initial surprise. Rosie's glowing face and Zachariah's immense pride as they had broken the news had convinced everyone that this marriage was going to be a blessing to them both.

Flora and Sally, who was Mrs McDoughty now, had arrived at Benton Street first thing, Sally insisting Rosie borrow her pearl necklace to fulfil the old rhyme *Something old, something new, Something borrowed, something blue*, and Flora with a small bottle of Chanel No. 5, a newly launched perfume by French fashion queen Gabrielle 'Coco' Chanel, and tiny seed-pearl earrings which had been her grandmother's for the something old and something new. Rosie had promised they could leave the blue part to her, and when she had tweaked up her dress to reveal a saucy blue garter complete with tiny velvet rosebuds, which she had made, the three girls had shrieked with laughter. And Flora and Sally had kept the morning full of fun and hilarity in the time before the wedding car – which Zachariah had ordered for Rosie, her mother and Hannah, and her two friends, he himself having spent the night at Tommy Bailey's – had drawn up outside, knowing that Rosie would be conscious of the missing face on this special day.

In the four months since Molly's departure all Zachariah's investigations had proved fruitless, and although the matter had been reported to the local constabulary the police had displayed a marked lack of urgency once the full details had come to light.

There were times when the thought of her sister wrung Rosie's heart, and others when she was filled with rage against Charlie Cullen, Ronnie Tiller and all such men. Strangely she never felt angry with Molly, something she had fully expected to do once the shock of her disappearance had worn off, but as the weeks and months had gone by she had become reconciled to the fact that Molly was gone. Her sister had chosen to step out of their lives with a ruthless decisiveness that suggested she had no intention of ever stepping back in, and unless Molly had a change of heart, or a miracle occurred, she would continue to be lost to them.

But if she had lost her sister then she had found her mother. When Rosie reviewed the happenings of the past four months it was with a deep sense of gratitude for the good which had emerged from all the turmoil. She had expected Molly's going to be the final push in her mother's downward spiral, but she couldn't have been more wrong. From that very night, when she had sped upstairs fresh from Zachariah's arms to find her mother still awake and the two of them had cried and talked the night away, Jessie had changed. The drinking had stopped, she had started taking an interest in Hannah and their home, and when Rosie had asked Joseph Green to give her away, and the upright and sprightly fifty-year-old had visited the house to meet Zachariah and the family, Jessie had actually gone and got her hair done for the first time in five years. Rosie felt all this augured well for the future, although occasionally she felt an aching sadness that the transformation couldn't have taken place earlier, before Molly had gone.

But now it was the evening of her wedding day, and the only thoughts running through Rosie's head were ones of apprehension mixed with curiosity and nervous anticipation about the night ahead. She knew the mechanics of what went on once you were married; Sally had jumped the gun with Mick months before she officially became Mrs McDoughty and hadn't been in the least bit reticent about what the two of them had got up to. 'You grin an' bear it the first time, lass, no pun intended,' Sally had giggled when Rosie had confided she was in the grip of wedding-night nerves earlier that morning. And then, when Rosie's puzzled smile had revealed she didn't understand, Sally had nudged her in the ribs as she'd chortled, 'You know, lass – *bare* it,' with a ridiculous leer. 'It gets better the more you practise an' I dare bet your Zac knows what's what. For all Mick's workin' with his flippin' horses he was as green as grass the first time we did it in his mam's scullery when they'd all gone to bed. Do you remember? You asked me why I was walkin' funny the next mornin', but what with havin' me backside jammed up agen their sink an' Mick thinkin' he was ridin' the winner in the Derby, it was a wonder I come in to work at all.' Rosie and Flora had been helpless with laughter as the other girl had elaborated further, but now Rosie didn't feel like smiling.

'Penny for 'em?'

Rosie jumped, she couldn't help it, but as she turned her head and saw Zachariah's engaging grin she relaxed a little. He had just walked through from the sitting room of their hotel suite to where she was standing looking out at Hartlepool's sea front from their bedroom window. The hotel was a grand affair and the imposing establishment had rendered Rosie speechless when they had first arrived earlier that evening. There had been bellboys to carry their valises and cases through to their ground-floor suite and when, after a quick freshen-up, they had gone straight through to dinner

213

in the formal dining room, the elegance of the other women's clothes and the general air of refined prosperity had filled Rosie with awe. Zachariah, on the other hand, had seemed singularly unimpressed.

'I was just thinking about . . . the day and everything.' As Zachariah approached her Rosie heard herself begin to gabble. 'It was so nice that everyone could come, although Mrs McLinnie seemed a bit subdued, don't you think? But Flora's Peter Baxter seems very pleasant, I really liked him.' The moment was fast drawing near when she would have to take off the pretty going-away suit she had made with such care, and put on the nightdress and matching negligée in ruched blue lawn and lace, and she wished, she so *wished* they were at home at Benton Street. It was so strange here, so splendid and opulent, and it had the effect of making Zachariah almost a stranger.

'I don't care about Flora's Peter Baxter.' Zachariah's voice was very soft, and when he took her hand and led her over to the bed the look in his eyes made her go willingly. He sat down beside her before fishing in his pocket and producing a small velvet box, but before handing it to her he leant across and kissed her in a way he had never done before, until when at last he released her she was limp and quivering. But she wasn't frightened any longer.

'Here.' He handed her the box as his other hand reached up and stroked the smooth silk of her cheek. 'Wedding present, Mrs Price.'

'Oh, Zachariah. I haven't got you anything.'

'I didn't buy it, lass. It was me mam's.'

He watched her as she opened the small hinged lid to reveal an exquisitely dainty ring worked in fine lacy gold with a half band of tiny diamonds and rubies, and at her delighted gasp he reached out and plucked it from its nest, sliding it onto the third finger of her left hand next to the shining gold wedding band. 'This is your engagement ring, lass, but I wanted you to have it tonight. Me mam would've liked that, bein' as how she felt about marriage an' all.'

She turned to him, flinging her arms round his neck as she pressed her lips to his for a moment, and then he held her close as he said, 'Me da an' me mam might not have bin wed, Rosie, but they loved each other all right. There was only ever one man for me mam, she worshipped the ground he walked on.'

Rosie knew what he was trying to say and she nodded slowly. 'I know your mother wasn't a bad woman, Zachariah. How could she have been to have had a son like you?' she said softly. And she must have been strong to have braved the wrath of her fellow northerners. No respectable woman did what Zachariah's mother had done – not unless they wanted filth flung in their faces by their virtuous neighbours when they stepped outside their front doors, or could put up with being spat on and reviled by all and sundry. But then no one had been absolutely sure about Zachariah's mother and she had firmly stuck to her story of being wed overseas, Rosie told herself silently. That had been her salvation.

'Me da was a sailor. No.' He shook his head. 'More than that, he was a captain, had his own ship, an' in Denmark where he come from he'd got his own business. He was well set up when he met me mam, but with a wife an' umpteen bairns over the sea she knew he couldn't wed her. He set me mam up in her own place – Benton Street – bought it outright in case anythin' happened to him. An' once I was on the way he set up a bank account for her along with some

215

bonds an' such like. The thing is she was scared to death about havin' a bairn with him away so much an' she took somethin'. That's why . . .' He gestured at his legs. 'It fair killed her later when she realized what she'd done. She was a good mam.'

His voice was defensive and when Rosie said again, 'I know she wasn't bad, Zachariah, and it must have been hard for her,' he nodded slowly.

'Aye, no doubt, but there would be some who'd say she'd brought it on herself.' A pause, and then, 'Me da liked to run the odds with the customs blokes, got a right little enterprise goin' he had, an' after his ship went down, when I was just startin' school, me mam started to handle the Sunderland end of it.'

Rosie was wide-eyed now but suddenly a lot of things were making sense. 'She didn't have to do it, me da had left her nicely set up, but she . . . she liked the excitement, I suppose, an' it kept her pally with all me da's mates an' such. They used to eat us out of house an' home when their ships were in but me mam liked company. She never got over me da goin', not really, an' the way they talked an' all . . . It comforted her. Not that she was a weak woman, by, no.'

'Did you get involved in any . . . ?' Rosie didn't quite know how to describe it. Smuggling seemed a bit strong and yet that was what they were talking about.

'Would you mind if I had?' Zachariah asked quietly.

She thought about it for a moment or two and then shook her head. 'I don't think so, not if it was in the past, but if you were doing it now I'd be worried.'

'Well I didn't anyway, me mam wouldn't have it an' likely she was right.' He touched the ring on Rosie's finger and his voice was soft when he said, 'It was me mam's one regret that she didn't have his name, legal like. He gave her that ring along with a gold band the day he moved her into Benton Street, an' although she called herself missus an' held her head high the gossip hurt her. I used to hear her sobbin' sometimes when he was away, an' after, when his boat had gone down, she was bad for months. She still used to have her times of weepin' for him right up to the day she died. It—' He stopped abruptly, and when Rosie said, 'Yes, what?' he shook his head.

'Zachariah, what?' He had turned away from her and now she reached out and cupped his face, meeting his eyes as she said again, 'What?' her voice insistent.

'It reminded me of her that night you cried for Davey Connor.'

'Oh, Zachariah.' She didn't know what to say.

'I found meself thinkin' it'd be worth dyin' to have you cry like that for me.'

There was a wealth of pain in his voice and now it was Rosie who shook her head as she said, 'Oh, Zachariah, don't you see? I don't want to cry for you, I want to live for you.'

Now they were clinging together and he was muttering against her lips, 'I've money enough for us to live however you want, lass, however you want. Anythin' you want, it's yours.'

She drew back slightly, touching his mouth with her fingertips, and when he stilled, his vivid blue eyes half closing, she felt the shiver that passed through him. This was a complicated man. A man who had been deeply scarred by life and yet who still had the capacity for great compassion and tenderness. And she loved him. She didn't know what the next few hours would bring, but she loved him. And her love told her that it was Zachariah who needed reassurance about the night ahead, not her, and she would give it to him.

When he took her into his arms she melted into him, her whole being striving to encourage and comfort and when he kissed her she kissed him back.

And it was later, much later, when she lay awake in her husband's arms in the big soft bed and listened to his measured, rhythmic breathing, that Rosie allowed herself to think of Davey. Davey Connor had left her – say what you will, dress it up how you like, he had, he'd left her. All right, he was dead now and you shouldn't speak ill of the dead, but Davey had made her think he cared about her in a hundred little ways that hadn't needed words. He had made her love him and then, when she was at her lowest, he had gone. But Zachariah . . .

He had been so gentle tonight. She shut her eyes tight for one moment, then opened them wide again in the darkness. And after that first brief pain it hadn't been so bad in spite of her shyness. Sally had been right, he had known what he was doing. A brief smile touched her lips. And now they had years and years ahead of them, years in which to have a family, to live peacefully with their friends and family, to travel a bit if they wanted, to do anything . . .

She was going to like being married.

Chapter Thirteen

'Hold your horses, lass, hold your horses, I can't take this in. You're tellin' me your Shane has always liked our Rosie?'

May the good Lord give her strength 'cos you needed a measure an' a half of it when you were trying to talk to Jessie. Annie McLinnie took a deep breath before she said, 'Aye, that's what I'm sayin', an' it's more than likin', Jessie. He come in the night afore their weddin' like a man possessed, we've never had such a do. He was rantin' an' ravin' we should've let him know—'

'Let him know?' Jessie's brow wrinkled. 'You knew where he was then? I thought . . .'

'We've had an address the last couple of years,' Annie admitted, 'but we had to keep it quiet like, our Shane didn't want anyone to know. Apparently there was some trouble afore he went, somethin' to do with his sideline, you know?' Jessie nodded; she'd put two and two together years ago and made four. 'An' he still wasn't satisfied they'd be off his back if he came back.'

'But if you had his address why *didn't* you let him know?'

How did she answer that? Annie hesitated. Her thoughts were one thing, but to malign her Shane to Jessie was quite another. If she answered truthfully she would have to say that she had been frightened to write Shane about the little lass's news. And the way he had carried on that night a week ago had proved her right if nothing else. The fact that Rosie and Zachariah had wanted a quiet do with no fuss and that it had all happened so quickly had been to their advantage, added to which there had been no engagement, not official like anyways. It had been too late for Shane to do anything when he'd found out. Do anything? She felt her stomach turn over at the thought. She didn't really think her Shane would have done anything, did she? Annie took a big gulp from the mug of tea Jessie had just handed her and sat down heavily at the wooden table covered with a clean oilcloth. Aye, she did. By, this was a rum do all round.

'Annie?' Jessie sat down opposite her and now her eyes were tight on this old friend of hers. 'Why didn't you let him know, lass?'

'He likes her too much, Jessie. He always has.' Annie's voice was low and rapid but she needed to do this, she needed to put Jessie wise. Shane was back and according to what he'd screamed at them that night afore the wedding he intended to stay, and that meant . . . Jessie had to be put wise. She dare not let herself think beyond that. Jessie was better now, the last few months she'd been herself again which was strange really, with her Molly goodness knows where and Rosie marrying Zachariah and all, but she could cope with this now. She couldn't have done before. And for her part she had never thought to see the day when she'd admit to being glad her boys had been laid off, but she wouldn't have wanted to be in the house alone. Oh, what was she saying? She took another gulp of the strong black tea. May God forgive her. Her Shane wouldn't hurt her, now then. But she'd spell it out to Jessie, you always needed to hammer something home with her. And then, if nothing else, her own conscience would be clear in that she'd done all that she could.

Jessie was silent for a long time when Annie finished speaking. She was staring at the other woman fixedly, thinking, For this to happen now when everything was going so well. Not that she hadn't been knocked sideways when Rosie had first told her about Zachariah the night Molly had gone; she had to admit she'd wondered what the lass was taking on with his handicap and all, but when she'd seen them together the next day and the days thereafter she'd had her mind put at rest. It was love all right, and love covered a multitude of sins. The saying was one of Joseph's, and now the thought of him again emphasized how life had taken a turn for the better.

Annie, who was always uncomfortable with silences, said, 'When are they comin' back off honeymoon anyway?'

'What? Oh, tomorrow. But they're not comin' back here.'

'Not . . . ?' Annie's face was perplexed.

'It's a secret, Zachariah didn't want anyone to know in case they let on to Rosie an' spoiled the surprise, but he's bought a house in Roker.' Jessie couldn't keep the pride out of her voice.

'Roker?'

'Aye, overlookin' the promenade. Lovely it is, an' he's had it furnished right grand, an' there's a run of garden at the front an' a patch of nice lawn at the back. But don't let on, Annie, not yet,' Jessie added hastily. 'Not a word, lass.'

'You know me, pet, me lips are sealed.' It said a lot for Annie that she didn't speak her mind at this point, because if she had it would have been along the lines of, 'Well, me lads have heard the odd tale about Zachariah, or his mam to be more precise, an' it looks as though the stories about her saltin' a packet away might be true, eh? Your Rosie has landed on her feet an' no mistake.' But it was none of her business, Annie told herself firmly, and any road, who was she to talk, with her Shane being in dirty dealings up to his neck? Them that lived in glass houses . . . 'You goin' with 'em to Roker, lass? You an' Hannah?'

Jessie shook her head. 'No, Annie. Zachariah's quite happy for us to stay here as long as we want an' I'm of a mind a young couple should have a year or two on their own if they can. There's not many round these parts can run to that.'

'You're right there, lass, by you are.' Annie thought of the groups of men visible at every street corner these days, their coats, caps and mufflers on whatever the weather, and the same dead hopeless look on their faces. The shipyards and the mines were cutting back by the week, and it didn't matter if you were a labourer, a riveter, a trimmer or a miner, you swallowed your pride and joined the dole queue or you and your family starved, and even with the dole the hordes of bairns scavenging on the coaltips for buckets of cinders bore evidence to the desperation of some families. 'It's a luxury, so it is.'

Jessie nodded but her face was sober, her thoughts having travelled the same way as Annie's. There was only Arthur in regular work now in the McLinnie household and they were feeling the pinch, no doubt about it. Since she had pulled herself together she'd tried to slip Annie the odd few shillings when she could, and a bit of this and that, but it was a drop in the ocean. The lads got the odd shift

now and again, but although that might go some way to
alleviating the soul-destroying hopelessness and bitter shame
that was tearing the guts out of the men of Sunderland and
Newcastle and South Shields and aye, the whole country, it
didn't pay the rent. There would be riots before long; they'd
already started in some places, and the unions were nigh on
useless. When she thought back to the wages her James had
earned through the war and such she couldn't believe what
men were expected to keep families on now. Wages were
supposed to go up, weren't they? By, them days had been
the heydays, even if each wage packet had been earned with
blood, sweat and tears. The country was dying now.

'I'd best be away, lass.' It had been a sombre visit what
with one thing and another and Annie wasn't loath to end
it. 'My Arthur will be home soon an' the lads'll be ready
for their dinner.'

Jessie nodded again and then, as the two women walked
out onto the landing and Annie glanced down the stairs,
she said, 'You gonna move downstairs, lass, if they're not
comin' back, an' have these two rooms as bedrooms?'

'No.' Jessie smiled. 'Zachariah suggested it but Sally an'
her Mick are livin' with his lot in Salem Street, an' there's
fifteen of 'em squashed in them four rooms accordin' to
Rosie. She's bin sayin' for months she wished they could
have a place of their own. Me an' the bairn'll move
downstairs an' let Sally have these rooms. She's a nice lass,
an' my Rosie thinks a bit of her an' Mick, an' rightly so.'

By, the difference a few months could make. And this
thought was brought home again to Annie when Jessie
followed her down the stairs to the doorstep where she
thrust four ten-shilling notes into her hand.

'What's this, lass?' Annie stared at the money as her throat closed and her eyes filled up. 'You've given us more than enough the last little while, I can't take all this now then.'

'Oh aye, you can. Who was it who filled our bellies more than one night when James and the lads went, Annie McLinnie?'

'But two pounds, Jessie.'

'Aw, go on with you. Zachariah saw me all right afore he went away, he's insistin' we're family now an' Hannah an' me won't want for nothin'. Take it, lass. Please?'

The last was said in such a way that all Annie could do was nod as she indulged in a rare show of affection and hugged Jessie tight for one moment, before stepping down heavily into the hot dusty street. God was good. Oh aye, God was good. Here she'd been fretting how she was going to fill her men's bellies the week, and He'd filled her cup to overflowing.

Annie was half talking, half praying, as she made her way down Benton Street, but as she reached the Dog and Rabbit on the corner and turned left towards the tram stop, the sound of a ship's horn in the far distance barely registering on her consciousness, she suddenly stood stock still as her eyes alighted on the tall young man coming towards her in the muggy afternoon air. *Davey Connor?* It was, it was Davey Connor! She'd know him anywhere in spite of him being as brown as one of them from the Arab quarter down by the docks. She pressed her hand to her heart which had tried to jump out of her chest with shock and it was like that she watched him approach her. When he was within easy earshot she said, 'Eee, eee, lad, is it really you? You gave me the gliff of me life! If I was after bein' a lady I'd have had a fit of the vapours an' no mistake.'

'Hallo, Mrs McLinnie.' The first old face he sees and it

has to be Shane's mam. But he liked Mrs McLinnie, he always had.

'I don't believe it, after all this time. How are you, lad?'

'I'm fine, Mrs McLinnie, and I see you're still as bonny as ever.' Davey grinned at the fat shapeless figure, his eyes twinkling.

'Go on with you!' Annie made a gesture with one hand as though flapping something aside, and then she said, 'Where you bin the last few years, lad? We heard tell you'd copped it . . . oh, it must be four years or more now. Drowned, when your ship sunk.'

'You heard that?' The smile had been wiped off Davey's face and now he said, his voice sharp, 'Who told you that, Mrs McLinnie?'

'Rosie. Rosie Ferry, as was, an' she heard it from Flora. Flora works in the Baxter shippin' office an' there was a report of a ship sinkin' with all hands lost. Your name was registered on the crew list.'

Davey flexed back on his heels as he let the breath out between his teeth. The *President*, it must have been the *President*. It looked as if he had something to thank Captain McGrathe for after all. But for his decision to jump ship he would have gone down to Davy Jones's locker alongside the rest of the crew, the poor devils. But he didn't refer to the doomed ship or his timely escape, instead he asked, 'Rosie Ferry as was? She's married then?' his voice casual, as though he hadn't just been on his way to Benton Street to find out that very thing.

'Oh aye, lad, just last week.'

Davey felt the blow register in his solar plexus but didn't reveal it by so much as the blink of an eyelid.

'They'll be comin' back from their honeymoon in the

next day or two, lovely weather they've had for it an' all, bless 'em.'

It was taking all of Davey's considerable willpower to stand still and nod quietly as though the news meant nothing more to him than it would to any old friend, and his stomach was threatening to throw up its contents, but still he managed to say, 'That's grand, Mrs McLinnie. You'll be pleased to see them back no doubt.' Five years. It had taken Shane McLinnie five years to get her to the altar and he had missed stopping it by one week. By, Someone up there was having a laugh at his expense all right, but he'd only himself to blame.

'Aye.' Annie's voice was faintly puzzled. That was a funny comment to make, wasn't it? 'Well, I'd best be makin' me way home, lad, my lot's stomachs'll be thinkin' their throats have bin cut. They can still put it away in spite of there only bein' Mr McLinnie in work most days.'

'Oh I'm sorry to hear that, Mrs McLinnie, about the lads being laid off,' Davey said dully.

'It's the same for everyone, lad, you've decided to come home at a bad time. The so-an'-sos are sellin' ships off for less than they took to build these days an' there's no new orders, an' the same spirit's in the mines an' everywhere else. Don't think you'll walk into work, lad, 'cos you won't. Oh, listen to me' – again Annie's hand flapped outwards – 'you don't need a prophet of doom the minute you're back, do you. Well, goodbye, lad, it was nice seein' you.'

Davey answered automatically, and long after Annie had waddled away he stood exactly where he was, his kitbag at his feet and his eyes staring blindly ahead down the long terraced street. It all looked exactly the same; he could have been away for five days instead of five years. There were the same raggedy-arsed bairns playing mas and das, one of them in charge of a dirty, dilapidated pram from which a bare-bottomed child had escaped or been lifted and was now sitting on the hot pavement with a five-year-old would-be mother trying to ram a mangled dummy into its mouth; a group of boys playing chucks in the gutter and another few fighting over the rights to an old rusty wheel they had found. He had sailed the ocean, travelled halfway round the globe, seen another world and lived a life that, although far from easy, had been one of satisfaction and fulfilment on the land, and here . . . Here time had stopped. Although it hadn't, had it? She was married. To Shane McLinnie. But that wasn't the end of it. His eyes narrowed and his lips drew back slightly from his teeth. That scum didn't have it in him to make any lass happy. He'd wait around a while, see how the land lay. Courting was one thing, being wed was another.

'Davey!'

It was evening of that same day, and Davey hadn't been at all sure if Flora would still be living in the house in Fulwell, but when he had tentatively knocked on the door she had opened it, and such was her greeting that it took some of the sting out of his homecoming.

'Oh Davey, Davey. Oh, Davey . . .'

It appeared it was all she could say as she stood on the doorstep, her hands gripping his and her lovely grey eyes staring up into his face with wonder in their depths.

'Hallo, lass.' He knew he was smiling somewhat self-consciously but it was either that or the lump in his throat choking him.

'But, but . . . how?' Her mouth had fallen open in a gape. 'We heard that . . .'

227

'Aye, I know.' He nodded his head in answer to the unspoken question. 'I saw Mrs McLinnie and she said, but I wasn't on the *President*, Flora. I'd skedaddled afore it left port for England.'

'Oh, Davey.' She shook his hands gently, her face radiant and her eyes wet. 'I'm so glad you did!'

'Me too, Flora.' Davey was laughing now but he was deeply touched.

'Oh come in, come in.' She had seen his eyes pass her into the hall beyond, and now she pulled him through the doorway, calling over her shoulder, 'Mam! Mam, you'll never guess what the wind's blown in.'

Thank heaven it was her da's night at choir practice. As Flora pushed Davey down the long narrow hall, past the immaculate and rarely used front room on their right and the family sitting room on her left, she said, 'Mam an' I were bakin', you don't mind comin' through to the kitchen, do you?'

'No, no of course not.' Davey had never been in the Thomases' house – all the bairns had known her da was something of a tartar – and now as he stepped into the big wide kitchen that stretched over the back of the house, with a small scullery and washhouse built in an L-shape at one side, he was struck by the space and general air of prosperity. 'Hallo, Mrs Thomas.'

Megan Thomas was standing at the scrubbed kitchen table, her sleeves rolled up and her hands deep in a large bowl of dough she was kneading, and despite the warmth of the summer evening a bright fire was burning in the open fireplace within the blackleaded range at the back of her, and the delicious smell indicated the bread oven was already in use.

'It's Davey, Davey Connor.'

At Davey's greeting Megan had turned enquiring eyes to Flora, and now the older woman said, 'Of course it is, I'm sorry, Davey, I didn't recognize you at first,' in the quick, bird-like, nervous voice that characterized Flora's mother, before adding, as she turned to Flora again, 'But didn't you say . . . ?'

'It was a mistake, he wasn't on the ship.' Flora's voice was excited, with a lilting note that caused her mother's eyes to sharpen on her daughter's pretty animated face. Oh no, no, please God, no. Things had been going so well, and she'd thought Flora was getting to like Peter more and more in the last twelve months since they'd been walking out. Of course nothing had been said for definite, not as far as she knew at any rate, but Peter's face when he looked at her lass made it crystal clear how he felt. He'd got marriage on his mind and it would only take the slightest encouragement for him to say so.

'Sit down, Davey, sit down.' Flora was fussing over him, her face still wreathed in smiles. 'I'll get you a drink, the kettle's on the hob, an' there's a shive of spice cake, or perhaps you'd rather have a bit of parkin?' She gestured towards the northern cake made of treacle and oatmeal that was cooling at one side of the table. 'I've just made it.'

'Please, don't go to any trouble.' Davey was feeling distinctly embarrassed, and this was reflected in his voice when he looked directly at Megan and said, 'I didn't intend to stay, Mrs Thomas, and I can see that you're busy. Perhaps a quick cup of tea and then I'll be on my way.'

He was different. As she watched her mother smile timidly and insist that no of course he must stay for something to eat and it was *so* nice to see him again after all this

229

time, Flora's mind was racing. He looked different; older, more handsome and very striking with his brown skin and sun-bleached hair, and he talked different too; the northern drawl was less pronounced and his intonation was clearer, crisper. But it was more than that. She felt her heart pound as the rusty-green eyes turned to her and smiled, and she smiled back quickly before turning and busying herself with making the tea. He had an authority about him now, a virility that made her knees wobble. The rawness of the thought shocked her and she almost dropped the teapot.

It was only half an hour later that Davey rose to leave, but he could sense the waves of agitation coming from Flora's mother even if he didn't fully understand them, and he felt sorry for the pathetic little mouse-like woman who was nothing at all like her vivacious daughter. The conversation had been all about his time in Egypt and his experiences overseas, but now, as he got to his feet, Flora said, 'Oh you can't go yet, there's still so much I want to know. Where are you staying anyway?' as she rose with him.

'With Mrs Riley, my old next-door neighbour. I called in earlier to say hallo, and with her Douglas married and it being just the two of them she was insistent I take the spare room. She thought a lot of my mother.'

He smiled now and Flora said, 'Aye, yes, of course.' She couldn't let him go yet, she just couldn't, although she understood why her mother was beside herself and perhaps it would be better to get him out of the house. 'I'll walk with you a little way, if I may?' she asked now, the words prim but her eager face anything but. 'It's a lovely evening and I want to ask you some more about the farm and Cairo.'

'Fine.' Davey blinked a little before turning to Megan

Thomas, his smile kind, as he said, 'Goodbye, and thank you for the tea and cake.'

'It was nothing, lad, nothing.' Dear God, dear Lord Jesus, don't let him see them, please don't let Llewellyn see them. Since Flora threatening him with Peter and the rest, it had kept him off her most of the time and the once or twice he'd gone back to his old ways, when he'd been in a rage about something or other, he'd come to his senses before he really hurt her. She glanced at the little finger of her left hand which was contorted out of shape. He hadn't done anything like that since Flora's warning anyway, and he hadn't dared lay a hand on the lass herself the last two years, but if Flora took up with a miner and this with Peter didn't work out Llewellyn would go insane.

Once Flora and Davey had gone and Megan was alone she continued to sit limply at the kitchen table instead of clearing away as she was apt to do; Llewellyn was averse to anything but the most immaculately clean and tidy house, and all baking and other such chores had to be done either in the day or on the evenings he was out at choir practice or committee meetings.

Her face was pale and lined and her faded blue eyes gazed wearily across the warm fragrant kitchen, and anyone seeing her sitting there could have been forgiven for thinking that she was exhausted or ill, but beneath the enervated exterior Megan's mind was screaming and shouting. If anything should happen to shatter this fragile haven which Flora's fortitude had brought them into, she didn't know what she'd do. Oh, she knew what Flora thought. Her daughter believed she was too petrified of Llewellyn to make a stand against him, that she was content to be bought off with the material possessions he loved to flaunt and crow about. She hadn't tried to disabuse Flora of any of it, how could she? It had been true once. She had allowed him to get away with near murder at times.

She stood up now, leaning with the palms of both hands on the table as she bent her body until her head was almost touching the table top. Twenty years, *twenty years* she had endured his rages. They had started just three months after they were married, when she had been late back from visiting her mother one afternoon and Llewellyn had arrived home to an empty house. He had been waiting in the kitchen for her and he had punched her so hard in the stomach she had been sick for a week. She shook her head slowly, tendrils of hair brushing the white film of flour on the table. But in these last two years she had had some semblance of peace and she couldn't, she *couldn't* go back to what it had been like before. Her glance rested on the big wooden-handled breadknife with which Flora had cut the cake earlier, and remained transfixed on the sharp jagged blade as the screaming in her mind died down to a soft murmuring that reverberated gently on her eardrums, and then one quiet whisper. And the whisper told her quite clearly what must be done if it looked as though the beatings were going to happen again. And she nodded to it, like an obedient child, and began to clear the baking tins away.

Davey stood still in the middle of the pavement and stared at Flora, and the look on his face caused her to say, and with some anxiety, 'But you said you *knew* she was married?'

'I . . . I thought . . .' Davey took a deep breath and forced the words through the constriction in his throat, 'I thought it was Shane, that Shane McLinnie was her husband.'

'Shane McLinnie?' Flora couldn't have been more

astounded if he had said the devil himself. 'Why on earth would Rosie marry Shane McLinnie?' And when he continued to stare dumbly at her she said again, with gentle insistence as she took his arm, 'Davey? Why Shane of all people?'

He had to pull himself together, she must think he was mad. The thought was there but the power to follow it through was quite beyond him, and when Flora tugged on his arm, leading him across the street and into a small park which was simply some few hundred yards of neatly cut grass and regimented flower beds, he went as meekly as a lamb. It wasn't until they sat down on the small wooden bench and Flora asked again, 'Why Shane, Davey?' that he found his tongue and managed to say, 'I thought he was sweet on her. I saw them one day . . .'

'You saw them? Rosie and Shane? I don't understand.'

And so he told her. He didn't look at her as he spoke – if he had done so he would have seen a whole host of emotions pass over Flora's face – and when he had finished there was silence. It was getting late, twilight was beginning to settle over the scene and the warm balmy smell peculiar to hot summer nights was scenting the air. In the distance beyond the park there were the muted sounds of a community settling down for the night – children shouting, a dog barking – but apart from one or two courting couples strolling the winding paths arm-in-arm, and a family with two small children rolling hoops making their way homewards, the park was quiet, as befitted this better part of Fulwell where the eminently respectable citizens kept their doorsteps scrubbed as white as snow and their curtains starched in permanent flounces. If any housewives in Fulwell were worried that their man's next pay packet might be his last it wasn't spoken about publicly – there were standards to adhere to, proprieties to be upheld.

She had to tell him. Davey was leaning forward, his elbows resting on his legs and his hands clasped beneath his chin as he stared straight ahead. She had to tell him what Shane McLinnie had tried to do that night, and about him visiting Zachariah's house and all the hoo-ha that had followed. But as Flora stared at the bowed profile the words wouldn't come. Rosie was married now, she had Zachariah and she said she loved him. She was *happy*, she was. It was better to let sleeping dogs lie, for Davey to continue to think along the lines he'd thought for five years, it'd do no good to tell him the truth and maybe stir up all the old feelings he'd had for Rosie – that wouldn't help him at all. And then the innate honesty that was a basic part of Flora's character added, And it wouldn't help you either, more to the point, would it?

But Davey was back, he was back, and she wouldn't have another chance like this again, she knew she wouldn't. And Peter? She felt a sharp stab of guilt that she immediately quashed. She had never said to Peter that she loved him. All along, right from when she had first agreed to walk out with him, she had said she wanted them just to be friends and see what developed. She hadn't made any promises. And they could still be friends, if he wanted that. In fact she would be sad to lose his friendship, if she thought about it.

'This Zachariah, I saw him one time.' Davey paused now, as though searching for the right words, and then he said, 'I don't understand, Flora. Does she love him?' And before Flora could answer, 'What does he do anyway?'

'Do?'

'A job. What sort of line is he in?'

'I don't know, not exactly. I know he spends quite a bit of time at the Maritime Almshouses, Rosie said he's on the board or something, and he owns his own house, I know that. Mrs McLinnie—'

'Aye, what about Mrs McLinnie?' Davey asked as Flora stopped abruptly.

'Well, Mrs McLinnie said – and I don't know if it's true, mind, and I've not discussed it with Rosie – but she said at the wedding when she'd had a few that she had heard Zac's mam used to be in with them that did the shifting down in the docks when the Danes' boats were in. She said Zac's mam had made a packet according to some folks. His da was a Danish sea captain so it might be true. He . . . he seems well set up anyway.'

So she had let one paw her for pleasure and the other because she had set her sights on a life of ease? And then, when Flora said hesitantly, 'Don't look so sad, Davey,' he turned to her, a bitter twist to his mouth as he replied, 'I'm not sad, Flora.' Angry – furiously, murderously angry – and disappointed, oh aye, disappointed, but he was damned if he would let himself be sad.

'They'll be back soon, from honeymoon, and I know Rosie would like to see you.'

Maybe. His eyes had left her to roam the neat little park as though searching for an answer to the sick turmoil that had gripped him, but now, as Flora placed a light hand on his arm he looked at her. She was waiting for his eyes. 'Aye, lass, well maybe I won't be staying over long. I hear tell it's bad here, the work situation? I might make my way down south and see how the land lies there.'

Flora gave an involuntary jerk, and her voice was rushed and high when she said, 'Oh no, don't do that, not yet when you have only just got back. I can have a word with Peter – he's . . . he's the son of the man who owns the shipyard I work for, and he's in charge of selecting men for the different shifts – and ask him to help if it's work you need. He won't mind.'

'Well, we'll see, lass.' Davey rose to his feet, offering her his hand, and again his attraction swamped Flora and it was all she could do not to shiver as she placed her fingers in his warm flesh.

He couldn't go, she wouldn't let him go, no matter what she had to do to make him stay. This was her chance, *it was*; the way things had worked out it was all meant to be, and she would make him fall in love with her if it was the last thing she did. Oh, Davey . . .

Chapter Fourteen

'Zachariah, where *are* we going?'

Rosie had known Zachariah was excited and keyed up about something from the moment she had awoken in the big double bed at the hotel and found him lying on one elbow watching her, his eyes as bright as a bairn's on Christmas morning. He had made the excuse that he was eager to get home now their honeymoon was over and start being Mr and Mrs Price, and at first she had believed him. But now their horsedrawn cab had passed Hendon and she smelled a rat.

'Trust me, lass, eh?' He grinned at her, raising his eyebrows before adding, his voice conciliatory, 'It's a surprise, a nice 'un, an' that's all I'm sayin'.'

Rosie grimaced at him but her eyes were soft. They had something special, very special; they were friends as well as lovers. Now if she spoke that out loud to any of her friends – even Flora – they wouldn't have a clue what she was on about. As far as they were concerned life followed a certain pattern: you started courting, and only on particular nights mind, ones that didn't interfere with the lad's darts matches and such like, and in due course you got married. Then the wife started having bairns and the man continued with his regular nights at the local club along with Saturday afternoons watching football which he'd take his bairns to – them being lads of course – as soon as they could toddle.

Would Davey have been like that? The thought came from nowhere and made her blink, but immediately she answered, Aye, yes, he would have been. He had been a working-class northerner – he would have thought and spoken in a certain way and she would have expected him to, and in spite of his desire to get out of the pit and work above ground he would still have been as narrowminded as the rest of them, as *she* would have been if Zachariah hadn't broadened her understanding and encouraged her to think for herself more and more.

When they drove into Roker the sun was out and the light was luminous on the glittering blue sea beyond the sea-wall facing the dignified houses of The Terrace. Their driver stopped the cab at number seventeen, and Zachariah almost bounded onto the pavement, his handsome face lit up from within as he held out his hand for Rosie to step down.

'We're home, lass.' The vivid blue gaze showed an intensity of purple, and Rosie, staring deep into the beautiful eyes, saw a depth of love that almost pained her.

She made a barely perceptible motion with her head, but what he saw in her face appeared to satisfy him and he smiled, unclasping her hand and drawing her arm through his as he said, 'Come on, Mrs Price. Come an' inspect your new habitat.'

And so it was like that, their fingers entwined and their bodies close, that they entered their home.

And now it was their first Sunday at number seventeen, The Terrace, and the bright August sunshine and mild warm breeze furthered Rosie's sense of wellbeing as she prepared the vegetables for lunch in the big stone-flagged kitchen at the back of the house. Zachariah had thought of everything when he had had the house furnished, she thought tenderly. From the lovely carpet and rich three-piece suite in the sitting room, right down to mundane essentials like the shining set of kitchen knives in the well-equipped cupboards in the kitchen.

She was lucky, she was so, so lucky, and not because of this house and her sudden newfound wealth either. No, it was Zachariah she was thankful for. What other man would have been happy for her to continue working when they were married? Not one, not *one* she knew of, especially if he was as well set up as Zachariah was. The men round here would have expected their wife to be at their beck and call, there would have been no question of their spouse working outside the home unless dire necessity commanded it. But Zachariah knew how much she loved her job and that it would have sent her mad to sit around and twiddle her thumbs all day.

And of course it helped that he had his own interests and outlets, begun years before he'd met her. He was a stout member of the Hendon working men's club, and she knew his financial contribution and time spent organizing the club's various activities were generous, but his main concern – the Maritime Almshouses in Bishopswearmouth which stood between Crowtree Road and Maritime Place – was a responsibility he took very seriously.

As the name suggested the almshouses were intended for the care of the widows and unmarried daughters of master mariners, and with Sunderland's high proportion of seamen the problem was not a small one. The almshouses had been built in 1820, but by the beginning of the twentieth century they were providing relief for an average of three hundred widows and eight hundred children.

Zachariah spent several half days a week at the grim line of terraced dwellings which were enclosed by a high wall and approached through an arched gate, and, as chairman of the board, had fought to raise living conditions for those the almshouses were supporting, and create a sense of purpose and encourage initiative for those inmates attempting to better themselves.

He was a good man, such a good man, and she loved him so much. She wanted everyone to be as happy as she was; Flora for instance. Rosie's smile dimmed and her hands became still. She had sent a note inviting Flora and Peter to lunch but had heard nothing. Her mother and Hannah and Joseph were coming, along with Sally and Mick, but it wouldn't be the same without Flora, not for her at least. She had thought of asking Mr and Mrs McLinnie but her mother had told her Annie was ill in bed with influenza and so she hadn't bothered. But this with Flora, she didn't understand it. She would make sure she saw her friend this week and find out if anything was wrong.

'You finished in here yet, lass?'

Zachariah's voice caused Rosie to turn and smile at the fair-haired figure in the doorway before answering, her tone cheeky, 'Oh, I've married a slave-driver, I should have known it was too good to be true. If you're so worried there's another knife on the side there and the carrots to do.'

'Aye, all right.'

As Zachariah approached the kitchen table Rosie said quickly, 'I was only joking, you know I was only joking. Go and sit down.'

'Why?' asked Zachariah with lazy good humour, his eyebrows raised.

'*Why?*'

'Aye, why? I'm sittin' there like King Canute in the sittin' room an' missin' you, an' you're workin' in here. It's daft, lass. We might as well sort out the dinner atween us.'

'But . . .'

'What?' The raised eyebrows dared her to say it.

'It's not done. I mean, it's a woman's job to get the meals and all . . .' Her voice trailed away as he shook his head sorrowfully.

'By, I can see there's still plenty of work to be done in the education line with you, Rosie Price.' Zachariah grinned at her, but then his tone changed and the look on his face made her warm as he said, 'I'd be with you every minute if I could, lass, you know that, an' there's no his an' hers, not in this house. I don't care what the rest of 'em outside these four walls do an' think, I only care about us two, an' we both know I'm the man an' you're the woman, all right?'

'All right.' She smiled slowly and then, when he moved to her side and began undoing the front of her blouse she protested, but weakly, 'They'll be here soon an' I've all the vegetables still to do.'

'There's more important things than vegetables to see to.' He had peeled back the cups of her bra and was supporting the ripe fullness of her breasts on the palms of his hands, and as he bent his head she trembled and arched at what his mouth began to do to her. She was panting when he raised his head again, her lips half open and moist, and when he drew her over to the large thick clippy mat in front of the enormous range she went willingly.

*   *   *

241

Dinner was half an hour late but no one seemed to care; with Sally on top form, it was doubtful if anyone even noticed. Once lunch was over Rosie shooed everyone out into the garden, promising a tray of tea once she had done the washing up, and accepting Sally's offer of help with a smile and a nod.

'I reckon Mr Green's fair gone on your mam.'

'Sally, shush.' Sally's voice carried and the window was open.

The two girls were alone in the kitchen but Rosie still made a flapping motion with her hand as she glanced out of the kitchen window to the little group settled under the shade of the beech tree at the far end of the small thin stretch of lawn.

'It's all right, they can't hear, but I'm tellin' you I'm right. Haven't you noticed him moonin' over the biscuits an' sighin' into the cheeses these days, an' he's dead keen for her to take Mabel's position now she's leavin'. He's called round at the house twice this week an' all, an' when I answered the door the last time he was all red round the collar.'

'I'm not surprised, with you answering the door,' Rosie said drily. 'I bet you put the poor man in a spot.'

'No, not really.' It was too airy, and Sally came clean as she grinned wickedly and added, 'I only asked him who the flowers were for an' began whistlin' "It had to be you", that's all.'

'He bought her flowers?'

'Oh aye, nice big bunch an' all, an' you know how tight he is. He's got it bad, I'm tellin' you, lass.'

Joseph Green and her mother. Well, hadn't she been thinking the same thing? She had sensed they liked each other from that very first meeting. He'd be a kind stepfather to Hannah and the child had already taken to him without any reservations, and for her mother to have someone again . . . It would be the best thing that could happen. Joseph was strong enough to handle that difficult side of her mother without suppressing the capable element that was taking hold again.

The kitchen having been restored to gleaming brightness, Rosie had just placed the milk jug on the tea tray when both girls were arrested for a moment by the sound of the front-door bell. Rosie looked at Sally, wrinkling her brow as she said, 'Who on earth . . . ?' and then, with an eager note, 'Oh, it must be Flora. I wrote her if she couldn't make lunch she was welcome to come this afternoon with Peter. Let them in, Sally, would you, while I mash the tea and put two extra cups on.'

Rosie heard the sound of voices, one of which was unmistakably Flora's, and as footsteps came along the hall she lifted a bright smiling face to the doorway, words of welcome hovering on her lips. But they were never voiced. She saw Flora pause in the doorway, her arm in that of a tall suntanned man. She heard her friend say, her voice nervous and high and giggly, 'I didn't know how to tell you, Rosie, but seeing is believing, isn't that what they say!' But the words were remote as though she was hearing them from a great distance. All she could focus on were a pair of achingly familiar hazel eyes set in a face that was older, much older, and unsmiling. She felt for a second that they were all suspended in space – each tiny detail of the frozen tableau crystal clear and bitingly sharp – and then the moment shattered into a million tiny pieces and the blood pounded into her head so fast it made her dizzy as

Davey said, calmly, even stiffly, 'Hallo, Rosie. It's been a long time.'

She felt her fingers lose their grasp on the teapot and again it seemed to fall to the floor in slow motion, which was part of the strangeness of it all, but then, as the thick brown ceramic pot smashed and the boiling tea splashed over her feet, she let out a scream shrill enough to wake the dead.

From that point it was all action for a few minutes. Rosie was aware of Sally thrusting the two in the doorway aside so roughly Flora almost overbalanced, and rushing to her side, of answering shouts from the garden and following that, Zachariah appearing next to Sally, but such was the pain in her feet she couldn't concentrate on anything else. 'Wash the tea off, wash it off with cold water an' then get some butter on her feet.' This was from Jessie who had just joined them and taken in the situation with one glance, and after Sally had pushed her down onto a kitchen chair, and her mother had washed the tea off with a wet cloth before dabbing them dry, it was all Rosie could do not to give in to the feeling of faintness the pain was inducing. It was Zachariah who knelt at her feet and applied the butter gently to her burnt red skin, but light though his touch was she could barely stand it.

'I'm sorry, Rosie, it was the shock, wasn't it. I was the same.' Flora was babbling away in the background and when Sally asked her what she meant, and Flora explained, there was a moment's silence before Sally said, in her usual forthright way, 'You stupid blighter, Flora,' which summed up what everyone was thinking but no one but Sally would have dared to say.

For her part Rosie was urgently aware of Zachariah's eyes on her face when the initial pain in her seared feet settled into a just bearable pulsating throb, and the words he had spoken on their wedding night were ringing in her mind. What she said and did over the next few moments would determine his peace of mind in the future, and it was this awareness that caused her to lean forward and touch Zachariah's cheek with the palm of her hand before she did anything else. When she spoke her voice carried a soft intimacy that was not lost on the others present, and what she said was, 'Thank you, my love, I'll be all right, don't worry.' She smiled at him, keeping her gaze on his face for some seconds more before she raised her head and turned to embrace the rest of the room.

'I'm sorry for all the drama, but it's the first time someone has come back from the dead in my kitchen.' She forced herself to smile, and her gaze swept over them all, not lingering on any one person. Then, when she finally allowed herself to look into Davey's face, it was only for as long as it took her to say, 'Hallo, Davey. You've met my husband before, haven't you, when I first went to lodge at his house in Benton Street?' and then she purposefully turned her eyes from hard challenging hazel to bright piercing blue.

This was no marriage of convenience. Davey experienced an actual physical pain in his chest the moment Rosie turned away. Whatever it was, it wasn't that. And the devil of it was, he had liked Zachariah when he had met him five years ago.

Damn it all, what was he doing hanging around these parts anyway? He should have gone as soon as he had found out how things were. It certainly wasn't the shipyard that was keeping him, that was for sure. He was grateful enough to Peter Baxter for giving him work when it was denied the milling throng of casual pieceworkers who stood outside the shipyard gates each morning, but the last few days had been hell on earth, with the deafening banging and hammering that was a constant background to the exhausting, filthy and dangerous work in Baxter's yard. It was addling his brains and sending him barmy. Or perhaps it wasn't the shipyard that was sending him barmy.

He gritted his teeth and then, as Jessie urged them all through to the garden, took Flora's arm and followed the others out of the kitchen, leaving Rosie and Zachariah together.

'It's been quite a day, hasn't it,' said Rosie quietly.

It was nine o'clock that evening and everyone had gone home. Zachariah was sitting on their bed fully dressed next to Rosie who was in her nightie on top of the covers, the windows open to capture the cool night breeze.

Rosie's feet were paining her, but it wasn't her sore and blistered skin she was thinking of. Flora and Davey had only stayed a short time, but the others hadn't made their goodbyes until a few minutes ago. Rosie hadn't had a chance to talk to Zachariah about Davey's reappearance with the company still present, but she knew it had to be done promptly and without any equivocation.

'Aye, you could say that.' Zachariah's voice was grim. He had been furious with Flora about the accident and it had taken him all his time to be civil to her in the twenty or so minutes she and Davey had stayed. 'If that lass wasn't such a good pal of yours I'd have bin very tempted to put me boot up her backside.'

'Oh, Zachariah.' Rosie leant against him for a moment. If she were to speak the truth she would have to admit she hadn't understood Flora's behaviour today. In fact it wasn't

246

too extreme to say that the girl who had arrived and left with Davey Connor had been a stranger to her. *Davey Connor.* He was alive, *he was alive.* She still found it hard to believe, but then the whole half an hour or so had been surreal. Flora had been nervous and animated and skittish, and Davey had been so *different* – self-assured, cold even – viewing them all as though they were insects under a microscope. She felt it had been a relief to everyone when the two of them had left.

And she couldn't understand why Flora hadn't given her some prior warning – a note, anything – when she of all people should know how much of a shock Davey's resurrection would be.

Oh, Davey. For the first time since she had seen him standing in the doorway of the kitchen Rosie admitted the depth of the feeling which had assailed her and her stomach turned right over. But she loved Zachariah too, she did, and he must be wondering about all this. And he must not wonder. He mustn't be afraid. She would rather die than hurt him. That thought brought a measure of relief and perspective into the situation that had suddenly exploded into their lives, and was an echo of the declaration she had made to herself in the kitchen earlier.

'I love you, you know.' The words came easy now as she turned to him, lifting her face in a manner that invited him to kiss her.

When he withdrew his lips from hers he didn't say anything for a moment, and then his voice was very soft when he said, 'Love seems too weak a word, too well used an' ordinary to express how I feel about you, but if ever your feelin' for me changed I'd want you to tell me, lass. I mean that.'

She was lying very still, cradled in his arms, and she kept

her gaze on his face when she said, 'It won't, it couldn't.' And then she further emphasized her words as she knelt up in front of him, ignoring the pain in her feet the movement produced, and cradled his face in her hands as she said again, her voice urgent and low, 'I mean it, Zachariah. There is no one and nothing that could change the way I feel about you. I'm so proud to be your wife.'

'Aw, lass, lass.' And his mouth came down on hers again.

Later, when Zachariah had gone downstairs to lock up for the night, Rosie walked over to the bedroom window with careful, tentative steps which was all her sore feet would allow, and standing with the palms of her hands resting on the windowsill she breathed in the salty night air through the open window.

Her eyes narrowed on the view that The Terrace residents enjoyed – the wide road, the stone-slabbed pavement beyond with its lantern-style street lamps, and then over the neat, chest-high stone wall the unending vista of sand and sea. She would keep the unspoken promise her mouth and her body had made tonight. This other thing, this wild, ecstatic, terrifying other thing, had to go back into the dark secret regions it had sprung from, and it must never, never be talked about. She was going to make Zachariah happy, whatever it took, whatever it needed, she was going to make him happy.

But, oh – she straightened, her arms going round her waist as she hugged herself, her eyes tightly shut now – that moment of wonder, of paralysingly fierce joy she had felt when she had seen Davey standing there. He was alive – alive and warm and breathing. She swayed slightly as her heart thumped and raced. What was it about him that made her feel this way? She didn't understand it. She didn't *want* to feel it, she didn't, but somehow he was as much a part of her as her own flesh. But she couldn't afford to think like this, not even for a minute. He was part of her past, an old friend, and that was all he was. *That was all.*

Rosie stood at the window for some minutes more until the swiftly deepening twilight and Zachariah coming upstairs sent her back to bed, and it was only then that a tall shadow some twenty or thirty yards down the nearside pavement and almost completely obscured by the high brick wall and hedge of the front garden of the house it was sheltering behind moved.

It began to walk down the street, passing number seventeen with just a casual glance as though that house held no more interest than any other in this pleasant salubrious part of Sunderland, but although the face would have been just a white blur to any passerby, the eyes, and the black satanic emotion they held, would have stopped them in their tracks.

He thought he had won, that little runt. He actually thought he had won, and he was in there now, holding her, touching her . . . The muscles of the hard square jaw worked, teeth ground together. But he could be patient. Oh aye, he could, he'd had years of practice hadn't he, and all at the hands of that conniving scum if his suspicions were right, and he would bet his last penny they were.

How much had Price paid to get his dirty work done and then for his cohorts to keep quiet about the set-up? A small fortune; it must be a small fortune because all his bribes had brought forth nothing to date. Mind, Price might have something on them, it might be blackmail he'd used, that was always more effective than pounds shillings and pence, as he knew to his own advantage. He'd turned the screws on many a man in his time because of what he knew about them, and it was amazing what you could learn if you knew how to handle folk.

He might never have clicked on how Price was behind him having to leave if the little fellow hadn't made the mistake of marrying her. But looking back in the light of the present it was clear – oh aye, crystal clear. But he'd found out one piece of useful information in all his digging and he was working on the result of that. Did Price's ex-fancy woman know anything? Maybe. And if she did he'd get it out of her, she was already eating out of his hand. Shane McLinnie paused, looking back the way he had come before turning and walking on towards Monkwearmouth as he fought the frustration that drew him to The Terrace every evening and kept him awake half the night. He'd left a nice thriving set-up in Glasgow to come back to this dead stinking hole, but he could always go back when he was ready. And he wouldn't go alone this time either. He was damned if he would.

Rosie was used merchandise now. The thought stuck in his throat and caused him to breathe harder. No better than some of the whores that worked the docks and the back streets. He'd take it out of her hide, by, he would, her giving herself to that – that *runt* of a man. No. No, he wouldn't. He shut his eyes tight against the knowledge and leant against the gable end of a house for a moment, his legs limp. He wouldn't harm a hair of her head, not Rosie. She was a sickness with him, she was in his blood, his marrow, he'd been born wanting her.

His eyes opened wide now and he started walking again, his mouth thin and tight. How could she? How could she have preferred that cripple to him? And of all places he had had to install her in The Terrace.

'All right, man?'

He was nearing Forcer Road now and about to enter a back lane which was a cut between two streets, and despite the late hour there were a few men, half a dozen or more, grouped at the top of it under the weak light of a flickering street lamp. They were all in the grim uniform of shapeless coats, caps and mufflers; some sitting on the pavement against a house wall, and others leaning against it, and the òne who had spoken to him Shane thought he recognized as a lad who had been at school with him.

'Aye, I'm all right.' Shane stopped as he nodded abruptly. 'Cyril Young, isn't it?'

'Aye.' The voice was wry in answer. 'Not that you're young for long round these parts, man.' There was a moment's pause and then, 'You back for good or passin' through, Shane?'

Shane shrugged. He wasn't about to divulge his private affairs to anyone. 'Depends.'

'Oh aye?' Cyril stepped forward, coming fully under the pale golden glow, and in spite of himself Shane was shocked. The face he was looking at could have belonged to a man twice the age of himself. 'Well, if I was you, man, with no wife an' bairns, you wouldn't see me for dust. The future's in the south, there's nowt here no more.'

'Oh I dunno.' An older man who looked seventy and was probably no more than fifty chipped in, his rheumy eyes a witness of years of working in black coal dust. 'I've heard say we're the backbone of the nation, lad. Or perhaps me ears are still ringin' with the promises of ten year ago, when they needed the coal an' the shipyards an' all. Aye, we were

251

the blue-eyed boys in them days right enough.' It was bitter, very bitter, and Shane saw the old man's trousers were held up with string and his boots needed cobbling.

'Funny seein' you back the same week as Davey Connor's come home. You remember him, Shane?'

'What?' Shane turned to Cyril now, his eyes narrowing. 'Davey's back?'

'Aye.' And then Cyril's eyes spoke for him as he added, 'Not as well set up as you though, man. You've done right well for yourself by the look of you.'

'I'm not complainin'.' Shane remembered this lad as something of a joker, one of them bright sparks who was always ready with a quip and a laugh, but there was nothing of the vigorous youth he recalled in the tired, beaten man in front of him. He felt something stir in him, something he didn't want to examine, and to assuage the feeling, and what he would term as weakness, he thrust his hand into his pocket and brought out a note as he said, 'Here, man, have a drink on me to celebrate me return, eh?'

'Aw, man. Ta, thanks.'

Shane didn't look back as he walked down the lane, but by the time he had reached the end of the brick-walled tunnel and emerged into the dimly lit street beyond, his shoulders had straightened and he was saying to himself, If ever you needed an answer as to whether you've done the right thing you've had it tonight. By, it was every man for himself all right. There was no black and white, it was all shades of grey, and the sooner you learnt to play the game by your own rules the better chance you had of climbing out of the mire. And wasn't that what Rosie had done? Aye, it was, and who could blame her? The little fellow was well heeled and he'd wanted her, and no doubt he'd used any sort of persuasion he could bring to bear to get her. He didn't blame Rosie, no, it was that runt that stuck in his craw and he'd see his day with him. Oh aye, if it was the last thing he ever did. But this needed to be done right. He needed to take his time over this and make sure there were no mistakes, and then . . . He felt his loins tighten and a surge of excitement make him as hard as a rock. Then it'd be him and Rosie.

Chapter Fifteen

'You mean to say Mrs McLinnie told you a few days ago that Shane was back and you didn't tell me?'

It was the next morning and Rosie hadn't gone into work, such was the condition of her feet, and now, as she padded to the stove, poking the fire into a blaze, lifting the kettle from the hob and setting it in the fire to bring it to the boil, she turned an exasperated face to her mother, who was sitting at the kitchen table. 'Why on earth didn't you say something before, Mam?'

'Oh I don't know.' Jessie was uncomfortable. The truth of the matter was she had meant to, but in the furore of the newlyweds' homecoming and then the performance with Flora and Davey it had slipped her mind, but she hadn't been able to sleep the night before for worrying she hadn't tipped Rosie the wink as Annie had expected her to.

First Davey and now Shane McLinnie. Rosie was frowning as she spooned tea from the caddy into her second-best teapot and then went to the range, lifting the kettle from its steel shelf above the fire as she shook her head at her mother's offer to help. 'I can manage, my feet are easier today, but I couldn't get my shoes on with the swelling first thing, and as Joseph wasn't expecting me in I thought I'd give them a chance to go down and go barefoot.'

'Oh aye, lass, aye. Joseph wouldn't have you struggling.'

Her mother's voice had been warm, and Rosie mashed the tea, pulling the big bulky teacosy over the teapot and sitting down at the table before she said, 'He's nice, isn't he, Joseph?'

'Aye.' Jessie looked straight at her as she said, 'You know he's asked me if I want that lass's job?'

'Mabel? Yes, I know.'

'An' you wouldn't mind?'

'Mind? Of course not, I think it's an excellent idea. Hannah is old enough to look after herself for an hour or two when she comes home from school, and apart from the money it means you're away from those four walls all day, and seeing people. No, I think it's a very good idea, Mam.'

'It's just that . . .' Jessie hesitated, and then as Rosie poured them two cups of tea she said in a little rush, 'Your da wouldn't have liked it, an' I still think of your da, Rosie. But . . . but things are different now, aren't they?'

Jessie was saying much more than the mere words that had been voiced, and it was in answer to the unspoken plea for understanding and approval that Rosie said, as she reached out and covered her mother's hand with her own, 'Quite different, Mam, and Da would have understood that, you know he would. He wouldn't have wanted you to spend the rest of your life alone.'

Mother and daughter surveyed each other for a long moment and then Jessie relaxed, nodding slightly. 'No, likely you're right, lass. You always know what's best.'

And then, as though it had occurred to her for the first time, 'Where's Zachariah, lass?'

'He's gone on his monthly visit to Gateshead, he couldn't keep his normal appointment because we were on honeymoon so he's gone today instead.' Rosie's voice was reserved, she knew her husband wouldn't like her discussing his business affairs – or their affairs now, as he'd pointed out more than once since their marriage – with anyone, even her mother. But he enjoyed his sojourn at his solicitors and the bank, and the buying and selling that often transpired as a result of his visits. She had been amazed and not a little awed at the extent of Zachariah's wealth when it was fully revealed, especially in view of how he was living when she had first met him. But she had since learnt that to him it was a thing apart from his normal day-to-day life. He bought shares and he sold them, he invested in this and that and thoroughly enjoyed keeping up-to date with every little happening in the world, but the accumulation of riches was not the important thing to him – it was playing the game and winning. And in that he was tenacious, even ruthless. This side of her husband had surprised her and even disturbed her a little.

And now, as though the two things were connected in her mind, Rosie said, 'So Mrs McLinnie doesn't know if Shane is back for good?'

Jessie shook her head. 'I haven't seen her lately, with her bein' bad an' all, so likely it'll all have panned out by now. I think she was hopin' he'd be away again, with the lads laid off an' all there's no room to swing a cat in their house. Mind you it was worse years ago, when the bairns were small an' her brother an' his wife lived with 'em for a time. Made Annie bad in the end an' her Arthur told 'em to clear out. They went to Australia, believe it or not. Funny how family outs, tain't it, lass, 'cos her Shane is the spit image of her brother.' Jessie took a loud slurp of tea before adding, 'I might pop in on Annie on the way back, lass, an' see how she's doin'. She's got a packet an' a half at the moment with one thing an' another, poor lass.'

'Jessie.' Annie's eyes widened with pleased surprise as she opened her back door in answer to Jessie's rat-a-tat-tat of a moment before. 'Come away in, lass, come away in. Aw, it's nice to see you. This flu's knocked me for six, I'm tellin' you, I've bin feelin' right middlin'. Haven't got the strength of a kitten.'

'Aye, it's nasty right enough. Here –' as Jessie entered the kitchen its faint musty smell and general air of uncleanliness was all the more apparent after Rosie's gleaming house – 'few bits I thought you might be able to use with you not bein' able to get to the shops.'

She placed two heavy shopping bags on the clutter of the kitchen table, and the gesture stopped Annie's bustling, causing her to stare first at Jessie's face and then the bulging bags. But it was when she began to empty the groceries on the table that her voice came, low and broken, saying, 'Oh, lass, lass, I can't take all this. There's nigh on a week's housekeepin' here an' that for my lot, not yours. It's too much, lass.'

'Go on with you.' Jessie's tone was brisk but when Annie didn't respond she said, her voice gentle now, 'You'd do the same for me, lass, now then, an' have in the past when things have bin tight. An' I've got a bit of news an' all. I'm gettin' a job.'

'You!' Annie raised startled eyes to her friend's smiling face. 'Never.'

'Aye, aye, I am, at the Co-op. One of the lasses is leavin' an' Mr Green's offered us the job.'

'Lads alive! I'd have sooner expected the Pope to get wed than you takin' a job.' Annie's face was the picture of amazement. And then, when Jessie's face dropped and she said, her voice uncertain now, 'You don't think I could manage it?' Annie's voice was loud in reply. 'What? With all them gormless gowks of bit lasses you see these days? You could do it standin' on your head, Jessie Ferry – not that I'd recommend that of course, not unless you make sure your drawers are clean anyways.'

'Oh, Annie.' Jessie was shaking with laughter and when Annie joined her they were wiping their eyes by the time they'd finished. 'Oh, I miss you bein' next door, lass. I do that.'

'Aye, me an' all. Sit yerself down an' I'll make the tea, the kettle's boilin'.'

It was as they were sipping Annie's black brew that Jessie asked, her voice elaborately casual, 'Your Shane made up his mind if he's stayin' yet, Annie?'

There was a second's pause, and Annie was looking towards the fire glowing in the blackleaded range as she spoke. 'Aye, he's stayin'.'

'For sure?'

'Aye.' Annie turned towards her friend but didn't look at her as she said, 'I think he's got a woman, he's stayed out a couple of nights since he's bin back anyways, an' the lucky blighter's already pickin' up regular shifts at the shipyard. There's the rest of 'em bin queuin' week after week an' sent home regular as clockwork, an' our Shane walks in after nigh on five years away an' bob's your uncle. Mind, our Patrick said years ago he reckoned Shane'd got somethin' on the foreman, old Jones, an' it looks like he was right.'

Jessie's eyebrows rose in comment but she said nothing.

'An' he's not short of a bob or two, I tell you, lass. He's talkin' about buyin' a car, would you believe? Can you imagine, a car parked outside me front door? That'll upset her across the road for a start, she won't be able to keep up with that.' Annie's voice was jocular but there was bitterness beneath the laughter. Their Shane could brag about buying a car and flaunt his fine clothes in front of Arthur and the lads, but he hadn't so much as slipped them the odd bob or two to buy some baccy, not even his old da. Granted he'd stumped up good as gold with his board and without her asking, but it wouldn't have hurt him to see his da and the lads all right. And as always, when thoughts like this assailed her, they were followed with, He couldn't suspect anything, could he? But he couldn't, no one could. There were only two people that knew and one of them was across the other side of the world, thank God. Oh aye, thank God all right.

If ever there was a sick perverted swine of a man Walter had been it, and the only good thing that had come out of that night was that the end result of it had frightened him out of her life for good. But at what a cost . . .

And then the training of years stepped in, and Annie deliberately turned her mind from the guilt and self-abasement that had threatened to break her years ago, and which even now, in her low moments, surfaced in screaming nightmares and dark fits of depression.

It was just after three o'clock when Jessie rose to make her way home, and the sky outside Annie's kitchen window was overcast and threatening rain. When Annie opened her back door the light was a muted, splintered grey with a strange hue reflected on the roofs of the houses, and she looked up into the sky as she said, 'By, there's goin' to be a storm all right, Jessie, I can smell it. You'd best get yerself away home smartish, lass.'

'Aye, I think you're right. So long, Annie lass.'

'Bye, lass, an' thanks, thanks again.'

By the time Jessie was halfway down Chapel Lane the first fat raindrops were beginning to fall from the low heavy sky, and several growls of thunder had rent the air. She saw the tram trundle to a halt at the end of the street but she didn't hurry – it had to go two more stops to the terminus and turn round so she had plenty of time – but as she neared the corner of Chapel Lane and Mapel Avenue the rain really took hold. It obscured the billboards on Garrison's wall opposite, advertising Remy's Starch and Batey's, John Bull's favourite ginger beer, and, as the little group of passengers who had alighted from the tram began to disperse, the pavements were awash.

In spite of the downpour Jessie recognized Shane immediately; he was a good-looking lad and taller than average. But when she spoke to him as he went to pass her without a word, saying, 'Hallo there, lad, I've just bin to see your mam,' his face was blank as he turned towards her. It was a good five seconds before he said, 'Oh, Mrs Ferry, it's you. Hallo,' before continuing on his way down the street, his broad shoulders hunched against the driving water.

By, he was in a right spin about something or other. Jessie stood stock still and stared after him. He looked as though he'd had a shock, a bad one, she thought musingly, and it was only when the rain began to drip off her felt hat down the back of her neck that she turned and crossed the road to the tram stop.

But all the way back to Hendon, as the tram rumbled and creaked its way along, her mind chewed at the conundrum, and even when she was in the house and stripping the soaking wet clothes off her back she was haunted by the look on Shane McLinnie's face.

On Monday, 24th August, Rosie got home from work to find Zachariah sitting in the garden. It was her custom to call to him as soon as she entered the house, and his to answer immediately, and so she had been perturbed until she spied him from the kitchen window sitting under the shade of the beech tree.

She made a pot of tea and put it on a tray along with a small plate of oatmeal biscuits she had made at the weekend – they were having panhaggerty for dinner later that night with some of the leftovers from the weekend – and then took it out to Zachariah in the garden. He didn't notice her until she was almost upon him, and then his smile was strained as he said, 'Hallo, lass. Good day?'

It was his usual greeting and she smiled as she bent and kissed him. 'Typical Monday. Fred dropped one of the butter casks, and half the cheese we had delivered was off. Joseph is furious. And Sally was forever nipping over to the stables because Mick's favourite horse has got colic and they didn't know if she was going to pull through, but she's all right now, thank goodness. Sally reckons if she learns to neigh and snort through her nose she'll get a lot more sympathy from Mick when she's ill. Zachariah . . . ?' His silence finally registered. 'What is it? What's wrong?'

'It's nothin', lass.' And then he shook his head at himself as he said, 'What am I sayin'? Of course somethin's wrong. What I mean is, it's nothin' to do with us, you an' me.'

Something had happened. There followed a stillness which was broken by Rosie saying, her voice soft, 'Zachariah? Can you talk about it?'

'It's Janie. You remember, the lass I used to see a bit of at one time.'

'Yes, I remember.'

'Apparently she was found in her house sometime over the weekend. They reckon she fell an' bashed her head in on the bedroom grate.'

'You don't mean . . . ?' Rosie stared at him aghast. 'She's not dead, is she?'

'Aye.' He shuddered, shaking his head again as he said, 'She wasn't old, Rosie, she'd still got half her life afore her. It was her pal who found her, Peg Keel. The two of 'em used to go out of a Saturday night an' when Peg called round the back door was unlocked but there was no answer. She found her in the bedroom an' the police reckon she'd bin gone a good few days.'

'Oh, Zachariah.' Rosie swallowed hard. 'How . . . Who told you?'

'The constable.' And at her start, 'It's all right, lass, don't worry, but apparently in a case like this, when no one sees what happens an' all, they check everyone who's had a bit to do with her.'

A bit to do with her. This Janie had loved him, Tommy had said so. Had he loved her? Rosie gave herself a mental slap on the hand as she told herself harshly, What are you thinking of, what does it matter? She's dead, dead, and that's a big enough shock for anyone who knew her. 'I'm so sorry, Zachariah.' She bent down and put the tray on the grass at the side of his chair, and then knelt in front of him, taking his hands in her own. In spite of the muggy warmth of the evening his flesh was cold. 'When did the constable call?'

'About an hour ago.' His voice was dull and quiet.

Rosie tightened her hold on his hands as she whispered, 'Oh, Zachariah. I'm so sorry. What a terrible thing to happen.'

'She was a nice woman, was Janie. Kind, you know? An' she'd had a rum deal one way or the other. Her husband, he was a flamin' maniac; used to knock her about an' all sorts, but she stuck with him 'cos she'd got married in church an' it meant somethin' to her; chapel, she was.'

When he stopped speaking there was a tense, pulsating silence, and then Rosie, her voice quiet, said, 'It wasn't your fault, Zachariah. You know that, don't you?'

'Aye.' He swallowed. 'In me head, lass. In me head, but me heart is tellin' me I'm all sorts of a swine.'

'No, not you.' She hesitated for a moment and then said, 'It was because of me that you finished with her, wasn't it? I didn't understand that until I realized how you felt about me. But feeling like that you couldn't have continued to . . .'

'Aye I know, I know.'

'So you did the only thing you could.'

There was no denial from him, only a slow nod of his head, but she could see he was still torturing himself.

'Zachariah, in telling her, you left her free to have the chance of meeting someone else. There's that too.'

'Aye.' He raised his head and looked at her now. 'The constable reckons she'd bin seein' someone the last few weeks; she'd told this neighbour of hers about him. A young bloke, a lot younger than her, but he'd taken a shine to her, she said.'

'There you are then.' It was scant comfort but Rosie

clutched at it, her voice eager. 'It's awful, terrible, but she was probably happy, Zachariah.'

'Aye.' He shifted restlessly in his seat, shaking his head as he said, 'By, the questions he peppered me with, lass, they don't leave a stone unturned, but maybe that's a good thing.'

'It *was* an accident?'

'Oh aye, aye. Well, it couldn't be anythin' else, could it, no one would want to hurt Janie. Aye, it was an accident all right, lass, but it's true what they say, the good die young.'

Rosie sat with Zachariah in the pleasant warmth of the quiet garden for some time, the sounds from the promenade beyond the front of the house barely penetrating the idyll, but through all their conversation, when she let him talk about Janie and his past life with just the odd monosyllable from herself to keep the therapeutic flow going, her mind was working on quite a different plane. What was happening? Molly running away had been bad enough; she didn't dare let her mind picture what might be happening to Molly. But now Davey had returned, and Shane, and then this terrible tragedy with Janie. It was as if the ordinary humdrum world she had known for the last few years had been rent apart and everything had been turned upside down. And Flora. Her stomach churned at the name. What had happened to Flora? She had known things would be different once she was married, she hadn't expected to see Flora several times a week, but apart from that one time when Flora had come to the house she hadn't seen hide nor hair of her. It was as though she had ceased to exist for her friend.

Rosie's soft mouth tightened as the possibility she had tried to ignore for the last few days tugged at her mind again.

Flora and Davey? Well, they were both free agents. The truth was inescapable. And she had no right to object. Poor Peter, he'd be devastated if it was true. Although there had been nothing definite between them, no ring or anything, she knew Peter had expected he could persuade Flora to marry him in good time. But she was running ahead of herself here, she didn't know anything about Davey and Flora, not for sure, but her gut instinct was telling her that Flora liked him. Liked him very much. She breathed in deeply as she realized her hands were clenched at her sides and forced herself, very slowly, to uncurl her fingers.

It was over an hour later that Rosie left Zachariah still sitting in the small garden and went indoors to begin preparing their evening meal, but all the time she grated the cheese and sliced the onions for the panhaggerty her mind was chewing things over. Davey had left Sunderland – and her – without a second thought all those years ago. She didn't mean a thing to him and she had faced that fact within weeks of his leaving, so nothing had changed. Not really.

And Shane McLinnie's sudden reappearance in the town? This question, apropos of nothing she had been thinking of a second before but which was somehow intrinsically linked with everything, caused Rosie to bite on her lower lip as she opened her eyes wide. This worried her more than anything else. She couldn't speak of it to anyone, they would think her deranged if she did, but she felt deep in the heart of her that Shane's dark propinquity bore no good for any of them. There was no way that man was coming within six feet of her or hers.

She flexed her shoulders at the thought, almost as though she was preparing to do battle, and it was that frame of mind that caused her to finish preparing the evening meal in half the time it normally took.

Part Four

Till Death do us Part

Chapter Sixteen

It was the middle of December and Rosie was twenty-one weeks pregnant. The child had been conceived on their honeymoon, and once Rosie's initial surprise had faded she found she was pleased, very pleased. She had paid a visit to Dr Meadows and he had put her – until then unspoken – fears to rest that Mary Price's attempted abortion would in any way affect Rosie's unborn child. 'Not possible, not possible as far as I know, lass,' the good doctor had said cheerfully. 'She damaged herself as well as Zachariah with that devil brew she took, but I've never known it to affect future bairns. Don't let it prey on your mind.' It had been good advice and Rosie was determined to live by it.

The baby cemented her marriage in a way nothing else could have done. It was a statement, a declaration of the abiding nature of her and Zachariah's union. Rosie didn't ask herself why such a declaration was necessary, neither did she question why she had allowed any contact with Flora to lapse without demur since the summer. She had seen her friend once since the fateful Sunday, and that had been three weeks after Flora had brought Davey to The Terrace when Rosie had been looking at curtain material in Blackett's store. In the course of their conversation it

271

had emerged that Davey had made the decision to stay in Sunderland for a while, and that he was working at Baxter's shipyard. The latter fact was more portentous than the first to Rosie, along with Flora's edgy manner and over-bright voice.

When Rosie had got home she had spent some ten minutes in the bathroom, eventually emerging with a scrubbed face and slightly pink-rimmed eyes but with her shoulders straight and her chin high. She had not discussed the meeting with anyone, nor had she ventured into Bishopswearmouth again for a good few weeks.

How long this state of affairs could have continued is uncertain, but on Tuesday, 15th December, just two weeks after the more unpleasant manifestations of her condition had ceased and Rosie was feeling well again, there was an urgent knocking at the front door of number seventeen The Terrace just as she and Zachariah walked from the sitting room into the hall preparatory to retiring for the night.

Rosie was feeling more relaxed that evening than she had in weeks. She had finished work the week before and she had arranged to collect Hannah that morning and take her sister into Bishopswearmouth as a Christmas treat.

The two of them had had lunch at Binns in Fawcett Street and then wandered round the shops so that Hannah could choose her Christmas present from Rosie and Zachariah. Most of the stores had paper chains hung in loops from the ceilings along with brightly coloured concertinaed paper balls and bells, and in Binns store, next to the cake shop and restaurant, the decorations included beautiful little glass swans, fairies, horses and all types of animals hanging on fine threads from the ceiling which waved in the air and made a tinkling sound when they touched. Hannah had been entranced.

The sisters had looked at miniature sewing machines, smiling dolls in all shapes and sizes, tram-conductor sets of hat and ticket puncher, boxes of mosaics with their horde of small coloured balls, toy shops with 'real' scales, kaleidoscopes with their mirrors and pieces of coloured glass that produced such wonderful patterns, tiny carousels with little painted horses that really moved, picture books with stories of Little Black Sambo and Mingo and Quasha, wooden-handled skipping ropes and fat teddy bears and a hundred and one other things besides, but Hannah had eventually chosen her heart's desire – a doll's house complete with furniture and a tiny family, which Rosie had paid for and arranged to collect the following week.

They had called in Haydock's sweet shop from which Hannah had emerged with a bag of ogo pogo eyes and black bullets and a shorbet dib-dab, before continuing to the Palace Theatre for the early evening pantomime where Zachariah was waiting for them.

It had been an exhausting day but fun, and Rosie had found that the hours with Hannah, as she had watched the unbridled childish enthusiasm and experienced the magical anticipation of Christmas again through her sister's wide eyes, had done her the power of good. But now the world outside had encroached once more, and as the banging came again and Zachariah made a move towards the door, Rosie found herself hanging on to his arm as she said, her voice soft with just the hint of laughter, 'I don't suppose we can pretend we're not in?'

'Shame on you, lass.' Zachariah grinned at her before he walked to the door, but as Rosie watched him, her face outwardly calm, a part of her was feeling slightly uneasy about the late caller and she had to warn herself not to let her imagination run riot.

Zachariah thought it was because of her condition, but for some weeks now she had had the feeling that someone was watching the house. It had started when she had drawn the bedroom curtains one night and thought she saw a shadow lurking in the dimly lit street beyond the front garden. She hadn't thought too much of it at the time; the evening had been a windy one with dark clouds scudding across a full moon and such nights could play tricks on your eyes, but then the same thing had happened a few nights later when it was as still as the grave. Zachariah had gone out armed with his trusty club which had travelled with them to their new home, but returned with nothing to report. On the third occasion, just a week or so ago, she had not mentioned what she thought she'd seen to Zachariah, but the incidents had been enough to put her on her guard.

She hadn't divulged Shane McLinnie's presence outside the Co-op in Hendon Road once or twice a week since September to Zachariah either. Shane had bought himself a car, a Morris Cowley, a shining black beauty with two brass headlamps on the front of the bonnet.

On the first occasion when he had been parked and waiting outside the Store she had not realized who it was in the car until some sixth sense had made her turn and look back. The start she'd given had been visible and he had smiled, nodded, and continued sitting impassively. From that day she had ignored him.

Zachariah only opened the door an inch or two at first, and then she heard him say, in tones of deep surprise, 'Why, man, what is it?' before he flung the door wide and said, 'Come away in, man. Come away in.'

Rosie raised her hand to her throat, and then as Davey Connor stepped through the doorway and she met the greeny-brown eyes head on it took every ounce of her willpower to remain standing perfectly still and say, her voice only one of polite enquiry, 'Hallo, Davey. Is there something wrong?'

'Aye, yes, I'm afraid there is.'

Davey turned to include Zachariah but then seemed lost for words, and it was Zachariah who said, 'Come on, man, come through to the sittin' room, we've only just left it an' the fire's still burnin'.'

'I . . . I feel bad disturbing you.' He was beside himself, they could both see it, and now Rosie felt her concern overriding everything else and she added her voice to her husband's. 'Don't be silly, that doesn't matter. Come and sit down and I'll make some tea.'

'No, no please, don't worry about tea.' Now that the flush of dark red colour that had stained his cheekbones when he'd first entered the hall had drained away, Davey looked white, and Zachariah actually took his arm and guided him through the door of the sitting room to the right of the front door, his voice soothing as he said, 'Sit yourself down afore you fall down, an' get your breath.'

Once Davey was seated in one of the big armchairs close to the glowing fire Zachariah indicated for Rosie to sit down but remained standing himself as he said, 'Well? What can we do for you? You don't look none too good if you don't mind me sayin' so.'

'Oh, I'm all right, it's not me.' Davey took a deep breath but his voice was still shaking when he said, 'It's

275

Flora, Flora and her mam and . . . her da. There's been an accident.'

An accident? Flora had been in an accident? The intervening weeks were swept aside as though they had never been and everything in Rosie wanted to fly to Flora's side. 'What sort of an accident, Davey?' she asked urgently. 'Is she all right? Is Flora all right?'

Davey nodded once as he said, 'Aye, of a sorts. Her da, he was leatherin' her and her mam went for him. Did you know Mr Thomas used to knock 'em about?'

'Flora and her mam?' Rosie's shocked face spoke for itself even as she thought, So that's what it was! All these years, that's what it had been.

'No, I thought not. Apparently he's been hitting them both for years but neither of them said a word to anyone. Anyway, there was a row this evening and Flora was getting the worst of it. She'd managed to get away from him and up to her bedroom and he'd come after her, trying to batter the door down by all accounts. When I got there the neighbours were out in the street and the old lady next door said there'd been all hell going on inside but it'd gone quiet just as I got there. And then in the next minute we heard Flora start screaming . . .'

'If this had been going on for years did the neighbours know about it?' Rosie asked shakily.

'It's been going on all right but this was the first time anyone had heard owt, according to the police after they'd questioned everyone. I don't reckon they believed 'em but everyone keeps themselves to themselves in that part of Fulwell.'

'The police? They got the police involved?' This was from Zachariah, his voice sharp.

'Aye. Her, the mother, Mrs Thomas, she's dead. Broken neck. According to Flora's da she came at him with the breadknife.'

'She *what!*'

'And in the struggle she fell down the stairs, at least that's what Flora's da is saying 'cos there's no witnesses, Flora still being in her bedroom when it was all happening.'

'Saints alive.' Zachariah looked at Rosie and she at him, and then they both turned back to face Davey who was still ashen and clearly in shock. And no wonder. Mr Thomas had been hitting them? And now Flora's mam was dead? And he was actually saying that that little mouse of a woman had attacked him?

'Flora's in the infirmary.' Davey shook his head, drawing the breath hard through his nose before continuing. 'They thought it best 'cos she went crazy when she saw her mam, screaming and trying to get at him. She kept calling for you, Rosie, all the time she was there, but they wouldn't have any of it and they sedated her so she didn't know what she was doing in the end. But once it wears off . . .'

'I'll go to her. Of course I'll go to her.' Rosie glanced round abstractedly as though she was going to take off that minute and then, as Zachariah's hands covered her own and he said, 'Come on, lass, she'll be all right. Don't fret,' she leant fully against him, her head on his shoulder as she murmured, 'Why didn't she ever *say*, Zachariah? She should have *said*.'

'Aye, lass. Look, we'll go to the infirmary first thing but I can't see the point of you goin' now when they've given her somethin' to make her sleep. She'll be out for the count.'

'But what if she wakes up and asks for me again?'

'She won't.' Zachariah's voice was firm. 'An' there's

277

someone else to consider besides you an' Flora in all this you know.'

Rosie thought for a moment he meant himself and then when he nodded pointedly at her stomach his meaning became clear.

She couldn't look at Davey, and when his voice came a moment later saying, 'Do I understand congratulations are in order?' she still didn't raise her head as Zachariah answered, 'Aye, too true, man. It's due the end of April.'

His voice was so proud it made her want to weep.

'Then of course she must get a good night's sleep before she goes in.'

They were talking over her now as though she wasn't there and normally she would have reacted strongly, but tonight Rosie didn't mind. All her thoughts were with Flora.

Davey left after a few minutes, again refusing the offer of tea and then Zachariah's suggestion of something stronger, and Rosie herself did not press him to linger, something that Davey noticed.

He walked briskly down the street away from the house and the lighted doorway with its two occupants, and after raising his hand at the end of the street in farewell he walked on a few more yards before pausing and drawing the icy air deep into his lungs. He had felt sorry for Flora tonight, gut sorry, her screams and her cries had turned him inside out, and if the police hadn't turned up when they did he would have gone for her father right enough. So why, when he had been in the midst of such a tragedy with such awful consequences, had the news of a future new life affected him so adversely? That wasn't right, was it?

He shook his head at himself, swearing softly before he

started walking again. He should never have come back to Sunderland.

The Sunderland Infirmary had been founded in May 1794, and after moving from Chester Road to Durham Road in 1867 had been extended several times throughout the 1880s and 1890s, but as Rosie and Zachariah approached the vastly imposing building with its grand steepled towers, Rosie was barely conscious of the magnificent hospital. Her heart was aching for the emotionally battered young woman within its benignant confines.

What was she going to say to Flora? How was this monstrous abomination – her da killing her mam, *her mam* – going to affect her friend? And this gulf that had come between them, she had lain awake half the night agonizing over that, along with the fact that you never really knew someone, not deep deep down inside. She had known something was wrong at Flora's house, but that? Never. And Flora wanting Davey . . . The tram creaked and rattled down the street, past the wall with its railings above and bare-limbed trees beyond which formed the perimeter of the Infirmary grounds. She would never have imagined that in her wildest dreams but it was a fact. She had faced it last night, head on and without any shirking, and in the facing of it she had felt a deep, consuming sadness envelop her. But along with the poignant sense of grief had come the knowledge that she didn't want to lose Flora. She loved her. You couldn't do away with nineteen years of friendship just like that.

'Penny for 'em?'

The tram had rumbled to a halt and now, as Zachariah helped her down off the step and the raw air caused Rosie to take an involuntary gasp, she pulled her hat further over her ears before she said, 'They aren't worth a penny, Zachariah.'

'Now that I doubt, lass.' But he didn't press her further, simply taking her arm and tucking it in his as he said, 'Careful now, we don't want you visitin' an' then stayin' on as a patient, these pavements are all ice.'

Once inside the antiseptic confines of the Infirmary, Rosie found the sheer size of the place overwhelmed her, and she was glad of Zachariah's presence as he made the necessary enquiries and they eventually made their way through the endless maze of cold corridors to Flora's ward.

They had been warned – by the reception staff and also a nurse and then a porter they had stopped to ask directions of – that there was little chance of their being allowed to see Flora outside normal visiting hours, but on reaching the ward and speaking to the sister in charge, the whole situation altered. Yes indeed they could see Miss Thomas, the small, sharp-eyed sister informed them abruptly, her voice clipped and tight. If nothing else it might serve to alleviate the distress Miss Thomas was causing the other patients with her undisciplined behaviour. The sister had had to post a nurse at the side of Miss Thomas the whole time, such was her conduct, and didn't Miss Thomas realize that that meant other patients were being denied the care they needed?

But perhaps the other patients hadn't just lost their mother in violent circumstances which had necessitated their father being taken into police custody? Rosie kept her voice calm and even as she spoke, but from the glare the sister gave her the message had gone home and was not appreciated.

'I'll wait here, lass.' As the nurse the sister had designated to lead them to Flora's side gestured for them to follow her, Zachariah pointed to one of the three straight-backed wooden chairs in the small waiting area outside the ward. 'It's you she wants to see.'

For a moment, as the prim-faced nurse gestured towards the far end of the utilitarian ward to the narrow iron bed which had an equally prim-faced nurse sitting on a chair at the side of it, Rosie didn't recognize the occupant. And then Flora saw her, sitting up and facing her fully as she said, 'Rosie, oh, Rosie,' and holding out her arms, and Rosie saw her friend beneath the puffy swollen face and wild tangle of hair.

She was at Flora's side in an instant, her heart melting with pity, and for long minutes she just sat on the bed holding Flora close as they cried together, and even when Rosie's face became dry she continued to enfold Flora as a mother might her child and murmur soothing words of comfort into the knotted curls of her hair.

'I . . . I didn't know if you would come.'

When at last Flora moved away to look into her face, Rosie's eyes were soft as she said, 'Don't be daft.'

'I've done it all wrong, haven't I? You . . . you must hate me.'

'Do you hate me?'

'No, but—'

'Well then, how could I possibly hate you, you daft hen?'

'Oh, Rosie.' Flora was holding on to her again as she sobbed against her shoulder. 'My poor mam, my poor, poor mam.'

'I know, I know.'

The nurse had been standing at the end of the bed through all this and now, as Rosie caught her eye, she saw the young girl wasn't so prim-faced after all, and there was sympathy in her eyes as she said, 'You're her friend? She's been hoping you would come. I'm afraid she's taking it hard, which is understandable in the circumstances. Are you staying for a while?' And at Rosie's nod, 'Perhaps you'd call me when you have to go? We don't want Miss Thomas left alone at the moment.'

'She won't be left alone.'

It was another twenty-four hours before the Infirmary would release Flora into Rosie and Zachariah's care, but mid-day Thursday, once a white-faced Flora was installed in one of the spare bedrooms, Rosie broke the news the doctor at the hospital had divulged to her when she and Zachariah had arrived that morning. Mr Thomas had been allowed home the night before. The police were satisfied that Mrs Thomas had fallen accidentally when Mr Thomas had been attempting to defend himself from his wife's attack. There was absolutely no evidence, according to the police, to substantiate Flora's claim that her father had beaten his wife and daughter in the past. And the fact that the argument had begun because Flora had refused to be interrogated by her father on the subject of her relationships with a wealthy shipyard owner's son on the one hand, and a penniless ex-miner on the other, had even seemed to elicit some sympathy for Mr Thomas with the powers that be.

Flora had sat ashen-faced as Rosie had spoken and then she had slipped down beneath the covers, turned on her side and shut her eyes. Rosie had continued to sit with her until she was sure Flora was asleep – the medication the doctor had insisted on was strong – and then she had tiptoed downstairs and told Zachariah of Flora's reaction to her father's release.

'Likely she's still in shock, lass, an' the journey home was enough for mind an' body to cope with. She'll discuss it when she's ready.'

And it was later that day, when the murky grey light of the winter's afternoon had begun to fade into evening, that Flora appeared in the kitchen as Rosie was kneading lumps of dough into loaves and putting them into small bread tins.

'There you are.' Rosie spoke as though Flora had popped out of the room a moment before. 'Come and sit down and I'll make some tea once I've finished this bread. How are you feeling?'

'Awful.' But Flora managed the semblance of a smile.

Rosie left the dough for a moment and walked across to give the wan figure a quick hug, saying as she did so, 'You're doing fine, lass. Awful though it is you'll get through this, I know you.' She pushed her down into one of the straight-backed chairs at the table before returning to the tins, and Flora glanced about her.

'This is a lovely kitchen, Rosie, and you've got it looking real nice.' Her eyes took in the big blackleaded range with its glowing fire, the rosy reflection on the steel-topped and brass-tailed fender and row of copper saucepans, and the general air of sparkling cleanliness married to warm cosiness.

'It was like this when we moved in, I just keep it up to scratch.' Rosie placed the tins along the fender and covered them with two clean tea towels before she placed the kettle on the hob. 'It won't take a minute to boil.'

'I'm in no hurry.' Flora tried to smile again but as her lips quivered Rosie hurried to her side, putting her arm round the narrow shoulders as she said quietly, 'It's all right to cry, Flora. Don't try and hold it in.'

'I just can't believe they've let my da out.' Flora looked up at Rosie, her eyes reflecting her bewilderment. 'And as for him saying that my mam went for him, that's such rubbish, Rosie, it is. I reckon he brought that carving knife upstairs to use on me, and when he couldn't get at me he lost his temper with her and hit her and she lost her footing. Mam wouldn't even *think* of going for him, I know that better than anybody. My mam's put up with hell on earth over the years 'cos she was so scared of him. But I'm not going to let this drop. I want him done for murder 'cos that's what it was.'

Rosie nodded, even as she thought, How would Flora cope with having to stand up in court and reveal the ill treatment she and her mother had suffered in silence for years? And Mr Thomas obviously wasn't going to admit to it, he would lie and Flora would have to challenge him. It would be a dreadful strain on top of the terrible tragedy of losing her mother.

Flora's mind seemed to be moving along the same channels because she next said, ''Course he'll lie through his teeth, he's started already. I . . . I did tell him that Peter was just a friend, but I didn't say there was anything between Davey and me. He just assumed that 'cos he saw me out with him. Davey's never said anything about us courting or anything like that.'

'But you like him,' Rosie said steadily as she walked across to the hob and lifted the kettle, bringing it to the kitchen table where she poured water on top of the tea in the brown teapot. Flora didn't reply, and now Rosie turned to her, looking her full in the face as she repeated, 'You like him, don't you? It's all right.'

'You don't mind?'

Mind? She minded so much she ached with it. 'No, of course not. I have Zachariah, don't I, and . . . and I want you to be happy.' That sounded ridiculous in view of the present circumstances and Rosie quickly qualified it with, 'Well, you know what I mean. I want you to have someone.' And she did, she did. She just wished it had been anyone other than Davey so that she didn't have to live a lie. But she and Zachariah could move away. She had already talked to him about a change of lifestyle away from the town, a smallholding or farm maybe, and he hadn't been averse to the idea, only qualifying it by saying he would want them to wait until the bairn was born and she was completely back on her feet again. And if they left they would probably only see Flora and Davey once in a blue moon. She could cope with that, couldn't she? And there would be the child, and others – God willing. That thought prompted her to say, 'Did you know I'm expecting a baby?'

'You are?' Flora's face lit up, the haunted sad expression lifting for a moment, and she sprang up from her seat, reaching across the table and taking Rosie's hands as she said, 'Oh I'm pleased for you, I am, Rosie. Oh, that's wonderful.'

Did she detect a certain element of relief as well as gladness in Flora's voice? A recognition that a child, her and Zachariah's child, was further substantiation that she was a married woman, soon to be a mother as well as a wife? Oh, what did it matter anyway? It was the truth. There could be no 'wondering' as to how things might have been, it simply wasn't an option.

The two women continued to sit and talk as the sky outside became black and the wind began to howl a warning of the snowstorm that had been forecast earlier in the day. Flora cried some more as she spoke about the years of violent beatings she and her mother had suffered, and Rosie found herself marvelling at the endurance in the slim frame of the girl sitting across the table to her. She had thought her da and the lads dying, their subsequent poverty, her mother's insobriety and Molly's defection into degradation were enough problems for any family, but this with Flora, this was awful. To whom did you run when the very person who should be protecting you, loving you, was the source of all your pain?

Rosie took Zachariah a cup of tea at half past five and found him dozing in front of the sitting-room fire, and as she sat with him a moment before returning to Flora she told herself, fiercely and silently, that she was lucky, she was so so lucky. Half of the folks round these parts – no, more than half, a darn sight more – didn't know where their next meal was coming from. The mass of black-capped, dark-clothed men standing outside the pits and steelyards was growing every day, the dole queues were lengthening and it was only the soup kitchens keeping some families alive. The mine owners were talking of longer hours for less wages and holding out pit-head baths as some sort of inducement; better working conditions they called it. She knew how her da and the lads would have viewed that – the same as the rest of the men round here did. Insulting. 'Carrots for donkeys' she had heard one old miner's wife describe it as in the Co-op, and everyone had agreed with her. How could pit baths fill hungry bairns' bellies? And here she was in clover, with her bairn being born into luxury she couldn't have dreamed of even a year ago. Aye, she was lucky all right. The broad idiom, which always came in moments of high emotion, made her think of her mother, and that led on to Flora's mother, and she said, 'I'd better get back to her, Zachariah.'

'How is she?'

'Fair to middling. I'll call you once dinner is ready, we'll have it in the kitchen, shall we? It's cosier in there tonight.'

'Fine, lass. Whatever suits you is all right by me.'

Yes, she was lucky all right. Rosie stood, bending and kissing the top of Zachariah's fair head before she left the room.

Mr Thomas called three times in the following few days to speak to his daughter, and each time Flora refused to receive him. She had followed through on her threat to take the matter of her mother's death further, and had gone to the police station and made a statement in which she accused her father of consistent unprovoked violence over a period of some fifteen to sixteen years, and also of attacking her mother on the night of her death with a view to doing her serious injury.

Following Mr Thomas's third visit to the house Flora had verged on the hysterical; the strain of her grief and impotent rage and bitterness had boiled up as she had watched from an upstairs window while her father had argued with Zachariah on the doorstep. After that, Rosie made up her mind to go and see Mr Thomas. She would ask him to stop pestering his daughter and allow her some peace until the court case, which would now be inevitable due to Flora's allegations. She didn't tell Zachariah of her intentions, knowing he would disapprove; neither did she mention the matter to Flora who was still struggling to get through each day minute by minute, but she really feared for her friend's state of mind if the visits were allowed to continue. Flora's heartache at her mother's passing was bad enough, but the gnawing resentment and fury she felt at her father's refusal to admit to the true facts was eating her up.

On leaving the house the following morning with the excuse that she wanted to spend her Christmas club from the Co-op, Rosie went to Mr Thomas's place of work, the Castle Street Brewery in Bishopswearmouth. On reaching High Street West she stood a while debating what she was going to say. The brewery, founded more than half a century before by the Vaux family, was a large and successful concern covering an area of some two acres with an extensive frontage to Castle Street, and Rosie knew Mr Thomas held a prestigious post in the business. She also knew he would not appreciate her visit. But . . . nothing ventured, nothing gained.

She took a deep breath and entered the grounds, walking past the rows and rows of large barrels that stretched as far as she could see, past the stables which housed the dray horses, looking for someone to direct her to the offices. She had no intention of wandering about in the brewery itself, which was vast with its spacious barley stores, kilning rooms, fermenting rooms and other departments. When she saw Mr Thomas she wanted to be cool and controlled, not hot and flustered. He had never liked her, and he was going to like her less after this visit.

The snow which had fallen the night before was inches thick outside the confines of the brewery, but Rosie saw that an army of workers must have been at it first thing because the cobbled grounds were swept clean, and a sense of order prevailed. It was an intimidating establishment and somehow set apart from the struggling world beyond its perimeters; she could see how Mr Thomas would revel in his authority in such an imposing and well-run business.

After a stable lad had pointed the way to Mr Thomas's office – a route which required her to retrace her footsteps – Rosie was just about to enter the building when the man himself came out of a door just in front of her.

'Mr Thomas?' Rosie's voice was high. There was a moment's silence and then he turned and she knew immediately he had recognized her voice. 'I . . . I need to talk to you.' No, this wouldn't do, she couldn't hesitate or stammer with this man. 'It's important.'

'It would have to be to bring you here.' Strangely there was none of the antagonism or rage she had expected, his whole manner was quiet, even subdued, and Rosie stared at him uncertainly for a moment or two more before Mr Thomas said, 'I was just leaving. Do you want to walk along with me?'

Rosie swallowed hard and then she spoke just as quietly saying, 'Yes, all right, thank you.' He had taken her aback. None of this was going at all as she had envisaged, and Mr Thomas himself bore no resemblance to the strutting, upright, cold individual she had always known.

When they stepped into High Street West it was beginning to snow again, small whirling flakes blowing haphazardly in the bitingly cold wind, and although it was only just gone nine o'clock in the morning the street was already bustling with Christmas shoppers. They walked in silence for some minutes. Rosie just didn't know how to start and Mr Thomas seemed immersed in thoughts of his own, but as they reached Blackett's, at the junction of Union Street and High Street, Mr Thomas turned to her and said, 'Beck's café is open and it's clean and warm. Shall we have our discussion over a pot of tea?'

Once seated at a small table for two near the window Mr Thomas ordered a pot of tea and toasted teacakes, and Rosie found a feeling of unreality had gripped her. If anyone had told her twenty-four hours before that she would be sitting with Flora's da having tea and buns she would have laughed in their face. She came down to earth with a bump as Mr Thomas turned to her and said, his voice holding a note she remembered from the past, 'Well? I presume you are here in the guise of Flora's envoy? You know she has filed a libellous report to the police in which she accuses me of virtually killing my wife?'

'Flora doesn't know I've come to see you.' Funnily enough Rosie found that Mr Thomas's return to supercilious mode had the effect of putting steel in her backbone. 'And you might as well know that my husband and I are behind her every inch of the way and support her decision wholeheartedly.'

He stared at her for a moment and then said, 'My employers were informed of Flora's accusations yesterday evening. I have been told this morning to take some weeks' "holiday" until the matter is settled, but what they mean is I am finished there. Will that satisfy my daughter's lust for blood, do you think, or is she determined to force us both to suffer the ignominy of a court appearance?'

'Is that the only thing that concerns you?' She couldn't believe this man. 'When Flora's mother—' Rosie stopped abruptly as a frilly-aproned waitress bustled up with the requisite tray holding a silver-plated tea set and a two-tiered cakestand with the teacakes at the bottom and small pots of preserves on the top, which she proceeded to place on their table with great ceremony.

'Of course I'm upset about Flora's mother.' Once the waitress disappeared Rosie looked up to find Mr Thomas's eyes tight on her. 'You think I don't care, is that it? I loved my wife, Mrs Price.'

Rosie was surprised that he gave her her title – she hadn't even known he knew her married name – but her voice was cool when she said, 'I'm sorry, but I find that hard to believe.'

He seemed about to fire back some retort but then he leant back in his seat, the breath leaving his body in a long drawn-out sigh. After a long pause he raised his eyes again and said, 'All the men in my family have been fighting men as far back as I can recall, army, all of them, they loved it. I used to think it was the military life they liked, the order and discipline, but I'm not so sure now. Do you think weaknesses, flaws, can be passed down from generation to generation?'

'What?' And then as she collected herself, 'I'm sorry, I don't quite understand what you are getting at.'

'I lived in terror of my father, Mrs Price, we all did, my mother included. We boys, my brothers and I, used to be in fear and trepidation when we knew he was coming home on leave, and we knew we'd be black and blue at the end of it. My mother' – he paused a moment – 'he would think nothing of striking her in front of us all. Maintaining standards, he called it. He was a violent man; my grandfather was violent, my brothers too, but until I got married I thought . . .' Again he shook his head. 'I thought I was different to them.'

'Are you saying . . .' Rosie paused, her tea untouched.

'Are you telling me you couldn't *help* hitting Flora and her mother? That it was your *father's* fault?'

'You don't think that is possible?'

'No, I don't.' Rosie tried very hard to keep her voice low but it was trembling with indignation. 'I can accept that an upbringing like the one you've described would bring its own set of problems, but I've known people – Sally's Mick for one, the girl I worked with, her husband – who were regularly knocked about and are as gentle as lambs. Even if you felt like hitting Flora you needn't have, but you didn't try to fight it, not really. You bullied Flora from when she was a small child and you know it, Mr Thomas.'

'And Flora intends to follow through and declare such things in court?'

'Yes. Yes indeed she does, Mr Thomas.'

As Rosie watched his eyes wander past her to the scene outside the window it came to her that Mr Thomas had been sounding her out, finding out exactly how the land lay. He was a cold fish; he was a very cold fish, she thought as a little shiver flickered down her spine. It was almost as if he didn't have a conscience at all. A man like Mick's father was one thing – she had met the big brute of an Irishman who was all mouth and trousers with a wicked temper – but he was a different kettle of fish to Flora's father and she knew which she preferred. Mick had told Sally he had heard his da cry and beg his mam for forgiveness when he had sobered up after a drunken violent bout, but apart from the fact that Mr Thomas didn't drink to become brutal, she couldn't imagine him ever asking anyone for forgiveness. His violence was a tool to control the mind as much as anything else, and he was trying to manipulate her now with this softly-softly approach.

As the thought hit, everything in Rosie rebelled and she said, 'Leave Flora alone, Mr Thomas. She won't see you, she's determined on that, and my husband and I don't want you calling at the house again.'

Mr Thomas's eyes returned to her face. 'I won't allow her to drag my good name through the gutter. Tell her that, would you?' His voice was still soft and low, but there was a quality to it that made Rosie's stomach muscles tighten. 'And my wife did attack me, Mrs Price. In that respect, at least, I am an innocent man. Tell Flora that, make her understand.' His voice was insistent. 'She is wronging me with this court action.'

'She's wronging *you*?'

'Yes. She's ruining everything I've worked for, everything I hold dear.'

'You killed her *mother*.' And then, as he went to speak, Rosie bent forward as she half rose in her seat, and her voice was a quiet hiss. 'I don't care whether Flora's mam went for you or not, that's almost immaterial. The fact remains, you killed her nonetheless. But you aren't going to spoil Flora's life, Mr Thomas. She's free of you now and she intends to stay free.'

His eyes had narrowed with the attack but he didn't react at all beyond saying again, 'Promise me you will tell Flora what I've said. I won't let her soil our name and I am innocent. I want her to know that. Tell her I've lost my job because of her, and that I'm being called before the church committee next week because of these allegations. Tell her.'

'It won't do any good.'

'But you'll tell her?'

'Yes.' Rosie had absolutely no intention of telling Flora.

'Today?'

'Yes.' Rosie straightened. She had to get out of here. In the last few minutes, it wasn't too extreme to say, she had been feeling as though she were in the presence of something evil.

'Good.' He relaxed back in his seat, his eyes still on her face as she stood looking down at him. 'That is all I ask, Mrs Price. In that case I won't call on Flora today as I had planned to do.'

Rosie didn't answer him as she gathered up her bag and gloves, nor did she look at him again as she made her way from the table and out into the street. She walked steadily along the pavement until she turned into Walworth Way, which linked Union Street with Crowtree Road, and here she leant against the brick wall on the corner under a large sign stating that Crowther and Co. in High Street West specialized in artificial teeth, with a graphic picture which illustrated the fact in glorious colour, and took several pulls of the icy air deep into her lungs. Had she done the right thing? The snow was coming down in thick white flakes now and the sky looked laden with it. At least she had spared Flora the trauma of another visit if nothing else. And if he had been going to accuse her in that way it wouldn't have done Flora any good.

She took one last deep breath and straightened. She had to go home armed with packages if her story of Christmas shopping was to be believed, so she'd better get cracking. With it being Christmas Eve tomorrow the shops would be packed to bursting all day even if a good deal of the purchases would be courtesy of help from the pawn shops, and half of Sunderland would still be in debt come Easter.

*   *   *

Rosie didn't mention her meeting with Mr Thomas to anyone other than Zachariah, and when she told her husband what had transpired she made it clear she didn't want Flora to know the meeting had taken place. She was doubly glad of the sixth sense that led her to that decision at nine o'clock on Christmas Eve when, in spite of the drifts which were now waist-high in some parts, there was a knock at the front door.

'Not more carol singers? I didn't hear anythin', did you?' Zachariah frowned enquiringly at the two women as he stood up. They had had 'God Rest You Merry, Gentlemen' at five o'clock and 'Hark the Herald Angels' followed by 'The Holly and the Ivy' at six, but since then the blizzard conditions had served to keep even the most intrepid carol singers indoors.

'Miss Flora Thomas?'

The constable resembled a walking snowman, his helmet a giant white busby, and as Zachariah followed him into the sitting room he shrugged his shoulders at the two women, indicating the policeman hadn't been forthcoming as to the reason for his nocturnal call.

Flora's hand had gone to her mouth and she merely bobbed her head in reply, and as Rosie moved to her side Flora's free hand gripped Rosie's and thus they faced the constable together.

This was to do with that man, it was, and he had contrived it to happen on this special night. Even before the policeman started talking Rosie sensed something of what was to come. It appeared Mr Thomas had arranged for a friend in the choir to collect him at five o'clock for the carol service at the chapel. The friend had arrived to find the door slightly ajar, and on entering he had discovered Mr Thomas in his favourite armchair in front of the sitting-room fire, the evening paper folded neatly at his side and a picture of Flora and her mother in his hands. He was quite dead, having consumed the contents of a bottle of sleeping draught which had been prescribed, so the constable informed them, to help combat his grief at his wife's passing. The short note was very simple, 'Let the guilt rest where it should.' There was no signature.

'Let the guilt rest where it should.' Rosie's eyes met her husband's, and they were both thinking the same thing.

Mr Thomas had planned that the full weight of his suicide should fall on the shoulders of his daughter. If Rosie had repeated anything of what Flora's father had said to her, the accusations against Flora and his holding her to blame for what he saw as his public undoing, this note would have had a very different connotation. He had wanted Flora to carry the burden for the rest of her life. Oh, Flora might have known it was unfair and untrue, that this master manipulator and cold tyrant had orchestrated his death for maximum effect in an effort to control her even from the grave, but some tiny seed of guilt would always have been waiting to root itself in the fertile regions of Flora's persona. He was a monster.

'"Let the guilt rest where it should."' Flora had fallen against Rosie as the constable had finished speaking, her hands pressed into her stomach beneath her breasts as Rosie's arms held her tight. 'He had to die before he could admit he was wrong, Rosie. What was the matter with him?'

They would never know, and Rosie for one was unutterably thankful that now they did not have to try to find out.

Chapter Seventeen

Christmas was over and it was New Year's Eve, and Rosie was regretting the open-handed invitations she had ladled out to all and sundry at the end of November for this night. She had been feeling vulnerable and a bit low at the time – the weeks of morning sickness had drained her spirit and the situation with Flora had been nagging at the back of her mind – and she had thought a party would be just the thing to start the New Year aright; but now she wasn't so sure. Flora was staying with them still, for one thing, and on the third occasion that Peter had called after Christmas she had felt obliged to ask him to join the jollifications. And then Davey had called the day after Boxing Day with little presents for them all, and somehow the conversation had got round to New Year's Eve, and another invitation had been issued . . .

All in all there would be fourteen besides herself and Zachariah. Flora, Peter and Davey – if Davey came, that was, he hadn't seemed too sure at Christmas – along with her mother and Hannah and Joseph Green. Sally and Mick were coming, and Beryl from the Co-op and her young man. Annie McLinnie and Arthur – Rosie would have invited the lads too, she hadn't forgotten their kindness when Molly had disappeared the first time, but with Shane McLinnie at home that had proved impossible – and lastly Tommy Bailey and his lady friend.

She had wondered if Flora would prefer a quiet New Year's Eve, the circumstances being as they were, but it had been her friend who had insisted the party go ahead. 'I can't hide myself away, I've got to face folk sometime so I might as well start now,' Flora had said when Rosie had voiced her misgivings a few days before. Rosie agreed wholeheartedly with the overall sentiment, she just felt a party, with all the chit-chat and social niceties it entailed, could be a little much at this early date, but she had been happy to leave the decision to Flora.

Jessie, Hannah and Joseph Green were the first to arrive at just gone half past eight, along with Sally and Mick, and as Rosie opened the door to them Sally was jumping from one foot to the other in her excitement as she said, 'Ask us how we got here, Rosie. Go on, ask us.'

'How?'

'Come and look.' Sally couldn't prolong the moment a second more. 'Mr Green's bought himself a car, what do you think of that?'

Rosie glanced down the frosted garden and beyond the gate, and although her voice was enthusiastic and she was smiling as she said, 'It's lovely, beautiful. Where did you get it?' her stomach had turned right over. Joseph's car was a Morris Cowley, identical to Shane McLinnie's, and it made her feel sick. Twice since Christmas she had seen a similar car parked across the road outside the house, and only last night she had been sure the tall dark figure standing in the shadows when she had drawn the bedroom curtains at gone ten had been Shane. For two pins she would have gone down into the street and confronted him, but with Flora still so up and down she hadn't wanted any possibility of her friend being involved in further upset.

She followed the others back down the path now, after calling for Zachariah and Flora to come and give dutiful homage, and as she looked at the car she made up her mind that once Flora was gone she was going to take the bull by the horns, go and see Shane and tell him to leave them alone. If nothing else, it would make her feel better.

'This is grand, Joseph, grand.' As Zachariah and Flora joined them her husband's voice was hearty.

'Aye, I thought it time I looked after meself a bit.' Joseph's eyes were soft as he looked across at Jessie, and everyone knew it wasn't himself he intended to look after. And then his tone was faintly apologetic as he added, 'There's only been meself for nigh on fifteen years now, and there's been nowt to spend me money on. I thought a bit of comfort wouldn't go amiss.' Joseph's first wife had died after eight years of marriage and there had been no children.

'I don't blame you.' Zachariah nodded his head several times as he thought, By, it's a rum do when a bloke has to apologize for spending his own money, but that's what it boils down to in this climate. It's got so you can hardly pick up the paper or pay a visit to the pub without some strike or dispute or other staring you in the face. He'd heard they'd opened a soup kitchen in High Street West over Christmas so some families could at least have their bellies filled once a day. But now wasn't the time for such sober thoughts, and he began to usher them all back indoors, saying, his voice jolly, 'Come on, come on, the drink won't come to you out here, an' me wife has done enough food to feed an army in there. I'm goin' to be eatin' me way through ham sandwiches an' mince pies till Easter if you don't all tuck in.'

Annie McLinnie and Arthur, and Tommy Bailey and his lady friend, a small stout woman called Matilda who had a sweet face and rosy red cheeks, were walking along the street together having caught the same tram, as they turned to go back into the house, and within minutes Beryl and Reginald had arrived too.

The party was in full swing at ten o'clock when Peter Baxter arrived, full of apologies for his lateness which had been caused by an emergency at the shipyard. One of Zachariah's more ostentatious presents to Rosie, a modern gramophone enclosed in its own wooden cabinet, was blaring out one of the hits of 1925, 'Show me the Way to Go Home', with ribald accompaniment and much merriment from the assembled company, and Peter soon found himself singing with the best of them.

Rosie and Flora had been making more sandwiches in the kitchen when the knock had sounded at the front door, and Rosie had let Flora answer it, knowing it would be either Peter or Davey. When Flora re-entered Rosie lifted her head from her task, forcing a lightness to her voice as she asked, 'Who was it?'

'Peter.' Flora's voice was flat.

'You had better go in there with him, he doesn't really know anyone very well.' Rosie inclined her head towards the shrieks of laughter. 'Get him a drink and a sandwich, Flora, and I'll bring this lot through in a minute. And the second bowl of punch is ready, could you ask one of the men to come and carry it through? And check if we need more beers while you're about it, would you.'

'I'd better get Sally to eat something too, she's already

three parts to the wind.' The two women smiled at each other but Rosie didn't voice what she was thinking, namely that she hoped Sally continued on form and kept everyone laughing. Sober she was funny, tipsy she was hilarious, and Rosie had a feeling they would need Sally's outrageous sense of fun. Well, she certainly did anyway, she thought wryly.

It was as she was mixing tinned salmon with vinegar to add to the already buttered bread that Davey's voice sounded just behind her. 'The door was open so I let myself in. I hope that's all right?'

She froze for one moment, her heart stopping and then giving a mighty kick start that brought it up into her throat, and then she turned carefully, keeping her voice very steady as she said, 'Of course it's all right, you know that. Peter has only just arrived and Flora couldn't have shut the door properly. It's a funny latch that one, you think it's shut and then it opens again.'

Davey nodded but he didn't speak, and as the moment stretched and tautened their locked gaze became painful, and it was Rosie who smiled, as naturally as she could, and said, 'Flora will be pleased you've come, she was beginning to think you'd changed your mind or got buttonholed by some neighbours or friends. There are always so many invitations flying around on New Year's Eve.'

'I couldn't get away from the Rileys. Douglas came over with his wife and bairns, and then some of the neighbours came in. You know how it is.' *Why hadn't it been Shane McLinnie?* The words were so loud in his head that for a moment he thought he'd voiced them out loud. He would have taken her away from Shane McLinnie, aye, he would, and without a second thought, whether she'd been married or not.

'Yes, I know how it is.' Rosie's voice was prim-sounding as she turned back to the table. 'Well now you're here perhaps you'd like to take that bowl of punch through, they're waiting for it.'

'Right.' And then his voice was soft behind her as he said, 'Don't be frightened of me, Rosie.'

'What?' She swung round so quickly she almost over-balanced and his hand came out swiftly to steady her, only to pause within an inch or two of her arm before dropping to his side again. The denial she had been about to make hovered on her lips but then she was looking into his eyes, and a softening, a melting of her mind and body rendered her dumb. She forgot that he hadn't been there when she had needed him most, that he had walked away from her and Sunderland without a backward glance and stayed away for five years; the look in his eyes depicted what was in her own heart and it thrilled her even as it terrified her.

'Don't.' It was a whisper but he seemed to understand it because he nodded slowly, taking a great intake of breath and then wrenching his gaze from her white face to the bowl on a side table. 'Is this it?' he asked gruffly, walking across to the table as he spoke.

How could he look at her like that? How could he? Rosie was fighting the feeling that had taken over her body and her mind with all her might. He had looked at her like that once before, when she had been a young naive lass of fourteen and desperately in love with him, but his subsequent actions had proved that what his eyes had said was not real. And she didn't want it to be real, not now, she *didn't*. She could control this feeling deep inside, this elemental core of her, if he didn't care for her. But if he did . . . She breathed hard through her nose. It couldn't be loosened, it couldn't become tangible. Even recognition that it was real was a betrayal of Zachariah.

She was trying to bring some sort of answer regarding the punch to her lips when the volume of noise beyond the kitchen swelled, indicating the sitting-room door had been opened, and as she turned back to the sandwiches without speaking Flora came hurrying into the kitchen. 'They've gone barmy in there, Rosie. I don't know what you've put in that punch but Sally and Mrs McLinnie are—'

There was a moment of deep silence, and Rosie nerved herself to turn, her voice airy as she said, 'You left the door open earlier, Flora, so Davey let himself in. He was just going to bring the punch bowl through.'

'They're ready for it, and those beers, Rosie.' Flora recovered almost immediately, and when Davey said, 'Hallo, Flora. How are you feeling?' she answered, 'Oh, you know, bearing up,' as she turned to smile at him.

Rosie handed Flora the plate of salmon sandwiches and let the other two go through to the sitting room while she busied herself slicing up the ham pie, but once she knew she was alone she stopped what she was doing, leaning heavily on the table as she lowered her head and shut her eyes tightly. *Flora knew.* No, no, she couldn't know – there was nothing *to* know, was there? Flora had just been surprised to see Davey in the kitchen, that was all. And Flora liked him. She had set her cap at him, they both knew it, so she was just jittery in his presence. But there had been recognition in that one glance Flora had given her when she had taken the plate, an awareness of the atmosphere that had existed between her and Davey when her friend had entered the kitchen. She wasn't imagining it.

Zachariah, oh, Zachariah. He must not be hurt, he mustn't

have a moment's unhappiness through her. Rosie opened her eyes, staring blindly down at the cluttered table, and in that moment she found herself wishing fiercely and vehemently that Davey *would* ask Flora to marry him. Flora would satisfy that physical side of things that men especially found so important, and once there were bairns that would widen the gulf between them. Her hand moved unconsciously to her stomach.

She loved Zachariah, she did, so much, but if *she* didn't understand how she could love him and still feel this way about Davey, how would he ever comprehend it? He wouldn't, he wouldn't understand how she could love them both.

But no, *no*, she didn't love Davey. She would not let herself love him.

'You all right, pet?'

When she raised her head to see Zachariah standing in the doorway it was almost as though her thoughts had brought him to her. She nodded slowly, holding out her hand as she sank down onto one of the hardbacked chairs at the table, and indicated with an inclination of her head for him to come and sit beside her.

'I'm a bit tired, that's all.' She smiled as he reached her side and sat down, and then, when he took one of her hands and chafed it gently between his palms, she added, 'It's been a difficult couple of weeks or so, hasn't it?'

'We'll take that as the understatement of 1925, lass.' He grinned at her, his beautiful blue eyes warm and loving. 'An' you're doin' way too much at the minute, you've bin on your feet since six this mornin'—'

'*Zachariah.*'

The look on her face cut off his words like a knife.

'Zachariah, I felt it. I felt it kick.' And then, as he stared stupidly at her, she said, 'Oh, there it goes again. It's really kicking, Zachariah.' She reached for his hand and placed it on the mound of her stomach. 'I've had these sort of flutters for the last few weeks but this is different. Feel it.'

'By, lass.' His face told her he was stunned.

It was making its presence felt all right, and the wonder of the new life they had created washed over them anew. They stared at each other for a moment, his hand still pressed to her flesh, and then they grinned and then laughed, before falling together as he hugged her tightly.

They remained like that for a minute or two, and then, as Rosie drew away slightly, she said, 'I want it to be just us again, do you think that's horribly selfish?'

'Probably, aye probably, but it does me heart good to hear you say it nonetheless, lass. Me happiest times are by me aan fireside with me aan wife an' the rest of the world shut outside.' He stroked her shining hair as he added quietly, 'But we'll do what we can to ease Flora's path, I know you wouldn't be content with less.' They continued to sit closely together for a few moments more and then Zachariah said, 'I've asked Davey to be first foot. He's the only dark one among us.'

'You have?' She raised her head to look into his face. Oh, he was so *nice*, her Zachariah. She knew he was still feeling a bit uncomfortable about Davey, and yet he had asked him to be first foot – the person who first enters the house on New Year's Day bringing food or fuel. Tradition called for a dark man, but she knew it wasn't just that that had made Zachariah ask Davey. It was his way of saying that everything was all right. 'I do love you, you know.' She smiled at him, her eyes soft, and she really meant it. 'Very much.'

305

'Just keep tellin' me, lass, just keep tellin' me. I can take all the spoilin' I can get.'

Twelve o'clock seemed to be upon them before they realized, and as Davey was pushed out of the back door, a small sack of coal on his back and his arms full of bread and a small ham and the requisite bottle of whisky, by a tipsy throng, there were shrieks of laughter as they turned round and hurried through the kitchen and into the hall, where they all squeezed, shoulder to shoulder, as they waited for the ships' hooters and the church bells to proclaim 1926. Rosie saw Peter Baxter had his arm round Flora's shoulders and she hadn't pushed him away, and that her mother and Joseph were holding Hannah between them, their gazes linked, but then the first hooter sounded, immediately followed by others, with the mantelpiece clock from the sitting room joining in as it chimed the old year away.

Annie was nearest the front door and as Davey knocked she opened it with a wide smile, saying, 'Happy New Year, lad, Happy New Year.' And then they were all kissing and hugging each other, treading on each others' toes and laughing – or, in Flora's case and also Jessie's, crying – as they continued to embrace each other.

Rosie found herself clinging to Zachariah as though she never wanted to let him go, and she couldn't have explained the consuming feeling of love and fierce thankfulness mixed with guilt and sadness, but she was praying silently, Thank you for keeping me, thank you for not letting me say anything to Davey, and don't let him say anything to me. It will be all right if we don't say anything. And then Sally prised them apart, saying in her own inimitable way, 'All right, all right, you two, come up for air. Married for nigh on six months an' you're still like a pair of rabbits,' and Rosie found herself laughing. There was no one in all the world like Sally for putting things in perspective.

'Right, records or piano?'

Zachariah was appealing to the assembled company, his head on one side, and when the concerted cry of 'Piano! Piano!' went up, he bowed in the manner of an orchestra's conductor and took his seat, beginning a medley of tunes that soon had everyone singing.

The bottle of whisky was long since empty, a third bowl of punch had been drained – and each bowlful had held half a bottle of gin deep in its innocent-looking pink fruity depths – and most of the beer had gone at five to two, when Rosie went out into the kitchen to make everyone a cup of tea. Peter had gone earlier, just after Flora had had a little cry on Davey's shoulder about her mam and da, and Rosie's heart had gone out to him. Beryl and Reginald had made their goodbyes just after one, but the rest had seemed set to make a full night of it when Zachariah had signalled to Rosie to make the tea.

'Make it strong, lass.' His eyes had been twinkling as he had nodded at Sally and Annie, who, arms round each other's waists, were singing a tuneless rendition of 'Who's Sorry Now' to their respective husbands, who were grinning inanely.

She smiled back as she inclined her head, and she was still smiling as she walked through to the kitchen. She stoked up the red glow of the fire before putting the kettle into its flickering heat, and fetching a tray from the big wooden dresser to one side of the kitchen door she put the six cups and saucers from her bone china tea set – a wedding present from Joseph – onto it. She only had six; the men would have to make do with the serviceable everyday set. After placing the teapot on the hob she spooned four good measures of tea into its brown depths, and, the kettle now boiling, mashed the tea.

It was just as she turned from the range with the teapot in her hands that something, some flicker of awareness, made her turn her head and look towards the small square window at the side of the back door, and it was only the subconscious memory of the agony of the hot tea splashing on her feet that prevented the same thing from happening again. The disembodied head was a monochrome of black and white, awful and terrible, and for the first time in her life Rosie knew what it was to be so frightened that she couldn't move or speak. She stood clutching the teapot in both hands, the hairs on the back of her neck prickling and her eyes riveted on the pale face at the window, and then it was gone, and in the next moment there was a tap on the back door.

She hadn't been aware she was holding her breath but now, as she drew the air deep into her lungs and stumbled to the table, setting the teapot down with shaking hands, she felt as though she had been swimming underwater.

When the knock came again she forced herself to move noiselessly to the door, one hand instinctively pressed against her stomach in an unconsciously protective gesture, and with her face close to the wood she said, 'Yes, who is it?' but made no effort to unslide the bolt.

There was a moment's silence and then, 'Shane. Shane McLinnie.'

Shane McLinnie? She took a step back from the door, her hand going to her mouth and her fingers half covering her nose as she pressed hard against her flesh. He had come here? Out in the open? He had actually dared to knock on the door? It had utterly thrown her, and now she half turned towards the hall and the sitting room beyond, before turning back again to the door. What should she do?

'I've come to see if me mam an' da want a lift home.' His voice was ordinary and cut through the spiralling confusion, causing her body to sag and her eyes to shut tightly for a second. Of course, Mr and Mrs McLinnie, that was all it was. But the relief was only temporary. In the next moment her eyes opened wide as the numbness that had taken hold of her reason was swept away by the voice in her head saying, You know exactly why he is here and his mam and da have nothing to do with it. It would be sheer foolishness to open the door when she was alone in the kitchen.

'Rosie?' He wasn't shouting but she didn't have to strain to hear what he was saying. His voice had always had a very clear, penetrating sound to it. 'Open the door, lass. This is New Year's Day.'

She knew what day it was and at last her brain was working. 'Go round to the front of the house, Shane, and I'll get your mam and da for you. I don't open the back door this time of night.'

There was a long pause and then, 'No? It opened well enough earlier.'

'I didn't say it didn't open, just that I don't intend to open it now.' Her heart was thumping with the implication of his last comment, but now was not the time to take him up on it. He *wanted* her to know he was watching her, all along he'd wanted it. That was the reason for his visits to the Co-op. But she wasn't going to give him the satisfaction of knowing how much it bothered her. 'Come round to the front and I'll tell your mam and da you're here.'

She fairly flew into the sitting room and such was her

entrance that everyone stopped talking and looked at her, which was not how she'd wanted it to be. She forced a smile. saying, 'The tea's on its way,' before looking straight at Annie and adding, 'Shane's arrived to give you a lift home.'

'Shane?' If Rosie had said the Grim Reaper Annie couldn't have been more surprised.

'He's coming to the front. He . . . came to the back door, but I asked him to go round to the front.' Rosie didn't offer an explanation as to why and no one asked her, but Zachariah and Davey rose as one, and then, when there came the sound of a sharp rat-a-tat-tat on the front door, Rosie caught hold of Zachariah's sleeve as he made to brush past her saying, 'Please, please, it's New Year's Day. He's only come to pick his mam and da up.'

Why the hell had he come here tonight? Annie's head was spinning with the effects of the punch but she knew she had to act fast. Zachariah was no fool, and Shane had said enough that night when he'd first come home to let them know he'd had some sort of run-in in the past with Rosie's husband. By, just when she'd had a lovely evening and all, she'd really been enjoying herself. 'I'll go, lad.' Rosie was still holding on to Zachariah and now Annie's tone suggested it was perfectly normal to have someone hammering on your front door while the occupants of the house had a tussle inside. 'An' we'll be straight off, it's late. Come on, Arthur.'

Arthur McLinnie lumbered to his feet to join his wife who was already in the hall, and Rosie and Zachariah followed her, Rosie saying, 'Thank you, Mrs McLinnie, I'm sorry,' as she helped the old woman into her coat, Zachariah holding Arthur's in readiness.

Annie didn't prevaricate or pretend she didn't know what Rosie meant. She looked straight at Rosie and said, 'It's me that's sorry, lass, heart sorry, an' on New Year's Day an' all. Thank you for a lovely evenin', lass. You an' all, lad.' And then, her voice sharp, 'Come *on*, Arthur.'

'Wh – what's the hurry?'

Arthur was definitely the worse for wear, his state emphasized by the fact that Davey and Mick were at his elbows steadying him as he lurched along the hall. Annie waited until he was beside her before she opened the front door with a wide flourish, as she said, 'Oh there you are, our Shane. A lift home, so Rosie tells me? An' there we was gettin' our coats on as you turned up on the doorstep.'

In all the time Shane had had the car she and Arthur had only ridden in it twice, and it had hurt Arthur, she knew it had. But now Annie could have killed her husband as he piped up behind her – the drink making him brave and bringing out the bitterness which had been lurking beneath the surface – 'An' to what do we owe the honour of ridin' in me lord's fancy motor then, eh? Sky caved in or somethin'?'

Shane had had a smile on his face when Annie first opened the door which had faded somewhat on the realization he wasn't going to be allowed across the threshold, but now, as his father finished speaking and no one said a word, his face was straight. He looked at them all, his mother with his father just behind and to the side of her, Davey and Mick still holding Arthur up, and Rosie and Zachariah just behind the three men, Zachariah's arm round Rosie's waist. He could see Rosie's mother and sister with the bloke from the Co-op, and Sally, whom he knew to be Rosie's friend, in the hall just outside the sitting-room door, with Flora framed in the doorway. They had been having a good time. He knew it from what he had gathered as he watched the house for the last three hours or so, but he would have been able to read it in their flushed faces anyway. There had been coming and going, laughter, noise, and at midnight the house had fair rocked with their jollity, and all the time he had been out in the freezing cold skulking about like a damn pimp on a bad night.

As his gaze moved over each face, it came to Shane that they were all linked by the very things he had been on the outside looking in on all his life: affection born of familiarity; friendship; genuine warmth and love, they were all there to a greater or lesser extent.

And there was his mother at the head of the bunch with her great fat body like a fleshy barricade to stop him entering the hallowed portals. The thought stabbed at him, causing his eyes to narrow. She was a strong woman, his mam, and not just in her body either. Normally, in any other woman, such an attribute would have brought a grudging respect if nothing else, but with his mother it merely reinforced the resentment and dislike that was at the base of his feeling for the woman who had given birth to him. And in that moment, in a flash of insight, he suddenly became aware that what she was doing in the flesh she had done in the spirit from when he was a little lad. She had always kept him on the outside, at a distance from herself, his father, his brothers. She had always allowed him so far and then no further. Why? *Why?*

His thoughts made it impossible for him to bring a smile back to his face as he said, his voice cool and penetrating, 'Well? Do you want a lift or not?' He was speaking to his mother but his eyes flickered to Rosie, and it was then that

Annie actually pushed at him, saying, ''Course, lad, 'course, never look a gift horse in the mouth, eh? An' take no notice of your da, all right? He's had a few.'

'Looks like you've all had a few.'

He had almost smacked Annie's hands off him, turning on the path to see Davey and Mick still helping Arthur – whose legs were completely gone – down the step, and the general movement had brought Rosie and Zachariah, their arms now entwined, onto the threshold. Rosie was twenty-three weeks pregnant and in the last couple of weeks the mound in her stomach had become definite proof of this, but with the light behind her, and the silhouette of her body shown clearly through the thin wool of her dress, her changed shape was highlighted even more.

Shane stood as one transfixed. Annie hadn't told him Rosie was expecting a child – knowing how he felt about her Annie had decided least said, soonest mended – and in all the times he had seen her outside the Co-op she had been dressed in outdoor clothes which had concealed her condition. His discovery gave him the biggest shock of his life. He stood as though in a trance, the blood draining from his face, and the emotion filling him was actual revulsion. He had accepted that she had used Zachariah for her own ends, he could understand that; money could enable you to put up with almost anything. But that she had allowed him to plant his *seed* in her. Him, that runt, that cripple! And his voice expressed his repugnance, along with his curled lip and narrowed eyes, as he looked straight at Rosie and said, 'Looks like you're fulfillin' your end of the deal. You've got some guts, I'll say that. A husband's one thing, but a bairn that's a freak—'

He had barely got the word out before Zachariah had

uttered a sound resembling a low growl, which sounded more like an animal than a man, but as her husband made to throw himself at Shane Rosie held on to him with all her might, crying as she did so, 'No, no, he's not worth it, don't you see? A fight is exactly what he wants.'

Arthur had lurched sideways and gone sprawling as Davey had let go of him to help Rosie hang on to Zachariah, causing Mick, who was still holding Arthur's other arm, to stumble and slip on the frozen snow. In his flailing to remain upright he grabbed at Annie, with the result that all fourteen stone of her considerable bulk landed on top of him causing his breath to leave his body in a strangled wheeze.

Tommy Bailey and Joseph went to the aid of the tangled three on the ground, but Rosie was oblivious to everything but Shane as she hissed at him, her eyes narrowed and flashing fire, 'You vile man! You get out of my sight. You're not fit to be drawing the same air as decent folk.'

'Me, vile?' Shane's voice was low and guttural. 'Me?'

'Yes, you.'

The three on the ground had now been lifted to their feet, Mick and Joseph supporting the inebriated Arthur, and as Tommy came forward to assist Davey, Rosie let go of her husband and moved forward a step as she continued to glare at Shane. But Shane looked past her to where Zachariah was struggling to break free, and his expression was malevolent as he spat, 'You! You. You see what you've done?'

'Get in the car! Get in the car.' Annie was beside herself, and as she brushed past Rosie and reached her son's side she pushed him backwards. As Shane, with a lightning movement, turned his body towards her everyone thought he was going to strike his mother, but Annie held her ground, her glare matching Rosie's, and after a long moment he turned towards the gate.

'Here, give him to me.' Annie took Arthur from Mick and Joseph who had followed her forward, and now she bodily whisked her small wiry husband down the path so fast his thin legs were dangling.

'By . . .' As the engine roared and the car drew off, Joseph turned to Mick at the side of him. 'He's a nasty customer if ever I saw one.'

A nasty customer. In the moment before Davey and Tommy released Zachariah and he reached her side the words vibrated in Rosie's head. Shane McLinnie was more than a nasty customer. She had never seen such hate in anyone's face as when he had looked at her husband. And then Zachariah's arms were round her and the others were all talking at once as they drew them both back into the warmth and light of the house.

'Eee, I never thought I'd live to see the day one of me own showed me up like that. What were you thinkin' of, lad?'

Annie was in the back of the Morris Cowley, Arthur sprawled drunkenly in the front and already snoring his head off. She had decided to play dumb as to the underlying cause of the mêlée, not so much to spare Shane's feelings or even her own, but because she was frightened of what would be said if Shane's obsession with the lass was put into words. *Obsession*. She knew all about obsession. Hadn't Shane's father been filled with an unholy lust for her from when she'd been nowt but a bairn? Walter had first taken her when she'd been no older than Hannah; crept into her bedroom one night when she'd been sleeping the innocent dreams of a bairn and, with one hand over her mouth to still her screams

315

and the other hoisting her nightie up round her waist, he'd entered her before she'd even known what was happening. That had been the end of her childhood. From then on her days had been filled with sick apprehension and her nights with terror. He had said that it was all her fault, that she had tempted him, led him on and, bairn that she was, she had believed him. He was her big brother, wasn't he, and everyone had always said how nice it was the two of them was so close what with her mam's other bairns all dying before any of them reached a year old.

And so she had kept quiet, year after year she had kept quiet, until, with the onset of her periods at the relatively late age of fifteen, her body – which had been very small and thin and childish until then – had shot into womanhood, and in the space of a few months she had become tall and heavy and better able to defend herself against his attacks. And she had defended herself, by, she had, she'd even gone to the lengths of threatening him with a cut-throat razor she'd bought from the pawn shop. And then she'd met Arthur at sixteen, and – desperate to get away from home – had married him within six months. And they had been happy enough, in a way. He was not a particularly physical man and had been content with a routine weekly coupling after their night out of a Saturday, and he had left her alone altogether when she was carrying the bairns. Aye, she could have married a lot worse than her Arthur, and she'd grown fond of him over the years.

Shane hadn't answered her or acknowledged that she had spoken, and Annie, sick with the shame and self-debasement that always accompanied thoughts of her brother, remained silent as her thoughts went on to the night Shane had been conceived. When Walter and his wife and their bairns had turned up on her doorstep that night twenty-five years ago, all the old feelings of guilt and pain and fear had kept her dumb at first as Walter had told the story of how they'd been turned out of their lodgings and they'd got nowhere to go until they left for Australia some weeks hence. Arthur had immediately offered them a roof over their heads as long as they didn't mind kipping in the kitchen – the lads had had the two bedrooms in those days, and she and Arthur the front room – and she hadn't had the guts to say anything different. By, she had paid for that act of cowardice sure enough.

It had been all right at first. Walter had been just as you'd expect a brother to be, nothing more, and the temptation to tell Arthur what had happened when she was younger – which she'd never breathed to a living soul – had faded as the days had gone by. And then one night, when her lads and his bairns were out playing, and his wife was at the shops and Arthur at work, he'd come up behind her when she'd been on her hands and knees scrubbing the kitchen floor.

It had been a brutal rape and afterwards, when she'd crawled into her bedroom and jammed the blanket box against the door, she'd been hysterical for hours. She hadn't come out that night and when Arthur called the doctor in the morning, and they had had to break the window and climb in from the street, he had diagnosed a mental and physical breakdown caused by overwork. Overwork! And so Arthur had got rid of Walter and his family, and Jessie and one or two other neighbours had looked after the bairns during the day when Arthur was working, and she'd lain in her bed and tried to hang on to what was left of her reason. And then she'd discovered she was pregnant.

It was only the fact that the baby could possibly have been Arthur's that kept her from suicide. She would have been prepared to answer for her immortal soul, even that of a child conceived by rape and incest, but an innocent bairn born under the marriage vows? The Holy Mother would look on that as murder. She'd gone to confession and for the first time ever she had spoken of the unspeakable, and Father Bell had confirmed her fears. She would be damning herself for eternity if she considered taking her own life and that of her child. The good Lord would see her through this, hadn't He known what it was to suffer degradation and humiliation at the hands of sinful men? He would strengthen her, she mustn't fear. And He had, aye, He had, even when the bairn was born and she'd looked into Walter's face, He had strengthened her, and – amazingly – put a love in her for the innocent product of a man's wickedness. But there had been fear there too, deep, consuming, mind-numbing fear that the innocent had the seed of something abominable . . .

'Did you know?'

'What?' Annie's eyes shot to the back of Shane's neck as his voice brought her out of the nightmare.

'Did you *know*?' he ground out through clenched teeth.

'About the lass expectin'? Aye, 'course I knew, it's no secret an' bairns have a way of presentin' themselves once two people are wed.' She wasn't about to tell him that Jessie had been round her door the minute she'd heard, all upset like. Not that Jessie didn't like Zachariah, aye, she did, but a bairn? Like her, Jessie had thought they wouldn't go in for children with him being the way he was, just in case. Things could be passed down in families from generation to generation, everyone knew that. Look at the MacFells with their trouble, one idiot after another they seemed to have, and there was the Wheatleys with each generation producing bairns with club feet. But she'd told Jessie not to worry, what else could she do? And it certainly wasn't something any of them could speak to Rosie or Zachariah about.

'Presentin' themselves!' Shane laughed, a high mirthless laugh, and then there followed something so crude and base that Annie's eyes stretched wide and her jaw sagged, but only for a moment and then she said, her indignation not at all feigned, 'I'll thank you to keep a civil tongue in your head, lad, an' remember who you're speakin' to.'

'Don't push me, Mam.'

It was for all the world as though she had been the obscene one, and again Annie's voice reflected her umbrage as she said, 'It's not me doin' the pushin', lad. To barge in there like that an' then to say what you said, an' on New Year's Day of all days. What must they all be thinkin'—'

'I don't care what they're thinkin', get that through your thick head. An' nothin' I could say can compare with what she's done.'

'What?' Annie rubbed her hand across her mouth where the beads of perspiration had gathered. 'I dunno what you're on about, I don't straight. They're married, for cryin' out loud.'

'Not for much longer.'

Annie pulled herself up straight, there had been something in his voice that went far beyond the rage and fury of the moment. 'What's that supposed to mean?' And when there was no immediate answer: 'Shane?'

'You work it out. You seem to have all the answers.'

'Now look, lad—'

'No! *You* look.' He stopped the car so suddenly that Arthur, who had been gently snoring and muttering to himself, would have shot forward into the windscreen but for Shane's arm restraining him. 'You look, Mam.' Shane turned in his seat, ignoring his father's 'Wh . . . what is . . . it? What . . .', as he said, 'All me life I've held me hand with her, all me life, an' where's it got me? But no more.'

He swore again, the sound ugly, but this time Annie didn't admonish him, and her voice was a whisper when she said, 'What are you sayin'? By all that's holy, lad, what are you sayin'?'

He stared at her hard, and she at him, and then as Arthur's snores began to reverberate in the narrow confines of the car once again Shane turned, very slowly and with measured control, and started the car.

Chapter Eighteen

Rosie was aware she needed to be strong as she sat facing Robert McLinnie over a pot of tea in the small café in a side street in Bishopswearmouth. It was the second Thursday in January, and he had written to her two days previously informing her he had some news about Molly but that it was imperative she told no one before she had spoken to him.

She watched him now as he swallowed the contents of his cup, wiped his mouth with the back of his hand and cleared his throat before saying, his voice very quiet, 'You didn't tell no one you were seein' me?'

'No. You asked me not to.'

'Aye, aye.' He cleared his throat again. 'It's on account of me mam you see, an' Connie, of course. I don't want them gettin' the wrong idea . . .' He straightened in his chair, screwing his buttocks into the seat, and in that moment Rosie realized he was highly embarrassed and wishing himself anywhere but where he was.

She bent forward, and now her voice was as quiet as his when she said, 'Robert, whatever you have to tell me will be between you and me if you want it that way, but of course I would like to tell Zachariah too.'

'Aye, aye I can understand that, but this can't be dealt with like a bull in a china shop.'

By that she surmised that Robert – who she had heard through Jessie who had heard through Annie had been more than a little affronted at being left out of the rescue of Molly years before – was referring to Zachariah's all-guns-blazing approach at Charlie Cullen's establishment.

Robert rubbed his face now as he said, 'Look, Rosie, I don't know quite how to put this, lass, I don't straight, but it's bin drivin' me barmy the last few weeks an' I need to get it off me chest. I remember you an' Molly as little bairns see, we was all brought up together in a manner of speakin', weren't we?'

'Yes, yes we were.' She looked at his red face for a moment and then said quietly, 'It's about Molly, you said?'

'Aye.' And then he began to speak rapidly. 'I happened to be in Newcastle afore Christmas with a couple of pals of mine. We'd had a few jars, you know how it is, an' one of 'em suggested visitin' a house he knows.'

'A house?' And then as Rosie looked into his eyes she said quickly, 'Oh yes, I see.' Annie had told her things were very bad again between Robert and his wife.

'The lads had gone upstairs an' I was sat waitin' for 'em, I didn't go up meself of course' – Rosie wasn't at all sure if she believed that but she nodded anyway – 'an' who should I clap eyes on but your Molly. It knocked me backwards, lass, I can tell you, an' she'd ducked away an' shut the door afore I could speak to her, but it was her all right. I'd stake me life on it.'

Rosie stared at him, her heart thudding, and she forced herself to speak very calmly when she said, 'When was this, Robert?'

'Ah now, that's the thing, lass. It was all of five weeks ago now, maybe six. I should've said somethin' afore but like I said, I didn't want it gettin' back to Connie or me mam an' them gettin' the wrong end of the stick, see. But it's bin like a ton weight on me shoulders since.'

Rosie adjusted the collar of her woollen coat which suddenly seemed to be strangling her before she said, 'Thank you, Robert, thank you so much for telling me, and I promise you I won't tell a soul apart from Zachariah where I heard it and neither will he. You have my word on that.'

'Aye, well that's good enough for me, pet.'

'Can you give me the address of this place?'

'Aye.' He shifted again in his seat. 'But I'm tellin' you, if your man barges in there like he did the other house, happen he'll get more than he bargained for an' it won't do the lass no good neither. That place is not like on the dockside, Rosie.'

Rosie nodded, her head whirling. What could she do?

'She's usin' the name of Marybelle, by all accounts.'

'Marybelle?' Rosie's voice was high now.

'Aye.' Robert nodded. 'Rum 'un, ain't it, but they all use fancy names – or so me pals tell me,' he added hastily.

They talked some more after Robert had given her the name of the street and some directions from the last tram stop, but after Robert had left, Rosie sat for some minutes as a plan began to formulate in her mind. She had told Zachariah she was seeing an old friend today – that was true enough in a way, Robert *was* an old friend – and he wasn't expecting her home until much later. She was going to tell him everything Robert had said, but . . . She wrinkled her brow as her mind raced on. If she could see Molly before that, *now*, wouldn't that be best? Robert had said it could turn nasty but not for a woman on her own, what threat was she? And if she could talk to Molly, just *talk* to her. Oh, Molly, *Molly*. Excitement mixed with fear and apprehension made her stomach churn. She had to try, and if she was going to do it she had to do it now. Once she had talked to Zachariah he would try and stop her.

Rosie got into Newcastle just before mid-day, and the bitterly cold winter's day and grey sky didn't add to the city's scant charm. There were the same rabbit warrens of factories, back-to-back slums, chemical works vomiting out foul-smelling smoke and steelworks in the poor part of town where Robert had directed her to go as in Sunderland, but on a larger scale.

Once in Newcastle, she had decided to take a horsedrawn cab rather than a tram – she would ask the driver to wait for her while she went into the house to speak to Molly; that way someone would be aware of where she was – and as it picked its way through the back streets and cobbled side roads she could barely sit still. She was going to see Molly – she simply wouldn't take no for an answer, she told herself stoutly.

It was some fifteen minutes before the cab arrived at Pauper's Row – an unattractive name but very apt, Rosie thought, for the grim narrow street of terraced houses. Robert had told her that the house she wanted was set at the back of this street, all by itself and adjoining the stables of a large laundry, and sure enough when the cab turned the corner a large brick house was in front of them.

The first surprise was that, in marked contrast to the endless houses in street after street through which she had just passed, this establishment's front door was freshly painted and smut-free along with the bright green windowframes, and the heavily ornate brass knocker was shining.

The curtains, which looked to be a dark patterned red, were draped across each of the five large windows – two either side of the front door and one directly above it – so that it was impossible to see into them, and there was a curl of grey smoke coming from one of the chimneys.

'You'll wait for me? I shouldn't be more than half an hour at the most.'

The cab driver looked back at the well-dressed young woman in front of him. She wasn't the type to be going into this particular house, not if he knew anything about it, but he kept his thoughts to himself as he answered, 'Aye, I'll wait, lass. As long as it takes.'

After a minute or so of almost continuous knocking, the door opened the merest crack and a somewhat quavery voice said, 'You're makin' enough noise to wake the dead, so you are. Be off with you.'

'Wait.' As the door made to close again Rosie's small boot shot into the space, causing the door to rattle somewhat, and the voice from within to say, 'Eee, hold on, what's your game?'

'I need to speak to someone, it's urgent.'

'Urgent, you say? You lookin' for work, lass?'

'No. No, nothing like that.'

'All right, don't sound so uppity, lass. It's the oldest profession in the world or so they tell me.'

'Please open the door.'

There was a pause and then, 'What's it about?'

'I need to speak to one of the girls. Marybelle. I've a message for her. Her mam's been taken bad and is asking

325

for her.' It was the story Rosie had decided on during the journey from Bishopswearmouth.

Silence again and then, 'An' who might you be?'

'I'm . . . I'm her sister.'

'Well, Marybelle ain't 'ere.' And then, as Rosie actually rattled the door, ''Ere, pack it in, you. I'm tellin' you she ain't 'ere, she's gone, just the other night.'

'I don't believe you.'

'Well, that's nice, ain't it.' There was another pause followed by, 'Look, if I open this door an' let you in, you ain't gonna cause no trouble are you? You are by yourself? I don't want to have to call Jimmy or Fred.'

'I don't want you to have to call them either.'

'Well, lass, I tell you straight, if it'd bin a bloke with 'is hoof in me door I'd have bin tempted to break his ruddy foot.'

The next moment the door swung wide on its hinges, and Rosie was confronted by the tiny wizened owner of the voice, but such was her surprise that at first she didn't move.

'Well? Ain't you comin' in now you've raised the whole 'ouse?'

'Oh yes, yes. Thank you.' Rosie was aware she sounded stunned but she couldn't help it. The little woman was minute, no more than four-foot-nine at the most, but it wasn't her thin frail frame in the black alpaca dress that had caused Rosie's mouth to gape, but the incredible painted face above. She must be seventy if she was a day, perhaps a lot older, but the white and pink face, that bore a resemblance to painted enamel, would have looked strange on a woman fifty years her junior, and the vivid blue eyeshadow and thick red lipstick turned the whole into a brightly coloured gargoyle mask. And the wig . . . Rosie found she couldn't take her eyes off it as she followed the little figure along the carpeted hall. She had never seen hair of such a vibrant orange in all her life.

'Come in 'ere, this is where the customers wait for the girls.' Rosie was led into a large and somewhat garish room, to the left of the wide curving staircase, full of low upholstered sofas and small occasional tables, and then the tiny woman turned to face her again, and the painted mouth smiled before saying, 'Sit down, lass, sit down. I don't bite. Me name's Bridget by the way. Now, you're askin' after Marybelle?'

'I know her as Molly.'

The woman nodded slowly at Rosie's flat voice, and then perched herself on the edge of a sofa. 'Aye, aye.' The watery blue eyes narrowed. 'An' you say you're her sister? You'd be Rosie then?'

Rosie's heart leapt. Right up to this moment she had half feared Robert might have got it wrong but it *was* Molly he had caught a glimpse of.

Rosie was aware of the painted gaze taking in every inch of her, and although her coat hid her condition to all but the most observant eyes she was sure the woman had noticed it, and now her face was slightly flushed as she said, 'Yes, I'm Rosie. I don't know if Molly is aware of it but I got married in the summer to Zachariah, the man we had been lodging with before Molly left.'

'An' does he know you're here today, lass?'

Rosie didn't hesitate. 'No, he doesn't.'

'I thought not.' The old woman surveyed her for a moment or two before she said, 'Well, you've 'ad a wasted journey an' that's the truth.' And then, as Rosie went to speak, 'It's the truth, lass. If you want to search each room you won't find 'er. She's gone, she's one of the lucky ones. Bin picked up by a gent.'

'A gent?'

'Aye. This is a better class house, in case you didn't know, we don't have no riff-raff in 'ere, none of your scum, not at our prices. No, we cater for them what 'as got a bit of taste.' And then she took Rosie aback for the second time in as many minutes when she said, 'You want a cup of tea? I always 'ave one about this time afore I get the girls awake.'

Rosie stared into the amazing face for a moment and then she cleared her throat. 'That would be very nice, thank you.'

The little bird-like figure jumped up with an agility that belied her advanced years and, after ringing a bellcord at the side of the fireplace in which an unlit fire was neatly set out, she resumed her seat seconds before there was a knock at the door and a young uniformed maid popped her head into the room. 'Tea, Carrie, for both of us mind, an' put on a plate of that spice cake Ada made last night. This lass is eatin' for two.'

The girl nodded, after an interested glance at Rosie, and shut the door again.

'Now, lass.' The voice was quavery but nevertheless determined. 'You tell me the real reason for this visit an' cut the blather, eh? I wasn't born yesterday an' I've 'eard the one about the dyin' mother more times than I've 'ad 'ot dinners.'

Rosie looked into the pink-and-white face and made an instant decision, and as she began to talk, outlining the circumstances which had led to this minute, she left out nothing, even mentioning Charlie Cullen by name. The old lady listened without interrupting, and it was only after the maid had served the tea and disappeared again, and they had had a slice of the fruit cake and a cup of tea, that she said, 'Well, lass, you've been honest with me an' like deserves like. I don't know where your Molly's gone, an' that's the truth, but even if I did it'd be more than me life's worth to tell you. You've 'eard of Charlie, you know what 'e's capable of, an' I've a good goin'-on 'ere. I know one of the gents was taken with your sister an' wanted to set her up proper like, an' that from Molly 'erself, she was full of it. He wanted 'er all to 'iself an' 'e was prepared to pay for the privilege, an' if the carriage an' 'orses that picked 'er up last Friday night are anythin' to go by, she's in clover, lass. Aye, clover.'

'She is sixteen years old, Bridget.'

Bridget settled back in her seat, and now the old eyes held a kind of weariness as they surveyed this pretty young woman. It was a good few moments before she spoke, and then she said, 'There's three types of lasses that go on the game, Rosie,' her voice almost conversational. 'There's them broken in as bairns, some of 'em no more than five or six, sometimes sold by their mam an' da or picked up random like off the streets; Charlie's arm is long. An' then there's them that need to feed their bairns, or their old mam an' da, or whatever. An' then there's the other kind, the kind that like it, that want it; like a drug or drink. Now this might be 'ard to 'ear but your Molly is like that, an' I know 'cos I was the same. An' she wants the money an' what it can do for 'er an' all, she's got 'er 'ead screwed on all right. She's good at what she does, young Molly, she used to 'ave their tongues 'anging out, I'm tellin' you. It caused some trouble with the other girls when the customers started linin' up for Molly.'

Rosie couldn't listen to any more. She stood up abruptly, shaking her head as she said, 'I'm sorry, Bridget, I know you mean well, but I just want to get her back.'

'So's she can run off again? Think on, lass, think on.' Bridget rose now and her voice was kind. 'She's gone, she's as dead to your mam an' the rest of 'em as if she was six foot under. Leave it alone, I'm tellin' you. She's where she wants to be, doin' what she wants. You're strong, lass, I could see it the minute you walked in the door, an' it took some guts for you to come here an' in your condition. But your sister ain't like you, lass. If there's an easy way out Molly will always take it.'

'You call this *easy*?'

'Aye, aye for her, I do. Like I said, there's all sorts on the game. Admittedly some of 'em are forced into it an' it near kills 'em but Molly'll be all right. She might even end her days like me, sittin' pretty with a maid at her beck an' call.' The wry note in Bridget's voice was tinged with bitterness. 'You're a bonny lass. You 'ave a fine bairn an' make a good life for yerself, but forget your sister. The lass you knew has gone for good.'

'I can't forget Molly, Bridget. She's my sister, I love her.'

'Oh, lass, lass.'

'Would you get a message to her? Please, Bridget, would you do that? If I write a letter—'

'No. No letters.' Bridget jerked away, walking across to the ornate fireplace and staring down into the neatly arranged coals. 'Letters 'ave a way of workin' themselves into the wrong 'ands an' then all 'ell'd be let loose. Believe me, lass, no one crosses Charlie an' gets another chance, an' that's how 'e'd see it if 'e found out. You don't know the 'alf, lass.'

Then the little figure straightened as it turned, and it was clear Bridget had reached a decision. She stared into Rosie's anxious face for a moment, then said, 'I'll get a message to 'er meself, personal like, all right? But I can't promise when.'

'You will?' Rosie's face lit up. 'Tell her I'm married to Zachariah and she's going to be an aunty in the spring, Bridget. I live in Roker now, number seventeen The Terrace. Ask her to come and see me. And . . . and tell her I love her, we all love her, whatever she's done. Make sure she understands that.'

'Aye, aye, but I doubt you'll 'ear owt, hinny.'

'Oh thank you, Bridget.' Rosie walked across to stand in front of the old woman, and took the wrinkled hands that were weighed down with rings and bracelets. 'You don't know what this means, you trying. Thank you.'

'Don't thank me yet, lass. It might be for nothin'.'

'But you're going to talk to her and that's the main thing.'

'You trust me word, then?'

The bright sharp eyes were tight on Rosie's face now, and when Rosie nodded, saying simply, 'I do, yes, of course I do,' the old woman shook her head.

'By, you're an 'eart stealer an' no mistake. Well, I'll keep me word to you, lass, by 'ook or by crook, but I'm sayin' again, don't get your 'opes up. I've seen life in the raw for too long to believe in miracles an' there's not much I don't know about folk. Your Molly is where she wants to be, lass, an' she's made up her mind 'er old life is a closed book. You won't be seein' 'er again.'

It was a long cold journey back to Roker.

331

Chapter Nineteen

The bright expectation and hope that a New Year engenders had evaporated like the dew on a warm summer's morning by the end of January 1926 for most northerners. Strikes, counter-strikes, flooding in parts of the country after continuous rain for eighteen days in February, and an escalation of the miners' dispute in March all continued the steady decline of the nation's morale. The Royal Commission's recommendations that the general level of wages must be cut and the 1924 minimum wage agreement abolished was the last straw for Sunderland's – and the rest of the country's – struggling miners, and their slogan of 'Not a penny off the pay, not a minute on the day' was fighting talk. However, by the middle of April, when 20,000 members of the Women's Guild of the Empire demonstrated in London for an end to strikes and lockouts, Zachariah barely noticed. Rosie's baby was due in another week, and since Shane's poisonous barb had brought all his own hitherto unmentioned fears to the surface he had been suffering the torments of the damned.

Rosie had reassured him in every way she knew how, striving with all her might to keep his mind off the awful foreboding Shane's maliciousness had caused. Whether it was because she needed to be strong for Zachariah, or simply because she knew in her heart she would love their baby whatever it was like, even if Dr Meadows was proved wrong, Rosie managed not to let Shane's venom overwhelm her, but at times it was hard. Her anger helped. She was furious that one man's viciousness should rob her husband of what should have been the happiest time in his life, but she comforted herself with the thought that for future babies – and she intended to have more – the ogre of the unknown would have been dealt with.

She had told Zachariah about her visit to the house in Newcastle immediately on her return home, and perhaps understandably it had resulted in their first real argument, as his concern for her welfare and what might have happened made him angry. But they had kissed and made up, and Zachariah had agreed to keep Robert's name out of it when Rosie told her mother the bare facts and that Molly was alive and well.

Flora had returned to the house in Fulwell early in the new year, and after a visit to the family solicitor she had discovered it was now hers, or would be when all the legal niceties were completed, along with some two hundred pounds in the bank. She had spent four weeks in the house, during which time Rosie had helped her make a thorough inventory of all its contents, and then Flora had walked out of the door and into lodgings close to Mrs Riley's. The solicitors had finished dotting the i's and crossing the t's the last day of March, and that very afternoon Flora had put the house on the market. She had given a list to J. Brickwell & Sons of Monkwearmouth of items to be disposed of, and another to her solicitors detailing keepsakes and gifts to her relatives in Wales. She herself had kept nothing but her mother's photo album, her mother's jewellery and her mother's sewing box. She had cut every photograph of her father from the album and she endeavoured, every day, to cut him from her memories, and this was something that would continue for the rest of her life.

She had seen Davey almost every evening since she had been in lodgings and she made no excuse to herself for her determined pursuit of him. That he regarded her merely as a friend she was well aware, but she also knew his warm regard was heavily laced with pity and a desire to help her since her parents' untimely deaths.

Slowly, very slowly, he was beginning to see her as an attractive woman too, though, and she could wait. As long as it took, she could wait. There was no one else in all the world like Davey. She didn't ask herself if he still loved Rosie, or Rosie him, she already knew the answer – she had seen it in both their faces on New Year's Eve. But in spite of that she knew this was her one chance to attain what had been impossible years before and she wanted to take it. It was that simple.

On April 21st, 1926, the Duchess of York gave birth to her first baby, a daughter, who was to become Queen Elizabeth II of Great Britain and Northern Ireland. And on that same day, at half past six in the evening in the master bedroom of number seventeen The Terrace, Roker, Rosie presented Zachariah with a son.

The labour had been long and difficult, lasting two days and nights, and at the end of it a distraught Zachariah had overruled the family doctor and midwife who were still insisting all was well, and ordered the doctor to send for one of his colleagues, a Dr Jeffrey of Newcastle, an eminent and highly respected gynaecologist, with the message that his immediate attendance meant he could name his own price for the consultation.

Dr Jeffrey had arrived at the house at six o'clock, and by a quarter past preparations were underway for an emergency Caesarean. Dr Jeffrey was just about to administer the chloroform to relieve his patient's intense suffering, when the tempo of the excruciating pains changed, and before anyone was aware of what was happening a huge baby boy was there between Rosie's legs, yelling for all he was worth.

Zachariah heard the sound from outside the bedroom where a concerned Dr Jeffrey had ordered him, but it held no wonder for him. All his thoughts were with his wife and he was frightened, more frightened than he would ever have thought possible. He couldn't bear to lose her; whatever else, he couldn't bear to lose his Rosie.

And so when Jessie opened the bedroom door some minutes later and beckoned to him, the tears still streaming down her face, he found he couldn't move. He stared at his mother-in-law, his face grey, and even when she said, 'It's all right, she didn't have the operation after all, she did it herself, lad,' he saw Jessie's lips move, but the actual words didn't register through the turmoil for another ten seconds.

Rosie was lying quite still in the clean, remade bed, her eyes fixed on the door as Zachariah entered. He didn't even see the two doctors and the midwife, who had been standing just inside the room, slip out of the door, and he wasn't conscious of Jessie standing by the window, nor yet of the small squirming shape in the crib at the side of the bed. His whole being was centred on Rosie, and when he reached her side and saw she was too exhausted to do more than smile and lift her hand to him, he fell down on his knees by the bed and took her hand, holding it against his lips as he murmured, 'Never again, lass, never again.'

'It should be me saying that.' Her voice, with its gurgle of laughter, reassured him somewhat, and then she said, 'Don't you want to see your son?'

'My son? It's a boy?'

Rosie nodded, her velvet-brown eyes soft as his gaze turned from her to the crib which was now emitting a wah of a cry.

He wanted to ask her. He wanted to, but he didn't dare. In all their conversations Rosie had emphasized that once they saw their child, whether it be boy or girl, perfect or imperfect, they would love it, but now the moment was here and he was terrified that he would let both Rosie and this new innocent life down.

As Jessie slipped from the room he rose slowly to his feet and walked round to the other side of the bed where the child lay in its nest of white downy covers. Its eyes were open and he saw they were a deep grey-blue with surprisingly long lashes, and the wisps of hair on the baby head were white blond and curly. The child's tiny fingers were grasping at the air as the small fists opened and shut, and as the miaow of a cry came again Zachariah stood looking down at this flesh of his flesh before he carefully put out a hand and drew back the fluffy blanket. And as he did so the baby kicked. It kicked with all the strength of its two beautiful, strong, perfectly formed legs.

'Isn't he beautiful?' Rosie's voice was soft with the trace of tears. 'Isn't he the most beautiful sight in all the world?'

Zachariah couldn't answer for a moment. He reached down and gently slid his hands beneath the small body, supporting the little head as he lifted the baby into his arms. And then he held his son close to his heart for a full minute, his throat full and his heart bursting, before he turned to Rosie, who was waiting for his look, her eyes luminous, and said, 'The second most beautiful, Rosie lass, the second. I'm lookin' at the most beautiful right now.'

'Well, I'd best be makin' me way, lass, else the day'll be half over afore I get there. Zachariah didn't know if he was on foot or horseback last night, bless him.'

Jessie was on tenterhooks as she sat in Annie's kitchen and she had been right from the moment, some twenty minutes before, when she'd knocked on the back door. It was the morning after little Erik James had been born – so named after his two grandfathers – and she was on her way to Roker. Dr Jeffrey had made it clear the night before that he wouldn't contemplate his patient leaving her bed for at least two weeks, and although Jessie had already arranged to have the last week in April and the first week of May off, when the baby had been due, Joseph was insisting on the extra few days. 'No good having the clout unless you use it occasionally,' was the way he had put it, 'and by my reckoning the lass needs you a sight more than the Store does.' Oh, he was good, he was, and marvellous with Hannah. Her youngest daughter loved him. The word brought a smile to her lips. She had never thought she'd fall in love again, not at her age, but the good Lord had surprised her with what He'd planned in the way of Joseph Green.

'I appreciate you comin', lass.' Annie's voice was low, in fact all their conversation had been conducted in little more than whispers owing to the fact that Shane hadn't yet left for his day shift at the steelworks.

The sky had still been shadowed with the last remnants of night when Jessie had boarded the early tram that morning, and it had been then that the impulse to call in on Annie before she made her way on to Rosie and Zachariah had hit her. She had struggled with it for a few moments – the furore on New Year's Eve had both shocked and sickened her and there was no way she wanted to run into Shane McLinnie – but she knew it'd put Annie's mind at rest to hear that all was well with the bairn. Well? She'd grinned to herself. It was ruddy marvellous, and one in the eye for Shane McLinnie. And why shouldn't she go and see Annie – her oldest and dearest friend – with the best news in the world? she asked herself as the tram trundled off. Annie was like a sister to her; the two of them had seen good days and bad and survived a war, aye, and all the heartache that'd gone with it.

Jessie had sucked in her lips and narrowed her eyes as she had contemplated the grey streets beyond the relative warmth of the tram. Shane McLinnie wasn't fit to draw the same air as decent folk. By, she'd never forgive him for what he'd said to her lass and Zachariah, but didn't she, of all people, understand that you couldn't always predict how your bairns were going to turn out? She'd never thought to see the day when she'd thank the good Lord He'd taken her man and her lads, but if they had been alive the day there would have been murder done over their Molly. It would have destroyed James. Even with them keeping it quiet like they had, it would have eaten away at him until it'd destroyed him.

Jessie finished the last dregs of her tea in one gulp and had actually walked to the back door with Annie and was standing with one foot on the step, when the door to the hall opened and Shane stepped through into the kitchen.

He was surprised to see Jessie in his mother's kitchen and his face reflected this, but along with the surprise there was a wariness – as well there might be, thought Jessie self-righteously. Her face was cold as she looked across the kitchen at Annie's youngest, and he, sensing the maternal wrath, straightened and returned the look, before turning to his mother and saying, 'You on strike or somethin'? Where's me breakfast?'

'It's comin'.' Annie's voice was agitated and the look she bestowed on Jessie in the next second was a pleading one. She'd been feeling bad since the New Year, right bad, and her usual medicine that she'd been taking on and off for years wasn't helping much. And Dr Meadows was no help, fancy him saying he wanted her to take it easy and then suggesting she go to the hospital for tests! She wasn't setting foot in that place!

Take it easy indeed. Would taking it easy get Arthur's and the lads' suits to the pawn every Monday morning so they could eat, and collect them of a Saturday once Shane and any of the others who'd got work during the week paid their bit? Or would it help her to scour the shops at closing for any stale loaves and scrag ends going cheap, or hang about near the market looking for bruised fruit and the like? And what about working all hours with the washing she took in, and then going round to Mrs Brent's on Higham Hill, and scrubbing her massive house from top to bottom twice a week? Take it easy! She'd paid out good money for him to tell her she'd got to take it easy, that was the top and bottom of it, and she wouldn't make that mistake again.

'I'll be seein' you, Annie.'

Jessie didn't look at Shane again as she said her goodbyes but as she stepped fully into the yard he appeared at the door alongside his mother, his tone confrontational as he said, 'What you doin' round these parts first thing in the mornin'?'

'She came to see me, there's nowt wrong with that is there?'

Jessie heard Annie's voice, and she knew her friend didn't want her to voice the real reason for her presence, but no power on earth could have stopped Jessie from throwing her satisfaction in Shane McLinnie's face as she said, her voice cold and very even, 'I came to tell your mam that Rosie had a bouncin' ten-pounder last night, a boy, as bonny a bairn as ever I've seen.'

Shane stared at her. He didn't say a word, he just stared at her, and such was the power in his gaze that Jessie took a step backwards as she thought, He's evil. He might be Annie's son, and certainly our Molly is no better than she should be, but this is something different.

She was aware of Annie's white face as she turned away, and also that Shane was watching her as she walked to the end of the yard and opened the gate into the mucky back lane, but she didn't look back, and it was only when she emerged into the street at the end of the lane and began walking towards the tram stop that she found she was shaking.

By, she could see why her Rosie had steered clear of that one right enough, aye, she could. And to think that she used to think him a nice lad, well set up in fact and a good catch for some lass. There had even been a time when she'd imagined him and Rosie . . . She shivered, but it was less to do with the chilly April morning that carried the odd drop of icy rain in its raw wind than the realization of her own lack of discernment. Her James always used to say she couldn't see the wood for the trees, and he was right, God rest his soul. He'd been right about a lot of things, her James, like her being her own worst enemy for one. She had been a silly woman the last few years, a very silly woman, but she had Joseph now and he'd already asked her twice to marry him. And she'd say yes, but in her own time. Maybe in a few months or so. But for now there was Erik. 'We've a grandson, James.' She breathed it out, her eyes misty with the joy and thankfulness that had been bubbling inside her since the evening before. 'A bonny little lad an' he'll never have to set foot inside a mine. That gladdens your heart, don't it, like it does mine.'

Once Rosie was on her feet again and the bitterly cold winds and snow and sleet of April and May had given way to a serene June and blazing July, number seventeen The Terrace was subject to a steady stream of visitors. Both Flora and Sally were quite smitten with little Erik, and their shared adoration of the tiny infant made for some merry tea parties on sunny summer afternoons.

Flora was still living close to Davey's lodgings, and he had accompanied her several times on her visits to Rosie and Zachariah and taken a great interest in the child. Likewise Peter Baxter, who also escorted Flora on occasion and who seemed quite reconciled to Flora's friendship with Davey. *Seemed.* But Rosie suspected differently. Peter was a gentleman and a quiet and unassuming individual, but Rosie recognized a tenacity in the mild-mannered man that was at odds with the placid exterior. He said little but observed greatly, and on the one or two occasions when he and Zachariah had been left alone they had apparently got on like a house on fire, despite their vastly differing political affiliations and the fact that Peter was third-generation 'money'.

Peter continued to employ Davey on a regular basis at his father's shipyard, and certainly on the one or two occasions Rosie had seen the two men together she had been unable to detect any noticeable ill feeling or rancour, but still . . . The old saying 'still waters run deep' was always at the back of her mind when she contemplated Peter Baxter, and Rosie was sure he had by no means given up his pursuit of her friend. It had merely gone under cover.

Little Erik James flourished under all the tender care and love which was lavished on him, and no one was more besotted than the infant's father. Zachariah was the epitome of the doting parent and he didn't care who knew it. The baby had been a good size at birth and had never had the fragility of a newborn child, and right from day one Zachariah had horrified the attending midwife, along with Jessie and a few others, by insisting he was involved in the daily care of his son. Rosie wasn't surprised; Zachariah was the only man she had ever come across who took it upon himself to share the housework and mundane chores as a matter of course. But to the other women, steeped in the age-old traditions of the north where 'men twer men' and even the lowest scavenger – the common nickname for the corporation soil men who cleaned out the dry closets or 'netties' with their long shovels – considered 'women's' work beneath their dignity, Zachariah's practical involvement with his son was nothing short of scandalous.

However, it was interesting that both Flora and Sally, who were often able to view Zachariah in action, waxed lyrical on the topic to Davey and to Mick, until both men became more than a little tired of Zachariah's halo.

* * *

But it wasn't Zachariah that Davey was thinking of as he walked home from the shipyard on a bakingly hot evening in mid-July. The extreme heat had brought back the flavour of Egypt and his life on Mohamed's farm. He could feel the warm, sun-soaked days and muggy nights, smell the intoxicating odour of freshly irrigated earth and thirsty vegetation and crops, the heady, sweet perfume of magnolia flowers.

The Sunderland street melted away, and in front of him in his mind's eye were hot dusty cart tracks in baked earth. He had felt out there, working on the land, that he had truly come alive for the first time. The work had been hard, very hard, and he had discovered that a farmer's life was a twenty-four-hour cycle of endless toil and labour – you lived it and breathed it all the time, there was no whistle telling you it was time to clock off and go home. But the overall satisfaction had been immense. He had been out in the fresh air, seeing the sky, feeling the breeze on his face. And here . . . Here there was the shipyard. And Flora.

What was he going to do about Flora? Davey wrinkled up his nose as he walked; the journey home to Mrs Riley's took him through the back lanes and alleyways and the bad smells from some of the hatchways were overpowering in the hot weather. He cared about her; she was a good lass, pretty and lively, and she'd had a rough deal the last few months . . . *Oh, stop your yammering.* The voice in his head was so distinct that he almost turned round to see if someone had spoken. What was he trying to skirt round the issue for?

Flora would make a lovely wife for the right man, and for a time he had thought that man was destined to be Peter Baxter, but over the last few months he had begun to wonder. Of course Flora wasn't— His brain closed down on that other name and now he actually ground his teeth as he walked, irritable with himself and the whole situation.

If he had stayed a week or two in Sunderland, just until he'd discovered how the land lay with Rosie, this wouldn't have happened. But now he had got further and further entangled in all their lives – Flora's, Rosie's, Zachariah's – and it wasn't doing him any good, not deep inside where his conscience and his reason lay. And there was the bairn, Erik. He could feel his guts twisting every time he set eyes on the child. In a way he could understand why Shane had reacted in the manner he had that night. Oh, not the twisted nasty side of it, that was just plain vicious and pure McLinnie. Nevertheless, when Zachariah had told him Rosie was expecting and he had had to face the fact that she was carrying another man's child in her body it had near crucified him. But he loved little Erik, he was a bonny baby and he could understand why Zachariah was so proud of his small son, he had every right to be.

He needed to make a fresh start, that was it at bottom, and perhaps Sunderland wasn't the place to do it. What was he thinking? He *knew* Sunderland wasn't the place to do it. But there was Flora; he enjoyed her company and, more than that, he cared about the lass deep inside. *Damn it all*. The feeling of confusion grew.

He couldn't go back to Mrs Riley's, not yet, he needed a drink, and not a cup of tea. Davey turned sharply at the end of the street and more by instinct than reason made his way to the Colliery Tavern which, being close to Southwick Road and the Wearmouth Colliery, was a regular haunt of miners and had been well known to him and Sam in the old days.

There were a few men in the bar when he entered, most

of them nursing a pint of beer, and one or two raised their hands to him and nodded, but it was Ralph Felton, whose father had been a pal of his da's, who said, 'Davey, man, over here.'

Davey nodded, ordering and paying for his pint before he joined the four men clustered round a table near the big square window of the taproom. 'How you doing?' He spoke directly to Ralph but his gaze included all of the party.

'Same as the rest of the poor blighters round these parts.' The bitterness was tangible. 'Never thought we'd see the day when we was sold down the river by our own, but it's happened. Aye, it's happened all right. Nine days the General Strike lasted in May, a paltry nine days, an' here we are still battlin' it out. Makes me sick to me stomach.'

There were murmurs of assent from all present, and then Ralph said, as Davey's face revealed what he was thinking, 'Oh, I'm not havin' a go at you, man, don't think that. You was out of it all years afore an' good luck to you an' all. No, it was the TUC that cut our legs out from under us when they went caps-in-hand to the government, the lily-livered so-an'-sos. An' that after we was called traitors an' worse for objectin' to a wage cut an' longer hours. *Traitors!* By, I'd like to ram the word down Churchill's throat, so I would. What did they expect with their threats of lockouts an' all?'

Davey nodded. His sympathies were all with the men sitting so despondently round the table. Winston Churchill's inflammatory speech for 'unconditional surrender by the enemy' in May had made him no friends among Britain's miners, and the government's import of large quantities of food at the beginning of July, along with the constant import of coal from abroad from the first month of the strike, constituted insult to injury. Add to that the recent Coal Mines Bill for longer working hours – something the militant Labour MPs had contested with such vigour that they'd stormed the House of Lords shouting 'Murder Bill' and 'Four hours for you, eight for the miners' – and it was no wonder men were prepared to starve, aye, and see their families starve, rather than give in to what they saw as blatant exploitation by a system that had used them like dogs for decades.

'How long do you think you can hold out?' Davey asked quietly.

'As long as it takes, man.'

Again Davey nodded, and then, after draining his glass, he stood up and walked across to the bar, ordering five pints and taking them back to the table. He passed them round silently and they were accepted silently. He might be an ex-miner but he was still one of them, and there was no need to thank your own. Every man at the table would have done the same in Davey's position and they all knew it. It was something that was imbibed with their mother's milk, this fierce shoulder-to-shoulder mentality, and the women of the north were no less fervent than the men.

It was just this inbred passion of looking after your own that was causing Annie such turmoil as she knocked at the door of Baxter's shipyard office immediately before Flora was due to leave that night. She felt torn all ways, and desperate – oh aye, desperate all right, she thought wretchedly, as the door opened. If she spoke, she was letting her lad down, and if she didn't . . . No. She had to. That was the end of it.

'Mrs McLinnie?' Flora's voice was high with surprise. 'What on earth are you doing here?'

'Oh I'm sorry, lass, I'm right sorry to be botherin' you at work. I can wait outside till you're done . . . ?'

'Don't be silly, come on in.' Fortunately Christine Wentworth had gone home an hour early to nurse a tooth-ache, and the day shift had been gone a good half-an-hour, so all was quiet. 'I was just about to leave anyway. What is it?'

Flora was shocked at the sight of Shane's mother. Annie had lost weight since she had seen her last at the beginning of the year, the big plump body seeming to have shrunk inwards, and her face, devoid now of most of its fat, showed every line and wrinkle. Flora knew Rosie and Jessie were worried about Annie and she could understand why now, but it was Annie's air of nervousness that struck Flora most, and this was enhanced when the older woman said, 'I've got to be quick, lass. I'm supposed to be out at the shops but they'll be wantin' their dinner.' And then she appeared to just run out of words and stood, gasping slightly and looking straight into Flora's bewildered face.

'Sit down, Mrs McLinnie.' Flora pushed Annie down into Christine's vacant chair, and when the old woman's shoulders remained bowed and her clasped hands – one thumb passing swiftly backwards and forwards over the fingers of the other hand – rested in her lap, again Flora thought, She's not well, she's ill.

And then Annie began to talk, and Flora found she had to sit down too. It seemed someone, a man, had called at the house the night before asking for Shane. 'Late it was, gone half eleven,' Annie said jerkily. 'Arthur an' the lads were in bed but I'd got a bit of ironin' I wanted to finish, it's no good tryin' to do it with my lot millin' about. Anyway, I'd just bolted the back door when he knocked an' nearly made me jump out of me skin. Appeared he wanted a word with our Shane like I said, an' when I told him the lad was abed he said for me to go an' wake him. "Tell him it's about that bit of Danish business, he'll know what I mean," he said. Well, I was a bit rattled, lass, to tell you the truth, him thinkin' he could call at that time of night, but when I said it'd have to wait till mornin' he got nasty. "It's me that's doin' your lad the favour, missus," he said, "an' it's in his interest not to have it broadcast." Well, I was still arguin' with him when our Shane comes down.'

Here Annie was starting to sway gently back and forth in her agitation, and Flora reached out and patted her arm, not knowing what else to do.

'Anyways, our Shane didn't look none too pleased to see this fella with me, an' he'd got him out in the back yard afore you could spit, tellin' me the while to get meself to bed. I went up, lass, but the window was open with it bein' so close an' all, an' I've always had a pair of cuddy lugs on me that could hear the grass grow, 'specially if there's any jiggery-pokery afoot. I couldn't hear everythin', the other fella was talkin' all muffled like, but although our Shane was whisperin' his voice carries, always has done, an' I heard enough to keep me awake all night. He's up to somethin', an' it concerns Rosie's husband, Zachariah. I heard his name a few times an' I reckon he was this Danish business the other fella spoke of. Our Shane means to do him harm, lass. I feel it in me water.'

'Do him harm?' Flora's voice was urgent. 'How, Mrs McLinnie?'

'I wish I knew, lass.' Again Annie rocked herself before she continued, 'But I was thinkin' if you had a word with Davey Connor on the quiet, he'd perhaps frighten our Shane

off? The lad could say he'd heard some talk in one of
the bars, somethin' like that. If our Shane thinks he'll be
fingered it'd put the wind up him sure enough. Oh, lass . . .'
Annie stared into Flora's concerned face. 'I'm worried out
of me wits where this lot could lead.'

So was Flora. She stared at Shane's mother for a few
seconds before saying weakly, 'Oh, Mrs McLinnie.' And
then after a longer pause, 'You've no idea when this . . .
attack is going to take place then?'

Annie shook her head, and they sat looking at each other
for a moment more before she said, 'I didn't know where
else to come, lass. I just couldn't bring meself to tell Rosie
with her so happy with the bairn an' all, an' there's nothin'
Jessie could do except worry herself silly. An' then I thought
of Davey Connor.'

'Don't worry, Mrs McLinnie.' It was a stupid thing
to say in the circumstances but Flora wanted to sound
reassuring. 'I'll see Davey, I promise, and he'll know
what to do.'

'Thank you, lass.' The words were scarcely audible.
'But . . .'

'Yes?'

'Best make it soon, lass.'

'Tonight. I'll see him tonight, Mrs McLinnie.'

Davey stayed for some two hours in the pub, and he wasn't
any nearer to making a decision on the thoughts which
had troubled him earlier as he listened to the men's talk
and catalogue of bitter grievances. When he rose to leave
Ralph said, 'You back home for good then, Davey?' and
he hesitated a moment before he answered.

'I'm not sure. Still thinking about it.'

'By, man, in your shoes I wouldn't have to think over-long.' There was a general nod of acquiescence as Ralph added, his tone harsh, 'You wouldn't see me for dust.'

Once in the street Davey walked quickly, looking straight ahead, but his blank countenance masked a sick tumult of emotion which curdled the beer in his belly. He was going to have to make a decision one way or the other, and soon. Those men had epitomized what he could expect of the future if he stayed round these parts. If he left, if he put everything – and everyone – here behind him, he could work on a farm down south maybe, start afresh?

It was just after eight o'clock when Davey strode down the back lane of Crown Street and into the communal yard which had been witness to him growing up from a babe-in-arms, but now it was number nine he entered, not number eleven. When he opened the kitchen door of Mrs Riley's and saw Flora sitting to one side of the blackleaded range sipping a cup of tea, it was all he could do not to groan out loud.

He hadn't wanted to see her tonight, not tonight. Tomorrow maybe, when he had had time to think about what he was going to do, but tonight his confusion and the churning emotions he was trying to contain made him poor company. Nevertheless, he smiled as he said, 'Hallo there, and what's brought you out the night?'

'I need to speak with you.'

There was no answering smile on Flora's face, and something in her grey eyes stiffened his expression as he said, 'Oh aye? Problems?'

'You could say that.'

He normally had his evening meal with the Rileys when he got home from the shipyard, but since the hot weather he hadn't been able to face the rabbit stew and dumplings

351

or other such fillers Mrs Riley favoured, so now, when the old lady said, 'There's cold meat an' bread an' cheese in the larder, lad,' he answered, 'I'll have it later, Mrs Riley, don't worry.' And to Flora, 'I'll just go and change and then perhaps we can go for a walk?'

There was still no smile on Flora's face as she nodded and then lowered her gaze to the cup in her hand, and when his eyes met those of his landlady, and she raised her eyebrows in mute enquiry, he shrugged his shoulders before leaving the room.

What now? He tried to curb his impatience as he swiftly changed his work shirt for a clean one, before slicking back his thick wavy hair with a touch of brilliantine. Since his sojourn abroad he had rebelled against the regulation caps and mufflers of the north without which no respectable working man would think of leaving the house.

He had to remember the lass had only recently lost her parents in terrible circumstances, and however well she appeared to be coping on the surface, she must still be going through hell underneath.

When he returned to the kitchen Flora had finished her cup of tea and rose immediately, making her goodbyes to Mrs Riley and preceding him to the back door without speaking directly to him, but once they were outside in the lane and walking away from the house, her manner, which had hitherto been constrained, underwent a lightning change. Her voice was charged with urgency when she said, 'I had to come tonight, Davey, I wouldn't have been able to sleep if I hadn't. I just didn't feel it could wait until tomorrow.'

'Steady on, Flora.' He took her arm as she stumbled over a ridge of baked mud in the narrow lane, and then, as they passed a group of children playing chucks in the dusty crevices, he said, 'Wait till we're out in the street, lass, you'll turn your ankle along here if you don't concentrate on where you're treading. Whatever it is it can wait a minute or two more.'

He took his hand from her arm once they reached the solid pavement beyond the dirt back lane, and for a few moments they walked rapidly down the terraced street. He was aware she was in a right stew about something and in an effort to comfort her he said, 'Come on, lass, this isn't like you. Calm down now.'

'How would you know what's like me?'

Her tone checked further commiseration and he stared at her as she continued, 'You don't know anything about me, not really. Good old Flora, bounces back from anything, nothing ever really gets her down. That's what you think, isn't it? Well, I do have feelings, Davey Connor.'

'Aye, aye, lass. 'Course you do.'

'And I'm sick of pretending otherwise while we're on the subject. You're a man, it's so much easier for you. Now isn't it?'

Davey had the feeling he wasn't going to win this one whatever response he made and his face must have spoken for him because in the next moment Flora said, 'I'm sorry, I am, that wasn't fair.'

Davey was feeling embarrassed and somewhat out of his depth, but he was aware there was an element of truth in what Flora had said. He had always tended to expect her to be, if not exactly the clown, then amusing and easygoing. And it wasn't fair.

'Look . . .' Flora's head was down and she didn't look at him as she said, 'Can we go to a café somewhere and sit down? There was one panic after another in the office today, and with this heat and all I don't feel like walking.'

'Aye, yes, all right. There's Prinn's at the end of the next street, or we can call in the Pike and Feather if you fancy a glass of shandy? They've got a little garden at the back with some tables and chairs.'

'Prinn's will be fine.' Her voice was so prim it made him want to smile but he restrained himself.

The café was small and very basic, simply six oilcloth-covered wooden tables with four straight-backed chairs tucked under each, and a large wooden counter down one side which led directly into the owner's kitchen. Apart from Mrs Prinn herself, who appeared immediately the little bell on the door tinkled their entrance, the café was empty, and once Flora had seated herself at a table by the window Davey fetched two cups of tea and two iced buns of dubious freshness.

Flora remained silent for a few moments after he had placed her tea and bun in front of her, and then she said, 'Mrs McLinnie came to see me this afternoon just as I was about to leave work.' As she continued to speak, relating the conversation almost word for word as best as she remembered it, Davey listened with growing incredulity.

'What does this "doing him harm" mean?' Davey asked quietly when she finished speaking. 'Knocking him about a bit, or worse?'

'She didn't seem to know.'

'Did you ask her?'

'Of course I asked her!' Davey's voice had been sharp but Flora's was more so, and now her small frame was bristling as she added, 'What do you take me for anyway?'

'I'm sorry, I'm sorry.' Davey reached out a hand and

gripped one of hers, and as he felt her jerk at his touch, and then become very still, the sudden revelation as to why Flora hadn't yet committed herself to Peter Baxter dawned on him. Why hadn't he seen it before? he asked himself silently. But he had always thought it was Sam Flora had liked; or maybe it *had* been in those days? Whatever, a hundred little incidents that had occurred over the last months suddenly fell into place. And hadn't he begun to think along the same lines anyway, and with Sam gone – and Rosie too, in a different kind of way – there was nothing to stop them.

'What are you going to do about Shane?' Flora's voice was little more than a whisper.

'I'm not sure.' Davey could feel her trembling now beneath his warm flesh and the depth of her feeling for him touched some deep ache of loneliness and need inside himself, even as he removed his hand from hers and settled back in his chair. He drew the air hard between his teeth before he said, his eyes narrowed on her face which somehow seemed small and pitiful, 'But I agree with Mrs McLinnie that something needs to be done. That son of hers wants locking up and they should throw away the key.'

Flora nodded. 'When I think of his face on New Year's Eve I wouldn't put anything past him where Zachariah is concerned.'

'But it's not reasonable, is it, not any of this.' Davey's voice was perplexed. 'Rosie and Shane were seeing each other before I left Sunderland and she didn't go anywhere, it was him who left. What's he got to gripe about now? It was years before she married Zachariah. He had his chance and he blew it.'

Flora lifted her head which had been bowed over her teacup and looked at him. He was so handsome and she loved him so much. He would never meet anyone who could love him as much as she did, and surely that justified what she was about to say? 'Perhaps men like Shane McLinnie don't need a reason as such,' she prevaricated in a small voice. 'He's always liked Rosie, right from when we were all bairns together – you know how it used to worry Sam. And Mrs McLinnie has never believed Shane actually chose to leave Sunderland anyway, she thinks there was some trouble and he was forced to go. Perhaps he expected Rosie to wait for him, I don't know.'

'But wouldn't she have told you that, you being her best friend?'

Flora shrugged. She should have told him the truth straight out when he first came back, she should never have started this lying. But it wasn't really lying, she comforted herself in the next instant. More not telling the whole truth. 'Rosie has never been one for wearing her heart on her sleeve,' she said uncomfortably, 'and perhaps she felt embarrassed, I don't know. I've never liked Shane McLinnie, it might have been that?'

'Maybe. Aye, maybe.'

Flora's face was burning with colour and in the light of his new understanding of how she felt about him Davey put her obvious awkwardness down to the fact that they were discussing the girl she knew he had loved.

How long had Flora felt this way? he asked himself now. Right from when he had first come back to the town? He remembered the warmth of her greeting at that time and it brought a surge of warmth and compassion that surprised him. He'd been a blind fool the last year but it wasn't too late, not for them. Suddenly everything he had been thinking about earlier fell into place and it set his heart hammering.

Flora had always known how he felt about Rosie and yet she still loved him. He'd be a fool to throw that sort of devotion away, wouldn't he? And his feeling for her was a kind of love, not the consuming desire he had felt for Rosie, admittedly, but then what had that sort of love brought him except misery and regret? Marriage was a composite of many things of which the physical side was just a part. He would be in control with Flora, he would never have to suffer the agonies of the damned with her.

'Don't worry, lass.' He bent forward as he spoke, reaching out his hand and lifting her chin with one finger as he brought her eyes up to meet his. 'We'll sort this with Shane out between us, never you fear.'

His face was warm and kind and it made Flora quiver inside. She knew she ought to say something, make a coherent answer, but it was beyond her.

And then, as her trembling became evident, Davey said quietly, 'I'm glad you came tonight although I'd have wished the reason was different. But there's been something I've been meaning to say.'

She froze at his words; only her eyes moved as they searched his face, and his intuition told him she was expecting him to say he was going to leave and his compassion increased. He wanted to make this easy for her. It was the only thought filling his mind now as he continued, 'I care about you, Flora, I hope you know that. I have cared about you for a long time.' He couldn't bring himself to say love. He wanted to – he knew it would please her – but he couldn't.

'I'm no great catch, lass, I know that, none better, but I can promise you I'll look after you and endeavour to do my best by you.'

As a proposal it wasn't the most romantic in the world although Davey thought he had made himself plain, but when Flora gulped, brushing a strand of hair from her cheek as she moved back in her seat, her brow wrinkled, and said, 'I don't understand? What are you saying, Davey?' he realized she hadn't grasped what he was asking.

'I want you to marry me, Flora.'

'Marry . . .' She looked utterly dumbfounded and for a moment he had the crazy notion she was going to refuse him, and then the old impetuous Flora was back as she, half laughing, half crying, said, 'Oh, Davey, Davey! Yes, I'll marry you! Of course I'll marry you,' her face shining like the sun.

He almost expected a rush of panic as it dawned on him what he had done, a feeling that he had made a dreadful mistake, but it didn't come. Instead relief filled him. This sealed the death knell on that other love: it was over; finished. He'd been in limbo for years, he had only fully realized it in the last few moments, but now his life could go on. He smiled at Flora, his eyes soft as he said, 'Can I kiss you? Right now in the open?'

'I don't think an empty café is the open.'

Her voice was eager and he knew that whatever else, they would have no problems regarding their coming together. She wanted him; desire was all too evident in her bright eyes and half-open lips, in the thrust of her breasts as she leant across the table towards him and the moistness of her flesh. She was ripe for marriage.

She shivered as his lips took hers, and although her mouth was responsive he could tell she was still totally innocent. Again the feeling of compassion was strong, but threaded through with a new element, that of protectiveness.

'I love you.' As she sank back down into her seat her eyes were bright and her voice was husky. 'And I'll be a good wife, I promise you that, Davey.'

'And I will be a good husband.' He smiled as he said it, his voice almost light, and Flora wasn't to know it was in the nature of a vow. She was his responsibility now; she'd had a rotten childhood from all accounts and the last six months had been the worst of all, but her life was going to change for the better. He would make sure of that.

Chapter Twenty

After talking the matter through again with Flora and remembering what she'd told him about the part Zachariah's contacts had played in the rescue of Molly, Davey had no hesitation in going straight to Zachariah instead of approaching Shane himself. There was no love lost between him and Annie's youngest, and although Shane's mother had made the suggestion in good faith he couldn't see McLinnie being frightened off by anything he, Davey, might say or do. This needed more force than he could bring to bear. Also, reading between the lines of what Flora had related, there was a possibility nagging away at him that put a whole new perspective on the strength of Shane's enmity against the man Rosie had married. And it was this he broached immediately he was alone with Zachariah the following evening, he and Flora having called at The Terrace ostensibly to tell Rosie and Zachariah of their engagement.

The first few minutes had been difficult but Davey hadn't expected anything else. Flora had been bubbling with happiness, although, as always when the two of them were in Rosie's presence, he detected a tenseness about her that manifested itself in her over-bright voice and inability to sit still.

Zachariah had been hearty in his congratulations, kissing Flora on the cheek and pumping Davey's hand like a piston engine. And Rosie . . . Davey hadn't been able to gauge anything from Rosie's warm felicitations and smiling face, other than the fact that not once in all the minutes before the two women disappeared into the kitchen to make a cup of tea had she met his eyes directly.

But now he came to the matter in hand, brushing away Zachariah's opening conversation on the concern that the recent developments in the coal strike were going to lead to riots, and saying, 'I need to ask you something, something personal, Zachariah, and bear in mind when you answer that I'm asking for a damn good reason and that it will go no further than these four walls.'

Zachariah stared at him for a moment and then settled back more comfortably in his chair before he said, 'Ask away, man.'

Davey raked back his hair from his brow, then rose abruptly and walked over to the ornate mantelpiece, where he stood looking down at the elaborate dried-flower arrangement in the empty grate for a few seconds. Then he turned, looking straight into Zachariah's waiting eyes as he said, 'When Shane McLinnie left Sunderland just after me in 1920, did you have anything to do with it?'

'Aye, an' again atween these four walls I'm proud of the fact.'

There wasn't a moment's hesitation and that made it easier for Davey to say, 'Can you tell me how you did it?'

Zachariah spoke swiftly and concisely as he outlined the events that had led to Shane's ignominious departure and when he had finished Davey nodded slowly. 'Well, I think he's rumbled it was you.'

'Impossible.' Zachariah shook his head decisively. 'The men I used would let their tongues be cut out afore they let on.'

'Maybe, but a careless word . . .'

'Never. They're used to sailin' close to the wind an' keepin' their mouths shut, besides which they're friends of mine from the old days. They wouldn't let on, I'm tellin' you.'

'And there was no one else you told? You didn't mention it to Rosie? Anyone? Think, man. It's important.'

'Rosie an' me weren't close in them days, I was still seein'—'

Zachariah stopped abruptly. And then, 'No, she wouldn't, not Janie.' And to Davey's enquiring gaze, 'I told a lass I was seein' at the time but she wouldn't have said anythin'. Anyway, she's dead now, died a while back.'

'Before or after Shane came back to Sunderland?'

'Not long after.'

'So it's possible he might have heard something from her?'

'No, I'm tellin' you, Janie was a good lass.' Zachariah now stood up himself and repeated, 'As good as gold. I admit she was a bit upset when we called it a day, but we never fell out or anythin'. She wouldn't have dropped me in it, not Janie.'

'A woman scorned, maybe? People can do funny things when they're bitter.'

'No, not Janie, she wasn't like that, an' if anyone had cause to be bitter with what they'd had to put up with, Janie did. Her husband was a swine. But she wasn't bitter, it wasn't in the lass's nature.' And then, as Davey shrugged, Zachariah narrowed his eyes, coming closer and lowering his voice as he asked, 'What's this all about, man? What's afoot?'

'It could be something or nothing. Sit down and I'll tell you.'

Out in the kitchen Rosie was finding it hard to make conversation as though this was just another night. *Engaged.* He had asked Flora to marry him. *They were going to be wed.* It was drumming in her head, along with the warning, Act natural, be glad for her, talk, laugh. She couldn't spoil this for Flora and hadn't she, at the bottom of her, expected just this thing for months? Aye, yes, she had.

Her plans to move further afield, to Lanchester maybe, or even Castleside or beyond, ostensibly to give Erik and any future bairns an upbringing free from the stench and noise of the town, had been partly rooted in this very thing. Not that she hadn't always longed for a rural life herself, but in the last months the need had become urgent. A smallholding or little farm somewhere, a place where she and Zachariah and their family could all work together.

There were times when she felt all their lives – hers and Zachariah's and Flora's and Davey's – were perched together on the top of a powder keg, and it would need only one little spark for the fuse to light and blow them all apart. And she knew what that spark could be. And life was good – it was – for all of them. She and Zachariah had each other and Erik, and Flora had Davey. It was the best thing, it was. That was what she had to tell herself. And before Flora and Davey's wedding she would make sure she and Zachariah had moved right away. And then, pray God, she would start to know peace of mind again.

*   *   *

The two men were having a conversation about nothing more controversial than Sunderland Football Club's successful last season, when Dave Halliday's forty-two goals had meant the club continued to be a force to be reckoned with, when Rosie and Flora entered the room again.

Davey and Flora stayed on for an hour or so, but all four were more than a little relieved, for reasons peculiar to each one of them, when the goodbyes were said. Once the door had closed behind Davey and Flora Zachariah made sure it was locked and bolted, and the downstairs windows secured with the wooden shutters tightly fastened.

As was his wont, Zachariah tiptoed into his son's room before he retired for the night, and he stood for a long while gazing down at the sleeping baby. He was glad Davey had told him about this latest, and although it might be nothing he would have it checked out.

There was a certain contingent down at the docks that were always ready for any sort of dirty work; they were nothing but scum, but scum could always be bought. For the right price they'd blab on their own grandmothers. Aye, he'd have it checked out, and carefully, because there was more than his own self to worry about these days.

Zachariah's expression softened as he gazed on the small form in the cot, who – so everyone was fond of saying – got more and more like him every day, and there came over his whole body an enervating wave that carried fear in its depths. He adored Rosie, he worshipped the very ground his wife walked on, but this feeling for his son – it was unlike anything he had ever imagined himself feeling for any human being. He was unable to put a name to it, the simple word love didn't even begin to cover the height and breadth of what burnt in his soul every time he watched

Rita Bradshaw

his son smile and reach out with his chubby little arms and kick his fat legs; he knew that however many other children he and Rosie might have, and whatever their dispositions and attributes, this child would always hold first place in his heart.

'I thought I'd find you in here.'

Rosie's soft smiling voice from the doorway brought his head swinging round and now he returned the smile, his eyes warm as he followed her out onto the landing. Rosie put her arm in his and like that they walked into their bedroom. She needed Zachariah to make love to her tonight. She needed to feel him inside her, strong and powerful, as he took what was rightfully his. He was a skilful lover as well as a considerate and thoughtful one, and she knew she was lucky in that respect. Although it was never talked about openly in an explicit way, the odd remark by this woman or that, and the many conversations that had gone on amongst the housewives when they were waiting for their orders at the Co-op or just standing about gossiping in corners, had suggested that some men treated their wives with as much finesse as a rutting stallion. But even in the throes of passion, when Zachariah did things she blushed to think about in the light of day, he made her feel treasured. And she was grateful for that, she was. It would have been so much harder if that side of things hadn't been good.

She didn't let her mind dwell on *what* would have been harder, she never did, not since that moment on New Year's Eve when her glance had locked with Davey's and she had read what was in his eyes, and now in repudiation of the shadow of the thing she had to keep buried and dead, she said, 'I love you, Zachariah. Come to bed,' and he, reading what was in her face, didn't need to be told twice.

* * *

Since her marriage Rosie had come to rely more and more on Sally's warm, uncomplicated friendship. It had been a means of brightening some of the dark moments her estrangement with Flora had caused before Christmas, but it was more than that. Sally's tall thin body and ugly face hid a capacity for love and understanding that was quite remarkable, and so Rosie felt it all the more keenly when, the evening after Davey and Flora had told her of their engagement, Sally and Mick called by with the news that they were leaving Sunderland for Ireland.

'I don't want to go.' Sally had wrinkled her nose as she spoke. 'But him, he sees himself as a gentleman farmer now! Isn't that right, Mick?'

'Aw, go on with you. It's daft you're talkin', so it is.'

'See? I swear his accent has got ten times worse since he found out his grandda's left him a smallholdin' back in the "old country". That's what you call it now, isn't it, Mick, the old country? An' here's him only been over "the watter" twice in his whole life!'

'All right, all right.' Mick was taking his wife's ribbing in his usual goodnatured fashion. 'I can't help it if me grandda liked me the best of our bunch, can I? You oughta be glad you've married into wealth anyway.'

'Wealth!' Sally's voice was scathing. 'A bit farm with a few pigs an' cows, an' chickens that don't know which end to lay an egg by the sound of it.'

'You don't want to listen to all me brothers say, now then. It's jealous they are, the lot of 'em. Me grandda's farm was a nice little place from what I remember of it.'

'Aye, from what you remember of it. An' how old was

367

you on your last visit?' his wife asked caustically. 'Refresh me memory.'

'Old enough.' And at her raised eyebrows, 'All right, ten.'

'I rest me case.'

'Aw, come on, Sal. Don't be takin' it like that, lass.'

'An' there's all the trouble out there, an' it's got worse, not better, since the Free State treaty. Tell him, Zachariah.' Sally flung her arms wide as she appealed to Zachariah. 'Tell him we'll wake up to find we've been murdered in our beds.'

'An' you call *me* Irish!' And then, as Sally went to say some more, 'Look, I know you're worried, lass, but me grandda's place is in a nice quiet spot in Southern Ireland, added to which there's plenty of me mam an' da's family still livin' near. We'll be goin' to family an' that makes all the difference. An' our own place, lass. Think of that.'

Sally was clearly unconvinced but just as clearly resigned to the inevitable, and as she looked into Mick's large rough face, his eyes bright with anticipation, she shook her head slowly before saying, 'Oh well, where thou goest, I goest.'

It wasn't what Mick expected and as he stared at her, his mouth slightly agape, she turned to grin at Rosie and Zachariah as she winked and said, 'See? I can still knock him bandy.'

Oh she'd miss Sally. Even as she laughed with the others Rosie felt a dart of pain at her forthcoming loss. Things were going to change and they would never be the same again. Her mother and Hannah were spending more and more time at Mr Green's little house on the outskirts of Hendon, close to Hendon beach. Hannah loved playing on the sands with Mr Green's next-door neighbour's children, and although her sister's timid disposition – so unlike Molly's – made her frightened of the sea, the stream running through Backhouse Park that went into the culverts, or cundies as they were known locally, in the Valley of Love and then came out on the beach, kept her down on the sands with the other children all day long.

Then there was Flora and Davey engaged to be married and already they were talking about moving away. Davey had made out the night before that it was due to the rising unemployment in the area caused by the increasing stranglehold on the mining communities and the steelworks by the government, but even she knew it was the same the whole country over. All right, maybe the north was being hit worse than most by the depression, but he and Flora would be comfortable enough with the money her parents had left her and all. But then, wouldn't it be better in the long run if they left for the south? Yes, it would. It most certainly would. Her thoughts were emphatic.

And now Sally and Mick were going too, and she couldn't blame them. Mick was right to go. Even the Co-op had cut back on its staff lately, and who knew who'd be the next to go? And Mick would find it impossible to get work if he lost his job there. There were a hundred or more men to every job nowadays, some of them having walked miles in the vain hope they might get set on. And it wasn't just the older men, the ones past working age, who hoarded their Woodbine ends in little tin boxes and raided the tips in the dead of night, digging for cinders to hawk about the doors at twopence a bucket. No, it was the young ones too now, some only in their twenties, but a white-faced wife and hungry bairns had made them swallow what little pride they had left after months and months out of work and do what they would have considered unthinkable just a couple of years before.

Rosie had always bought a bucket or two every time they called until, with a mountain of virtually unusable cinders piling up in the cellar, Zachariah had told her he would start answering the door. Word had got round she was an easy touch, he'd said, and it had become ridiculous. So she'd let him go to the door, and the mountain had continued to grow. 'Them poor blighters.' Every time he had doled out another shilling or two he had come and found her, his eyes screwed up with pity. 'By, no man should be reduced to bein' without hope.' Rosie had been thinking the same thing herself, and along with her plans for the move into the country she had been wondering how many jobs a little farm could provide. Her contribution might be a drop in the ocean in the mass unemployment gripping the north, but to the men they could give work to it would be the difference between holding their heads high or grovelling in the gutter.

Just before ten Sally and Mick rose to leave, and Rosie stood too, saying, 'I'll walk with you to the tram stop, I could do with a spot of fresh air.' She called up to Zachariah to tell him where she was going and that she would only be a minute or two – he was nursing Erik back to sleep, the baby having awoken earlier with teething pains – and shut the front door behind her as she followed Sally and Mick down the garden path and out onto the pavement.

They were laughing as they strolled arm-in-arm to the tram stop at the end of the street, Sally at her best as she regaled them with the latest stories from the Store, and as Rosie lifted her face to the cool salty breeze she was conscious of thinking, Things are only going to change, not necessarily be *worse*. I've got to be positive, that's the thing.

And then the next moment she heard Zachariah's voice and turned, her arms still linked in Sally's and Mick's and her face smiling, and saw her husband tearing along the street as fast as his awkward gait would allow, Erik clutched tightly in his arms.

'What is it?' She had wrenched her arms free and met Zachariah a few feet from the tram stop, her stomach turning over at the look on his face. 'What's wrong?'

She couldn't hear what Zachariah said at first – Erik was howling enough to wake the dead – but then, when he repeated, 'You should have *told* me you were leaving the house, I don't want you out here by yourself,' she stared at him in absolute amazement.

'I'm not by myself, I'm with Sally and Mick.' She indicated the other couple who were standing some distance away, clearly bemused by the turn of events. 'Whatever's the matter?'

He didn't answer her, saying instead, 'Here's the tram.'

'*Zachariah.*'

'Later, I'll tell you later. Say goodbye to Sally an' Mick.'

The tram had barely pulled away when Rosie turned to Zachariah, having taken Erik from his arms as she tried to soothe the baby with meaningless nonsense, and said over the fair downy head, 'Well?'

'It's nothin'. I just don't want you out here in the dark by yourself, that's all. Next time you're leavin' like that give me a bit of warnin'.'

'Nothing?' Rosie's voice was too shrill and as Erik began to wail again she lowered it an octave or two as she repeated, 'Nothing? Zachariah, you frightened me to death, and as for it being dark, it's hardly that.' She indicated the dusky twilight with a bob of her head. 'There's still plenty of light and it's really warm.'

'I don't want you out here by yourself, Rosie. That's all.'

'It's not all.' She clutched at him as he made to turn, her eyes enormous in the dim light. 'Something has happened, hasn't it? I want to know, Zachariah. Tell me.'

'It's nothin'.'

Her brows came together. 'Nothing? With you racing down the street yelling your head off?' She bent her body towards him and her voice, although low, was weighty as she said, 'I'm not a child, Zachariah, neither am I stupid. *Tell me.*'

Zachariah stared at her. They had been so happy the last few months, so marvellously, gut-wrenchingly happy. And if he told her, if he related what was no more at bottom than an old woman's fears and imaginings, Shane McLinnie would once again have an insidious and prominent place in their lives. And he didn't deserve it, the scum simply didn't deserve it, damn him. But if he didn't tell her, how could he stop her doing things like this? Natural, ordinary things, but things that just couldn't be done while there was the faintest possibility of that scab skulking around.

He told her. Out in the street, with the warm, flower-scented air from the front gardens vying with the sea-crusted breeze, he told her exactly what Davey had imparted to him the night before. Rosie's grip on her son tightened, and she swallowed twice and moved her head before she managed to say, 'I hate Shane. I do, I hate him.' Zachariah took her arm, bending close to her and pulling her into his body with the baby sandwiched between them.

'It will be all right. Trust me, lass.' He smiled, but for the life of her she couldn't dredge up an answering smile. 'I've put me feelers out an' me arm is longer than his, whatever he might think. We'll soon know if there's anythin' brewin'.'

'How dare he?' Indignation followed hard on the shock, and now Rosie's face was scarlet with anger as she repeated, 'How *dare* he think he can intimidate us, Zachariah? If there *is* anything in this, this is the last time he interferes with my life. I've had enough, more than enough, and I shall tell him so to his face.'

'You won't, lass.' His voice was sharp. 'Now I want your word on that. I don't want you within a mile of that scum.'

Rosie took a step backwards. Zachariah had never used that tone with her before, even in their argument about her going to the brothel to see Molly, and she didn't like it. 'He needs to be told,' she said tightly. 'He seems to think he can do anything he likes.'

'An' he'll find out he can't, right? But you seein' him will do no good at all. Now I'm not jestin', lass. I want your promise you won't get involved in any of this. Come on, promise me.'

'No.'

'No?'

It was their second serious altercation, but then Zachariah cut through her defences when he said, his voice soft and loving and his own again, 'Rosie, lass, I shan't know a moment's peace if you don't. Please, lass.'

In that moment she was tempted to promise him anything, but she couldn't. She stared at him for a second, her eyes soft, and then she said, 'I can't, Zachariah, not in all honesty, but I promise I won't do anything foolish like seeing him alone. Will that do?'

He shook his head slowly. 'Not really, but knowin' you when you get the bit between your teeth it's the best I'm goin' to get, eh?'

His tone was wry, and as he pulled her close again, the baby snuggled between them, Rosie relaxed against him.

He had known all along, hadn't he? Hadn't he? Aye, but he had hoped against hope he was wrong.

It was a few days later and the weather had broken, violent thunderstorms shaking the heavens in the last two days, but this particular evening, although cool, was quiet and still. Zachariah was in the kitchen and Rosie was upstairs in the nursery, and now Zachariah took a hard pull of air deep into his lungs before turning to the man sitting opposite him at the scrubbed kitchen table and saying, 'I appreciate you comin', Alec. An' you say there's no doubt he means to do for me?'

Alec Piper shook his head, his heavy lids unblinking as he looked straight at his friend and said, 'None, Zac. But the man's a fool for all his wheelin' an' dealin'. You've plenty of pals an' that's somethin' that don't seem to have got through his thick skull. You've got to sort this one out, man. You know what I mean? Big Abe could put the frighteners on the bloke who's helpin' McLinnie with his dirty work this time, but what about the next an' the next? If you dinna fix him you're gonna be lookin' over your shoulder for the rest of your days. No, you've got plenty of pals an' you need 'em for this, Zac, an' I don't mean givin' him just a beatin' either. It needs to be permanent.'

'Aye.' Zachariah swallowed deeply, his Adam's apple bouncing in his throat. He knew Alec was just waiting for him to say the word and Shane McLinnie would draw his last breath, but they were talking cold-blooded murder here, damn it. He didn't think he'd be able to sleep at night with a man's blood on his conscience, even blood as tainted and foul as McLinnie's.

'He's bin doin' business with the Gallaghers up in Glasgow, dealin' in all sorts. You know he was in with that bunch?'

'No, no I didn't.' The Gallaghers were notorious far beyond the boundaries of Scotland for their contempt for human life, which was reflected in their empire of hard crime and prostitution rackets. If Shane was one of their boys now he'd sold his soul to the devil.

'He's bin doin' deals for 'em down here, so I understand.'

Zachariah was thinking fast. Smuggling tobacco and the like was one thing, hadn't his own mam and da been up to their necks in the trade, but the Gallaghers were living embodiments of evil. Even so . . . No, he couldn't countenance murder. But if the right people dealt with this, Shane McLinnie wouldn't make the mistake of coming after him again. Alec's cohorts could be very persuasive; he had seen the results of some of their inducements and it wasn't pretty. It would do the trick; Alec could make Shane wish he'd never been born.

'He needs teachin' a lesson, that's for sure, but to tell you the truth, Alec, I'm not too keen on the other. I've not the stomach for it.'

'He wouldn't think twice about doin' you in, man. That's what this is all about, for cryin' out loud.'

'Aye I know, I do know, but it don't alter what I feel in me guts. A good hidin', somethin' he'll carry for the rest of his life is enough.'

Alec cast a sideward glance at his friend before shaking his head slowly. 'You're playin' a dangerous game, Zac. Far better to do the job clean. He's down at the docks most nights an' it could be quick an' painless if that's the way you want it. Meself I'd make the scum suffer a bit first if he was after me or mine.'

Zachariah didn't comment on this. He knew Alec wasn't jesting and there was nothing he could say. There was silence for a minute or two and Zachariah poured them both another tot of whisky from the bottle on the table before he said, 'An' it was planned for the day after next, you say?'

'Aye. Seems you go into Gateshead on the last Thursday of the month an' call in for a bevvy with Tommy Bailey on the way back? Well they must've bin watchin', 'cos they've got it all clocked. Makes sense when you think about it, them goin' for the pair of you when you leave the pub. Fights happen like that all the time.'

Zachariah nodded. Aye, it made sense all right. Two men involved in a bust-up was different to a man alone being set upon. And if one poor devil was left lying dead in a dark street that was just a fight that had gone too far, wasn't it?

'Seems you normally have a drink in the Dog and Rabbit?' Alec was still talking. 'Well, it would've bin your last one.' He leant back in the seat and surveyed Zachariah through slitted eyes. 'Still want to turn the other cheek?'

'I'm not talkin' about turnin' the other cheek, man, an' you know it. What if . . .' Zachariah tapped his fingers on the arms of the wooden chair in which he was sitting a number of times before he continued, his voice low, 'What if I went to Gateshead as normal an' got back at me usual time, everythin' nice and friendly. An' me an' Tommy have our darts an' pint, but there's a couple of extras in the pub that night, know what I mean? An' they happen to leave just after us but careful like. An' they see these fellas attack us . . .'

'Aye, I know just the type. Invisible when they want to be.'

'An' they'll keep their mouths shut?'

'Need you ask? But I still reckon you ought to have the job done properly. The more I hear about this bloke McLinnie the less I like him.' Alec downed his drink in one gulp and stood up. 'But there's no changin' your mind once it's made up, I know that of old. I just hope you don't live to regret it.'

'It worked with Charlie Cullen.' Zachariah grinned as he too rose from the table, but when there was no answering smile on Alec's face he leant across and tapped the other man's arm as he said, 'I don't have a choice, man, that's the thing. I couldn't look me little 'un in the face when he's older if I had blood on me hands.'

Alec looked at him for a moment before pursing his lips and shaking his head. 'By, I'm glad I'm not a family man, Zac, that's all I can say. If this is what bein' wed does to you, you can keep it.'

It was heartfelt, and now Zachariah was smiling broadly. 'Aye, well, everyone to their own, Alec, eh? I wouldn't swop my lot for all the tea in China an' that's the truth.'

Alec had gone and Zachariah was in the garden when Rosie came downstairs. The leaves on the trees were trembling slightly and the twilight was golden-hued, the air scented with the summer smell that comes after rain, as she plumped down beside him on the garden bench. 'What are you doing sitting out here? It's a bit chilly.'

'Is it?' Zachariah had turned to her as she sat down, and

now he continued to stare at her, taking in every contour of her face. He had already decided he wasn't going to tell her what Alec had discovered, so now, when Rosie said, 'Well? What did Alec have to say?' he answered, 'Just reportin' on how things are goin', that's all. Didn't want me to think he wasn't botherin', I suppose.'

Rosie looked at him long and hard before she said, 'And?'

'Nothin' to tell as yet.'

'I see.' She had suspected he was going to try and keep her out of this and so she had felt no compunction in listening to his conversation with Alec from her vantage point in the hall. And of the two men she had to admit she felt Alec had a more realistic understanding of Shane McLinnie. Not that she could countenance cold-blooded murder any more than Zachariah could. But there were other ways to deal with Shane McLinnie and make sure he was put away for good.

They continued to sit in the garden until it was quite dark. Not kissing, not even talking, just holding each other close in the cool soft darkness as the world outside their sanctuary fell silent and even the birds stopped their twittering and settled down for the night. But although she sat quietly, even serenely, Rosie was far from quiet and serene inside.

Shane McLinnie meant to do Zachariah harm; perhaps even her too? Or worse than anything, their baby? All these months of silent intimidation had been building up to something, and she was surprised and even a little shocked at the depth of her loathing for Annie's son.

It had been there for some time and she could pinpoint the exact moment that contempt and dislike had hardened to hatred. Since that moment on New Year's Eve when she had looked into Shane's contorted face she hadn't known real peace. And it had got worse since Erik had been born. Every time she contemplated that tiny face which was such a perfect miniature of his handsome father, she felt a fierce protectiveness that made her heart gallop. She would kill anyone who tried to hurt their child, she would, and without a moment's hesitation. But handled right, this could end without any bloodshed.

Alec was right in so much as you couldn't frighten Shane, and he wouldn't be stopped with a beating either – even the kind that Alec had in mind – so that left only one option as far as Rosie could see, because the man who had spat his venom at them on New Year's Eve was beyond reasoning with. He always had been.

Several miles away, Annie was saying exactly the same thing. 'You're beyond talkin' to, that's the truth of it. I dinna understand you, even if you are me own.'

Shane was sitting at the kitchen table stolidly eating his evening meal. The others had had theirs long ago and left the house for some meeting or other in support of the latest strike at the steelworks; Annie wasn't sure where, or even what it was all about. He didn't bother to raise his head as his mother finished speaking. 'No? Well I shan't lose too much sleep over that.'

Annie stood looking down at the fair head of her youngest and a surge of terrifying emotion filled her, causing her to turn quickly before she gave way to it. How could you love someone and hate them at the same time? Was it possible? And then the voice was harsh in her head as it said, Don't ask the road you know. Oh, dear God, dear Lord, help me. Father Bell promised me You would and You have, You have. Don't stop now when I need You most. He means to do that little lassie and her family some mischief . . .

She heard the sound of a plate being pushed across the wooden table and then Shane's voice saying, 'I'm ready for me puddin'.'

Normally she would jump to – he was the only one in regular employment and as such could reasonably demand that his meal be on the table whatever time of the day or night he came home – but this night the pain in her stomach was worse, added to which she knew she had to speak. And so she swung round and reached for the empty plate, picking it up before she said, 'I'm gonna ask you one more time. What did that dockside scum want with you the other night?'

'An' I'll tell you one more time, it's nowt to do with you.'

'I'll tell yer da an' the lads—'

'Me da an' the lads?' He parroted her words with sudden viciousness and in the moment it took for her to take a step backwards he had risen so quickly his chair went skidding across the stone-flagged floor to crash against the far wall. 'How many times have I heard that, Mam? Your da an' the lads? An' do you know what you always say when you're talkin' about us, all of us? "Our Arthur, the lads an' Shane." Or sometimes, "the lads an' Shane". I used to think it was because I was the youngest, but I dinna any more.'

'I dinna know what you're on about.' Annie had backed up against the range now, she could feel fierce heat against her back, but still he advanced. Did she say that? And all these years he'd never let on what he'd been thinking.

'I'm on about me bein' different, that's what I'm on about,' he ground out through clenched teeth, his face a mottled red. 'You, you've always seen to it I'm different, haven't you. Right from when I was a bairn you've seen to it. "The lads an' Shane." ' '

Annie could feel the skin on the back of her elbows where her sleeves were rolled up beginning to singe, but she didn't dare move. He was right in front of her, his face an inch or so away from hers as he bent over her, and it was like that he said, 'Me da's never made me feel like you do, not once.'

Maybe if he hadn't been looking directly into her eyes, or perhaps if she had had some warning of what he was going to say she could have prepared herself, but as she felt the words register in her eyes she saw his gaze tighten and she knew he must have noticed her reaction.

'What?' He took her arm, and now she actually cried out as he shook her so that her teeth rattled. 'Why did you look like that?' And then suddenly she was free, and he had taken a step backwards as he stared at her without speaking and she stared back.

'No, I dinna believe it,' he said at last.

'What?' His voice had been frightening.

'Not a great fat piece like you.'

'What are you on about?' But she knew what he meant and she also knew she had to deny it and keep on denying it if she was going to live to see another day. There was murder in his eyes.

'If I thought . . .' His voice trailed away and then he said, 'The wrong side of the blanket, aye, that'd explain a lot.'

'What are you sayin'?' And then, as though the import of his words had only just hit home, she bellowed, 'You dirty-minded devil! If I live an' breathe! For one of me own . . . I can't believe what I'm hearin'! Get out of me house with your foul thinkin'!'

It seemed to take him aback for a moment, but then he

said, very slowly, 'If I thought you'd done that I'd strangle you with me bare hands, aye, an' take pleasure in it.'

Annie's eyes were stretched wide now but there was no time for fear. She had to convince him, she had to, she didn't dare to contemplate anything else. She drew in a sharp intake of breath, and then, bending towards him and her voice low but weighty, she said, 'Lad, if you think that for one minute you can get out of me house an' stay out. I never thought to see the day when I'd turn one of me own out on the street, but so help me, I will. I've not had much in me life, an' God's me witness to that, but I've me pride. Aye, I've me pride.'

Again they were staring at each other and she could almost see his brain assimilating what she had said, probing, questioning. He was no fool, her Shane – hadn't his father been one of the craftiest so-and-sos who ever walked God's good earth? – so she had to force herself not to sink to the floor in relief when his eyes flickered twice and he said, 'All right, all right, don't take on.'

'Don't take on?' She felt the blood rushing over her face and her body in a great flood and prayed he would think it was with fury, and now her voice was high as she said, *'Don't take on?* Do you know what you just said to your own mam?'

And then she had to warn herself not to overdo the indignation because his gaze narrowed on her hot face and his voice was very cold, and not at all penitent as he said, 'Aye, like I said, don't take on. Likely I was wrong, we all make mistakes, but I tell you one thing—' And now he paused deliberately for some long seconds, his eyes telling her something she had been trying to hide from herself for years – that her son, her own son, didn't like her – before he continued, 'You an' me are gonna have to have a long talk sometime soon, Mam. Aye, a long talk.'

She knew she should have come back with something sharp but for the life of her it was all she could do not to collapse into a chair, and then he had turned and was gone, and she was left shaking from head to foot until the pain in her stomach became so bad she stumbled into the scullery and was sick into the deep stone sink.

The next morning Rosie awoke very early, and by the time Zachariah was awake Erik had been bathed and fed and was back in his cot fast asleep.

'You're sprightly this mornin', lass.' Zachariah sniffed appreciatively at the bacon and eggs Rosie placed in front of him as he sat down at the kitchen table.

'I need to go into town for a few things for Erik. He'll sleep till mid-morning now and I'll be back before lunchtime if I catch the nine o'clock tram.'

'No hurry, lass, you take your time an' browse a bit if you've a mind, you know me an' him will get along just fine.'

When Rosie arrived in the East End she made for West Wear Street, just off East Cross Street, where the police station was situated. Her heart was in her mouth as she approached the building, passing the terraced houses that stretched down the street without even seeing the children playing on the narrow pavements as she rehearsed what she was going to say for the umpteenth time.

She knew whom she was going to ask for – Constable Browning, the policeman who had dealt with Molly's first disappearance years before. Although she had only spoken with the ruddy-faced middle-aged man a few times he had been both sympathetic and friendly, and she felt it was something of a link, however tenuous.

When Rosie entered the arched doorway of the building she stood for a moment or two before proceeding to the reception area where a young policeman asked her her business.

'Constable Browning?' He stared at her as he wondered what this young pretty lass wanted with his colleague. 'Aye, I'll see if he's about, lass. You come and wait in here and I'll see what I can do.'

She was guided into a small room which had a bench attached to one wall and a wooden table and two chairs set in front of a barred window. The bars brought her stomach churning but she sat down quietly on the bench, her hands in her lap and her face composed, and then the door closed behind her and she was alone. It was a minute or two before it opened again and Constable Browning entered.

'You want to see me, lass?' She had given her name to the young policeman but now, when Constable Browning said, 'Price? You weren't Price the last time we met, were you, lass?' she realized he couldn't have recognized it.

'Oh no, no, how silly of me. I got married. You knew me as Ferry? You came to the house when my sister . . . got lost.'

If Constable Browning noticed the moment of hesitation he did not comment on it. 'Aye, I remember. Well, what can I do for you this time, lass?'

Where to begin? Rosie stared into the kind blue eyes somewhat helplessly as her mind raced, and then she spoke her thoughts as she said, 'I really don't know where to start.'

Constable Browning looked at her for a second before

walking across to the middle of the room and picking up one of the chairs. He placed it in front of the bench where Rosie was sitting and as he sat down he said, 'You take all the time you need, lass, and start right at the beginning, eh?'

Rosie told him it all, starting with Sam's warning to her when she had been a young bairn and finishing with the conversation she had overheard between Alec and Zachariah the night before, although she left out the unlawful suggestions Alec had made pertaining to Shane's future. Neither did she think it prudent to reveal Alec's name.

'Aye, well I can see why you were a mite worried, lass.' Constable Browning settled back in his seat as she finished talking and surveyed her through half-closed eyes as he shook his head slowly. 'And you did the right thing in coming here if only half of what you tell me is true. And you're sure this man, this Shane McLinnie, has been dealing with the Gallaghers?'

She had noticed him sit up straighter when she had first mentioned the name, and now she nodded firmly. 'Quite sure.' The name was obviously known to the Sunderland police. 'And even this man my husband was talking to seemed to think the Gallaghers were the lowest of the low.'

'He's right an' all, lass, and the fewer of their lackeys we have around here the better for all decent folk.' There was a moment's silence before the constable jumped to his feet saying, 'You wait here a minute while I get the sergeant, and then you tell him everything you've just told me. All right?'

Rosie nodded.

'And don't you be frightened of Sergeant Musgrave, he looks a bit grim but he's a good bloke.'

She nodded again. Sergeant Musgrave wouldn't frighten her. There was only one man she feared, and with good reason. It would be stupid for her to assume she was invincible, especially against a man who knew no boundaries of right or wrong and would stop at nothing to accomplish his ends.

Sergeant Musgrave was a slightly older version of Constable Browning, and once Rosie had convinced him it was useless to try to reason with Zachariah, and that her husband would only call off his visit to Gateshead and arrange something else at a different time with his informant if he caught wind of any police involvement, he listened to her without interrupting. 'And you're sure you don't know the name of this man who is going to help your husband?' There was a long moment of silence, and the sergeant's face was grim. 'Think on, lass.'

'No. No I don't.'

'Pity.' And when Rosie made no comment: 'In a case like this well-meaning friends can be more of a hindrance than a help.'

'Yes, I suppose so.'

He wasn't going to draw her out, and he must have realized this because his manner became more crisp and businesslike as he made a note of names, times and other details pertaining to the following night.

It was almost eleven o'clock when Rosie left the police station but she still couldn't buy what she needed to convince Zachariah she had been shopping. The real business of the morning wasn't finished, not by a long chalk, she thought grimly as she set off for the waterfront.

Very little surprised Alec Piper, but his mouth was agape as he listened to his friend's wife some thirty minutes later.

For her part Rosie had been taut with nerves as she had picked her way along the quayside in search of Alec's place, but she had found the building without mishap and although she had nearly jumped out of her skin when Alec's guard dogs – two massive brutes which resembled wolves – had all but torn the door apart at her knock, she had kept her composure, even if her heart had pounded like a drum.

As she finished speaking Rosie was aware of two things simultaneously: one, Alec was looking at her with more than a modicum of respect, and two, he hadn't altogether liked what she had related.

'You've got the polis in? Well, there's no way my lads will show their faces with the law sniffin' about, lass.'

'They will if you tell them to, Alec. We both know that.'

Alec stared at the slim young woman in front of him, and it came to him that in spite of her delicate loveliness she was tougher than most of the men he knew; but it was her unconscious charm that was the real killer. And this was confirmed when she reached out and gripped one of his hands in the next instant as she said, 'You're Zachariah's friend and I know you've helped us before, and I'm grateful, very grateful, but this is even more important, Alec. You heard Zachariah last night, he won't change his mind and he thinks he can stop Shane.'

'An' you don't think he can?'

'I know he can't.'

They were in a large room on the second floor of the three-storey building, and although the room was furnished in the manner of a sitting room there were numerous boxes and casks and sacks stacked all around its walls, the contents of which Rosie wouldn't have wanted to hazard a guess at.

'Aye, well I'd have to agree with you on that, lass, but I've never had no truck with the polis afore. We sort out our own problems in this neck of the woods, an' it goes agen the grain to do the law a favour.'

'You aren't, not really; only Zachariah.' Rosie's voice was quiet as she released his hand and walked across to the grimy window from which only a patch of blue sky was visible. Funnily enough this was the second window today she had seen with bars. The irony of it would have made her smile in different circumstances. She turned to face Alec, who was standing in the middle of the room, his eyes hard on her, and said, 'I love my husband, Alec. I love him very much, and the only way we will ever know any peace of mind is for Shane McLinnie to be locked away for long enough for us to make a new life, far from here. It's not enough that he might be arrested tomorrow for attacking Zachariah, he'd be out in no time, but if something was found on him when the police take him in . . . That would be a different story.'

'Meaning . . . ?'

Rosie sat down on a hardbacked chair to one side of the window feeling in need of its support, but she was taut on the edge of the seat as she continued: 'Something to do with his dealings with the Gallaghers. There is going to be a fight, isn't there, we know that, and he wouldn't feel something being slipped into his pocket.'

Alec let his breath out between his blackened teeth in a slow hiss. 'If this goes wrong an' the Gallaghers get involved—'

'It won't go wrong, Alec, I promise. If some of the stuff Shane is dealing in could be used against him I'd say that was poetic justice, wouldn't you? And you know the type of man he is, you'd be doing the world a favour.'

'An' you think I could get somethin', is that it?'

'Alec, I think you could get the crown jewels if you wanted to.'

When Rosie saw the slow smile on his face she knew she was winning, and his voice reflected this when he said, 'A bit of butterin' up works wonders, eh, lass? Aye, well I did hear of a job recently that caused a few red faces among some of Sunderland's finest. Seems Mr Farley, him that lives in Farley Hall an' is a magistrate an' close friend of the chief constable? Well, it seems his mansion was robbed an' his lady wife's jewellery went missin'. Beautiful pieces some of 'em, so I understand, an' naturally they'd be inclined to throw the book at the so-an'-sos that did the wicked deed, if they could catch 'em, that is. If somethin' from that little haul was found about McLinnie's person . . . Now, just supposin' that comes to pass, do I take it you don't want Zac knowin' owt aforehand?'

'You know him, he's as stubborn as a mule at times. He won't agree to this.'

'Aye, well right at this minute I'm thinkin' it takes one to know one, lass.' His smile widened. 'But one thing's for sure, I won't make the mistake of payin' you a visit an' speakin' in the kitchen out of earshot like.' Rosie had confessed to her eavesdropping the night before, which Alec had seemed to find amusing.

'I had to do that, I knew Zachariah would try and do something foolish. Will you do it, Alec? Will you help us again? Please? If Shane McLinnie could be locked away for a good few years, we could move far away from here, Zac and me and the bairn – far enough that he could never find us.'

389

They looked at each other for a moment, the slender, well-dressed and quietly spoken young woman and the hard, rough miscreant, and then Alec said by way of answer, a twinkle deep in his cold eyes, 'I've never felt inclined to tie the knot meself, lass, never fancied the idea of a woman layin' down the rules, an' by gum you've proved me right sure enough.'

But it was a compliment and Rosie recognized it as such, and when she grinned at him and said, 'I'll tell Zachariah afterwards, once everything's sorted and Shane is caught and behind bars,' he laughed out loud.

'Aye, well just make sure I'm well clear when you do, lass, 'cos he'll be after havin' me guts for garters sure enough.'

Chapter Twenty-One

'I don't like this, Zachariah. I hope you know what you're doing.'

'Stop worryin', man, you're as bad as him.' Zachariah thumbed at Tommy Bailey, who was sitting next to Davey at the pub table and looked scared to death. 'Look, I've told you, Alec has a couple of blokes watchin', an knowin' Alec they'll be able to cope with anythin'. I only told you about tonight 'cos I thought it was only right to put you in the picture, you havin' tipped me the wink in the first place. An' there's no need for you to come instead of Tommy.'

'It's better I do.' Davey's voice was quiet but his face was troubled. Tommy Bailey was a small man and very slight; if something went wrong he would be of no help to Zachariah against Shane McLinnie and his professional thug and they all knew it.

'It's near enough nine. If we're goin' we'd better be makin' tracks.' And then Zachariah looked straight at Davey and his voice didn't falter as he said, 'I appreciate this, man. You turnin' up like this.'

'Aye, well let's just stick close and keep our wits about us, eh?' Davey smiled as they rose to leave, and as the two of them stepped down into the street he tried to act as naturally as possible but it was difficult. There was something about all this he didn't like – it was a bit too much like stepping willingly into the lion's den.

It was still quite light and there was even the odd child playing out at the top end of the street where the terraced houses were, but Zachariah and Davey turned in the opposite direction towards the tram stop. The street was a long one and the Dog and Rabbit was situated halfway along on the left-hand side adjoining the high wall of a factory with a school beyond. On the opposite side of the road was another long high brick wall enclosing the grounds of a Catholic church, and beyond that a laundry, so effectively the street became little more than a tunnel at that point, with any activity at the top end where the houses were.

The tram stop was round the corner of the street they were presently walking down and part way into the next one, which was called Sadlers Row. Sadlers Row was even lonelier, being made up of shops on one side followed by a large area of waste ground, and facing this on the other side ran ten terraces called groves. There were eight houses with eight more back-to-back to each terrace, and they were dismal.

Just before they turned the corner, and as two young children of eight or nine darted past them in the deepening twilight, their bare feet making little sound on the dusty pavement, Davey risked a quick glance behind him. There were two figures some distance behind, but they were strolling slowly from what he could make out. They could be Alec's men but there was no way of knowing for sure.

'There's a couple of blokes behind us, Zachariah, but they're a long way off if there's any trouble.'

'Aye, well I can't see sight nor sound of the organ grinder

or his monkey,' Zachariah said quietly under his breath. 'Maybe they've bin frightened off. Alec said he'd be careful but it don't take much to— Hold on, what's to do?'

They had just reached the last shop with the waste ground stretching before them, and Davey was never very sure of the sequence of events in the following minutes. As two figures emerged like bullets out of a gun from behind the wall of the shop, a fist caught him full between the eyes causing him to rock backwards but then he was fighting for his life, or so it seemed, as the big, thickset gorilla with Shane was on top of him with fists and feet. He heard shouts which he took to be Alec's men, but he was having his work cut out merely to defend himself and he knew a moment's panic: his opponent was bigger and heavier and altogether nastier than him, and plenty of his own punches were missing their target.

Just as Alec's men reached them he saw Zachariah go down, but then the reinforcements were on Shane, bearing him to the ground even as Shane was aiming his big hobnailed boots at Zachariah's crumpled body.

The shrill whistle and shouts of 'Police, lads! Stay where you are!' cut through the pandemonium in a moment, but in the instant Davey's attacker turned tail and ran, one of Alec's men who was grappling with Shane gave a horrible groan and rolled over, and then the other was clutching at his arm and screaming blue murder. Davey saw the glint of silver and then the knife itself, but it still took a second more for the realization that Shane had used a knife on them to register. He'd meant work all right, Davey thought feverishly. It had been Zachariah he'd intended to use that on.

Davey saw two policemen do a flying tackle on the gorilla a few yards away but Shane was already up on his feet and preparing to run. Zachariah was now in a sitting position and shaking his head like a boxer after the knock-out blow, but as Shane sprinted down the street Davey didn't think twice. He thought he was going to get away, did he? Over his dead body.

He heard Zachariah shout for him to stop as he tore down the street after Shane, but his eyes were fixed on the figure in front of him. He could hear footsteps behind him as he wove in and out of the myriad back lanes and alleyways, but he didn't look back to see who was following. He knew instinctively where Shane was making for. The docks. He would make for the docks like a rat to its hole, and in the web of brothels and gin houses and tenement slums he would attempt to go to ground. He wouldn't be the first to disappear down there either. But McLinnie wouldn't get away, not if Davey had anything to do with it.

As he continued the chase his breath was fire in his chest and he felt his lungs were ready to explode; but for the backbreaking years on the farm and the hard grind of the shipyard he would never have been able to keep up the punishing pace. But he couldn't lose him. Shane'd intended to kill Zachariah the night – he hadn't been messing with that knife – and he'd try again if he wasn't stopped. It was the one thought, the only thought, in Davey's pounding head as he followed the fleeing figure into the rabbit warren surrounding the docks.

The July night was warm and muggy and the sweat was pouring off him, his hair as wet as if he'd been underwater, and in spite of the urgency he was moving slower now, totally spent – but so was Shane McLinnie. They were both stumbling rather than running, and as they passed house after house where dirty, runny-nosed bairns were sitting on stone doorsteps, sometimes with a black-shawled woman watching them but more likely than not left to their own devices, he was aware of the pungent smell of unwashed humanity.

It was now nearly ten o'clock on a July weekday evening, and the docks were alive with activity, but of a different sort from during the day when the tugboats, pilot cobles, cargo vessels and the like churned the water, and the slowly dying secondary industries of ropemakers, fish-curers and many others spawned the banks.

Now the dark shadows were populated with sailors and visiting merchants and local men out for an evening pint, as well as the thieves and whores and vagabonds who preferred the night hours to go about their business.

Davey had nearly lost his footing a few times on the remains of gutted fish and offal and excrement as he panted after Shane, so when he saw the other man sprawl full-length he knew immediately what had happened. Shane was already scrambling to his feet as Davey reached him, the pool of rancid debris causing him to slip and slide as he struggled for balance. For a moment all the two men could do was stare at each other as they laboured for breath, their limbs quivering with exertion.

Shane was the first to speak. 'Look, Connor, me quarrel's with the other 'un, not you. It's that runt I was after an' I'd have thought you of all people'd understand why. How can you bear the thought of him touchin' her, maulin' her? He's not a man—'

'He's more of a man than you'll ever be.' Davey's lower jaw was jutting out and his voice was a low growl.

Shane stared at him for a moment before he said, 'I'm tellin' you, you don't know what he is. It was him who put the screws on me six years ago. Did you know that?'

Davey didn't answer this directly but what he did say was, 'An' who told you that fairy story? You can't trust any of them round here, they'd as soon sell their own soul as spit.'

'It's the truth I'm tellin' you, I got it from the horse's mouth, or as good as. It was from his woman, his whore. He'd bin visitin' her for years afore he got rid of her when he set his sights on Rosie, an' he used to talk to her, this Janie, the two of 'em were as thick as thieves. She told me.'

'An' you'd trust what she said when she'd been given the elbow?'

'She didn't know I knew him.' Shane took a long hard pull of air. 'She had no idea who I was, I never give her me real name. I made on I was fallin' for her an' then one time when she'd had a drop too much an' was in a chatty mood I steered the talk round.'

They could both hear shouts coming nearer, and as Shane darted a quick glance behind him, Davey said, 'Where is she? I'd like to talk to this Janie.'

'Six foot under.'

'Six . . . ? You did her in?'

'No, no, man.' Shane's tongue flicked over his lips and then he said, 'It wasn't like that. Like I said, she'd had too much, she'd got to be a real soak an' she was one of them that couldn't hold it. She got maudlin an' started talkin' an' I must've said somethin', I dinna remember what, 'cos the next minute she's tumbled who I am an' the silly bitch starts screamin' enough to wake the dead. I was just tryin' to stop her screamin', that was all.'

'*You killed her.*'

Davey's tone told Shane he wasn't going to talk the other man round, and now the shouts and footsteps were almost on them. Shane's hobnailed boot came up into Davey's groin with enough force to send Davey stumbling backwards as he clutched himself in agony, but it was that movement that saved him from the thrust of the knife at his throat.

In spite of the pain ripping through his vitals he tried desperately to stay on his feet, and in the moment he raised his head and saw Shane bearing down on him and thought, I'm finished, I'm done for, he saw something catch Shane on the side of his head and send him spinning over the edge of the quay into the black water.

Only then did Davey allow himself to fall to his knees, and almost immediately the policeman who had thrown his truncheon at Shane reached him, two more pounding up a moment or two later.

He was going to be sick. Davey tried to fight the nausea but it was overpowering, and as he heaved his heart up on the filthy cobbles he could taste blood. He was shivering when he finished, and as the policemen helped him to his feet and he stood with them, and one or two interested onlookers to the incident who hadn't melted away as soon as the police arrived, he watched the first policeman, who had dived into the water after Shane, being helped onto the side of the quay. The man glanced across at his colleagues either side of Davey and shook his head slowly. Shane McLinnie was dead.

'And if I hadn't have got the police involved, what then? They said you were getting the worst of it and they only just arrived in time as it was. You could have been *murdered*, Zachariah.'

'How could I know it'd turn out like that, lass? I thought

we'd be all right with Alec's men to hand, it was all supposed to go like clockwork.'

'Clockwork! You expected it to go like *clockwork*?'

It was four o'clock in the morning, and Rosie and Zachariah had just got home, courtesy of Joseph's Morris Cowley. Jessie's beau had been marvellous. It had been Joseph – once Zachariah had asked the police to contact him – who had driven Jessie over to Roker so she could stay with little Erik while Joseph took Rosie to the Sunderland Infirmary. He had waited while Zachariah and Davey had their respective wounds stitched; Zachariah had a nasty cut from his temple down to his right ear, and Davey had a deep gash over one eye.

Then the police had taken statements from Alec's men, both of whom had lost a considerable amount of blood but were not in any danger, and Zachariah and Davey. Following that, Joseph had driven Davey home – Alec's men would be in the hospital for a few days yet – before taking Rosie and Zachariah back to Roker and collecting Jessie.

Zachariah looked at Rosie. He had known the woman he had married was one in a million, but he still found it hard to believe she had managed to make cohorts of Alec and the police, but as he – and maybe a couple more besides – might well be lying in the morgue tonight but for Rosie's intervention, there was very little he could say. 'I'm sorry, lass.' He suddenly sounded like a little boy and this impression was strengthened when he added, perfectly seriously, 'But it wasn't my fault, Rosie. I thought I was doing the best thing in keepin' it from you, I didn't want you worried out of your mind, lass. Besides.' He tried an appealing smile. 'You shouldn't listen to private conversations.'

Rosie didn't smile back. She stared at him unblinkingly as she said, 'Oh yes I should where you are concerned, Zachariah. You could have been killed tonight.' And Davey too. Yes, Davey too. The both of them. She would have gone mad then, knowing it was over her; and it was, at bottom. Was she glad Shane McLinnie was dead? The answer wasn't slow in coming, and it made her want to cross herself for protection against the punishment God would surely inflict for being glad someone was dead.

'But I wasn't.' The smile turned into a grin, his blue eyes brilliant in the muted lighting in the sitting room. 'An' I'm ready to admit me wife knew best in this instance. Now, I can't say fairer than that, can I? An' I swear on the bairn's life that I'll never keep anythin' from you again, whatever the circumstances. How about that, lass?'

'Zachariah, I know when I'm being soft-soaped.' But she couldn't help smiling. She had never known anyone who could turn on the charm like Zachariah.

'I love you, lass.' They were sitting on the sofa and he took her face in his big hands. 'I just wanted to get things straight for you an' the bairn. That man was hangin' over this family like a big black cloud an' it couldn't have gone on. Maybe it never would have been settled for good until one of us was dead, thinkin' about it now.'

'I believe that,' Rosie said a little shakily. 'After what Davey repeated to the police about what Shane had said, I know he'd never have given up until he had settled the score with you, and in his book that would have meant murder. He was a disturbed man, Zachariah. Looking back he always has been, even as a young boy. But I feel sorry for Annie. Whatever else, he was her son and she loved him. I must go and see her in the morning.'

'Aye, you do that, lass. I've nothin' against the rest of that family, far from it. It's amazin' to me that Shane's related to 'em. When I think of the way he wielded that knife . . .'

As Rosie began to weep for the first time Zachariah recognized the tears were remedial and held her tight in his arms. After a while they went upstairs and lay, fully dressed, on their bed as they continued to hold each other close.

'I love you so much, Zachariah.' Dawn was casting a pale pink glow across the room as Rosie spoke and neither of them had been to sleep. 'When I look back over the last few years I don't know what I would have done without you and that's the truth. You . . . you've been my salvation.'

'That's a bit ripe, lass.' He turned towards her and looked into her face as he continued, 'But it's the way I feel about you so I won't say you're exaggeratin'. I never thought to have a family, bairns an' such. The way I am . . . well, to tell you the truth, I was scared to try in case history repeated itself. An' then you came along an' suddenly it was worth tryin'.'

'If Erik grows up to be half the man his father is he won't go far wrong.' Rosie's voice vibrated with the depth of her emotion and for a long minute they looked into each other's eyes, and whatever Zachariah read in Rosie's must have satisfied him because he smiled the sweetest smile she had ever seen and settled down into her arms, his head against her breasts.

'We both need a bit of shut-eye, lass. There's a bairn not far from here who'll take no account of his mother's exhaustion come feed time. Mind you, I don't blame him. If I was feedin' where he's feedin' I'd yell me head off for me rights an' all.'

'Oh, Zachariah.' She nudged him with her arm, kissing

the top of his fair head where it rested under her chin as she did so before shutting her eyes and settling down herself.

She must have slept, and for once Erik didn't demand his feed dead on the dot of six o'clock, because it was nearly eight when she heard his first wah of a cry. She stretched carefully – Zachariah was still in exactly the same position cradled in her arms against her breasts, and her arms were cramped – before gently easing his head back onto his own pillow. And it was only as his head lolled that she took in his complete stillness.

'Zachariah?' It was a whisper, and then louder, '*Zachariah?*'

But there was no answering lift of his eyelashes to reveal those piercingly blue beautiful eyes, or the soft 'Good mornin', me darlin'' that had characterized all the mornings since her marriage.

He lay, a slight smile still curving his lips, as handsome in death as he had been in life, and even as she sank down and gathered him in her arms again, smothering his face in kisses as she frantically willed the breath back into his body, she already knew it was too late. He had gone, and nothing could bring him back.

After the post mortem and other necessary legal technicalities they buried Zachariah on the morning of August 18th. This was the day the miners reopened negotiations with the government to end their three-month-old strike, but the bitterness of the soul-destroying dispute was pushed to the background as Wearsiders, young and old, lined the route the hearse took. The ornate, flower-covered carriage was drawn by two fine black-plumed horses and the cortège was a long one – Sunderland had been shocked by the facts that had emerged over the young husband's death.

401

It was widely acknowledged that Shane McLinnie had killed Zachariah – he might not have plunged a knife into his heart but the blow that had caused the massive bloodclot was murder, nonetheless – and the papers were full of it for a few days. Some folk thought it odd that the mother of the murderer should ride in the same carriage as the deceased's wife and mother-in-law, and that two of his brothers should be among the six men who carried the coffin into the church. Rosie didn't care what they thought. She had done what her heart had told her to do and she knew Zachariah would have approved of her actions.

Zachariah. She couldn't believe she wasn't going to see him again. There had been times over the last few days when she had awoken with a start from one of the catnaps that were all her exhausted mind could take refuge in, and imagined she was hearing his distinctive-sounding footsteps; and others, especially when she was seeing to the child, when she'd thought she'd heard his voice calling her name. She hadn't told anyone of this, fearing they would either assume she was going mad or start pressing her to take the medicine the doctor had prescribed. And she didn't want to sleep all the time, she wanted to *feel* her agony and desolation, it was the last thing she could do for him.

'I found myself thinking it would be worth dying to have you cry like that for me.' The words he had spoken on their wedding night, and which had never left her, were at the forefront of her mind all the time now, and often when she paced the floor at night, stifling her sobs so she didn't wake her mother and Hannah who were staying with her for the time being, she found herself ranting and raving at Zachariah through the pain.

It was unreasonable, she knew that in the sensible part of

her, in her brain, but her emotions were a different thing. She was so *angry* at him for leaving her, she couldn't help it. She hadn't wanted to cry for him, she had wanted to *live* for him. She had told him that, hadn't she?

Rosie could only manage cool politeness to Davey on the day of the funeral. She hadn't realized until then that she was holding him partly responsible for Zachariah's demise, and again she knew it was unfair but she was as angry with him as she was with Zachariah. Her son would grow up without ever really knowing the wonderful man who had given him life, and it could all have been prevented. It was the one thought that filled her mind night after lonely night.

And yet with Annie she felt nothing but deep compassion. Shane had been buried a few days before Zachariah, and according to Jessie Annie had told her that only she and Arthur had been present at the graveside. Even Shane's brothers had refused to attend. Rosie felt no satisfaction in this; her emotions were strangely numb and frozen regarding Shane.

Rosie began to visit Annie fairly regularly in the days following the funerals – maybe it was their shared misery that drew her to her old friend's side, she wasn't sure; she only knew that in Annie's little kitchen she felt the odd moment of respite from the constant pain of her loss. That Annie herself was suffering was obvious. She was now skin and bone and her clothes hung on her as if on a broomhandle, but although Rosie encouraged her to eat Annie seemed to get thinner with every week that passed.

Sally and Mick left for Ireland four weeks after Zachariah had died, leaving behind scenes of riots and disturbances by striking miners, ever-increasing dole queues and a thick blanket of utter despair that had settled on Sunderland's working class.

In spite of this, Sally hadn't wanted to go; she had been all for cancelling the arrangements and staying in Sunderland for as long as she felt Rosie needed her, but Rosie had added her weight to Mick's arguments that they had to leave. This was a wonderful opportunity for the pair of them – a once-in-a-lifetime chance – and they must grab it with both hands, Rosie had told a tearful Sally. She owed it to Mick to go, she knew she did at heart, and Rosie would visit them as soon as she felt able to. She promised.

Rosie had meant every word, but once the boat had sailed she felt quite bereft and terribly alone. Her mother and Hannah and Joseph were now a family unit, and that was fine and how it should be. Jessie and Joseph were planning to marry at the end of the year and move into Joseph's neat little house and Rosie was glad for them. And Flora had Davey. There were no marriage plans as yet but it was only a matter of time, Rosie told herself quite frequently. She rarely saw Davey now but Flora called in regularly and spent time with Erik as his favourite honorary aunty.

Rosie had hoped his real aunty would make an appearance at the funeral, or at least write – something – but there had been no word from Molly and Rosie felt it keenly. Molly was always there, in the back of her mind, and when Valentino – Molly's idol – died just five days after they buried Zachariah, Molly was the first person she thought of on hearing the news.

A week after Sally and Mick's boat sailed Zachariah's solicitor called at the house. He took tea with her in the sitting room and sat and talked to her as though she was little more than a child, but she didn't mind. He was a kind man and Zachariah had liked him. Her husband's will had been very simple, he informed her gently. Everything was left to her. This house, the one her mother was presently occupying, some more properties in another part of the town she had only been vaguely aware of, it was all hers, along with a considerable amount of money and other funds tied up in bonds and such.

Zachariah had been something of a speculator – Rosie got the impression at this point that the solicitor had privately disapproved of such foolhardiness – but he'd had something of the Midas touch. Did she realize she was a very wealthy young woman? No, she had replied, she didn't, and if she was being truthful she didn't much care at this moment either. And he had patted her on the hand, clucked into his tea and told her he would write a full report so she could peruse it at her leisure when she was feeling a little better. For the moment he would arrange for a substantial sum to be paid to her each month for household expenses and so on, and she must contact him if there was anything she required, anything at all. He was *totally* at her disposal. And then he had drunk his tea and left.

When Rosie looked back on the weeks following Zachariah's passing she realized for most of that period she had been working on automatic and had little recollection of them. She had visited the Maritime Almshouses to assure them of her continuing patronage, knowing that was what Zachariah would have wanted, and dealt with other necessary duties, but most of her days seemed to have vanished into a shadowy never-never land where dark confusion reigned.

And then, at the beginning of November, when the approach of the harsh northern winter was already beginning to make itself felt in hard white frosts and frozen pipes,

Rosie received an urgent message one morning that Annie had collapsed and was asking for her. She flew to Annie's bedside, arriving just as the doctor was insisting Annie be taken to the Sunderland Infirmary. Rosie knew Annie's abiding fear of any sort of institution – to Annie every one smacked of the workhouse – and once she had Dr Meadows alone in the kitchen she spoke frankly. 'What's wrong with her, doctor? Is it serious?'

Dr Meadows knew Rosie; he had watched her grow up and had admired the way she had fought back against circumstances that might have ground another young lassie into the ground, so now his voice was quiet and he answered candidly. 'Annie is a very ill woman, Rosie, and has been for some time. When she started to lose weight a few months ago I suggested a specialist but she wasn't having any of it. I think she knew then what she'd got.'

'But . . . but she will get better?'

He looked at her, a long look, and as her hand went to her throat he said, 'There now, don't upset yourself.'

'How – how long?'

'A month, maybe two, but she will need round-the-clock nursing sooner or later and the best place for her is in hospital. It's in the stomach and that can be pretty unpleasant towards the end. Perhaps you'd have a word with her, she's got a soft spot for you, and you might be able to persuade her to see sense. Arthur and the lads mean well but the sort of nursing she'll need is beyond them even if they felt inclined to attempt it, which I doubt greatly.'

'She'll hate going into hospital.'

'It can't be helped, I'm afraid.'

'What if . . . Dr Meadows, I've room for her at my house. Why can't she come and stay with me? I can nurse her.'

'Rosie.' He paused, choosing his words carefully as he said, 'You've no idea what you would be taking on, my dear. It's beyond one person's capabilities and you have a child, haven't you? It really isn't possible. You have to be sensible.'

'I can pay for a nurse, two if necessary, whatever's needed. I would like to do that for her, really.'

'But why would you want to do that?' Like most people in the district Dr Meadows was aware of the circumstances of Rosie's husband's death, and although very little surprised him after forty years of working as a doctor, he was finding this young woman's concern for the mother of the man who had effectively made her child fatherless was beyond his understanding. Not that it wasn't commendable of course; it was, very, but not bearing a grudge was one thing, this was something else.

Rosie looked at him, and then she said, very simply, 'I can't bear the thought of her going into hospital knowing how she'll feel about it,' her calm countenance belying the fierce beating of her heart. 'Please, Dr Meadows.'

He shook his head slowly. 'It will be expensive.'

'That's all right.'

'And there is no way a nurse could stay here, you understand that? There simply isn't the room.'

'I've said I've plenty of space in my home.'

Dr Meadows opened his mouth to speak and then shut it again. Looking after a terminally sick patient was the last thing he would recommend for someone who had only recently been bereaved in such appalling circumstances as this young lass, but one thing life had taught him was that everyone was different. What crippled some folks made Samsons of others, and maybe this was just what was needed for this particular situation. But if he was wrong . . .

His mind was made up and the thing settled when Rosie said, her eyes holding his and her voice resolute, 'Please, doctor. Please agree to this. She needs me.'

'All right. If Annie wants to come to you and Arthur has no objection I won't stand in your way, but if at any time it gets too much for you you must promise me now that you will ask for help.'

'I promise.'

'And if she gets difficult, awkward – and they can you know, this thing affects the mind as well as the body – you must be prepared to let her go to the hospital. It's a matter of a few weeks at most.'

Annie didn't die in a few weeks, and at Christmas, when Rosie had her mother and Hannah to stay, Annie was still very much in the land of the living. She slept a great deal of the time, mainly due to the high quantities of morphine necessary to control the increasing pain, but when she was awake she was quite lucid and always, in spite of the circumstances, amazingly cheerful.

Rosie had one nurse living in and another who came during the day, and it was they who did all the heavy work involved in turning and washing their patient and other such necessary duties. Rosie cooked the meals for them all and dealt with the mountainous pile of dirty bedding every twenty-four hours produced, along with the normal running of the house and caring for Erik.

Arthur and the lads visited Annie every day, often having a bite to eat in the kitchen and invariably going home laden with fresh bread and cakes and other tasty morsels. The routine was very strenuous and life was hectic, but in spite of that there was the odd time when it was just Rosie and Annie in the pretty double bedroom at the back of the house overlooking the garden, and even with the prevailing situation the sound of laughter could occasionally be heard.

'You're a grand lass, Rosie. You know that, don't you?' Rosie was sitting by the side of Annie's bed, a roaring coal fire in the basket-style grate across the other side of the room casting a cosy glow over the furnishings. It was six o'clock on Christmas Eve.

After a word with her mother Rosie had decided she and Jessie could cope without the services of the live-in nurse over the Christmas weekend, although her associate would still be calling each day as usual, and Rosie had given the grateful woman the time off to see her elderly parents in Newcastle. Now Rosie had just finished washing Annie after giving her a few mouthfuls of soup which was all her grossly distended stomach could take. There were carol singers in the street a few doors away, their voices pure and clear in the cold frosty air, and the two women had been sitting listening to the strains of 'While Shepherds Watched their Flocks by Night' before Annie spoke.

Rosie now looked at her old friend, the once plump face skeletal from the illness which had ravaged Annie's flesh, her eyes dark and sunk back in their sockets, and she smiled as she said, 'Go on with you. You just want your Christmas box early, I know you. You think a bit of flannel will work wonders.'

Annie smiled back. 'There's one who can't wait for her stockin', that's for sure. You'd think the bairn was three instead of twelve years old. She's bin on the go all day long an' she still can't sit still. She'll be straight back up once she's done her cookin', you mark my words.'

Hannah was downstairs with her mother, the pair of them making Hannah and Erik's Yul-doos – baby figures made from Christmas dough with the arms folded across and two currants for eyes. There had certainly been no possibility of anyone in the house brooding over Christmas with Hannah about. The young girl had been dizzy with excitement when she and Rosie had decorated the downstairs of the house and Annie's bedroom earlier, hanging paper chains and honeycombed paper bells from the ceilings and placing berry-encrusted holly over the mirrors and pictures. She and Rosie had built a snowman that afternoon in the sparkling crisp snow, Erik – muffled and cocooned in his pram like a baby Eskimo – looking on, and talking away to them in baby gibberish to which they had replied perfectly seriously.

'I want to thank you, lass, for all you've done.' Annie reached out and took Rosie's hand in her two frail ones, her eyes soft. 'I've always looked on you as a daughter, right from when you was born, I couldn't help it, an' no daughter could've bin better. It might sound daft, lass, but these last eight weeks or so have bin the happiest of me life.'

'Oh, Annie.'

'No, I mean it, lass.' Annie lay back on the heaped cushions. She had been sitting forward and any slight exertion exhausted her. 'You don't know, you see, no one knows, but I want to tell you if you'll listen? It might help you understand about . . . about Shane.'

In all the weeks since the tragedy neither of them had mentioned him by name, and now, as Annie felt Rosie's fingers jerk in hers, she said, 'I don't want to upset you, lass, that's the last thing I want, but if you understand it might help in the future. Not now, it's too early now, but later. I'm ready to meet me Maker when He calls me, there's nothin' atween me an' Him that I knows of, but bein' here the last few weeks it's bin like He's tellin' me to get it off me chest. Will you listen, lass?'

The last thing in all the world that Rosie wanted to talk about was anything connected with the events of the summer, and especially Shane McLinnie, but as she glanced down at the feeble hands holding hers she knew she couldn't refuse Annie anything. And later, when Annie had unburdened herself about her suffering at the hands of her brother and the terrible night Shane had been conceived, both their faces were wet.

'It's strange how things work out you know, lass.' Annie was tired, her voice slurred from her last heavy dose of morphine. 'He was gettin' near the truth an' he'd have bin like a terrier with a bone, he wouldn't have let go. He'd have seen his day with me all right an' it'd have destroyed Arthur, findin' out he weren't Shane's da. An' Shane knew, that night in the kitchen; he clicked on he wasn't Arthur's, an' he wanted to do for me then. But I found the strength, and the good Lord only knows how, to hold him off – persuade him he might be wrong.'

'It wasn't your fault, Annie, none of it. You do know that, don't you? You do see?'

'I dunno, lass. If I'm bein' truthful, I dunno, but I'm content to leave it in the hands of the Almighty now. He'll judge aright. I just wish . . .'

'What?'

'Oh, lass, I shouldn't be sayin' it to you, not after what he did to your man.'

'Go on, Annie, it's all right.' Rosie held the terribly

frail body close as though her old friend was a little girl. 'Whatever it is, I don't mind.'

'I just wish I could take him in me arms one more time, like I did when he was nowt but a bairn, an' tell him I love him. An' I did you know, bad as he was.'

The power of love . . .

Rosie continued to cuddle Annie close as she gazed unseeing across the room, and like a small child Annie had gone off to sleep without her next dose of morphine and slept all the night through until Christmas morning.

It was another six weeks before Annie died, and despite what Dr Meadows had feared the morphine went a long way to controlling the pain right to the end. It had been expected Annie would become comatose but her will to remain with Rosie as long as she could triumphed over her mortal body. She died looking up into Rosie's face and cradled lovingly in her arms, and in the last minutes her face was wiped clean of all pain and anxiety and became that of a young girl again, a peaceful young girl; and such was her expression that it went some way to quieten the agony Rosie felt at her departure.

The announcement of Annie's death was almost lost in the one thousand people a week dying from the influenza virus that was sweeping the country and creating havoc, but to Rosie, and Jessie, and Annie's family and other friends, the world was less rich without her indomitable presence.

There was a special message in the little card attached to the wreath of pure white roses that Rosie laid on her friend's coffin.

Your purity was never besmirched in His eyes, and now you are like a young girl again, washed clean in the blood of His Son and forever lovely.

I love you and I miss you.

Your Rosie.

Part Five

Tomorrow

Chapter Twenty-Two

The last twelve months had seen a great change in Rosie, and when she thought about the woman she had been before Annie's death it was as though that girl was a stranger to her.

Oh, she'd all but raised a family when her father and the lads had died, she had married Zachariah and borne him a son, she'd been a friend and comforter to Flora in her troubles and a support to her mother, but she knew now that Annie's revelation about her childhood and the conception of her youngest son had opened a door in her mind that had hitherto been closed. Before then, she had seen the world very much in stark black and white. Even when Molly had left them, and she had faced the fact that her sister had embraced the oldest profession in the world, she had still retained an element of naivety deep inside.

It embarrassed her now to think about how she had blamed Davey, if only in part, for Zachariah's death. She had transferred her own feelings of guilt to his shoulders and she knew he'd guessed that. They had never spoken of it, however, and in the first few weeks after Annie's passing, when she had been quite desolate, Flora and Davey had been wonderful to her – like a sister and brother in fact.

Looking back now Rosie was sure she must have imagined those times when she thought Davey was still in love with her before Zachariah's death. It made her hot with mortification when she thought about it. He was devoted to Flora, quite devoted, and Flora was unashamedly madly in love with him.

Flora called to see her several times a week – her friend was Erik's favourite playmate and the two of them would disappear into the nursery for hours on end – but Davey only accompanied her on the odd occasion, maybe two or three times a month, and then he was always friendly and amiable. Nevertheless Rosie never felt at ease with him and she blamed herself totally for this. If she could have torn the feeling she had for him – which she had acknowledged was still there after Annie had died – out of her heart she would have done so like a shot.

It was wrong, self-indulgent, and she had so much to be thankful for, she told herself constantly. She had her son – and more than that, she had tasted great joy in her all-too-short marriage. Zachariah had been a wonderful man, she would never meet the like of him again, and therefore she was content to remain single for the rest of her days.

There was her voluntary work among the forty boys at the Sunderland Orphan Asylum; that kept her busy, as well as her half-days helping at the Royal Institute for the Blind in Villiers Street. The Orphan Asylum's little inmates were trained for seafaring careers. In the playground was an old wreck called the *Victoria* that the boys loved to play on, and Rosie always considered it an honour that on sight of her the children would leave the boat and run pell mell to her side, swarming around her like small monkeys. Of course the sweets and little treats that invariably appeared out of her bag might have had something to do with it, but the boys loved to sit on her lap, too, or hold her hand or walk with her, and the once or twice she had taken Erik to meet them there had been great excitement. The Asylum had a little band, comprised of some twenty children, and on one of the occasions she had taken Erik with her they had played for him, which had necessitated her buying the toddler a tin whistle on the way home to Roker.

On the three or four half-days a week she worked, Rosie paid a neighbour to take care of Erik. Ellen rented a room in a house a few doors away and had a baby daughter a few months older than Erik, which had been the means of the two women first getting to know each other. Ellen's husband had been drowned in a fishing accident shortly before Zachariah had died, and the young widow took in washing and ironing, besides cleaning several houses in The Terrace and elsewhere, to make ends meet.

Ellen was fiercely independent and Rosie had recognized a kindred spirit immediately, and as their children had become great friends so had they. To date Ellen had refused Rosie's offers to come and live with her, which were made at regular intervals, but the more than generous payments Rosie made for the hours Ellen took care of Erik had taken a great load off the other woman's shoulders.

And Rosie hadn't given up her plans of moving out of the town altogether, they had merely been shelved as she had adjusted to her loss. Now, at the back of her mind, the proposal included Ellen, and possibly Annie's sons who were still out of work and desperate. With that in mind she had bought a little car, a modest three-seater Citroën, and taken excursions into the surrounding countryside, the while keeping her eyes open for a suitable property. She was determined she was going to *do* something with Zachariah's legacy, she knew he would have approved of that, and a farm could provide so many jobs and a secure future for her son as he grew into manhood.

She had the means now. Jessie had married her Joseph in the spring of 1927, three months after Annie had died, and at that point Rosie had sold the house in Benton Street along with the other properties Zachariah had owned – a house in the middle of Ward Terrace in Hendon and another in Ryhope Road in Grangetown.

Part of the proceeds she had sent over the water to Sally and Mick. Their small farm was thriving but in dire need of new equipment and modernization, and it had pleased Rosie to be able to help her friends with a substantial gift.

She had received a rapturous letter thanking her from Sally, the contents of which had seemed to bring the tall, gangling woman in front of her and made her chuckle.

Mick's still loving every minute here, Sally had written in her barely readable scrawl, *and his Irish brogue is now so thick you can't understand a word he says. This week alone we have had a horse with pus in his hoof, a cow with a severe impaction of the rumen, and a sow with a blockage (I won't tell you where!), and the local vet is opening a new bank account. Mick smells of pigs as well as horses now, and I'm sure when this baby is born it will have two little hoofs and a swishing tail.*

Sally had been five months pregnant at the time, and had had a son at the end of September. The two women wrote to each other nearly every week, and Rosie looked forward to receiving Sally's letters, which were never dull.

At the end of every letter Sally would repeat her invitation for Rosie and Erik to pay them a visit, but as yet Rosie hadn't taken her friend up on it. She would, she told herself each time she read Sally's warm words that seemed to bring her so close she could reach out and touch her, but when Erik was just a little older. Maybe in the summer.

So all in all her life was full and busy, and as satisfying as it could be without her beloved Zachariah. Now Rosie was sitting in her sitting room preparatory to retiring for the night. She glanced up from the glowing fire into which she'd been staring for some time and glanced round the softly shadowed room. It was almost eighteen months since Zachariah had died – the day after tomorrow was Christmas Eve, and she had her mother and Joseph and Hannah arriving in the morning to stay for a few days, and Ellen and little Mary were coming on Boxing Day when they returned from visiting relations; yet at times she still felt utterly desolate at his loss.

And since Annie's death, as her new knowledge of herself had continued to grow and grow, she now recognized that an element of this feeling was guilt because she hadn't loved Zachariah enough when he was with her. Her one comfort was that he hadn't known that other secret passion had continued and taken some of the love that should rightfully have been all his as her husband. And when the moments of self-accusation came she was able to answer them with the recognition that she had done what was right in the impossible situation she had found herself in at that time. Which was all anyone could do, wasn't it? You couldn't force your heart to feel a certain way just because your head told you you must. Love, unfortunately, wasn't like that. It found its own outlet however much you tried to channel it in one direction. She made a deep obeisance with her head in answer to the thought and rose to her feet, her carriage straight and determined as she walked from the room.

Christmas Eve dawned bright but very cold, the frost-painted shrubs and trees in the garden holding an exquisite beauty all of their own in the crystallized air.

Because it was a Sunday, Jessie had insisted on dragging them all to church that morning, and now, as Rosie peered out of the kitchen window and drank in the frozen scene outside the warmth of the house, she knew she was glad she had gone. The Catholic church had been full and the half-remembered prayers from her childhood, when Jessie had taken her and the other children on high days and holidays, had comforted her. The Christ child had been lying in his crib, the shepherds had been kneeling in mute adoration, and the smell of incense and the hushed atmosphere had made her feel five years old again.

She could hear shouts of laughter and Erik's high-pitched squeals from the sitting room, and her lips curved in answer to the infectious sound as she turned from the window and walked over to the blackleaded range to check the Sunday roast. How Zachariah would have loved his son. At twenty months old Erik was a bundle of energy and into everything, and the absolute image of his handsome father. Everyone who came into contact with the child loved him, and he could twist his grandma and young aunty round his little finger. He was tired now though, he was long overdue for his morning nap, and he would start to get fractious and unsteady on his legs before long.

The thought moved Rosie across the kitchen and out into the hall, and when she reached the warmth of the sitting room it was just in time to see Erik, his round baby face red with excitement at all the attention he was getting, attempt to turn a circle as he waved his arms in time to the nursery rhyme her mother and Joseph and Hannah were singing.

As Rosie realized what was about to happen she leapt forward but he had already tottered backwards, banging against the fancy chiffonier and causing a heavy cut-crystal vase to overbalance and smash down on his head. In a moment there was blood everywhere, and as she reached the child and whisked him up into her arms his screaming rent the air. Joseph was already reaching for his car keys, for the cut on the baby's head was gaping and would certainly need stitches.

The roads were lethal with black ice and Joseph drove at a snail's pace that made Rosie feel she could have walked the distance in less time. She was sitting in the front seat with Erik cradled in her arms wrapped in a blanket, her mother and Hannah having stayed at the house, and the towel she was holding to the baby's forehead was already soaked when they had gone only a mile or two. Erik had fallen asleep as soon as the car started, whether due to tiredness or a result of the bang on his head Rosie wasn't sure, but then, when they were passing over the Wearmouth Bridge and he was violently sick, Rosie really began to panic. By the time they reached the Sunderland Infirmary Erik had vomited twice more and didn't seem to be aware of his surroundings, and Rosie felt a fear so deep and consuming that it made any other she had experienced in her life trifling by comparison.

They were kindness itself at the Infirmary, but Rosie already knew she wouldn't be returning home that day. It was a fight to get the doctor to allow her to stay at the side of Erik's narrow iron cot in the children's ward, but when Joseph took the doctor aside (she heard snatches of their conversation such as, '. . . widow, child is all she has', and 'will be amply rewarded with a generous donation'), a straight-backed chair was brought for her along with that British panacea for all ills, a hot cup of tea.

The long afternoon crept by. Joseph had gone back to the house once he had established Rosie wouldn't be returning home that day, but just before teatime Jessie appeared at the door of the ward with a basket containing freshly cut sandwiches and a container of lukewarm onion soup. Rosie tried to force a few mouthfuls down, but it was beyond her. Jessie stayed for an hour but her fear of the hospital was only a little less than Annie's had been, and after sixty minutes of Jessie's twisting and turning on her chair and nervous bursts of chatter followed by long uncomfortable silences, Rosie sent her home. Erik was sleeping most of the time and was aware of very little, but the once or twice he had recognized his grandmother Jessie's distraught behaviour had made him worse.

'We'll be home tomorrow, Mam, don't worry.' Rosie had walked to the door of the small ward with her mother and signalled to Joseph and Hannah, who were waiting in the corridor outside, to come and take her. 'We'll probably be back in time for Hannah and Erik to open their presents together.' They were brave words and the four of them looked at each other for a moment before Rosie said, in answer to the expression screwing up her mother's face, 'Don't, Mam, please don't. I've got to take it a minute at a time and be strong for Erik and believe he is going to be home tomorrow.'

'I'm sorry, lass. I'm sorry.' Jessie's voice had been quivering and Joseph had hurried his wife and stepdaughter down the dark, green-painted passageway after an encouraging pat of Rosie's arm and a reassuring, 'I'll take care of things, Rosie lass, don't you worry.'

Don't worry. *Don't worry?* What stupid things are said at times like these. Rosie felt suddenly tired, but it was an exhaustion of the spirit rather than the flesh. She couldn't take any more. *Are you listening, God?* She lifted her face to the whitewashed ceiling of the corridor as she continued to stand just outside the ward doors. I can't take any more. If anything happens to my baby, to my precious beautiful baby, I'm finished. It will be the end, it will. She lowered her eyes, shutting them tightly and biting hard on her lower lip.

She had lost count of how many times Erik had vomited during the afternoon and when he emerged, for a few minutes, from the strange sleep which seemed almost like unconsciousness it was always to crying and moaning with the pain in his head. Zachariah had had a bang on his head. What if there was some inherent weakness in Erik's makeup that made him particularly vulnerable? It was possible . . .

And this was Christmas Eve. Of all the times for it to happen, for her baby to fall sick, how could He allow it on the night His Son came into the world? 'Take everything I have, God.' She muttered the words out loud in the form of a prayer, still with her eyes tightly closed. 'Take everything, every last penny, but leave me my son. I don't care about the money or the house or any of it, and I'll never ask you for anything else as long as I live. I promise.'

'Rosie?'

Her eyes snapped open and she found herself staring at Flora and Davey, and then Davey said again, 'Rosie, lass. Are you all right? Where is he?'

Davey had been gripped by a terrible fear for Erik as they

425

had walked round the corner of the passageway and seen her standing there, her head bent and her face as white as a sheet. In all the years he had known Rosie, even in the caustic aftermath of Zachariah's death, he had never seen her shoulders bowed in defeat or such an expression of agony on her face, and now the unexpected defencelessness made him want to gather her up in his arms and smother her face with kisses.

'He . . . he's in there.' Rosie managed to lift her hand to the ward but she didn't take her eyes off Davey's face. In this moment of consuming need he was the person in all the world she most wanted with her, and for a moment she was quite oblivious to Flora's presence. 'He's so small and so poorly.'

'I know, I know.' And now Davey followed through on his initial impulse to take Rosie into his arms; he gently drew her close, bending his head and murmuring soothing words of comfort into the fine silk of her hair as he endeavoured to comfort the woman he loved.

They could only have stood together like that for a moment or two and then Rosie straightened and drew away, and Davey made no effort to restrain her. 'How . . . Who told you I was here?' Rosie was talking directly to Flora now and she took her friend's hands adding, 'Oh, I'm so pleased to see you, you don't know how pleased.'

'We called at the house this afternoon with Erik's Christmas present, didn't your mother tell you?'

Flora's voice held nothing but gentle concern, and when Rosie shook her head saying, 'She's in such a state herself she doesn't know if she's on foot or horseback,' and Davey's voice came brisk and even as he nodded and said, 'That's understandable of course, she is Erik's grandma when all's said and done,' Flora didn't look at her fiancé but kept her eyes on Rosie.

And in the few minutes that followed before Rosie went back to Erik – visiting time had finished so Flora and Davey weren't allowed in the ward – Flora didn't once glance Davey's way.

Erik remained in the Sunderland Infirmary for four more days before the doctors were satisfied Rosie could take him home. The enforced rest meant he seemed to have twice his normal energy in the days that followed, and he ran Rosie ragged, but she was so thrilled he had fully recovered she didn't even notice. He was very proud of his 'war wound' as Joseph had christened the scar on the child's forehead, and when Jessie's husband bought Erik a tiny soldier's hat – it was really a play tram conductor's cap, but Joseph had adapted it for his purposes – and whittled a small gun out of a piece of wood, Erik was transported to seventh heaven. He spent hours strutting around and giving orders in his baby jargon to all and sundry, and insisted on sleeping with both the cap and the gun at his side every night.

In that last week of December, 1927, Britain was swept by freezing blizzards and food supplies had to be air-dropped into villages cut off by snow. The atrocious weather seemed like the last straw to many of Sunderland's miners and steelworkers who had been out of work for months. Boots could only be cobbled so many times, clothes patched in so many places before they fell apart, and the squalor and decay that had been just about bearable through the warmth of the summer became intolerable in the harsh, unrelenting winter.

The childhood complaints that had begun to die out at

the end of the nineteenth century such as rickets and other wasting diseases were rearing their ugly heads again, and the non-attendance of doctors and midwives at births – and who could afford to pay for their services when there was no coal or even cinders for the fire, and no food for the table? – produced a terrible culling of the weakest among the stricken north's working-class families.

Men were angry and bitter – whole communities were angry and bitter – and yet it was a time when one man would lend another his only pair of boots for the day when the need was great, and know that they would be returned with some spit and polish on the patched leather. Housewives would band together to provide a pot of broth for a new nursing mother, and bread and dripping for the rest of the family. The colour and furore might be dying in the docks, and the steelworks and mines gasping for breath, but the northern people looked after their own where they could.

But now it was Saturday, 31st December – New Year's Eve – and Flora had come to a decision. She was meeting Davey at Mrs Prinn's café before they went to the Cora Picture Palace at the corner of Southwick Road and Newcastle Road, but as she slowly got ready she knew she had to face the truth she had been putting to the back of her mind whilst concern for the child had still run high.

She had always known deep inside, hadn't she, however much she had tried to fool herself over the last few months? Aye, she had. She'd known all along. Davey's easy acceptance of the unwritten law that they should wait a respectable period after her parents' deaths before they set a date for the wedding, his coolness on occasion, his lack of ardour and considerate, almost benevolent attitude towards her – it was all linked with Rosie. Davey had never been the eager

428

fiancé, and he had certainly never behaved as a man madly in love with his sweetheart.

If Zachariah hadn't died, if Rosie hadn't effectively become free again, things might have been different. She could perhaps have carried on fooling herself then. They could have moved away and started afresh. And when she'd had his children – and she longed for children, oh, she did – that would have been a bond between them that could have been nurtured and built on. But Zachariah *had* died. And she couldn't fool herself any more.

Davey would never look at her the way he had looked at Rosie that night at the hospital.

The knowledge she had been fighting against for days was like a physical pain in her chest and she flinched under it. It wasn't his fault, it wasn't Rosie's fault, it was just a fact. Oh, she didn't doubt she could bring him up to scratch if she so chose. Her lip curled slightly at the thought. He was a decent man, honourable and kind, and if she pressed him he would go through with the marriage. She could be Mrs Connor by the summer if she set her heart on it.

She buttoned her coat and pulled her hat down over her ears before picking up her gloves and her handbag, and leaving her room. She walked quickly down the stairs and opened the front door without speaking to her landlady; she couldn't have faced idle chatter today.

The raw December afternoon was so cold it took her breath away, and she was conscious of thinking, There's more snow in the air, I can smell it, before she came back to the dilemma she now knew she had been trying to ignore for months. She could have prompted Davey to marry her before this but she hadn't because she had wanted him to fall in love with her. And it wasn't going to happen. He cared about her, in his own way she didn't doubt he was very fond of her, but it wasn't *love* in the real sense of the word. Not like she had for him, like Zachariah had had for Rosie, like Peter had for her . . . The last thought caused her to bring her lips together and draw them inwards. Poor Peter. Poor, poor Peter.

Davey loved Rosie. Flora drew the freezing air deep into her lungs as she neared the end of the street. She herself had ceased to exist for him in those few moments when he had seen Rosie's distress. She had thought she could live with it, master her own feelings and *make* him fall in love with her, but it wouldn't happen. It couldn't happen. Deep in the heart of him it would always be Rosie.

She clenched her teeth against the pain. If she kept Davey to his word and forced this marriage through, she would live to regret it bitterly.

The wind was raw, and as she pulled her hat even further down over her ears the first fat snowflakes began to whirl and soar from a laden sky. She had to tell him. She had to let him go.

Davey was waiting outside Prinn's when Flora turned the corner, and as she saw his face break into a smile at the sight of her she felt her heart crack. He wasn't smiling by the time she reached him – the look on her face must have told him something was wrong. 'What is it? Is it Erik?'

Flora was surprised by the sudden anger that flooded her. Here was she, tearing herself apart, and still he could only think of Rosie – or her child, to be more precise. 'No.' Her voice was crisp. 'As far as I know Erik is absolutely fine.' And then, as he went to open the door of the café, she said, 'No, don't let's go in there. I . . . I need to talk to you. Privately.'

She turned and began walking back the way she had come without waiting for his agreement, and when he fell into step beside her, and before he could speak, Flora said, 'I need to tell you something, Davey, and just listen, will you? Without saying anything? It's about Rosie, Rosie and Shane, and that night you saw them in the snow.'

She didn't look at him as she related exactly what had happened that night so many years ago, and Shane's subsequent visit to Zachariah's house when his hatred of the other man had been born, and she finished with, 'She's always hated Shane, Davey, always. There was never anything between them except in his sick mind.'

It was some moments before he said, 'Why are you telling me this now, Flora?'

She glanced his way and although it might have been her imagination he looked different – younger, lighter and it made her voice sharp as she said, 'You know why. I think it's about time we faced facts, don't you? It isn't working between us and we both know it. We should have stayed friends, Davey, and that's all.'

The effect of her words on Davey was paralysing for a second. He stood stock still so that Flora was forced to slow her footsteps and then turn and face him. 'What on earth are you talking about?' he asked slowly.

'I'm talking about me getting on with my life, Davey. I think I shall start looking around for different accommodation in the spring, perhaps even a little house of my own. I think I would like that. I'm tired of lodgings.'

'Flora—'

She spoke quickly now in an effort to stop herself breaking down, but she had seen the relief and surprise in his eyes. 'I'd like us to go back to how we were before my parents died, that's what I'm trying to say. I wasn't thinking straight after they had gone, it was a difficult time all round, and I know you wanted to see me through it but I'm better now. I want . . .' She paused. This was hard, so hard, but she intended to come out of this whole miserable affair with a remnant of dignity if nothing else. 'I want there to be a spark with the man I marry, you know what I mean? And it isn't there with us, is it?' Not on your side anyway, she added silently.

'I don't understand.' He was looking hard at her now. 'Is this because of Christmas Eve? When I comforted . . .'

If he had said Rosie's name, if he had actually *said* it, she might still have thought there was some hope for them. 'When you hugged Rosie?' Flora shook her head slowly. 'Oh, Davey, what do you take me for? This isn't because of a hug.' And it wasn't, not really. When he had taken Rosie into his arms it had merely been the catalyst. 'I care about you very much, you know that.' She was standing straight and still and the snow was whirling about them in fierce gusts, and now she turned, saying, 'It's coming down thicker, we'd better keep walking.'

'Flora, listen to me.' Davey caught her arm, turning her to face him again. 'I'll try harder—'

'*I don't want you to have to try!*' It was fierce, and her face was white when she said again, but more quietly this time, 'I don't want you to have to try, Davey. Don't you see? That's the whole point. And I want you to know you are completely free to approach anyone you like.'

'What does that mean?' His voice was sharp but then, as he stared into the dark grey of her eyes, what he saw there humbled him. 'Oh, Flora.' He shook his head sadly. 'If you're thinking what I think you're thinking, I can tell you now you're barking up the wrong tree, lass.'

'You still love her.'

He did not deny it, but what he did say was, 'She's a wealthy young woman, and once the necessary proprieties have been observed there will no doubt be countless men of similar wealth beating a path to her door.'

It was a slight exaggeration but Flora didn't take him up on it. 'What's that got to do with anything?'

'Everything.'

Everything. He could say everything and mean it, and yet he had taken the job at Peter's father's shipyard that she had arranged, and he would have married *her*, knowing about her money, without a second thought. Not that her wealth was on the same lines as Rosie's, of course it wasn't, but in these days of increasing depression and poverty it wasn't to be sneezed at either.

But Davey had looked at it as though he was doing her the favour, that was the thing. And he had been. He had loathed every day working in the shipyard, she knew that, and but for her parents dying he would be long since gone. In the first weeks of his homecoming he had been full of working on a farm somewhere down south and he would have followed through on that.

Her thoughts hardened Flora's resolve, and now her voice was very controlled and even as she said, 'What you do is up to you, of course, but it doesn't alter what's been said. We'll still be friends?'

She looked up at him as she spoke and his eyes were waiting for her, and they were warm and soft when he replied, 'Of course we'll still be friends, Flora.'

'And . . . and you forgive me, about not telling you the truth about Shane and Rosie?'

'It wouldn't have made any difference, Flora. She was already married,' he said quietly. It wasn't the point and they both knew it, but then he took her hand and tucked it through his arm as he continued, 'But if it makes you feel better, of course I forgive you, you know that.' He tried to keep his voice even and steady, but the tumult of emotions filling his chest made it difficult. He should be feeling wretched – he thought a lot of Flora, he always had done, hadn't he – but it was as though a ton weight had lifted from his shoulders in the last few minutes, and the removal of it was making him light-headed.

It was over, done with. Flora forced herself to keep walking and talking although her mind was working quite separately to what her mouth was saying. Although it wasn't quite over, was it? There was something else to do before she could put all this behind her and start to pick up the pieces of her life, if that was possible. And this last thing would be more difficult than anything which had gone before.

The second sweep of furious blizzards and deep snow meant that Flora didn't get to visit Rosie until the end of the first week of January. The papers and radio were full of the fact that the Thames had burst its banks in London, flooding low-lying districts and killing fourteen people owing to the combination of a high tide and sudden thaw, but the north remained icebound.

Rosie was busy baking in the kitchen when Flora arrived. Since Annie's passing she had taken to stocking up Arthur and the lads with fresh bread, cakes, ham pies and other such necessities once a week, pretending each time she delivered the food parcels that it was simply to indulge her love of cooking and that their empty cupboards and bare shelves were unnoticed by her. She looked on Arthur and the lads as extensions of Annie and quite unconnected with Shane, and even when the numbness surrounding thoughts of Annie's youngest had worn off and she had felt a bitterness so deep it had been a dark abyss, it hadn't influenced the way she had thought about Annie's husband and other sons. In the last year Patrick and Michael had started courting local lasses, but Arthur had told her both were chary of committing themselves with the depression biting hard, and again Rosie's thoughts had returned to the little farm. But it would have to wait until the better weather, and even then she might not find anything suitable at the right price. It was an enormous undertaking at best.

Flora followed Rosie through into the warm fragrant confines of the kitchen, lifting her nose as she sniffed with loud appreciation. 'By, Rosie, you're making my mouth water.' And surprisingly enough Flora found it was true. Since New Year's Eve she had had no appetite whatsoever, but warm spice wigs fresh from the oven were hard to resist, broken heart or no broken heart.

'Help yourself.' Rosie indicated the yeasted teacakes with a wave of her hand. 'There's a slab of butter in the pantry although it'll be rock hard.'

'Peter's mam eats nine or ten of these in one go,' Flora confided as she bit into the teacake which was bulging with currants. 'And with each mouthful she always says, "I'll have one more bite and that's all, I've got to watch my weight." Peter says on the quiet that he reckons that's all she does do – watch it. Watch it go up and up and up.'

Flora was sitting in front of the kitchen range and her

voice was mild and conversational, but Rosie's eyes were penetrating as they focused on her friend's face. Flora hadn't mentioned Peter in months. It was all Davey. Always Davey.

'How is Peter?' Rosie kept her voice casual as she turned her hands to the pastry, and she didn't look at Flora now.

'Peter's fine.' Flora didn't have to force the thread of affection in her voice. She had told herself several times over the last days that she didn't know what she would have done without Peter Baxter. She and Davey had decided on New Year's Eve that there would be no formal announcement of the end of their engagement; she'd never worn an engagement ring anyway, she had just changed her mother's ring to the third finger of her left hand after Davey had spoken. But then she had broken down at work on the Tuesday following the weekend and it had all come out. Peter had been marvellous. There had been no I-told-you-so, or any indication that he considered she'd got her just deserts, he had just been the same old Peter – supporting her one hundred per cent. He had mopped up her tears, fetched her a cup of tea and then waited for her after work and driven her back to her lodgings. And now Flora took a deep breath after finishing the teacake in one gulp before saying, 'I'm sort of seeing him again actually. Davey and I . . . It wasn't working out.'

'*What?*' Rosie couldn't say any more, she just looked at Flora.

'Don't look at me like that.'

'Don't look at you . . . Flora, I *know* how you feel about Davey. What on earth happened? Did you have a row?'

'No.' And then to Rosie's surprise Flora suddenly stood up and took Rosie's floury hands in her own, blinking

436

rapidly as she said, 'He loves you, Rosie. He's always loved you. I won't pretend to be a saint and say I think it's fair, and if I thought there was any chance at all for me I wouldn't be here now. There, that's the truth. But it was me who finished it. I suddenly realized I couldn't face the rest of my life with a man who wanted to be with someone else, and . . . and I do care about you.'

Rosie's eyes searched her friend's face but although her mouth opened no words came out.

'And so now it's up to you.'

'Me?' When Flora let go of her hands Rosie plumped down on a kitchen chair. 'What do you mean it's up to me?'

'Do you still love him?'

'Love him?' Suddenly the moment when Davey had taken her in his arms at the hospital was there and Rosie could feel her face burning. But she didn't dodge the question. 'Yes, I do.' She inclined her head slowly with the affirmative. 'But like you just said, that's not fair is it? No one forced me to marry Zachariah, Flora, and if I was in the same position again as I was then I would do exactly the same thing. I – I loved him, very much. Not like Davey, but I did love him.'

'Aye, I know you did, and he loved you an' all.'

'And with your mam and da and everything—'

'No.' It was the old impetuous Flora who interrupted her. 'No, forget all that, lass, that's nothing to do with it. This is *now*.'

There was a long moment of silence when the kettle on the hearth spluttered and hissed and the low moan of the wind outside emphasized the warm cosiness of the kitchen. Rosie looked towards the dark window for some seconds before turning to meet Flora's eyes. And then she said, 'Flora, are you sure about this? About what you are saying?'

'Aye, I'm sure.' Flora relaxed back in her seat, her shoulders slumping. 'Davey thought you were seeing Shane McLinnie before, when he left all them years ago. He'd seen you that night in the snow – you remember you thought someone had passed by? – and he'd got the wrong idea, then he went to see Shane and you can imagine what Shane said.' She lifted her head and looked at Rosie's face and what she saw there made her continue quickly, 'And I let him carry on thinking it but he knows the truth now. The thing is, all this' – Flora waved her hand widely – 'will stop him speaking. So . . . it's up to you.'

Rosie looked into Flora's soft grey eyes and their gaze caught and held for long moments before she got up and put her arms round the other girl, saying simply, 'Thank you for telling me all this, lass.'

'Something's burning.'

'What?' It wasn't what Rosie had expected, and then, as realization dawned, 'Oh my goodness, Mr McLinnie's parkin! I made it special as well 'cos it's his favourite.'

The cake was black and smoking when Rosie rescued it from the oven and as the two women stared at the charred lump, Flora's comment of, 'Well, lass, he'd have to be mortalious to fancy that,' suddenly struck them both as funny. Their laughter was loud and long and it relieved the tension, and when Flora left just before nine o'clock to catch the tram home, they hugged each other in a way they hadn't done for years.

Flora had peeped in the nursery before she'd left and now, as Rosie watched her friend disappear down the street amid the swirling snow and icy wind, she recalled the soft longing in Flora's face as she'd said, 'I do so want a bairn, Rosie, and before I'm too old to enjoy it. I want lots of babies, one after the other. I want to fill a house with them.' And her voice had been a statement of intent when she'd added, 'Peter would make an excellent father.'

Rosie hadn't known how to reply for a moment, but then Flora had looked at her, and the tacit plea for approval in the other girl's face had helped her to say, 'Yes, he would. He's a lovely man, Flora.'

'Aye, I know it.' And then Flora's voice had come more strongly. 'I know it all right.'

It was another ten days before Rosie saw Davey, and then he only called at the house because she had sent a letter asking him to come. It had been a brief letter, terse almost, and anyone reading the few short lines would never have guessed that the writer had agonized over them for days.

Flora had related her conversation with Davey on New Year's Eve word for word before she had left, and as the days after her friend's visit had crept by and Rosie had waited in vain, she was forced to acknowledge Flora was right. It was up to her – again. What was it about her, she asked herself, that made men who loved her so tongue-tied? But that was silly; she had known what it was with Zachariah and she knew the obstacle that was holding Davey back. But it mustn't, the money mustn't keep them apart. She wouldn't let it.

Since Flora's revelation Rosie had alternated between wild elation and deep despair, often within the same sixty seconds. There was so much water under the bridge, they weren't the young lad and lass they had been back in the carefree days of their youth. He had travelled, seen foreign parts, met other women . . . He would have slept with them. He would have. And there was her, she had been married for goodness' sake, and she had a son to prove it. And she had loved Zachariah; she would never deny that love no matter what the cost. But he wouldn't ask her to deny it, he had liked Zachariah, she knew that. Maybe they could work things out? But what if . . . And so it had gone on, questions and answers, questions and answers until she had thought she would go mad.

What would people say if they knew she had asked a man to call on her – and with her first husband having been laid to rest only eighteen months before – with the express purpose of encouraging him to ask her to marry him? She would be labelled a brazen huzzy and worse. Oh aye, she could hear them. The rich young widow and the handsome penniless labourer. Oh, they'd have a field day and no mistake. The tongues would be clacking from here to Newcastle. Did she care what people thought? She had asked herself this more than once and the answer was always the same. Only in as much as it might affect Erik.

Davey arrived at number seventeen The Terrace at exactly seven o'clock in the evening. She had thought about asking him for a meal but her courage hadn't run to it, and now when she answered the door to his knock her face was burning with colour and quite at variance with the white frozen world outside, the glow suffusing her skin almost scarlet.

'It was very good of you to come.' It was formal, too formal, and she tried to lighten her tone as she added, 'I've just put Erik to bed, he was asleep on his feet. We've been out in the fresh air most of the day building an igloo in the garden, of all things.'

'An igloo?' He raised dark eyebrows. He might have known she would aspire to something more ambitious than the average snowman.

He looked at her for a long moment and then, when he realized his eyes were feasting on her face, quickly glanced behind her as he said, 'Shall I come in?'

'Oh I'm sorry, I don't know what I'm thinking of. Please, come in.' She was flustered and it showed.

Once in the sitting room she waved him to a chair, saying as she did so, 'Would you care for a cup of tea?'

'Thank you.' He stood in front of the crackling fire, his tall lean body straight and stiff, and there was a brief embarrassing silence before Rosie said, 'I'll just go and . . .' as she backed to the door.

Why had she asked him here? Once the door had shut behind Rosie Davey sank down into the proffered armchair, gazing round the bright attractive room as though it would provide the answer. Perhaps she was going to ask him what had happened between himself and Flora? She must know by now that the engagement was off; Flora had made no secret of the fact that she was seeing Peter again, but he had no idea how the news would have affected Rosie. Before Zachariah had died he would have bet his last penny that her feeling for him was still very much alive, in spite of the way she felt about her husband. But now? Since Zachariah's death she had been reserved, cool even, until the night at the hospital. But she had needed a friendly face then, and likely that's how she saw him now – merely as a friend.

And then he was disabused of this idea, and his mouth brought agape in the process when, on entering the room with the tray, Rosie said without any preamble at all, 'There is no easy way to say this, Davey, but knowing how I care about you, Flora told me why she felt it necessary to break off the engagement.'

He stared at her wordlessly while she busied herself with the tea things – or perhaps hid behind them would be a more accurate description – and then he said gruffly, the Tyneside inflexion very prominent in his voice, 'Did she now? Aye, well that's Flora for you, isn't it.'

'Don't be like that.'

'*Don't be like that?*'

It was a bark, and in answer to it Rosie's head jerked up and her mouth thinned as she snapped back, 'Yes, don't be like that. You haven't got the monopoly on feelings, you know. Flora thought she was doing the right thing in telling me what was going on.'

'Then she was wrong.'

'I don't think so.' As Rosie uttered the words she suddenly had a vivid mental picture of Zachariah's sitting room in Benton Street, and his face when she had pressed him to declare his feelings for her. There had been none of the aggressiveness that Davey was showing, no egotistical pride, but then the circumstances had been different. No, no. She checked herself quickly. She must be honest in her feelings from this point on whatever happened. It wasn't that the circumstances were different, that wasn't it, it was that Zachariah had been a man in a million and she had realized it even then. No one would ever love her as completely or as unselfishly as her late husband. There had been a well of love in Zachariah. And Davey . . . Davey was very human. Life would never be easy or plain sailing with Davey. He would never know how to handle her like Zachariah had done, and they would clash – both having strong, determined personalities – over and over again, but it didn't make any difference to this love she had for him. It was consuming, that was the only word for it, and if he felt the same he *had* to see things clearly.

'Is that why you asked me to come here tonight? To talk about what Flora has said?' He was on his feet now and Rosie put down the cup of tea she had been about to give him and faced him squarely as he continued. 'Because I trust she also told you that I'm planning to leave these parts once the weather's better? It's high time I made a clean break with Sunderland.'

Her voice was flat and her face was straight when she said, 'You must do as you please, of course, but can I ask you one thing? And please answer truthfully.'

He stared at her without replying and then, when she had swallowed hard and wetted her lips, she said, 'Do you love me, Davey?'

He couldn't believe this was happening. As Davey stared into Rosie's face he thought, She's an incredible woman, quite remarkable; but then he'd always known that, hadn't he? What other woman of his acquaintance, given the circumstances, would have asked him outright like that? Blatant, like. But she wasn't forward, not in the normal sense of the word. No, she was just very strong, and unique – oh aye, she was unique all right. And it was the knowledge of her strength that enabled him to say, without any softening of his voice, 'Aye, I do, but it counts for nowt in what we're talking about.'

'Nowt? How can you say that?'

'I'll never ask you to marry me, Rosie.' He saw the colour flood her face again but he dare not betray any sign of the raging turmoil that had had him walking the floorboards into the early hours every night since New Year's Eve, when one refrain had sung through his blood like a song. She hadn't let him touch her. Shane McLinnie – *she hadn't let him touch her*.

'Because of the money? That's what this is all about, isn't it? You're putting what other people might think before us.'

'No!' It was like the crack of a whip, and as her face blanched he said more quietly, 'No, that's not it, not entirely. Other folk I could handle, it's meself I can't stomach. I'm . . . I'm weak in certain areas.' The words were being torn out of him and when she made a move towards him he stopped her with a savage movement of his hand. 'Those years down the mine, I can't describe what they did to me. And the shipyard . . . There's lads of fourteen and fifteen working there and they handle the deafening row and the heat and the accidents that occur, but me? I'm scared, scared stiff every minute of every day. There was a man last week who had both his hands sliced off by a steel plate—' He stopped abruptly although Rosie had made no sound or movement, and then continued, his voice and face blank, 'I can't take it any more. I don't mind working hard, I'll work all the hours under the sun, but I can't be shut in. And what work is there round here like that? And I won't be a kept man.' He said the last as though Rosie had suggested it.

Rosie closed her eyes and when she opened them again she said, 'What are you going to do?'

'I'll go down south, see what's about. I hear work's available there. And if I make it, if . . . if I get on me feet in a year or two I'll . . . I'll write.'

No he wouldn't. Rosie stared at him in silence. And in spite of all he had said it *was* the money that was separating them. If she had been an ordinary young lass working in a shop or in service or something similar, without any ties or obligations, he would have asked her to go with him. But she wasn't an ordinary young lass any more, and there was Erik. However she might feel she couldn't expose her child to the perils of the sort of life Davey was describing. And then she said what was in her heart, in a little soft bewildered voice that made his jaw clench: 'But I love you.'

'And I love you.'

Her heart leapt as he pulled her into his arms and then their lips were clinging, the kiss fiercer and fiercer as their bodies strained together until it seemed they would merge. She could feel the power in his loins as her body moulded to his and she knew that this kind of loving, this wild, crazy, unearthly loving, was something she would never experience with anyone else. He was her other half, the half of a perfect whole. Any weakness of his would be covered by her strength, likewise hers by his strength, it was meant to be, *it was*. He had to see it. He couldn't kiss her like this and not see it.

When his lips moved from hers they trailed her face in hot burning kisses as he murmured words that a few minutes before would have made her blush, but now only served to fuel the passion that had her in its grip. She was gasping, frantic, her body arousing him still more as she rubbed against him in a fever of desire, barely aware of what she was doing.

And then it stopped. Just like that.

She stood where he had put her, at arm's length, and watched him as he walked to the door of the sitting room, and he would have gone without another word if she hadn't said, 'You will come and say goodbye before you leave for good? When exactly will you go?'

If he was surprised at her easy acceptance of the situation he made no sign of it as he answered, 'Late April, early May most likely. There'll be nothing doing before then.'

'And you'll come and say goodbye?' she pressed again.

'If that's what you want.'

'Yes, that's what I want.'

They faced each other from across the room and although Rosie's lips quivered her eyes were dry. He drew in a long breath that expanded his broad chest and lifted his shoulders before turning sharply and opening the door.

She didn't follow him into the hall but remained exactly where she was until she heard the front door open and then close behind him, after which she stumbled to a chair, one hand stretched out in front of her as though she was blind.

Chapter Twenty-Three

On 21st January, four days after Davey had been to see her, Rosie travelled across the water to Ireland to see Sally and Mick. The inclement weather and the fact that she wasn't at all sure about the conditions in which she would be staying persuaded her to leave Erik with her mother, and she was glad of this by the time she arrived in Dublin. The long journey by train to Holyhead had been bad enough, but the crossing had been rough and arduous and she had felt very ill most of the time. But the purpose of her visit had given her strength.

On her arrival in Dublin she had stayed overnight in a hotel, then resumed her journey to Ballymore the following morning. She had written to Sally and Mick informing them of her proposed visit but she wasn't at all sure if they would receive the letter before she actually arrived on their doorstep, and as the horse-drawn cab bounced and bumped its way along frozen mud roads piled high either side with banks of snow, she wondered at times if she *would* arrive.

But then, at last, she was standing at the door of the small thatched farmhouse that resembled an English country cottage, her heart racing with excitement at the thought of seeing Sally again.

'*Rosie!*' Sally's ear-splitting shriek of pleasure was all she could have hoped for and the next moment she was enfolded in the other woman's arms and being hugged like there was no tomorrow. 'I don't believe it. Rosie!'

'Did you get my letter?'

'Your letter? Rosie, lass, we're lucky if we get the sun in the mornin' an' the moon at night in this neck of the woods. Oh it's good to see you, lass, it is that. Oh bloomin' hell, I'm soundin' like one of the natives now! Heaven preserve us.'

Sally hadn't changed.

The next few days were a revelation to Rosie as to just how hard farming life could be. Sally and Mick rose before five and were rarely ready to sit in front of the fire in their little sitting room before seven in the evening, and then Sally's hands were working at darning socks or some such necessary but mundane chore. Little Patrick, the youngest McDoughty, resembled nothing more than a tiny smiling leprechaun, and never once, in the whole of the ten days that Rosie spent with the family, did she hear him cry. And in spite of the hard grinding work it was clear Sally was happy.

'Oh aye, I wouldn't swop a minute of me day for bein' back in England.' When Rosie spoke of her gladness at how things had turned out for them, Sally was very forthcoming. 'Farmin' life is a thing all on its own, lass, an' I never realized it till I come here. You either love it or hate it, there's no middle path, an' I reckon there's some who would consider themselves buried alive an' that's the truth. But as long as I've got Mick an' the bairn I'm all right. You know what I mean? An' he's a natural.' Sally glanced across at Mick, fast asleep in his armchair by the fire, his snores vibrating the air. 'He's a born farmer an' that's the truth. Aye, lass, we're doin' all right, an' in more ways than one. There's another one on the way.'

She grinned at Rosie, who gave the expected enthusiastic response. 'I'll have to be careful else I'll be turnin' 'em out like clockwork.' Sally grimaced cheerfully. 'But I tell you, lass, it was like shellin' peas, an' like Mick said, there's nothin' much else to do when the sun goes down an' if I have 'em all like I had the last one we'll soon have our own little workforce. Nothin' like keepin' it in the family, is there.'

'No, I suppose not.' Rosie smiled as Sally dug her in the ribs and then they both giggled as Mick woke up with a 'Wha? Who?' when a burning log spat like a bullet in the fire.

Rosie came back from Ireland on 2nd February with her mind quite made up about the course of action which would determine whether she just lived for the rest of her life, or lived abundantly.

She spent the following morning at her solicitors and arrived home early afternoon and, after Ellen and her daughter had left, settled down in front of the fire with Erik playing at her feet with his toys while she looked through the sheaf of papers she had brought home with her. An hour slipped by, with just the sound of Erik's vrum-vruming as he played with his toy lorry and car, then the peace was shattered as a sharp knock at the front door brought Rosie's head up.

Rosie had actually opened her mouth to speak to the slim, very well-dressed young woman standing on the doorstep clad snugly in furs and matching muff, when she felt the blood rush to her head so fast it made her dizzy. '*Molly?*'

'Hallo, Rosie.'

'Molly! Oh, come in, come in.' Rosie reached out and drew her sister over the threshold, and then, as she looked into the beautiful face framed by mink, she said again, 'Molly, oh, Molly,' before hugging her tight. There was one moment of stiffness and then Molly was hugging her back just as tightly and both women were laughing and crying as they stood swaying together.

And then a small voice brought them apart as it said, 'Mammy?'

'You had a little boy?' Molly's voice was very soft as she glanced down into the solemn little face surveying her with Zachariah's deep blue eyes.

'You didn't know?' Rosie was looking at Molly, and now the first rush of emotion was gone she found it difficult to link the composed young woman in front of her with the Molly she had known. A transition had taken place, and if she hadn't known Molly's circumstances she would have said it was for the better. Her sister's voice was different, clearer and well modulated and the broad Tyneside accent had mellowed into a warm burr, and her carriage was straight and dignified, her manner self-assured and controlled. In fact she was, to all intents and purposes, very much a lady.

'I knew you were expecting a baby; Bridget told me when she came to see me a few weeks after you'd gone to the house,' Molly said quietly, still with her eyes on her nephew. 'But I didn't try to find out . . . He's beautiful, Rosie, and so like Zachariah. That must be some comfort to you.'

'You know about Zachariah?'

450

'That's why I've come.' And now Molly turned back to her as Erik, suddenly bored with the proceedings, ran back to the sitting room. 'I have only just heard, Rosie. We . . . we've been away, Gerald and I, in Europe. He took me on a tour, it's been wonderful, but we've been out of the country for over eighteen months.' And then the poise slipped a little as Molly added, her voice soft, 'Oh, Rosie, I'm sorry I didn't come before when you gave Bridget the address, but I thought it best. I . . . I'd made up my mind it had to be a clean break for me to manage. But this with Zachariah, this is different. I'm so sorry at his passing, Rosie, heart sorry, and you with the bairn and all.'

'It's all right.' Rosie's voice was distracted and she was thinking, Europe? She said Europe. Did that mean this man, whoever he was, had married her?

And then Rosie's hopes were quashed as Molly, reading her sister's face, said, 'He's a good man, Gerald, and he treats me very well, but he has always made it quite clear that when he takes a wife she will be from his class with all the right connections. But as his mistress I have my own house and car, and we entertain frequently. He . . . he doesn't hide me away, they don't think like that, Rosie. It's quite acceptable for a man in his position to have a mistress and I'm treated with respect by his friends.'

Rosie was at a loss to know what to say.

'I've landed on my feet, and knowing what I know now it could have been mighty different.'

'Do you love him?'

'Love him?' Molly stared at her and for a moment Rosie felt very very young as she looked back into her sister's exquisite face with its wide sea-green eyes, but Molly's voice was gentle when she said, 'Gerald is twenty-five years older than me and a man of large appetites. What he loses at cards in one sitting would keep a family round here for a year, and I don't think he has ever bothered to find out just what he's worth. He regards his mistress in the same way he does his favourite horse, as a valuable possession, no more. But he is kind and generous, and through him, whatever happens now, my future is secure. When he tires of me, and sooner or later he *will* tire of me, I know that, I shall go abroad to live. France, or Italy. Their culture is quite unlike ours and so free, Rosie. The last eighteen months have been a revelation.'

She *had* changed and she was living in a different world. They stared at each other for a long moment, Molly nipping at her lip, and then their worlds were bridged as Rosie said, her eyes full of love, 'I'm so glad you came, Molly. You can stay for a while?'

'If you're sure you want me to.'

'You're my baby sister and I love you, you don't have to ask.'

Molly stayed for over two hours and once Erik had overcome his brief shyness with the beautiful lady with the furry coat, he was clambering onto his aunty's lap and putting his chubby little cheeks next to her smooth, scented ones as he hugged her tight and chatted away. Molly hugged him several times as though she would never let him go, and after he had gone to sleep on her lap she asked about her mother and Hannah, but expressed no desire to see them and Rosie didn't press her.

It was when she was leaving that the years really rolled away. She knelt in the hall, taking Erik in her arms again as she said, 'This will be the last time I'll come, Rosie. It's not fair. But mention me to him sometimes.' She kissed the silky blond curls. 'You can say I died, I don't mind, but don't not mention me.'

Oh, Molly, Molly. Rosie's heart was full and now she knelt too and the three of them were close as she said, 'I'll tell him about you often and that you held him in your arms, Molly, but my door is always open to you. Remember that. Wherever I am, whoever I'm with, there's always a place for you too.'

'Oh, Rosie.' Molly smiled at her through her tears. 'You've never given up on me, have you?'

'No, and I never will.'

'I had to follow my own star, and do what I needed to do. For right or wrong I did what my heart told me. Tell Mam that when you talk to her, try and make her understand.'

For right or wrong. They were born of the same parents, they had suckled at the same breasts and there was a wealth of shared memories between them, but it all came down to what they saw as right and wrong and it was *so* different. Rosie couldn't speak, but as they rose to their feet she cupped her sister's lovely face in her hands and kissed her.

And it was later, much later, when Erik was tucked up in bed and fast asleep and the night wind was howling down the chimney, that Rosie thought again of Molly's last words. 'I had to follow my own star and do what I needed to do. For right or wrong I did what my heart told me.' Maybe she and Molly weren't so far apart after all.

Jessie took the news of Molly's visit very well; she cried a little, but seemed reconciled to the fact that Molly had chosen the life she wanted and was gone for good. Rosie spent some time talking to Hannah and putting Molly in the best light she could as she explained how things were, and by the time she left her youngest sister she was satisfied Hannah both understood and accepted the situation and, whilst not approving of Molly's lifestyle, still loved her sister. It was the best Rosie could have hoped for.

As the weeks went on Rosie made no attempt to see Davey, neither did she divulge to anyone the plans she had set in operation after her visit to Ireland.

February and March saw the whole of England swept by ferocious blizzards which often took the temperature to nine or ten degrees below zero, and April was bitterly cold with icy rain and sleet and snow. Rosie was probably the only person in the whole of Sunderland who welcomed the atrocious weather, but the dreadful conditions meant Davey wasn't likely to change his mind about leaving at the beginning of May and go any earlier. And so she continued to make her plans for the inevitable day when the sun would shine and spring would herald Davey's departure from Sunderland and her.

Then, in the first week of May, spring came with a vengeance, all the more determined for being kept at bay so long. Overnight, it seemed, the yards and back lanes were alive with zealous housewives beating the long winter out of threadbare squares of carpet and clippy mats and flock mattresses, washing curtains and bed linen and clothes, and in some cases – certainly in the tenement slums of the East End – children were being unpicked from their winter underwear that had been sewn on sometime in November, and their encrusted skin introduced to water and air for the first time in months. Pavements were bleached, doorsteps scrubbed and whitened, floorboards scoured and windows washed. For a few days all was a positive hive of activity.

Whether it was the sap rising that gave Peter the courage to ask Flora to marry him was anybody's guess, but the first weekend in May saw Flora sporting an exquisite diamond-and-ruby engagement ring and talking about a summer wedding.

Rosie had chosen her words very carefully when Flora had come to see her, without Peter, and show her the ring. 'Oh, I'm pleased for you both, I am, really, but . . . but you are sure?' She took Flora's hands in her own, shaking them slightly as she spoke.

'Do you know, I am.' There was something akin to a note of surprise in Flora's voice. 'I thought he would ask me soon, and I kept changing my mind every two minutes as to what I'd say. But—' She broke off abruptly, pulling her hands free and walking across to little Erik, who was banging away on an old saucepan with a wooden spoon despite the toys scattered about him, and, after picking the child up and holding him close for a moment, continued. 'He asked me so nervously, Rosie, but he went down on one knee and everything. He said I was the only woman he had ever loved, ever would love, and if I said no he would keep on loving me till the day he died. He said I was beautiful and – oh, lots of things. Nice things.' She gave a little embarrassed smile and shook her head, placing Erik down and giving him the wooden spoon again. And then she turned, looking straight at Rosie as she added, 'It was everything that Davey didn't say.'

'Oh, Flora.'

'No, it's all right. Really. I'd have gone round the bend trying to be someone I'm not just to please him. It's funny you know, but I've always been able to say anything to Peter, anything at all, and yet with Davey I was forever

Rita Bradshaw

picking me words and biting me tongue and that's not natural, is it.'

'No, I suppose not.'

'Not for me anyway.' And now Flora grinned her old cheeky grin before she said, 'I told Peter's mam where she could stick her idea of us living with them after we were married, she'd got it all planned to the last tiny detail, and Peter didn't turn a hair.'

'Flora, you didn't!' Peter's mother was a formidable lady.

'He agreed with me. And when his mam started ranting and raving like she does, he stood up and said very coolly' – and now Flora gave a perfect impersonation of her intended's quiet, slightly upper-class voice – '"Mother, please conduct yourself with some propriety in front of my future wife." Honestly, Rosie, I thought she was going to swallow her tonsils!'

No, Flora could certainly never have survived a marriage where she had to choose her words, Rosie thought, as the two girls gave way to helpless laughter. She could have been Sally's twin in that regard.

The day following Flora's call was a Sunday, and at three o'clock in the afternoon when Rosie answered a knock at her front door and found Davey on the doorstep, she knew her intuition had been right. She had felt he would come this weekend, it was one of the reasons she had agreed that her mother should have Erik for the day when Jessie had suggested it after Rosie had declined an invitation for Sunday lunch herself.

'Hallo, Rosie.' Davey inclined his head towards her and it took all her considerable willpower not to betray the shock that had coursed through her at the sight of him. He looked ill. No, not ill exactly, more tired, exhausted.

456

'Won't you come in?'

Won't you come in. Just like that. Here he'd been, suffering the torments of the damned for weeks, and she was as cool as a cucumber. By, women were a different species all right. He had always known it, but never so clearly as in this moment. And she must know why he had come to see her. As Davey followed the demurely dressed figure into the sitting room his thoughts were racing. Didn't she care that he was leaving? If she did there was no sign of it.

'Please sit down.'

'I'd rather not.' He couldn't match her cool composure and his voice was rough.

'As you please.'

He couldn't take much more of this. He had worked himself up all week for this meeting and it wasn't going at all as he had expected. Not that he had known what to expect, to be fair, but whatever it'd been, it wasn't this . . . this ice-maiden.

'It's good news about Flora and Peter, isn't it?'

Flora and Peter? For a moment the names barely registered and then he nodded quickly, his voice curt as he said, 'Aye, yes. He's a good man and he's got his head on straight. He'll look after the lass.'

Now the time was here, the time she had prepared for for weeks, Rosie found her hands were trembling and she put them behind her back as she said, 'Can I offer you a drink? A cup of tea?'

Davey had never been a patient man and Rosie was aware of this, and she knew the effort it took for him to say, and with some civility, 'No, nothing thank you. Look, I've come—'

'I know why you have come.'

'Oh.' She had taken him aback, both by her cool tone and the manner in which she was looking at him. He couldn't work her out and that was an understatement, he told himself bitterly, but the sooner he was away from here the better.

'But before we go into that,' she flapped her hand as though his leaving was of no importance, 'there is something I want to ask you. A favour, I suppose you could call it.'

'Aye?' His back was very straight now and his face grim, but Rosie told herself she couldn't weaken. Not now. She had to do it all as she had planned. She had thought about this for a long time and she knew the success or failure of her plan was blowing in the wind.

'I want you to take a drive with me.'

'A drive?' If she had propositioned him to go upstairs and sport in bed he couldn't have been more astounded.

'Yes, a drive. It's what civilized people do on a Sunday afternoon if they are fortunate enough to have a car.'

For a moment she thought she had overplayed her hand as his face tensed and a muscle in his jaw worked, but then he said, 'Why would you want to go for a drive?'

'I will explain as we go, if that's all right, but it would help me considerably if you'd come.'

When he was a child it had been a trick of his, which had driven his poor mother half mad with frustration at times, to shut his eyes and make his face blank if he was being told something he didn't want to hear. He'd been able to keep it up through any amount of carry on, even when his backside was being walloped, and for a moment the situation he was facing made Davey want to resort to that same childish defence. The last thing he wanted was to go for a ride in her damn motor car! By, did she know what she was doing? Did she have any idea of the way she was rubbing his nose in it?

458

'Davey?'

She was looking at him, and now he caught a thread of pleading in her voice at the same time as a fleeting shadow in her eyes, gone in the next moment, told him she wasn't so sure of herself as she would like him to believe. But it would do neither of them any good to go for a drive, to prolong the agony, Rosie must know that? He had made his arrangements, he had said his goodbyes, and this was the last call before he was on his way, and nothing – and no one – could change that. She *had* to understand; and he hadn't hidden behind any subterfuge, now, had he? He'd made himself plain the last time, he knew he had. No, this had to end as if with the cut of the surgeon's scalpel – quickly, cleanly and without hesitation.

And then, in repudiation of all he had been thinking, he heard himself say, 'A short drive, then, if that fits in with your plans. I . . . I've things to do.'

Rosie made an almost imperceptible inclination of her head and again the regal lady was back with the nature of her acquiescence, and it grated like barbed wire on his taut nerves. He was barmy, clean barmy, to go with her, but how could he not? *How could he not?* The words were a groan from deep within where the essence of his love burnt, and he found it hurt to look at her. Her pale creamy skin, the dark eyes with their long silky lashes – she was beauty and warmth and bright tomorrows, and from this day on he knew he would never see her again. He wouldn't come back, they both knew it. The gulf was too wide; whatever happened in the future it was too wide.

'I'll just get my coat.'

In contrast to his feverish thoughts her voice was cool and low, and the need that was upon him to touch her, to feel

459

her skin beneath his fingers even if it was just the side of her face or the palm of her hand, kept his hands clenched in his pockets and his voice gruff as he said, 'Aye, all right.'

She must think him a loutish brute. The thought did nothing to take the frown from his face. And perhaps he was; certainly compared to Zachariah he was. Flora had told him how Rosie's husband had educated her, broadening her mind and her vision and giving her an understanding of the classics and the arts. What did he know about such things? Nowt. Double nowt. How could he imagine she would ever have considered spending the rest of her life with a man like him anyway? It wasn't until that second that he realized how jealous, how bitterly jealous he was of a dead man, and the knowledge caused him to grind his teeth before walking out into the hall where Rosie was pulling on her gloves.

'Shall we go?' She turned to smile brightly at him and for a moment he could have hit her. She made him feel like a worm, a nothing. She needed him so little and he needed her so much. And he knew now – the last grindingly slow weeks of misery and longing providing all the confirmation he could have asked for – that if things had been different, if she had been the old Rosie living in Forcer Road, he would have worked down the mine for the rest of his life if he had her to come home to in the evenings. Aye, he would. And counted himself fortunate.

There had been times in the last weeks when he had questioned himself, agonizing over whether he was doing the right thing. The right thing! He laughed inwardly, harsh, bitter laughter. But all his deliberations, his searching to find an answer to the unanswerable, had brought him back to one inescapable conclusion. If he had asked her to marry him he would have become nothing more than a lackey. She had this house, money in the bank – she was as well set-up as any of the toffs in Ryhope Road or Barnes Park. Zachariah had made sure she would want for nothing till the day she died. And what would he have said when the bairn got older and asked him what he did for a living? No, it was impossible. He couldn't stay with her and she couldn't go with him. End of story.

Once they were seated in the car Davey felt acutely uncomfortable, partly because of the bittersweet sensation of sitting so closely at Rosie's side and smelling the fragrant scent of her – a perfume which had nothing to do with a bottle but was all to do with a gracious way of living that started the day with a scented bath and finished with fresh linen and a clean bed – but also due to the fact that he had never been driven by a woman before, or a man either for that matter. He found it was not enjoyable, and on the second occasion that Rosie had to swerve slightly to avoid a car coming in the opposite direction which was taking most of the road, he said, in an effort at conversation, 'They are talking about putting road markings in some of the larger towns now, have you heard? Apparently it's proved successful in London in lowering accidents. There's over fourteen people killed every day now.'

'Really.' The brief reply made it evident that if he continued with the small talk he would be talking to himself, and after one glance at Rosie's face Davey allowed the previous uneasy silence to reign again, telling himself that the next word spoken would be uttered by Rosie or they wouldn't speak at all.

He was annoyed. Rosie had noticed his glance and understood the meaning behind it. But it couldn't be helped. She was normally a good driver, she knew she was, but today she felt so keyed up she was having to concentrate with all her might. He would understand when they got there. Pray God, oh, *pray God* he would understand. And if he didn't? If all her frantic manoeuvrings, and the palaver that had gone with them that had nearly driven her mad at times, if it was all for nothing – what then? For a second her stomach hit rock bottom and she had to clutch the wheel so tightly her knuckles showed white. No, no, she wouldn't think of that. This had to work, it had to. She would consider nothing less. She couldn't lose him twice in one lifetime. God wouldn't be so cruel.

The route Rosie had taken soon took them out of Roker and towards Southwick, the rows of streets and houses giving way to the tender green of the countryside, where the thickly fringed fields and hedged lanes caused Davey to wind down his window and breathe in the fresh air. When they passed Southwick he still made no comment and neither did Rosie, but as the car trundled along narrow mud roads, passing the odd gated field enclosing grazing cattle and sheep, he was finding it increasingly difficult to maintain his composure. What had she said exactly? he asked himself as the minutes ticked by and the strain of having her so close made him begin to sweat. It would help her if she went for a ride with him? That'd been it, hadn't it? How the hell did coming out here help her? By, it was bonny though. The sky was bluer, the air sweeter . . . The drab stale existence in the towns might belong to another world when you were breathing in lungfuls of this stuff.

'You must think it very strange that I've asked you to ride with me today.' As Rosie spoke she turned the little car off the winding lane on which they were travelling and along a bumpy track that opened almost immediately into a wide farmyard.

It wasn't a prosperous farm by the look of it, Davey thought, before he turned to her and said, 'Not strange, surprising maybe.' And then, 'Look, should we be in here? I mean someone might object.'

'I know the owners.'

Again her voice was very cool and even and he didn't have the intuition to know it was strain, not composure, that made it so.

Rosie brought the car to a halt on the cobbles which, if the cow pats gently steaming in the May afternoon were anything to go by, had recently seen a herd of bovines pass through. 'Come and have a look round.'

She smiled at him but that shadow was back in her eyes and it caused him to say, 'What is it? What's the matter?' before he realized the stupidity of the question.

But Rosie didn't treat it as stupid. She twisted in her seat to face him fully and then she became quite still, the stillness seeming to fill the car with a tenseness that became unbearable. He swallowed deeply, and then he swallowed again, but still he couldn't bring himself to speak although he didn't quite know why.

'The farm is a nice size.' Her voice was quiet, but with an underlying throb of emotion that made him stretch his neck and make to ease the collar of his shirt before he checked the action. In the far distance he could see a golden meadow, bright with a shimmering yellow haze of buttercups, and the delicate smell of May blossom vied with the more pungent aroma left by the cows.

'But as you can see it has been terribly run down. To get it back on its feet it will need to employ at least a dozen men

463

or so, and even then it will take time to turn things round, but it can be done. And there are some definite benefits, one of which is that there is a row of six farm cottages just behind the rear of the farmhouse garden, and although they need a good deal of renovation they are habitable now. Of course they aren't furnished, but then most people would like to bring their own possessions anyway, don't you think?'

Was she saying she had asked about a job for him? Was that it? He was going to be offered the job of cowhand or something similar? Well, he had had enough of well-meaning females poking their noses into his affairs, the last twelve months or so had taught him that if nothing else. He would sooner starve. Aye, or even go back into that hell underground than have her to thank for his employment.

'Lambing time is finished,' Rosie continued after a pause, 'but with the livestock being shut inside for a good part of the winter they're not as healthy as they could be. I know a little about the basics now from what I learnt from Mick and Sally when—'

'Rosie!' Her name was snapped into the space between them and he saw her jump, but he didn't apologize, neither did he alter his tone when he said, 'Turn the car round.'

'What?' Rosie's hands were clutching at the front of her coat and she must have realized this, because in the next instant they were lowered sharply to her lap, and now there was a fierce ring to her voice as she said, 'No, I won't. I need to talk to you.'

'You won't?'

'Not until I've talked to you.'

'Then you'll drive home alone.'

'*Davey.*'

Oh, this was all going wrong, terribly wrong, and then, as

464

though to emphasize the point, Rosie saw two border collies bound round the corner of the farmyard from the direction of the cottages and barns situated behind it. Within a second or two three burly farmworkers followed, and she breathed a sigh of relief when she saw who they were. These men were unknown to Davey.

'All right, we'll go, but just wait here a moment.' She spoke urgently, her voice low and rapid, and then to Davey's surprise she was out of the car and approaching the men, careless of the muck and filth. He couldn't hear what was being said but when they nodded at him, doffing their caps before turning and retracing their footsteps, he sat stock still.

'Will you come into the house for a moment? Please, Davey?' When Rosie reached the car again all her previous defiance was gone, and to Davey's eyes she suddenly seemed disturbingly vulnerable. It was the same demeanour he had seen at the hospital that day, and it cut through his aggressiveness like a knife through butter. 'There's no one there and I know it will be all right. Please?'

'Aye, yes, if you want.' His voice was still brusque, but now it was because of the weakness that was constraining him to agree to the request. But two minutes in the farmhouse and then they were on their way – he'd make sure of that. Whatever she had set up for him with the owners of the place – and if those men's attitudes were anything to go by it wasn't something at the bottom rung of the ladder, which made it worse somehow – he wasn't having any of it.

He got out of the car slowly and followed her across the cobbles. There was a four-foot-high drystone wall enclosing what should have been some twenty feet of lawned garden directly in front of the large stone dwelling, but the waist-high nettles and thistles hid any grass. Rosie opened the old wooden gate that was propped on one hinge and passed through onto the narrow path, and now Davey walked to where she was waiting for him in front of the big oak door. He had noticed one of the three tall chimneystacks was leaning drunkenly to one side, and it looked as though a few slates were missing from the roof, but he made no comment on this.

The door was unlocked, and when Rosie lifted the latch and it swung open, a large stone-flagged hall was revealed with a massive square of coconut matting on which to wipe dirty feet.

'It's a big place.' There was a tremor in her voice now and it checked his impatience when she continued, 'There's a kitchen and scullery at the back of the house, and two washhouses along with the dairy. On this side' – she waved her hand to the left of them – 'is a dining room and a study, and this' – she moved forward and opened the first door to their right – 'is the sitting room.'

She might call it a sitting room but it was unlike any sitting room he had ever seen. The room was a large one, long but also wide, and its overall volume would have swallowed the whole downstairs of any house he had been in. The ceiling was oak-beamed, the walls newly whitewashed, and the mullioned windows in the side wall made him realize the house must be built on an incline. He could see rolling fields pastured by grazing cattle and sheep dipping down to a glinting river, and beyond that a wooded hillside from these windows, and the scene was very pleasing to the eye. The other two big windows overlooked the front garden and the farmyard where the car was presently parked.

The fireplace was a massive one and deep-set, its ornate surround of wood beautifully decorated with small individual carvings depicting animals, birds and flowers. The furnishings in this room were of good quality and at odds with the overall air of neglect he had seen so far, and he could imagine that once the thick heavy velvet drapes at the windows were pulled and the fire lit, the room would take on a tranquillity that would be very comforting to live in.

'Do you like it?'

He was still standing in the doorway, and now he became aware that Rosie had turned a few yards into the room and was quietly watching him, and something in her face made his uneasiness return tenfold. 'This room? Aye. There's nothing not to like, is there?'

'No, no there isn't. And the rest of the house could be made like this and the farm become productive again. It would be a wonderful place to bring up bairns, don't you think?'

He didn't answer this but said instead, 'And you say you know the owners?'

'In a manner of speaking.' Rosie walked across to a small occasional table under one of the leaded windows at the side of the front door and picked up a bundle of papers which was lying on it, next to a crystal fruit bowl which was empty. 'But one of them not as well as I would like to.' She walked over to him, handing him the bundle as she said, 'These are yours.'

He didn't say 'Mine?', he didn't say anything at all, he just looked at her without moving. Rosie took his arm and drew him over to one of the armchairs. 'Please look at them.'

Davey sat down, still without speaking, and carefully undid the ribbon holding the papers together. They comprised documents relating to the purchase of the farm and the furniture in this room, with further receipts detailing the pending acquisition of new equipment and other such matters. All the documents were in his name and Rosie's. Even the car he had travelled in that day was in joint ownership.

He was quite unable to move.

The feeling that was gathering in the core of him was indescribable. It embodied all the beauty and colour he had ever seen, every note of music he had enjoyed, every soft word, every good and perfect deed that had gladdened his heart, and it was all the more poignant because he knew he had to let it go. Let her go.

'What have you done?' His voice was so low she could scarcely hear it.

'I've sold everything.' The words hung in the air. 'The house in Roker isn't mine any more, I've got to move out in a week's time. I'm leaving it fully furnished except . . . except for Erik's things which will come here. That's the only other room I've had time to see to, the nursery. And the bonds and shares have all gone, and a good deal of the money. As well as the three men you just saw, who were the original workers here, I've hired another couple and . . . and the McLinnie brothers and Arthur. Even Robert is coming – his wife's gone back to her mother's and taken the child, Robert knows she's had someone else for some time—'

'Rosie—'

'We will need some more men of course, but that will have to wait until the farm starts to make a profit. The three originals have been struggling for years to keep the place going for the last owner, but they assure me if we all muck in it will only take a couple of years to get the farm viable again with the new equipment and such. Oh, and there's Ellen and her child. She's coming too, and she'll help me in the dairy and the house and—'

'I'm not going to let you do this, Rosie.'

'I've done it. Whatever you say now, whatever you do, this is partly yours, Davey.'

He turned his head and looked up at her where she was standing by the side of his chair, and she saw his face was as white as lint. 'No, it is yours. These mean nothing—'

'You're right, they don't.' She knelt down by the arm of the chair now, much as she had done with Zachariah years before. 'Papers and documents don't mean anything, *all* this doesn't mean anything, not really. It was never *my* money, it was Zachariah's, and even he held on to it lightly. It should be used, Davey, and to benefit everyone, and . . . and Erik and other bairns. Out here—' She could not go on to say, 'Out here we can be Rosie and Davey again and go back to how it used to be,' because she knew there was too much water under the bridge for that, but said instead, 'Out here we can have the life that you and Sam used to talk about. We can make a success of it for him too. If it makes you feel better, look on it as though you are in partnership with him through me, that we're fulfilling what he wanted.'

'Better?' He made a swaying movement with his head and his voice was thick. 'This is madness, lass. You're committing yourself to years and years – a lifetime – of hard work when you could have taken it easy and never lifted a finger.'

'It would drive me mad not to lift a finger.' She sat back on her heels as she continued to crouch at the side of the chair. 'I could never live like that, Davey. And Zachariah knew I wanted to move out of the town and find somewhere like this, and he was all for it. This way, with this farm, we can really make a difference, don't you see? I first saw this place last year on one of my trips out and it put me off, it being so run down and all, but when I asked Mick's advice and we started discussing facts and figures, I knew we could do it, Davey. You and me and the others together.' She was gabbling in her need to make him see, and now she forced herself to stop, her heart pounding with the force of the emotion she was trying to contain. But he had to see, he did.

'Don't, Rosie.' Her name was wrenched from him. 'Don't say any more. I can't—'

'*You can!*' Her voice was fierce but she was fighting for everything she had ever wanted. 'If I had been Sam you would have thought a partnership was all right, wouldn't you? And surely you care about me as much as you did about him? It's straight down the line, Davey – every stick of furniture, every beast on the farm, every blade of wheat in the fields, whether . . . whether you want me or not.'

'Whether I want you . . .' His voice was deep, guttural, and now the feeling was pouring out of him, melting the core of his being with its heat and strangling the words in his throat as he got to his feet.

She looked up at him, into his face, and something told her it was going to be all right. She had the strangest impression that Davey was surrounded by an aura of light in the moment before he touched her. Not a white light, but a warm pulsating radiance that made his face glow and his features blur. And then his arms were round her, crushing her into him as he smothered her face in wild burning kisses before taking her mouth with a hunger that was almost savage in its intensity.

Rosie could feel his heart racing, pressed as she was against the hard solid bulk of him, and she returned kiss for kiss, her breath sobbing in her throat. She had the sensation they were spinning in a place where time was not – it was another era, another dimension, and for a moment they were in the same skin.

'You're sure about this? You're sure this is what you want? Absolutely sure, lass?'

And now she dared to say what she had always wanted to say. 'All I have ever wanted is you. When I thought you were going to go away again—'

'Oh, my Rosie, my love.' He cut off her words with his mouth, pulling her into him as though he couldn't get enough of her and muttering endearments against her lips, her cheeks, her hair, as they stood locked together in the centre of the room.

He was her world, her universe, he was every tomorrow she had ever wanted. 'Davey, Davey, I love you. I love you so much.'

'And I love you, Rosie. Do you hear me? I'll love you to my dying day and beyond.'

Now you can buy any of these other bestselling books from your bookshop or *direct from the publisher*.

FREE P&P AND UK DELIVERY
(Overseas and Ireland £3.50 per book)

My Sister's Child	Lyn Andrews	£5.99
Liverpool Lies	Anne Baker	£5.99
The Whispering Years	Harry Bowling	£5.99
Ragamuffin Angel	Rita Bradshaw	£5.99
The Stationmaster's Daughter	Maggie Craig	£5.99
Our Kid	Billy Hopkins	£6.99
Dream a Little Dream	Joan Jonker	£5.99
For Love and Glory	Janet MacLeod Trotter	£5.99
In for a Penny	Lynda Page	£5.99
Goodnight Amy	Victor Pemberton	£5.99
My Dark-Eyed Girl	Wendy Robertson	£5.99
For the Love of a Soldier	June Tate	£5.99
Sorrows and Smiles	Dee Williams	£5.99

TO ORDER SIMPLY CALL THIS NUMBER

01235 400 414

or e-mail orders@bookpoint.co.uk

Prices and availability subject to change without notice.

Epilogue

On 31st January, 1933, on the day the papers were full of the news that Adolf Hitler, the flamboyant leader of Germany's controversial Nazi Party, had been appointed Chancellor of the German Reich, a small notice appeared in the births column of Sunderland's *Daily Echo*.

Connor David and Rosie Connor of Becks Farm, Castletown, are proud to announce the arrival of twin sons on Saturday, 28th January, 1933. The boys, christened David Zachariah and Samuel Philip, are baby brothers for Erik James.